HEIR TO FALCONHURST

Lance Horner
Heir to Falconhurst

Pan Books London and Sydney

First published in Great Britain 1969 by
W. H. Allen & Company Ltd
This edition published 1971 by Pan Books Ltd,
7th printing 1979
ISBN 0 330 02628 3
© Kenric L. Horner 1968
Printed in Great Britain by
Richard Clay (The Chaucer Press) Ltd, Bungay, Suffolk

HEIR TO FALCONHURST

CHAPTER ONE

DRUM MAXWELL – although he preferred to be known as
Drummond Maxwell, he always thought of himself as Drum –
stepped from the high-backed tin bathtub out on to the chilly
marble tiles of the floor. Curse Boston, which could be this
cold when spring was already here. Shivering after his im-
mersion in the warm water, he yelled, his deep voice echoing
in the small room.

'Mede, you black bastard, bring that towel and be sure it's
warm. Hurry, damn you, I'm freezing.'

'Yes, sir, Mista Drum. Coming, sir. Towel nice 'n' warmed
up fronta the fire.' A black face appeared in the doorway,
grinning to show a row of dazzling white teeth. Mede walked
in, the towel in both hands, and folded it around his master,
scrubbing with it briskly until Drum's olive skin glowed. They
were about the same age, these two, and there existed between
them an easy camaraderie, which, however, seldom transcended
the bounds laid down between master and servant.

Kneeling to place his master's feet into the carpet slippers
that were lined up on the floor, Mede grinned. 'Mighty cold
for April, ain't it, Mista Drum?'

'Damn cold in here. Let's get into the bedroom.' Drum took
several quick steps into the other room and waited for Mede to
close the bathroom door behind him. It was warmer here in
the big bedroom. A cheerful fire burned in the fireplace and
Drum went over to stand before it, drying his skin thoroughly.

'Pull the curtains, boy, and light the gas. It's getting dark.'

There was a rattling of curtain rings as the heavy draperies
of wine-coloured velour were pulled together, the scratch of a
sulphur match, the faint whistle of escaping gas, and then the
room was bathed in a warm light.

'Laid out your clothes, Mista Drum, that is' – Mede pointed to the garments lying on the bed – 'if'n those the ones you want to wear.'

'Doesn't make much difference what I wear tonight. Dinner at home with Uncle Chris and Aunt Mary – typically cold-boiled Boston. Then, after we finish, Uncle Chris will suggest that he and I have a glass of port in the library and we'll go in and close the doors. That's the signal for all hell to break loose. Of course, Uncle Chris will not raise his voice, nor will I raise mine. We'll both be gentlemen, Mede, in the best Beacon Street tradition. You can always bet on one thing.'

'What's that, Mista Drum?'

'When Uncle Chris becomes overwhelmingly a gentleman, he's going to lay it on good and tonight's the night I'm going to get it.' Drum walked away from the fire to stand before a long pier glass supported on tall mahogany pillars. The light from one of the gas jets shone down on him, illuminating his body, and he smiled at his reflection in the glass. To hell with Uncle Chris and his lecture! He'd heard lectures before and survived them. Uncle Chris would storm and rant – quietly and gentlemanly, of course – and then Drum would be duly penitent and promise never to do such a thing again. Drum would manage to squeeze out a few tears, which was more difficult now that he was twenty-one than it had been when he was sixteen, but they would have the wanted effect on Uncle Chris. Then Aunt Mary would knock gently on the door and come in, stand behind Drum's chair, and let her fingers twine themselves in his hair. All would be forgiven and he'd be free to do as he damn well pleased. Aunt Mary would kiss him and take her fingers out of his hair.

His hair! Goddam his hair! He stepped closer to the big mirror. How he hated his hair. Not necessarily because it was the colour of spun gold but because it was so curly. More than curly; it was wiry, even kinky. Where in hell could he have got such hair? Even with liberal applications of Macassar oil and pomatum, he always had difficulty in getting it to lie down and the long sideburns on his cheeks, instead of being as sleek and smooth as he wanted them to be, were sparse and coarse. His

mother had been a blonde – so Aunt Mary had told him – and
he had inherited his hair from her. Well, then, he must have
inherited his olive skin from his father, whose name had been
Drummage Maxwell and about whom neither Aunt Mary nor
Uncle Chris had ever talked very much. He knew his father's
name had been Maxwell and his mother's too, but according to
Uncle Chris it was merely a coincidence and they were not
related by blood. Anyhow, as Uncle Chris was fond of saying,
the Maxwells of Falconhurst Plantation in Alabama were one
of the first families of the South.

Drum himself remembered very little about Falconhurst. He
had not seen it since he was six years old, when he, accompanied by Mede, had come to Boston. Mede didn't remember
much about it either. No, Drum didn't know much about
Falconhurst and he didn't care a hell of a lot either, as long
as it kept producing the money that Uncle Chris deposited in
the trust fund for him. Falconhurst had prospered under
Uncle Chris' management, even though his uncle had run it
from Boston.

Apart from his hair, Drum was pretty well satisfied with his
appearance. In fact, he was damn well satisfied with it, not only
from the standpoint of his own vanity, which was immense,
but from the fact that women – all women, so it seemed – liked
it. He stood back from the mirror, tilting it so that his entire
body from feet to head could be seen. It was a good thing that
it was a tall mirror because he stood just a half inch over six
feet, with wide shoulders, a flat belly, and a narrow waist.
Admiring his reflection in the mirror, he clenched his fist and
raised one arm, poking at the swelling bicep with the fingers of
the other hand to reassure himself of its hardness. Inhaling
and sucking in his belly, he admired the twin swells of his
chest with the dark copper pennies that adorned them. He
nodded in approval, his lips twisted in a little smirk of pride,
as his eyes took in the other details of his body. Damn! No
wonder women liked him.

The dark olive of his skin, he decided, was far more attractive
than the milk-white skin of his friends, which always reminded
him of the underbelly of a dead fish. He would have preferred

9

black hair, which would have given him a dashing Latin look more in keeping with his olive skin, but women seemed to like the contrast of his yellow hair with his dark skin. After all, that was what mattered. Too damn much it mattered! That was one of the reasons he was in for a raking over the coals tonight.

Picking up an ivory comb from the table near the mirror, he ran it through his hair, trying to make it smooth, cursing as the comb snarled in the tight curls. Wet as it was now, his hair lay flat and he wished it would stay that way all the time.

Drum Maxwell was not a narcissist, but he could appreciate his own beauty as quickly as he could that of a woman. He approved of the eyes that stared back at him, which were so darkly brown as to be almost black and fringed with long sooty lashes that were in direct contrast to the gold of his hair. He admitted that his forehead was too low, as the widow's peak came down too near his brows. Also, his face was too square and the high cheekbones made it seem even wider. His nose was short and straight and the nostrils, although wide, were sensitive. Under them the lips appeared a trifle too thick, too moist, and too red, but when he parted them to smile, the gleaming whiteness and perfection of his teeth minimized the sensuality of his lips.

True, he would have preferred to have a moustache. Most of his friends sported them, but he had never been able to cultivate one. Only a few sparse hairs had ever grown on his upper lip and he had almost no beard at all. In fact, he shaved rarely more than once a week and this was a ritual he indulged in more from enjoyment of it than from necessity. It had been difficult for him to get the sideburns to grow. Yet he realized that in an era when most young fellows sported moustaches and beards his smooth face made him doubly distinctive.

Mede was standing behind him, holding his linen drawers, and he lifted one leg and then the other as Mede slipped them on and buttoned them. A thin undershirt of French lisle went on next and he waited for Mede to kneel and draw on the black socks of fine silk. A meticulously ironed but unstarched shirt, ruffled with lace down its front, slipped on over his arms and then, the better to get into the narrow trousers of fawn-coloured broadcloth, he stood upon a chair and let Mede ease them over his feet, which were so large that he had difficulty getting them through the narrow pants. His hands and his feet, he had often thought, were far too large, but, as Aunt Mary had told him, it required big feet to support a fellow as big as he was.

With his feet worked down through the trousers and with his hand on Mede's shoulder, he got down from the chair while Mede tugged to force the trousers up over his hips, tucking the shirt-tails down in and waiting for Drum to take a deep breath before buttoning the waistband. Again he kneeled, using a shoehorn to slip Drum's big feet into the soft leather shoes, then pulling at the straps on the bottom of the trousers so that they would go down over and under the heels of the shoes.

Waving Mede away, Drum took the black satin cravat and adjusted it under the smooth white collar, tying it in the newly popular four-in-hand, which he knew Mede was unable to do. Stepping away from the mirror, he opened a leather box on the big chest of drawers and selected a pin with a large baroque pearl, which he centred in the cravat. Holding his arms out behind him, he waited for Mede to slip on his coat, which, since he was dining at home, was a short jacket of dull garnet brocade with a wide velvet collar and cuffs.

As he was dressing, his hair had dried and had curled into small ringlets all over his head, so he had Mede massage pomatum into his scalp and then he combed it again himself. A gold watch with an elaborate fob was checked first by Mede to see that it corresponded with the clock on the mantelpiece and then slipped into the small pocket in the trousers. Another look in the long mirror assured Drum that his dressing process was finished except for the folded handkerchief that Mede handed to him, which he slipped into his hip pocket with some difficulty, owing to the tightness of his trousers.

It was still a few minutes too early to go downstairs to the dining-room and Drum had no desire to face either his Uncle Chris or his Aunt Mary until they were seated at the table. He lowered himself down into one of the big leather chairs, carefully adjusting his trousers so that they would not wrinkle, and looked up at Mede. When he spoke, the tone was one that he might have used with one of his own friends rather than what he had been using to Mede as a servant.

'How're you making out with that Johanna wench that Uncle Chris had sent up from Falconhurst?'

'She awfully goddam black.' Mede was rather proud of his own tobacco brown colouring. 'Seems like those Alabama niggers all awful black.'

'She's rather pretty, though, not bad for a nigger wench that never had shoes on until she came north.' He levelled a finger at Mede. 'Come on now, answer my question. I'm not Aunt Mary. You can tell me just like you always do.'

'We getting along fine, Drum' – at times like this Mede dropped the 'Mister' – ''cept that I can't nohow understand her nigger talk. Don't know how come all those Alabama niggers talk like that. But the first day she was here, I got her on the back stairs and backed her up against the wall. Didn't have much trouble kissing her and then one thing led to another and the next day as soon as I started up the back stairs, she started after me. Believe me, Drum, if you've never tried doing it on the stairs, you'll never know how hard it is, but I did it.'

Drum winked at him. 'Figured you had. Sometimes I wish I had a taste for black meat. We're the only house on Beacon Street that has nigger help. Sam Witherspoon's mother always hires young, pretty Irish girls and Sam manages to get into them before they've been there a week. Wish Aunt Mary'd change and stop bringing help up from the South.'

'Might be you'd like a wench onc't you'd tried one.'

Drum shook his head. 'Don't like those frizzled heads and they're all so stenchy. As a matter of fact, boy, you're the only nigger I ever got near that wasn't stenchy.'

'That's 'cause I always use your bath water after you get through.'

'And my cologne too. Smelled it on you.'

'Wenches like it.' Mede grinned back. He glanced up at the

12

clock on the mantel. 'Dinner gong 'bout ready to ring, Mista Drum.'

As if it had heard him speak, the Chinese gong sounded two flights below. Drum stood up, slapped Mede on the shoulder, and pointed to the bathroom.

'Go ahead, boy, wash yourself and use the cologne if you want. And' – he pointed to the small room of his own, where Mede slept on a couch – 'whyn't you invite Johanna in there now. Nobody going to disturb you while we're eating. It's a lot better than the back stairs.'

'Just might, Mista Drum, just might. Sure itching for that wench tonight.'

Drum regarded him momentarily. 'Somebody made a big mistake when they named you Ganymede. You're about as far removed from a Ganymede as anyone could be.'

'My mammy back at Falconhurst, she name me that. Pappy he wanted me named Zanzibar after him, but Big Pearl, what's my mammy, she say no. She naming me after my uncle, her brother, what was called Ganymede, though folks always called him Mede.' He opened the door and watched Drum traverse the hall and descend the broad staircase. Once sure that Drum had reached the lower floor, he ran the length of the hall and opened the tall door that led to the back stairs. In a small room, lined with shelves and cupboards, a black girl was stacking sheets and pillowcases, freshly ironed from the laundry. 'Hey, gal.' Mede knew the correct tone for addressing those under him. 'Mista Drum needing clean towels.'

'Yassuh, Mista Mede suh. Bring 'em right in soon's I finish stackin' these yere sheets.'

'When I speaks, gal, yo' jump. Ain' waitin' for yo' to stack no sheets. Git them towels 'n' hop to it. Give yo' jes' two minutes to git in Mista Drum's room.' Unconsciously Mede had lapsed into the Southern vernacular. 'Jump!'

CHAPTER TWO

NEITHER THE GAS jets in their cut-glass shades in the ornate chandelier nor the two silver candelabra on the table were able to disperse the gloom that seemed a permanent part of the dining-room. Its walls were panelled in a dark, lustreless Santo Domingo mahogany; the furniture was of the same wood; and the curtains, drawn now, were a green- and mustard-coloured velvet brocade that absorbed the light. The long buffet was covered with fine pieces of silver that shone with subdued highlights and over the buffet there was a depressing painting by some Dutch artist that depicted a basket of dead pheasants and defunct rabbits.

The table was laid with a priceless cloth of *point de Venise* and in the centre a tall epergne held polished specimens of fruit that appeared more decorative than edible. Three Chippendale chairs were at the table, one occupied by a middle-aged man with a pleasant face, who would have looked considerably younger had it not been for his nearly white hair, and another by a handsome woman in her forties, whose dark hair was severely parted in the centre and done in the style favoured by England's Victoria.

As Drum entered the room, he smiled a greeting to the man at the head of the table, then leaned down to kiss the woman.

'Aunt Mary' – his voice held a caress – 'I haven't seen you yet today.'

She reached up a hand to stroke his face, worshipping him with her eyes. 'Not when you get up at ten o'clock in the morning, Drum dear. I was off to a meeting of the Unitarian Society, then to luncheon at Maria Brewster's, and after luncheon we all went to the Horticultural Society to see the spring flowers.' She patted his cheek. 'Consequently you'll have rather a picked-up supper tonight, Drum. I told Hebe to make do with what we have in the house.'

'Anything Hebe cooks is fine.' Drum walked back to his chair and waited for the grey-haired Negro in dark green livery to pull it out for him. He sat down and turned to the man seated at the table. 'And you, Uncle Chris, how have you been today?' His tone was respectful, but it lacked the warmth with which he had greeted his aunt.

'My rheumatism has been bothering me, son.' Christopher Holbrook looked up as the butler brought in the elaborate Sèvres tureen and set it before his wife with a flourish.

'Poor darling.' She waited for the servant to lift the cover of the tureen and hand her the big silver ladle. She peered inside. 'Clam chowder! You got it from sleeping on the ground during the war – the rheumatism, not the chowder, I mean.'

'Drum's father once told me of a cure for rheumatism they used to have in the South. They'd take a slave boy about ten years old and place him at the foot of the bed. The rheumatism sufferer would place his feet against the boy's body and the theory was that the child would drain the rheumatism from his master.' He laughed without mirth. 'Maybe I should try out Drum's father's theory.'

Drum hesitated before dipping his spoon into the chowder. 'What did my father look like, Uncle Chris? I have a pretty good mental picture of my mother, but I never did know what my father looked like.' As he bent his head to sip from the spoon, Mary Holbrook sent a warning look to her husband.

'He was a fine-looking man, Drum. About an inch taller than you are and quite a bit heavier – more muscular, I mean.'

'What colour hair did he have?' Drum asked.

'Black,' Mary Holbrook answered. 'Black as coal. He always said he inherited it from his grandfather, who was Cuban. I do believe' – she smiled at Drum – 'he was one of the handsomest men I've ever seen.'

'Can't understand where I get this curly mop of mine, then.'

'You've got beautiful hair, Drum' – Mary was persuasive – 'but nobody ever likes his own hair. Look at mine! All my life I've wanted curly blonde hair and mine is black and straight as a string. I'd trade you in a minute.'

'Must have got this dark skin from my father's grandfather, too.' Drum savoured the chowder. 'Guess most Cubans are dark. Last summer, down on the Cape, my arms and legs

15

turned nearly as black as Mede's. Going to keep out of the sun this summer or people will think I'm a nigger.'

'Hebe's put too much salt in the chowder.' Mary Holbrook made a valiant effort to change the conversation. 'Ipswich clams are salty anyway and need almost no seasoning. I must speak to her about it.'

She prattled on until the soup had vanished and Scipio had brought other plates, warm from the oven in the butler's pantry.

The meal proceeded, accompanied by a monologue from Mary Holbrook. She knew that Drum was in for a dressing down in the library after dinner and she drew on her fund of trivialities to keep up some semblance of conversation, to which her husband and Drum responded when asked direct questions but contributed little. At last, when the big silver coffee urn was brought in by Scipio and placed before Mrs Holbrook, Drum waved away his cup of coffee and addressed his uncle.

'You left word this morning, Uncle Chris, that you wanted to see me after dinner tonight.'

'I do, Drum. Scipio, bring the coffee and the decanter of port into the library. Excuse us, dear' – he bowed to his wife – 'Drum and I have something to discuss.'

'You men and your discussions.' She tried to make light of the matter, then became serious. 'Remember your promise, Chris.'

He merely nodded and led the way into the library. Scipio placed the coffee and the decanter of wine on the big table and departed noiselessly, closing the door behind him; Chris Holbrook pointed to one of the two big wing chairs that flanked the fireplace, where a bright log fire was burning. It was the only light in the room and Drum was glad. It would be easier to face his uncle in the dim light than it would be in the glare of the gas chandelier.

Stirring his coffee, Holbrook looked across at Drum. 'What are we going to do with you, Drum? You no sooner get out of one scrape than you get into another.'

'I don't feel it was my fault, Uncle Chris, that I was kicked out of Harvard. I just can't make any sense out of Latin and Greek. Latin and Greek! What good are those things going to do me? We've already gone over it before, and since I left school I've behaved myself. Yes, sir' – he grinned at his uncle – 'for a whole month I've toed the line.'

'What I have to speak to you about, Drum, happened some six or eight months ago.' Holbrook's voice was serious. 'It's the same story all over again. First when you were barely sixteen. Then when you were nineteen. Now it's this Dorothea Reynolds from Worcester.'

'Dorothea Reynolds? From Worcester?' The name meant nothing to Drum.

His uncle nodded gravely. 'She was a nursemaid for the Forbes children last summer at the Cape. Rather a pretty girl. And hardly a nursemaid, either, as she comes from a respectable family in Worcester. Her father is pastor of one of the smaller Congregational churches there.'

Drum snapped his fingers. 'Oh, you mean Dottie? I don't know if I ever did know her last name. Red hair, a few freckles on her nose, and the greenest eyes I've ever seen. Now I remember her. You don't mean—?'

'Yes, she's pregnant and she claims you're the father of her child.'

'I'll admit I knocked up Sue Dennis – or, if you prefer the more elegant expression, "got her in a family way". We were just kids and we didn't know any better. And I'll admit to doing the same thing to Hope McIntosh. But as far as Dottie is concerned, I'm not going to take the blame. At least not entirely. Sam Witherspoon and Tad Forbes were both playing around with her. In fact, it was Tad that told me about her. He had her first. We all shared her last summer, but she claimed she liked me best of the lot. Can't blame her much when you think what Tad looks like.'

'Her father and his attorney appeared at my office yesterday. They demand that you marry her. I told them that would be impossible.'

'I have no desire to marry her. She's too willing to spread her legs for anyone, but' – he looked at his uncle, puzzled –

17

'why would it be impossible for me to marry her?' There had been an accent of finality in his uncle's words that puzzled him.

'Absolutely impossible! She's not the kind of girl either your Aunt Mary or I would like to accept into the family. But you don't have to marry her. A statement from your friend Sam or from Tad to the effect that they both had relations with her will settle the matter and we'll add a thousand dollars, which will seem like a small fortune to a poor minister. But . . .' Holbrook hesitated, looking at Drum.

'But what, Uncle Chris?'

'I'm going to force you to make a very strange promise, Drum. And, strange as it is, I cannot give you a reason for it. You've got to promise me that you will not marry.'

'Not marry, Uncle Chris? Not marry ever? I can't promise you that. You know I can't. No fellow my age could.'

'But you must, Drum. You must.'

'Then, tell me why I must.'

'That I cannot do now. I just cannot, so please do not ask me. Perhaps some day I can.'

'Not now?'

'No.'

Drum got up from his chair and walked to the big table, poured himself a glass of port, and downed it, followed by a second and a third.

'Good God, Uncle Chris! Stop talking in riddles. Is there something wrong with me? Is there some reason why I should not marry? Am I different from all my friends? Why can Sam or Tad or Jedidah marry and why not me? Sam is engaged to Charity Nichols and Tad is devoting all his time to Martha Bottomley and, as you know, I've been going with Nancy Fotheringill for some time now. She's in love with me or so she says. I've even thought of proposing to her. She's a girl that both you and Aunt Mary would approve of. She's rich and her father and mother are friends of yours.'

'Nancy Fotheringill is a fine girl,' Chris Holbrook agreed, 'but I must insist that you make me this promise. I'll tone it down a little. Promise me that you will not speak of marriage to any girl until you have talked the matter over with me first. Is that too much to ask?'

'Not if you insist. But what does all this have to do with Dottie? If she's knocked up, I'm sorry. Probably I did it. She went out more with me than she did with the others. After all, our little affair went on all summer. We used to meet down on the beach after she'd put the children to sleep and you know how it is on a beach on a hot summer's night with the moon shining. Besides, she was more than willing. It was neither rape nor seduction.'

'I know you, Drum. I know that all you have to do is get a girl alone and you lose all control over yourself. You're too hot-blooded.'

'That Cuban great-grandfather!' Drum essayed a weak smile. 'It's true, Uncle Chris. The minute I meet a girl, I start planning on how I can get her into bed. But all fellows are like that. I'll bet you were too.'

'Maybe,' Holbrook admitted, 'but I think I exercised a little more control in keeping my breeches buttoned than you do. The trouble is you're young, good-looking, and rich, and that's a combination that's hard to beat. Women will chase after you, but you've got to make me that promise.'

'That I'll never propose to any girl until I talk it over with you and Aunt Mary?'

Holbrook nodded. 'And one more thing – that about keeping your breeches buttoned. Of course, I don't mean for you to be a monk. There are ways and I know you are as familiar with them as I am. There are places—'

Drum waggled a finger at his uncle. 'Shame on you, Uncle Chris! You're not even supposed to know that such places exist.'

'Listen, boy, I was brought up here in Boston and went to college here. I've been around in my day. Now, about the promise?'

'I promise. Cross my heart, Uncle Chris. I'll dance with them and flirt with them, and play games with them and maybe even kiss them, but I'll not ask any one of them to marry me until I talk it over with you and Aunt Mary.'

There was a rap on the door and before Holbrook could call out 'Come in,' the door opened and his wife entered. She went to Drum's chair and stood behind it, letting her fingers touch his hair.

'You haven't been too hard on Drum tonight, have you, Chris?'

'No, Mary. I find Drum not to be quite as blameworthy as I had suspected. It seems that the Reynolds girl was rather common property last summer at the Cape and Drum was only one of several. Therefore she cannot claim his exclusive parentage of the child. I think we can fix the matter up to the satisfaction of all concerned.'

From behind Drum's chair she formed with her lips an unspoken question to her husband.

'Drum has promised,' he answered her.

She seemed relieved. 'And the other thing you were going to mention?'

'I was waiting for you to be with me, dear, when I spoke about that.'

Drum reached up and took his aunt's hand in his. 'Ye gods, Aunt Mary! Have I done something else?'

'No, darling, your Uncle Chris and I just happen to have an idea.'

'We thought, Drum,' Holbrook continued, 'now that you are of legal age and Falconhurst is your property without my trusteeship, that you might like to go down there. It's a valuable property and we've made it one of the best plantations in the South. Fortunately it escaped damage during the war, principally because I was quartered there. The big house is really beautiful and it has been kept in fine condition. For many years prior to the war the soil was not used for planting cotton. The main business of Falconhurst was the raising of Negro slaves for the Southern market. Therefore, though all other plantations in the neighbourhood have exhausted the soil for cotton, Falconhurst is raising bumper crops. Fertilizer and scientific methods of crop rotation have made it a big producer. Cotton is high now and you're a rich man, Drum. I've invested your money carefully over the years and in addition to the plantation you have a sizeable amount of cash. You should go down there and take charge.'

'Your uncle has always been so fond of the place, Drum,' Mary interrupted. 'He's looked after it all these years and I sometimes wonder if he doesn't care more for Falconhurst than he does for Boston.'

Drum got up from the chair and walked slowly up and down the room, pausing to stare alternately at his aunt and uncle. Yes, he loved them. He had never known his own parents, who, he was told, had both died while he was still a baby. All that he had, all that he was, he owed to these two people. They were good people and had always had his own best interests at heart. They had tried to do everything for him and now he could see how poorly he had repaid them. Aunt Mary had been a mother to him and he realized the full extent of the love she had for him.

He was at a loss to understand his uncle's strange request that he should not marry. Admitting it to himself for the first time, he had been looking forward to marriage perhaps more to get away from the stuffiness of Beacon Street and have a home of his own rather than for any compelling love for a woman. Now that he had reached his maturity, he rebelled against the authority that Uncle Chris continued to exert over him and the maternal solicitude that Aunt Mary always showed. He felt like a small child. Several of his friends, on reaching the age of twenty-one, had set themselves up in bachelor flats, where they were away from the constant jurisdiction of their parents. Drum had had more freedom when he had lived in the Harvard dormitory. He had even considered taking Mede and renting a flat for himself somewhere.

But now all this could be accomplished by going South. It would be a new way of life to him, a new adventure, a severance of all ties. At Falconhurst he could lead his own life.

'Perhaps, Drum dear, you'd rather take a nice trip to Europe.' Aunt Mary had been eyeing his frantic pacing.

'Are you both trying to get rid of me in a nice way?' he asked. 'First you propose that I go to Falconhurst. Now you want me to go to Europe. Again, I ask you – what's wrong with me? Have I suddenly developed leprosy or something?'

'Now, now, Drum' – Uncle Chris' voice was placatory – 'nothing's wrong with you, but you must admit it's hardly the right thing for a young fellow your age to have no particular interest in life. Everyone should have some work to do. I'd take you into business with me and that is what I had considered when I entered you in Harvard, but without a law degree you'd be no good in a firm of lawyers.'

'We want you to be happy, Drum dear.' Aunt Mary motioned for him to sit down. 'Just living here with us and spending your summers on the Cape isn't much of a life for a young fellow.'

'I've no particular desire to go to Europe and make the grand tour,' Drum said, shrugging his shoulders. 'And I'll be a stranger at Falconhurst. But—' He looked at them both, first his aunt and then his uncle, realizing as he did so, almost for the first time, that they were neither his aunt nor uncle, nor were they, in fact, in any blood relationship to him.

'But what, Drum?' Mary awaited an answer.

'But I'll go. You're right. Since I left Harvard I've been bored. Every day seems too long. I've even missed trying to get Latin and Greek through my thick skull. I'll go South.'

'We're not trying to get rid of you, Drum.' Chris was serious. 'You know this is your home and always will be. But keeping you here doing nothing is like keeping a spirited young stallion in a stall. You need to get out in the world and accomplish something. Remember, though, this is your home. It always will be. We love you, Drum. Never forget that. No matter whatever happens, remember that one thing.'

'I know,' Drum agreed, 'and I know all you have done for me and how little I have done to repay it. I don't know what's the matter with me, Uncle Chris, I don't know. I try to act like my friends, but there's some devil down inside me that makes me act differently. I'd like to be Beacon Street and Bostonian and proper and the kind of person you want me to be and I try. Damn it all, Uncle Chris, I do try. And then something comes along and I forget all my good intentions.

Perhaps Falconhurst is the place for me. Perhaps I'll be more at home there than I've ever been in Boston. It's time I found out. I'll go.'

'Then I'll write Sylvester, the overseer, to get things ready for you. You'll find him a good, trustworthy man who knows his business. He's not been there very long, but he was highly recommended. He was born and brought up in Benson, the nearest town to Falconhurst.'

Mary Holbrook arose from her chair and stood before Drum. Suddenly she threw her arms around him and kissed him and he felt his uncle's hand in his. He still did not understand everything, but he knew he was doing something to please them. For the time being that was sufficient. Walking between them, he crossed the library and opened the door to the hall.

'The Simmonds are coming in tonight to play whist, Drum. Don't you want to join us?'

He laughed. 'Five people for whist, Aunt Mary? No, I'll go out for a while.'

'But you'll be home early?'

He nodded affirmatively and started for the stairs. He ran up them, then down through the hall to the door of his room. The door to Mede's cubbyhole was closed and he opened it without knocking. Mede was sitting on his mussed bed alone, looking through a stereopticon, which was his particular pride.

'Johanna she gone.' Mede removed a photograph of Niagara Falls from the wire clasps of the stereopticon and laid it down on the bed. 'You know, Mista Drum, you kin look at that picture and almost hear the water a-rushin' over them falls. It look so real. Want to see it?'

'No, boy, get my other coat. I'm going out.' Drum turned on his heel, stripping off the house jacket and flinging it to Mede.

'Yes, sir, Mista Drum sir. You wantin' me to go with you?'

Drum shook his head. 'I'm heading for Mother Carey's. No use in your going there, Mede. Not one of her girls would take on a nigger.'

'Not wantin' any white girls neither, Mista Drum. Never did have one and never did want one. Know one thing? Ain' no white girl what can come up to a brown skin. Coloured girls just love it, Mista Drum, but just can't 'magine any white girl loving it.'

'They do, boy, they sure do, once you get them warmed up. But you'll be having plenty of dark meat from now on. We're going to Falconhurst.'

'Glory be! I'm going to see my mammy again! Glory be, Mista Drum. You mean it?'

'I do.'

'We going to like it at Falconhurst, Mista Drum. We sure going to like it there.' Mede eased Drum's long arms into the coat of dark green broadcloth, then handed him his white beaver hat and wallet.

'You-a-goin' to Mother Carey's, you're sure going to need plenty of money. Them white girls don' give it away, they sell it. And you know something, Mista Drum? That what you buy ain' never so good as what you gets given to you.'

'Maybe you're right, Mede, but I've found this out — when you get it given to you, you usually have to pay in the end.'

CHAPTER THREE

TRUE TO APRIL, the lowering skies of the afternoon had turned into a cold drizzle when Drum closed the heavy front doors behind him and stepped down the few granite steps that led to Beacon Street. An ancient Jehu, his sodden hat turned down all around and dripping water on his caped coat, was seeking shelter under one of the budding elm trees that lined Beacon Street on the Common side. A whistle from Drum caused him to slap his nag with the reins and draw up to the curb. Drum stepped inside the decrepit vehicle, which smelled of mouldy leather and the countless sweaty bodies that it had transported over the years. The cabbie slid back a little panel.

'Where to, mister?'

'Mother Carey's,' Drum answered. 'It's down on—'

'Don't need to tell me where 'tis,' the old man chuckled. 'Half o' them young toffs that come out at night is headin' there, but 'pears to me you're a mite early. Things don't start hummin' at Ma Carey's till about midnight.'

'None of your damned business what time I go there,' Drum snapped back. He had no desire to carry on a conversation with the cabbie.

'Jest tryin' to be friendly, young feller. Jest tryin' to be friendly, that's all. No offence meant.' The cabbie slammed shut the panel, but Drum opened it again, passing his hand through it with two bits in his fingers.

'Sorry. I'm a bit edgy tonight.'

'Then Ma Carey's the place to go to take the edginess outa you. Get you there's quick's I can. Giddap!' Once again the panel closed but this time gently.

The horse clip-clopped up over the hill, past the State House, and then down School Street, towards the market, arriving finally at a dark street where the fishy smell of the harbour hung heavy in the rainy night. There was one fair-sized house on the street, better kept than its neighbours, and through the fan light over the door a gas jet in a red shade sent a ruby light out on to the glistening cobbles.

The old man got down off the box, opened a large umbrella, and escorted Drum up the steps until he was in the shelter of the narrow porch that extended out from the doorway. Smiling over the tip that Drum gave him, the cabbie departed, and Drum pulled the long chain beside the door, hearing the echoes of the bell inside. He could hear heavy footsteps approaching inside and the door opened only as far as the guard chain on the inside permitted. An enormous woman, dressed in decent black with a caricature of a maid's cap of white lace on her frizzled hair, peered out at him, immediately taking the chain off the door and welcoming him inside.

'Mister Maxwell' – the Irish brogue was pleasantly thick – 'come in, Mister Maxwell. Step right in and I'll be after telling the madam that you're here. My, but she'll be glad to see you.'

25

The warm and brightly lighted hall was eloquent with closed doors. One might imagine all sorts of things happening behind them, but they held no secrets for Drum, who had been in all of them. Biddie, the maid, knocked on the first door and at a responding 'Come in' she opened it for Drum to enter. It was a small room, overheated by a Franklin stove, with a discreetly shaded lamp that revealed a woman, fantastically arrayed in a ball gown, reclining on a rose-upholstered gilt chaise longue. Her brassy hair was elaborately coiffured, heightened by a spray of paradise feathers that sprung from a diamond clasp. She was as large a woman as her maid Biddie but so tightly corseted that her breasts were pushed up high, nearly escaping from the froth of lace that edged the front of her gown. The vivid magenta of the dress accented her florid complexion and the coarseness of her face. It was impossible to judge her age because of the depth of her maquillage, but she was probably nearer sixty than the forty she hoped she appeared to be. She was smoking a slender cigarette and raised one hand in a languid greeting, making sure that the lace over her elbows was not displaced to show the flabbiness of her upper arm. Her fingers were a coruscating mass of vari-coloured jewels.

'Drum, darling!' The brogue that was so apparent in Biddie's speech was nearly concealed in her own. 'How good to see my boy. I've been sitting here and, believe it or not, I was thinking about you. I was just asking myself "Who's the handsomest fellow that ever came into your house, Mother Carey?" and I decided it was you. There's nobody I'd rather see than my own dear boy, Drum.'

'Mother.' Drum took the bejewelled hand and kissed it with a cavalier gesture, realizing as he did so that this was the only woman he had ever called 'mother' in his life. In some ways, he felt, she had a right to be called that because there had always been a peculiar rapport between them from his very first visit to her establishment on his seventeenth birthday. 'Beacon Street got a little too stuffy for me tonight, so I raced over here early to get my pick of your lovelies. How about my Rosalie?'

'Rosalie?' Mother Carey shrugged her shoulders. 'Just between you and me, Drum, Rosalie is nothing but a two-bit whore. She's pretty, yes, and she happens to be young, which is an advantage, but she's got no talent in bed. She's not for you tonight, darling, even though she's your favourite.'

'Then Bettina?'

Again Mother Carey shook her head. 'Bettina is supposed to be Spanish, but she's nothing but an Eye-talian I picked up over in the North End. Oh, she gives a man his money's worth, but again I say she's not for you, Drummond Maxwell, you darling you, you're something out of the ordinary, therefore you must have something out of the ordinary and I'm going to give you a great big surprise. I've got just that for you, Drum darling.'

'Something you've been keeping up your sleeve?' Drum let his hand glide up to her elbow.

'Hell, no, dear. The baggage just arrived yesterday and she's so goddam independent and exclusive that she's taken on nobody as yet. She reserves the right to pick and choose and at twenty dollars, yessiree, twenty dollars, but she insists she's worth every cent of it. She's French – or so she says – and she comes from Belle LaBelle's house in New Orleans. She's on her way to Montreal, but she's stopping off in Boston for a few days to rest up from the ocean voyage and make a little extra money.'

'Twenty dollars, Mother? What is she, gold-plated?'

'Solid gold, I'd say. She doesn't look a day over fourteen and could pass for a virgin any time, but she admits to being eighteen and that means she's probably twenty-five. But she's little. *Petite*, the Frenchies call it. Pretty as a picture and looks just like a little doll.'

'Sounds interesting.' Drum was getting enthusiastic.

'Anyway, she's taken over my best room and she won't appear downstairs with any of the girls. I'm to send them up to her, them that can afford twenty dollars, and she'll look them over and see if they're to her taste. Fussiest goddam whore I ever had in my house. Thank God she's only going to be here a few days, her and her milk baths.'

27

'So' – Drum looked at her and winked – 'do you think I might meet with her approval?'

'And if you don't, who would? Biddie'll take you up. Her name's Gigi, and remember, she insists on being treated like a lady until she gets into bed.' She tinkled the small bell on the table beside her and waited for the door to open and Biddie to enter. With instructions to Biddie to take Drum upstairs and introduce him to Mademoiselle Gigi, she again extended her bejewelled hand and this time Drum kissed it with real feeling.

'I just hope she's worth a gold eagle, boy. In my best days I never got more than five dollars and I thought I was pretty high up on the ladder then. But prices are going up. Yessiree, prices are going up.'

Drum ascended the stairs behind Biddie and waited for her to knock on one of the front doors. At an almost inaudible murmur from within, she opened the door and ushered Drum in. After the bright lights of the hall, it took him a moment to adjust his eyes to the dimness of the room – Mother Carey's so-called Royal Room because of the enormous bed with the ceiling mirror over it, the flowered Brussels carpet, and the curtains at the window. The room was lighted by only two fairy lamps, those tiny oil lamps of the period with coloured glass shades, which cast a dim, rosy glow in the room. Stretched out on the chaise longue similar to the one that Mother Carey occupied downstairs was a girl clad in a négligé of some sheer black material through which her flesh showed rosy pink. She was an elfin creature, a little French doll, so beautiful that Drum had no regrets over the twenty dollars it was to cost him.

She half rose, adjusting the pillow behind her. 'The Madame she picked well,' she said, studying him as he stood inside the closed door. 'One, you are young. I hate old men. Two, you are handsome and I like handsome men. Three, you are blond, and I like men with blond hair. *Mais oui!* Gigi is satisfied, but you must promise one thing. You must be very kind and gentle with Gigi. I am so tiny' – she made a little moue with her lips – 'so very tiny that you must be careful, do you promise?'

'I do. And let me tell you that I like small girls with black

hair and that I shall be careful, but I think I can satisfy you.'
Drum bowed, remembering his instructions to treat her like
a lady.

'That we shall see. Gigi is not the one to be satisfied, you are,
and Gigi knows many ways to satisfy a man. But come here,
mon cher, sit beside me and let us talk.'

'Talk?' Drum had already begun to remove his cravat. This
pretence of gentility was becoming a little tiresome.

'And why not? There are many things a man and a woman
can talk about that will make what is about to happen more
interesting. Come!'

He strode across the room, pushed one of the frothy pillows
from the chaise longue, and sat down beside her. Immediately
her hand reached out and touched his, drawing it to her. 'This
is more comfortable, yes?'

Drum glanced towards the bed. 'I can think of a more
comfortable place.'

'Oh, you are in such a hurry. You men! Always in a hurry.
Love can be so much more *amusant* if one does not hurry.
There are so many little things that heighten one's pleasure.'
She sat up, leaned towards him, and pressed her lips to his.
One of her hands untied the bow at her throat, so that her
négligé fell from her shoulders, and the same hand guided his
to her breasts. For long moments he explored, marvelling at
the size of her breasts for so small a person and at their
perfection. There was no sound but the rustling of the silken
pillows and her almost inaudible moans. Finally with a
determination that apparently had caused her some effort, she
pushed him away.

'As you say, *mon cher*, there is a more comfortable place than
this and certainly the clothes you are wearing must be most
uncomfortable. See!' She stood up, leaving the wisp of black
silk behind her. 'While you are getting rid of those horrid tight
clothes I shall light the lights.'

'The lights?' He was peeling his clothes off fast.

She came close to him, letting her hands slide over his body.

'*Mais oui*, the lights. The good *mère* knows that one's
pleasure is far greater when one not only feels but sees.' She

pointed to the mirror over the bed. 'And so, m'sieur, with this most marvellous gas that you have for illumination here in your city, we shall be as bright as midday.' She took a rolled paper spill from a vase and held it over one of the tiny lamps until it burst into flame, then went around the room lighting the gas jets and the chandelier in the centre. As she turned to replace the charred spill she stopped suddenly and looked at Drum in his nakedness. The professional smile on her lips – it was not altogether professional, as she was anticipating this encounter as much as he was – vanished. Instead there was a shadow of consternation on her face and her smile vanished to be replaced by a scowl of hatred and disgust.

'Who are you?' she demanded, backing away from him.

'I'm Drummond Maxwell, but I don't see what that means to you.'

'It means nothing. But please dress and leave.'

'What?'

'Get your clothes on and get out.'

'What's wrong with you all of a sudden?'

'Please do as I say. I have no reason. I only ask that you get out.' She picked up his trousers and shirt and flung them at him.

'Now, look here. If this is a game, I'm getting tired of it. What are you doing? Playing with me? Do you want me to chase you around the room or something? Is that your way of doing things?'

She backed up to the chest of drawers and slipped open one of the small drawers on top. From it she drew out a stiletto whose thin blade of steel glittered in the brilliant lights.

'It is no game. And, although you are a strong man, if you try to force me, you will be sorry. I'll gash your face. Now, dress and get out!'

Suddenly Drum had lost all desire for her. He slipped into his clothes quickly. As he fumbled with buttons, he realized he had never before been made such a fool of. His narrow trousers gave him some trouble and when he had managed to get them on, he found he had forgotten to put on his socks, so he drew his boots on over his bare feet. Without tying his

30

cravat, he donned his coat, grabbed his hat, and started for the door. He had an insane desire to take her over his knee and trounce her, but the sharp blade in her hand could cause damage and actually he felt so foolish under her staring eyes that he wanted nothing more than to leave her as quickly as possible. Her body, which only moments before had set him on fire, now repulsed him. With one hand on the door-knob, he reached into his pocket with the other and drew out a gold eagle.

'I always pay a whore for her time,' he said, as he flung the coin down on the floor at her feet.

'Take your money.' She kicked it back to him. 'I know that I am a whore. You know it and probably the whole world knows it, but I chose to be one and I am. I enjoy it. I enjoy bedding myself with men that I choose and if they pay me money, that is only right because I give them their money's worth. Yes, I am a whore and in the eyes of the world that is about as low as a woman can get, but let me tell you just one thing. I am a white whore, understand, and if there is anything lower than a white whore it is a white woman that beds herself with a nigger.'

'A nigger? Are you calling me a nigger?'

'Do you think I have lived in New Orleans all my life and I cannot tell a coloured man when I see one? Look in your mirror. Your hair! Your eyes! Your nose! And above all – that.' She pointed to Drum's trousers. 'No white man ever had a monstrosity like that. That's a sure sign of a nigger.'

'I've never had any complaints before.'

'That's because these northern girls are ignorant. Now, get out.'

In his anger he wanted to strangle her, choke that white throat until she denied the words she had spoken. He knew they were not true and yet he was too stunned to react to anger. His stiffened fingers closed around the knob of the door while words struggled in his brain for utterance, but he was mute. Mechanically, his eyes still on her, he stepped out into the hall and closed the door behind him, walking the length of the hall without realizing that he was lifting one foot and placing it down and lifting another. He made his way down the stairs and, with no conscious effort on his part, opened the door to Mother Carey's room and stumbled in. Something inside him cried out for comfort – some consolation, some denial of the horrible words with which the woman upstairs had branded him. Still holding his cravat in his hand, he lurched like a drunken man on to the floor beside the chaise longue where Mother Carey was sitting, burying his head in her satin lap, and then, unable to control himself, he burst into tears – racking sobs that made it impossible to speak.

'Why, Drum boy, what's happened to you?' In vain she tried to raise his head, but he clung the closer to her, ashamed of the tears he was unable to control.

She soothed him, stroking his head and letting her fingers wander down to the warm flesh at the nape of his neck. Finally she noticed a lessening in his sobs and he became quieter, although he still clung to her, his fingers digging into her flesh through the tight corsets. Gently she lifted him up beside her, pillowing his head on her sequinned bosom. With the other hand she reached out to the small table, took out the crystal stopper from a decanter, and held the decanter to his lips.

'I don't know what's the matter with my boy, but whatever it is, drink this and then tell Mother all about it. Land sakes, I feel almost like your own mother. You've been coming here since before you started to shave and I've always looked out for you. Now, come on! Nothing's ever so bad as it seems after you tell someone about it. Come on, tell Mother.'

'It's that girl upstairs.' He finally managed to get the words out.

'That dirty little slut! Did she do something to you? Her and her hoity-toity airs, coming in here and setting herself up like some goddam princess. Tell me, Drum, tell me!'

'She said' – he took another gulp of the whisky to give himself courage to speak – 'that she wouldn't go to bed with me because I was a nigger. She called me a nigger.'

It took a moment for the import of his words to sink into Mother's consciousness. With more agility than one would have thought possible from her tightly corseted body, she was up

32

on her feet, opening the door, and screaming down the hall. 'Biddie, Biddie, come here!'

Sensing some emergency, Biddie came running down the hall and into the room. Mother was still standing in the middle of the floor, her face purple under the heavy powder.

'You go upstairs to that slut's room – that goddam two-bit whore Gigi – and you bring her down. Drag her down by the hair of her head if you have to, but get her here – quick!' She turned to Drum. 'Never heard of such a thing in my life. The girl's crazy – off her rocker! I know why she will only take certain men. She claims she is too small to take most men and I know you, Drum. That's what all this fuss's about. She was just afraid of you, that's all, and she said the first thing that came into her mind. Hush, don't say a word. Here she comes. Let me handle this.'

Gigi, her black négligé clutched around her shoulders, was pushed into Mother's room by Biddie's hamlike hand. Her eyes were blazing and she turned and gave Biddie a slap across the face.

'Slap me, you bitch.' Biddie drew off and let her have it, hitting her so hard she reeled across the room. 'No whore's a-slappin' me.'

Gigi straightened herself up to the full majesty of her five feet, assuming as regal an air as she could with the mark of Biddie's hand on her face. 'What is the meaning of this? *Mon Dieu!* I shall pack my bags and leave this house this instant. Never in my life have I been so treated. You send a goddam nigger up to my room and then you send this she-devil up to drag me down. I want you to know that I am Gigi—'

'Shut up!' Mother raised her hand and would have knocked her down, except that Drum, despite his hatred for the girl, held Mother's hand. 'Now, what's all this about? What do you mean by calling Drum Maxwell a nigger?'

'Look at him,' Gigi was screaming. 'Look at him! All you have to do is look at him, especially with his clothes off. No white man was ever like him. Ask anyone in New Orleans the sure proof for a coloured man. Even though he may look white, when he has his clothes off, you can tell that he's nothing but a

33

nigger beast. Then look at his hair. Look at his lips. Look at his nose. He's coloured, I tell you, and where I come from a coloured man's a nigger.'

'Look at this and look at that and look at the other thing.' Mother was still ready to clout her. 'Now you look at me, you high-falutin' French trollop. Drum Maxwell is no coloured man and he never was and he never will be. Drum Maxwell comes from one of the richest families in Boston. His uncle is Mister Christopher Holbrook of Beacon Street and if you knew anything about Boston, you'd know that Beacon Street's better than Buckingham Palace in London. Drum's a gentleman, a toff, a real swell. He's the best society in Boston, and Boston society would make your dirty New Orleans crowd look like a bunch of Johnny-come-latelies. What do you mean by all this?'

'But I saw him undressed. I know. He would have killed me.'

'Too goddam bad he didn't. I don't know much about niggers because I never had one in my house, but just because a man's well hung is no sign he's coloured. We got a Swede named Olaf what comes here about once every six months. Never saw anything like it on a human being before, but he's no nigger. Look, sister, you're in the wrong business. If you wanted to get ahead in this business, you've got to be able to take what comes along.'

'But I come from New Orleans. I know.'

'You don't know a goddam thing. Now, look at Drum. Take a good look at him. Look at his hair! Did you ever see a nigger with yellow hair? Look at his skin! He's whiter than my Bettina, who's an Eye-talian. I've never in my life seen a handsomer man than Drum Maxwell and if he's like you say he is, so much the better. Take a long look, dearie, a long, long look.' Mother clawed at Gigi's hair and dragged her to within a few feet of Drum. 'Look, you little slut, take a good look or I'll clobber you like you've never been clobbered before. I'll mess up that pretty face of yours so you'll be fit only for some two-bit sailors' dive. Look at him!'

Gigi, her sangfroid entirely departed, now frightened out of her wits by Mother's belligerence, looked long and searchingly at Drum. He returned her stare.

'I could be mistaken,' she admitted. 'Now that I look at him carefully, I can see that I could be.'

Mother gave a vicious yank to her hair.

'You *could* be mistaken. You *could* be? You know goddam well you are. Look at him again.'

Gigi stared. Even in her present state of agitation she was not unaware of Drum's good looks. No, his hair was not kinky, despite its tight curl. His lips no longer seemed Negroid, nor did his nostrils. She had evidently made a serious mistake. Possibly the fellow might have some Spanish ancestry, which would account for his Latin appearance.

'Have you any Spanish blood, m'sieur?' she finally asked.

'My great-grandfather came from Cuba,' he answered.

'Then, I must apologize to you, m'sieur. I judged you wrongly. I can see now that you are not a Negro and have no trace of Negro blood, but I have always been afraid of big men. Once a man like you nearly killed me and that is why I must choose my own men. So I do apologize to you. I regret, m'sieur, that I was hasty. Please consider my words as never having been said.'

'And please pack your baggage and get yourself to hell out of my house.' Mother felt Drum relax under her encircling arm. 'I'll not have the likes of you around here. I'll give you half an hour to get out or Biddie'll throw you out. Git.' She pushed her out of the room.

'Of all the goddam foolishness I ever heard of.' She offered Drum another drink of whisky, this time pouring it into a glass, and she took one herself. 'You need something to get yourself back on your feet tonight. Spend the night here, Drum. A pint of good whisky and one of my girls will make you forget all this.'

'Can I have Rosalie? I've always liked her, Mother.'

'You can have Rosalie and Bettina and Clarice – all three of them if you want them.'

'No, Rosalie is enough. She's not like the rest. She's sweet and good and makes a man feel comfortable.'

'Then, Rosalie it is. Drum, did you give that slut any money?'

'I gave her twenty dollars, Mother.'

'Biddie, go up and get that twenty dollars. Knock her down and take it away from her if you have to. Then give it to Drum. Tonight's on the house, Drum. Rosalie and the whisky too.'

'Thank you, Mother,' Drum smiled for the first time. 'I guess that's what I need – Rosalie and the whisky too.'

'Then, you just sit here and I'll go out and have Rosalie get ready for you. Thank God it's early yet.' She walked over to Drum and reached up and patted his face. 'You're my boy, Drum. Don't forget that. If you ever need a friend, remember Mother.'

'I shall,' he promised.

CHAPTER FOUR

WHEN DRUM AWOKE, it was dark and cold. The fire in the grate had gone out and even the warmth of Rosalie's body, curved to fit his own, was not enough. He reached down to the foot of the bed and pulled the quilt up over him, tucking it in around Rosalie's back and adjusting it so that it did not cover her head. Her face was closely pressed against his chest and the curls of her chestnut hair only partially covered his arm that encircled her. Without waking her, he slid his arm down under the pillow and pulled her closer, so that he could feel her moist lips and her warm breath against one of his paps. He did not know what time it might be but he had left word with Biddie to call him at six. It was important to be home in time for breakfast.

He would have warmed himself further with a drink from the bottle on the floor beside the bed, but he knew it was empty. He had drunk it all himself – Rosalie never drank. He knew that because he had tasted her drink one night, when he ordered one for her in Mother's salon, and had discovered that it was nothing but cold tea. She confessed to him that she never drank liquor like the other girls but, as the customers paid the regular price for it, Mother made even more on Rosalie's drinks than on the others'.

Now, snuggling down into the pillow, feeling the warmth of her body against his own under the protection of the quilt, he realized that he was not only comfortable but happy. That he was happy was something he could not understand after the events of the night before, but the very fact that Rosalie was beside him had seemed to make his worries disappear. Despite the amount of whisky he had drunk, he felt no ill effects from it. In fact, his mind was so sparklingly clear that he had no wish to sleep again nor, despite the warmth of her body, which was arousing his desire, did he particularly want to wake Rosalie. Somehow everything seemed to be so very much all right that he didn't want to disturb anything.

Presently she stirred on his arm and he knew that she too was awake because her lips nuzzled against him and he pulled her up in the bed until her face was on a level with his own. Their lips met and their hands explored and their flesh was hot against each other's under the thick quilt until Biddie's rap on the door interrupted them.

'Six o'clock, Mister Maxwell,' she whispered, opening the door a crack.

'I'm awake, Biddie. Give me another ten minutes and I'll be up. Call a cabbie for me if you can find one.' There were usually one or two hacks waiting outside the door in the early morning to carry away the occupants of the night.

Now Drum had reached a point where he could not leave Rosalie and the ten minutes lengthened into half an hour before he was up and dressed and racing down the stairs. By the time he reached home, it was nearly seven and he let himself in silently with his key, tiptoeing up the broad stairs, past the still-closed door of his aunt's and uncle's room to his own on the third floor. Mede was sleeping, but Drum roused

37

him, bidding him to lay out clean clothes while he washed and shaved. At seven-thirty he was in his place at the breakfast table, beaming a good morning to his Aunt Mary, behind the silver coffee urn, and to his uncle, who lowered his morning newspaper long enough to greet him.

Hebe had outdone herself this morning with buckwheat cakes and fresh maple syrup, crisp bacon, and little sausages. Scipio, on silent feet, served them deftly, waiting behind Aunt Mary's chair until they had eaten; then, just as silently, he took the plates out to the butler's pantry. As he left, Drum got up from the table and slipped the bolt on the swinging door between the pantry and the dining-room. His uncle stared at him, a question on his lips, but as Aunt Mary's back was to the door, she had not noticed.

'I'm sorry if I'm going to make you a little late for your office this morning, Uncle Chris, but there's something we've got to talk about.'

'Is it so important that it cannot wait until evening? I've an appointment this morning.'

'Let your uncle go, darling, and talk it over with me if it's so important it cannot wait.' Aunt Mary took her husband's coffee cup to be refilled.

'Perhaps I won't detain you too long, Uncle Chris. It's just one question I wanted to ask you, and the answer can be a simple "yes" or "no".' Drum waited a second while the coffee flowed from the spigot into his uncle's cup. 'Uncle Chris, am I a nigger?'

There was a crash as the coffee cup dropped from Mary's hand. She looked first at Drum and then at her husband, pleading with her eyes.

'Is that why you forbade me to marry, Uncle Chris? Is it?'

Chris handed his napkin to Mary to sop up the coffee from the tablecloth.

'I'll answer your question in the one word you mentioned, Drum. No, you are not a Negro.'

'Then, I shall ask you another question, Uncle Chris. Am I a white man? I don't mean just white skin. Am I a pure white man?'

Chris Holbrook looked at his wife and she stared back at him. Almost imperceptibly she nodded her head.

'I can only say this,' he said finally, 'it is true that you have coloured blood in you.'

'Then, that makes me a nigger.' Drum brought his fist down on the table with such force that the dishes rattled. 'That makes me just as much of a nigger as Mede or Scipio.'

His uncle shook his head slowly in denial. 'You certainly don't think of yourself as a black man, do you, Drum?'

'I never did until last night?'

'And what happened last night?'

'I think I'd rather spare Aunt Mary the details. Sufficient to say, I was accused of being a Negro.'

'Let's all go into the library,' Mary said, grasping the edge of the table to help herself to stand up. 'Chris, send Mede to your office with a message that you will be late. Nothing could be more important than this is to Drum or to ourselves.' She walked round the table and took Drum's arm for support. 'Just remember one thing, Drum, we love you like our own son. We couldn't love you any more than we do. Whatever happens, remember that.'

They walked out through the drawing-room, across the hall, and into the library, where Chris closed the door. Drum sat in one of the big leather chairs facing Chris, but his aunt insisted on sitting on the arm of Drum's chair, her hand on his shoulder. For a long time they talked, while Chris tried to explain to Drum some of his past history. They had intended, he said, to tell it all to Drum on his twenty-first birthday, but Mary had been reluctant. Now it was evident the time had come. It was not going to be easy for any of them.

Chris Holbrook went back to the time that he was serving as a captain in the Union Army in the war. He told how one night Drum's father, whose name was Drummage, had saved his life.

'I wouldn't be here this morning, Drum, if it had not been for your father. And let me say right here that he was one of the finest men I have ever known. Yes, Drum, he was a Negro, but he was not a full-blooded Negro. We would call him a

39

mulatto, although I am just not sure what percentage of white blood he had in him.'

'And he was one of the handsomest men I have ever seen,' Mary added.

'Your mother, Drum, was Sophie Maxwell of Falconhurst Plantation. The Maxwells were an important family in the South. They were wealthy as well as important. Falconhurst slaves were known far and wide as the best in the South.'

Yes, Drummage, Drum's father, had been born a Falconhurst slave. Beyond that, Chris knew very little about Drum's ancestry except what he had heard from Drum's grandmother, whose name was Pearl – Big Pearl, if he remembered correctly. She was a Negro but not an ordinary Negro – a Mandingo. Mandingos were the aristocrats of the slave world. They were a special breed from Northern Africa, part Arab and part Negro, noted for the strength and beauty of their superb bodies, their intelligence, and their fine characters. They were scarce, these Mandingos, and highly prized, bringing fabulous prices in the slave market. And, Chris added, smiling as though it might mitigate somewhat the seriousness of what he had to say, that Drum's grandmother, Big Pearl, was Mede's mother; which actually made Mede, Drum's body servant, his own uncle.

Hammond Maxwell, Sophie Maxwell's father, had been killed in the war. Sophie was a young widow and was the sole heir to the plantation. As the entire wealth of Falconhurst was in its slaves, there was of course nothing left. It was then that Drummage, Drum's father, came to the front. Impressed not only by his rare good looks but by his brains, Sophie had married him and that in the presence of Chris Holbrook himself. Truly, Sophie was in love with her husband and Drum need have no fear that he was a bastard; he was entirely legitimate and the sole heir to Falconhurst.

Drum's mother had died at his birth and Drum's father soon after. Drum's father had been murdered by the white people of the neighbourhood, who were incensed over the fact that Drummage had married a white woman, that he was the owner of Falconhurst, and that he was running for Congress and would certainly have been elected. Drum need not, Chris assured him, ever be ashamed of his father. Why, Drum's father was actually a member of the Union League and if he were in Boston today, he could walk right up the steps and into the Union League Club.

So this, Aunt Mary explained, was the reason why she and Uncle Chris did not want Drum to marry, at least until he had talked the matter over with them. It would hardly be fair for any girl to marry him without knowing that there was Negro blood in him.

'Which means,' Drum answered with some bitterness, 'that I can never marry a white woman. And since I am sure I could never marry a black one, I shall never be able to marry at all.'

'That, my dear Drum, is why we suggested that you return to Falconhurst.'

'So that I could marry some black wench?'

Mary shook her head in denial. 'No, Drum, you do not need to marry a black wench. The octoroon girls of New Orleans are considered the most beautiful women in the world. You are only partly coloured and I do not lie to you when I say you are a handsome man. So, then, there are girls whose blood is the same as yours who are just as handsome as you are.'

'She'd still be a nigger, just like me.'

Chris allowed an edge of anger to creep into his voice. 'I forbid you ever to use that word again in this house, Drum. There is no such a thing as a *nigger*. A black man is a Negro. *Nigger* is nothing but a corruption of the Southern dialect that preferred to say *Nigra* for *Negro*. Now, let's go into this matter a little more. I respect the Negroes. Remember this, Drum, I put in four years fighting a war to free them. Do you think I would have done that unless I felt that they were worth fighting for?'

Drum had to admit that there was some truth in his uncle's statement.

'Then, during the last part of the war, I met your father, Drum, and, as I told you, he saved my life. White men were going to kill me and a black man saved me. That obligation initiated my friendship with him and I accepted his invitation to make my headquarters at Falconhurst. Soon I felt towards

Drummage more like a brother than a friend. We were very close, closer than I have been to any other man in my life. I saw him take a run-down plantation and make it into a thriving, prosperous business. I saw him take the Falconhurst slaves and make them into upright, self-respecting people with their own community and their own code of laws and living. I even saw him give them names and the pride to hold their heads up high. Now I want you to respect him as much as I do, regardless of what colour he was. He was a man, Drum, a fine man, and he was cruelly murdered by white people who were jealous of him.'

Drum looked from his uncle to his aunt. Nothing they could ever say would assuage the awful shock of knowing what he really was, but their confidence made him feel somewhat better. 'So, you think I should go to Falconhurst, where I shall be among people of my own kind?'

'No, Drum, that is not the reason, at least not the entire reason. Falconhurst is your property now that you are of age. It is a valuable property. You should be there to take care of it. Remember this one thing. You speak of "people of your own kind". You are not a Negro, nor are you black. And more important than your colour, Drum, you are an educated, cultured man, even if you did not master Latin or Greek.' He essayed a weak smile.

'You'll be so happy at Falconhurst, Drum darling,' Aunt Mary said, trying to be helpful. 'Of course we are going to miss you and you'll miss all your friends and your home here, but it will be a whole new life for you. Today you learned something about yourself that I daresay you had never even suspected before. It's been a shock to you, but remember this, Drum – it has not changed you. You're the same handsome boy you were before you knew about it. You can always come back here whenever you wish – it's your home, Drum – but Falconhurst will be your home too.'

He gently removed her arm from his shoulder and stood up, staring into the log fire that blazed in the fireplace. His uncle and aunt both watched him, waiting for him to speak. It was a long moment before he turned and faced them.

'Yes, I am the same man I was yesterday before I knew about this. But now I want to prove that I am the same man. I think perhaps I'm a little bit in love with Nancy Fotheringill. I know she's in love with me. Tomorrow night there is to be a small ball at her house and I am invited. I think I shall propose to her, but I shall tell her the truth. If she accepts me and if her parents accept me, I shall marry her and we'll go to Falconhurst together and start this new life you talk about. Yes, it may be a new life, but just at this moment I'm not so very anxious to start a new life. I'd rather end my old one because I have a feeling this new life will not be a good one for me.' He turned to leave them, unable to stay the tears that his aunt was shedding or assuage the abject sorrow on his uncle's face.

CHAPTER FIVE

THE FOTHERINGILL FAMILY had previously lived on Chestnut Street on 'The Hill' – that is, Beacon Hill – which was a most proper Boston address, although not quite as socially important as Beacon Street, Mount Vernon Street, or Louisburg Square. But, with the opening up of the Back Bay, or rather the filling in of the back bay to make THE Back Bay, Commonwealth Avenue had started to attract the attention of the very rich, among them Mr Fotheringill. True, those who lived in the fine old homes on Beacon Street rather turned up their noses at Commonwealth Avenue ('horrible brownstone atrocities, my dear'), while those living in the new houses on Commonwealth Avenue looked down their noses at the old Beacon Street houses ('such horrible drains, my dear'). But, while the houses on Beacon Street had the historic advantage of purple window panes and Bullfinch fronts, the houses on Commonwealth Avenue did have real bathrooms and central heating along with their carved oak woodwork and stained glass windows.

So Mr Fotheringill, lured by the more expansive plots on Commonwealth Avenue, had built himself a corner mansion that, true to the prevailing style of the 1880s, somewhat resembled a French château or an Italian Renaissance palace, depending on which angle it was viewed from. It could also be considered faintly English baronial and had one or two corner towers that were almost Spanish. And the house boasted a ballroom – one of the few private ballrooms in the city. It was only natural, therefore, that most of the Fotheringill entertaining since the opening of the new house a few short years ago took the form of balls. It was really not a very large ballroom, however, and only about a hundred couples could be accommodated comfortably, so the Fotheringill dances were always referred to in the social columns as 'intimate affairs'.

Some twenty-four young people were to sit down to dinner in the dining-room before the dance began and, since Drum had been invited at Nancy Fotheringill's special request and as her escort, he was placed next to her at dinner. Nancy Fotheringill, had she been a poor girl, would have been called 'plain, poor thing'. She was nearly as tall as Drum, which made her feel awkward, and she was inclined to slouch to minimize her height. Her face was well-boned and she had a look of more than ordinary intelligence, but she would never be considered pretty. Tonight, however, she had taken particular pains with her toilette and the polonaise she was wearing, of heavy cream satin, was appliquéd with lace and fell in elaborate drapings over a skirt of the same heavy lace. Pearl earrings and a string of pearls – modest in size, as befitted an unmarried woman – were her only jewellery. Her mouse-coloured hair had been done in a waterfall of curls behind and the only colour she wore was the bunch of Parma violets that Drum had sent her, which she carried in a filigreed bouquet holder that dangled from a silver finger ring by a slender chain.

Drum too had taken unusual pains with his appearance. His suit of black broadcloth with revers of corded silk was relieved only by the snowy whiteness of his shirt and the fringed white satin bow tie, which was embellished with a diamond stud that exceeded in size but matched the diamond studs of his shirt front. Tonight his hair was sleek, heavy with pomade, and his olive skin was deepened by the stark white of his shirt collar. When he had purchased the violets for Nancy, he had ordered a *boutonnière* for himself, choosing, as though anticipating a certain occasion, lilies of the valley, which were seldom worn except by a groom.

They sat beside each other at the long table in the Fotheringill dining-room and Drum outdid himself in his cavalier attentions to her. Once or twice he almost exceeded the accepted standards of good taste of the times, because his attitude towards her had a certain appearance of possession, which would indicate that there had already been an understanding between them sufficient to precede the announcement of their engagement. But this, too, Drum had anticipated and a slight bulge in his pocket was the only thing that marred the perfect symmetry of his tailoring. The bulge was a small red morocco ring box in which reposed a ring with a single diamond. After buying the violets and the *boutonnière* he had strolled round to Shreve, Crump, and Low's and picked out the diamond. It was neither too large nor too ostentatious and the clerk had informed him it was a perfect stone. It would, Drum hoped, persuade Nancy to marry him. He was quite certain that he was not in love with her – not madly, head-over-heels in love with her anyway – but he had a feeling that if he could be married to her, it would give him a certain sense of security that would offset his anguish over the recent discovery he had made about himself. He would tell her. Yes, he would do that, but he would minimize it as much as possible and the fact that they had known each other all their lives might cause her to overlook his ancestry. After all, there had always been a rumour about the Cole family – that there was a hint of the tarbrush in their background – but it had never diminished their social prominence.

But the fact upon which he relied most heavily was the surety of her love for him. He had always sensed it, even from the days when they were children, and as they had grown older he could sense it more and more. He was always sure of a date with Nancy, even if he called her at the last minute. Besides, he felt that regardless of what he was himself, the Fotheringills might have as much money as the Holbrooks, but they were not quite as definitely out of the top drawer, and in Boston in those years that meant a great deal, a very great deal.

When the long and elaborate dinner was over and the guests for the ball had arrived, it was Nancy and Drum who led the grand march. So many people commented on them – such a handsome couple, Drummond Maxwell, nephew of the Christopher Holbrooks, and Nancy Fotheringill. What a brilliant match! It was rumoured that he was rich in his own right and one only had to look at him to see that he was by far the handsomest man at the ball. And, of course, there was all that Fotheringill money and only Nancy to inherit it. Already many were anticipating the big wedding that would probably be coming in the fall.

After the grand march Drum took Nancy's programme and filled in every dance with his own name – all the polkas, the waltzes, the quadrilles, and the lancers. She made no objection, although, being the daughter of the house, she should have shared her favours. Drum was a good dancer, full of rhythm, and Nancy, almost his own height, followed him perfectly. They had been dancing together since they had both attended Miss LeClaire's dancing school. Now their dancing seemed even more intimate and he noticed that her cheeks flushed from the extra pressure he gave her hand from time to time and the way he clasped her waist in the waltz.

At the conclusion of the second dance he led her from the ballroom out into the conservatory, where he brought her a glass of punch after quickly downing two glasses of champagne himself. He would have preferred whisky, but he knew that that would be served only in the library upstairs. They found a secluded retreat behind some potted palms but even in their seclusion they were constantly interrupted.

'Let's go upstairs,' Drum suggested, 'where we can be alone.'

But once upstairs in the stately second-floor drawing-room, they found the older people sitting at small tables playing whist. The library was no better because it was blue with the smoke of cigars and filled with men drinking whisky and discussing business. Reaching out her hand to him, Nancy pointed to the staircase leading up to the third floor. She drew him up the stairs and down the hall to her own room, a white and gold room that was so appallingly virginal it made him shudder. Its very innocence made Drum feel, upon entering it, that he had already deflowered her merely by stepping across the threshold. Once inside, she closed the door.

Now, as he regarded her in this icily virginal room, he wondered if he really wanted her after all. He was beginning to doubt it. Surely no girl reared in this white and gold immaculateness could ever accommodate her cool body to the heat of his passions. But, then, their joining would be merely marriage; it would not necessarily be either love or desire. Women of Nancy's ilk were not supposed to enjoy sexual relations with a man; they merely tolerated such intimacy for procreation. Men did not so much love their wives as respect them. Nancy represented a way of life to him, secure, prosperous, and quite in keeping with the Boston tradition. He could always go elsewhere for his pleasure. There was Rosalie at Mother Carey's and after her there would be others. Now he could and must pretend the ardency of a lover. He held out his arms to her and she came to him, lifting her lips to his to be kissed.

The kiss, unfortunately, was as chaste as the room – a mere brushing of her lips against his. It was proper and decorous but hardly what he had expected. Drawing her closer, he pressed his lips against hers, seeking with his tongue an entrance, which was at first denied him and then granted. Much to his surprise, after the first entry of the tip of his tongue between her teeth she responded even more ardently than he. It was difficult for him to reconcile this now passionate young woman with the always proper Nancy Fotheringill he had known. Her hands stroked his cheeks, pulling his face towards hers, and he, clasping her to him, initiated her into lovemaking that he was

47

sure she had never known existed before. Her nearness and her warmth had an embarrassing effect on him and now he did not dare separate himself from her, although he knew she was all too aware of what was happening to him.

It necessitated a little struggle for him to force her lips away from his own, even though their bodies continued to touch.

'Nancy, darling!' His voice was low and husky with the desire he now felt throbbing within him. 'You do love me. You do, you do, you do!'

'Oh, Drum, my very dearest.' She looked up at him through lashes moist with tears. 'I've always loved you. Always. There has never been anyone for me but you, Drum. When all my friends had crushes on this boy and that boy, I always knew there was only one for me and that was Drum Maxwell.'

'And for me too, Nancy.' He lied gallantly, thinking even now of Rosalie and the many others with whom he had shared his body. 'There's never been anyone but you.' Without her lips on his, he had cooled down sufficiently to draw away from her without exposing himself to her gaze. Now he reached in his pocket and drew out the little red box, snapped it open with one finger, and held it for her to look at.

'May I put it on your finger, Nancy? Will you marry me?' He slipped the ring slowly down on her finger.

She stared at it, moving her hand ever so slightly so that the light struck a myriad of coloured reflections from it. Scarcely taking her eyes from the ring long enough to look at him, she answered him in a whisper. 'Oh, I am so happy, Drum. So happy that you of all people put that ring there because I promise you, Drum darling, that if you had not put it there, nobody else ever would. If I could not have had you, I would not have wanted anybody.'

'Nor I,' he said, actually believing his words now. His hand crept to her neck, fingering the pearls, and then slowly travelled down to the lace of her dress, his fingers forcing themselves under the tight bodice. She moved away from him slightly, frightened at his boldness, anxious for the moment to divert him.

'And now there remains only one thing, darling. We must speak to Papa. I know what he will say. He has always admired you. Come, Drum, we'll go downstairs and I'll send for him. We'll talk in Papa and Mama's bedroom and then he can announce our engagement to all our guests.'

But it was several minutes before they left. Although she was willing to kiss him as passionately as he kissed her, she demurred to his seeking fingers and when he took her hand and pressed it down between them against his own throbbing body, she drew it back quickly, recoiling from the momentary contact she had made with him. Disengaging herself from his arms and trying hard not to look at him, she opened the door and led him down the stairs to the large bedroom at the back of the house. This time she did not close the door but sent the black-uniformed chambermaid flying downstairs with an urgent message to fetch her father and mother.

'And,' Drum instructed the maid before she left, 'ask Mr and Mrs Christopher Holbrook to come up also, please.'

Nancy would have flung herself again in Drum's arms but he very gently pushed her away, motioning to the lace of her dress, which was in disarray, and straightening his own cravat. He reached for her hand, squeezed it tightly, so that he could feel the pressure of the gold band he had just placed there. They had not long to wait. Mr and Mrs Fotheringill, accompanied by the Holbrooks, arrived and were ushered into the room by the maid. Evidently Mr Fotheringill had taken in the situation at once, because he was beaming proudly and so was his wife. There was, however, a look of consternation on the faces of Chris and Mary Holbrook.

'Drummond has something he would like to say to you, Father.' Nancy gave Drum a little nudge forward.

He stepped up to the Fotheringills. Now, despite his efforts to convince himself, he almost regretted he had asked her, but it was too late to back out. She was already wearing his ring.

'Yes, Mr and Mrs Fotheringill, it is indeed something important. I have asked Nancy to marry me' – he reached down and brought up her hand with the ring sparkling on it – 'and she has accepted me. Now all we need is your consent.'

'Gladly, my boy, gladly.' Mr Fotheringill nudged his wife and she echoed him.

'But first' – Drum glanced at his aunt and uncle – 'there is something I must say to you. That is why I asked Uncle Chris and Aunt Mary to be here, too. Perhaps it would be better if they said it for me.'

'No, Drum, speak for yourself,' Chris Holbrook answered. 'It is your marriage that you are speaking about. It should come from you. But your Aunt Mary and I want to thank you for keeping your promise to us.'

Mr Fotheringill looked blankly from Drum to his uncle and back again to Drum. 'Well, whatever it is, it certainly cannot be very important.'

'Of almost no importance at all, Mr Fotheringill,' Drum answered. 'The fact of the matter is that I am . . .' – he looked to his Aunt Mary, hesitating for a moment until he caught the encouraging glance from her eyes – 'that I am, as you might say, not entirely white. I have some Negro blood in me.'

Mr Fotheringill's mouth opened wide as he stared at Drum. 'You mean . . .?' He was at a loss for words.

'He means' – Chris Holbrook spoke up – 'just what he said. There is a slight strain of Negro blood in Drum. Drum himself never knew it until a day or so ago. We have never told anyone else. Yes, there is a mixture of blood in Drum.'

'And knowing this, you had the effrontery to ask for my daughter's hand.' Fotheringill almost spat at Drum. 'Why, you're nothing but a mulatto!'

'Let's just call it "nigger",' Drum said. He reached forward to keep Mrs Fotheringill from falling, but Fotheringill brushed him away and supported her. 'Keep your dirty black hands off my wife.'

'Father!' Nancy's voice was a scream that choked in her throat and became a sob. 'It's not true, it's not true and even if it were true, it wouldn't make a bit of difference to me. I love Drum, Father, I love him.'

Fotheringill had dumped his wife into a nearby chair and motioned to Mary to attend to her. She was chafing the woman's wrists and shaking her.

'And I suppose you'd settle for nigger pickaninnies for children.' He silenced his daughter with an impervious wave of his hand. 'Oh yes, you'd have babies as black as coal and they'd be my grandsons.'

'That's ridiculous,' Chris Holbrook said.

Fotheringill turned on him. 'How have you dared to do such a thing to us, Holbrook? Foisting off a mulatto on us, allowing him to associate with white people, even permitting him to ask our Nancy to marry him. I blame you, Holbrook. You're more at fault than this fellow you call your nephew. Why,' he sputtered, 'you should be—'

'Tarred and feathered, I suppose you are going to say. Didn't we fight a war, Fotheringill, to free the Negroes and make them men instead of animals? I am proud of Drum. He is a fine young man.'

'Am I any different now than I was five minutes ago before I told you about it?' Drum interrupted. 'Have I undergone any change in those past few minutes? Do I look different? Do I act differently?'

Mrs Fotheringill was moaning in her chair and Mary was fanning her. Nancy had sunk to the floor, a heap of lace and satin, her arms round Drum's knees. Fotheringill, trying to control his anger, spoke slowly, measuring his words.

'You will leave my house, young man. Immediately! And I would appreciate it if you would also go, Mr and Mrs Holbrook. I'd rather see my daughter dead than married to this man. In fact, I'd rather put a bullet in her head than see her take such a step. Do I make myself plain?'

'We are leaving, Mr Fotheringill,' Holbrook said, motioning to his wife and Drum.

'And believe me, sir, this infamy will be published abroad throughout the whole city tomorrow.'

'That is up to you,' Mary said. 'It cannot hurt Drum, as he is leaving Boston, but before you start telling the world about Drum, you had best remember your daughter. She is remaining and it will hurt her far more than it will hurt Drum or us.'

'No!' Nancy struggled to rise. 'He is not leaving without me. I am going with him. I don't care what he is, I love him

51

and I am going with him. I love him, I love him, I love him.'

Mr Fotheringill grabbed at her left hand, yanked the ring from her finger, and handed it to Drum.

'The matter is finished. For Nancy's sake I shall not report it if you leave Boston. Now, please go.' Half dragging Nancy, he pushed her into a small dressing-room off the bedroom and locked the door. As Drum and the Holbrooks left the room they could hear her pounding on the door and her wild screaming. Even when they descended the stairs, they could still hear it. The orchestra had stopped in the ballroom and all the dancers had crowded into the hall, listening. All eyes were on Drum and the Holbrooks as they slowly descended the stairs. There was a moment's hesitation as the butler brought their wraps and during those few seconds the strained silence was punctuated by Nancy's muted screaming. Then the front door opened and they walked down the steps to their waiting carriage.

'I kept my promise,' Drum said to his uncle once they were seated inside.

'You poor, poor boy.' Aunt Mary leaned forward and kissed him on the cheek. 'Oh, you poor, poor boy. I blame myself now. I do. We should have told you long ago.'

'Drum can take it,' Chris said. 'He's a man. He knows it's not his fault. He'll be able to live with it. I suggest, though, that he start for New Orleans. There's a ship leaving day after tomorrow. Buck up, Drum.'

'You know' – Drum tried to laugh – 'Nancy was rather pretty tonight. In fact, she was prettier than I have ever seen her before, but I'll bet in another twenty years she'll look just like her mother. So, dear Aunt Mary, don't feel too sorry for me, please don't.'

CHAPTER SIX

CHRISTOPHER HOLBROOK was right. There would be a boat sailing for New Orleans and now, after the fiasco at the Fotheringill's house the night before, Drum was only too anxious to take it. Last night, after he had left his aunt and uncle on the second floor, he had gone to his own rooms on the third, routed Mede out of bed, and had him tiptoe down the service stairs to the dining-room and bring up a decanter of whisky. Not wanting to drink alone, he had invited Mede to drink with him, something he would never have thought of doing a week ago. Then he was the white master and Mede the Negro servant. Now – what was it his uncle had said? – his own grandmother was Mede's mother, which made Mede his uncle. Ridiculous! Yet it was undoubtedly true, true but difficult to believe. Mede's hands were black with pink palms. Mede's fingers were long and spatulate and the nails oversized in proportion to the fingers. Mede's head was covered with a skullcap of black wiry wool. How could they be related? Yet they were. They were no longer master and servant; they were kinfolk, related to each other with some of the same blood flowing in their veins.

Well, to hell with it!

By the time he and Mede had finished the decanter of whisky, he didn't give a damn and went to sleep in the same clothes in which he had taken such pains to dress himself the evening before. But in the morning he was up and dressed in time for breakfast, even though he had to do it himself – Mede still sleeping off his drunken stupor.

When he appeared in the dining-room, he was able to greet his uncle and aunt as affably as though nothing had happened. He wanted neither his Aunt Mary's tearful sympathizing nor his Uncle Chris' hearty nothing-has-happened-after-all attitude. He could not blame them for what he was. They had given him everything, done everything possible for him, and he knew that if by some mysterious alchemy they could have

53

drained the colour from his blood, they would have done so willingly. No sacrifice would have been too great for them. That they had never told him was only their way of loving and protecting him. But now he wanted to be away from them. An insurmountable barrier had suddenly sprung up between them. They were white and – let him face it squarely – he was a mulatto.

When the carriage came to take his uncle down to his offices on State Street, Drum accompanied him, accepting a bundle of bills from his uncle's book-keeper, and then walked alone to the offices of the steamship company, which were on nearby Broad Street. He engaged passage for himself and Mede in two adjoining cabins, one a large double cabin for himself and the other a mere cubbyhole with a single berth for Mede. The steamship agent had suggested that he engage only the cabin for himself and let his servant sleep in the steerage, but Drum informed the man that he did not travel that way; he wanted his servant near at hand to wait on him.

The *Delaware* was to sail the next morning and now all Drum had to do was return home and oversee the packing of his clothes. He decided he would take only a few things with him. New Orleans was a hot place and, as he understood that Falconhurst was not too far away, that would be hot too. Therefore the woollens and the tweeds and the heavy broad-cloths would be of little use there. He'd take enough for the voyage and have more made up in New Orleans. Certainly there must be a decent tailor there who could make up a suit. Perhaps he'd even stay in New Orleans for a few weeks before he set out for Falconhurst. There was nothing in particular to call him and he had very little idea of what it would be like when he arrived there. Uncle Chris had a photograph of a brick house with white pillars and a lot of Negroes standing on the steps. The house looked big and attractive, but beyond that he had little idea of what he might encounter in his own home.

As he closed the door of the ticket office behind him and stepped out on to the pavement, the damp, salty tang of the ocean reminded him that he was not far from Mother Carey's.

Ten o'clock in the morning was certainly no time to visit her establishment, but the heat of desire, which Nancy had aroused in him last night and which had never been quenched, produced a compelling need to visit Mother's house. He felt that going there would do even more for him than the whisky had last night. To be sure, either one was merely a temporary escape from the reality of life but a short escape was better than nothing. As a result, he turned his steps towards the waterfront and to the obscure street that housed Mother Carey. She, at least, would be glad to see him. Mother Carey! The only woman he had ever called 'mother'.

Biddie, the maid, her voluminous petticoats hiked up above her knees, was out scrubbing the front steps of Mother Carey's house and Drum realized that it was the first time he had ever seen the place in daylight. Although the house was kept up better than the others on the street, it looked dismal in the bright light of morning. Its drab exterior gave little promise of the delights it offered. He stopped for a moment to watch Biddie sloshing the water on the steps and she, conscious of someone looking at her, turned and scowled, ready to spit out some coarse invective until she realized it was Drum.

'Why, if it ain't Mister Maxwell himself! And what be you a-doing here at this hour of the mornin'?'

'Is Mother up?'

'Herself? Up? Glory be to God, Mister Maxwell! We don't keep bankin' hours here. Up all night and sleep all day, that's us. I'd not be up myself 'ceptin' I like to get to early mass. But to answer your question, I can tell you this, she's awake and having her coffee in bed while she counts over last night's take.'

'Can I see her?'

'Listen, me laddy. Nobody ever sets eyes on Ma Carey till she gets her war paint on 'cept me. She ain't much to look at in the mornin'. Fair to scare the wits outa you just to get a glimpse of her.'

'Let me in, Biddie, and then go up and tell her that I don't care what she looks like. I want to see her. Tell her it's on business.'

'You and your business!' Biddie closed one eye in a prodigious wink. 'You don't have to see Ma Carey 'bout that.
Just tell me which girl you want and I'll kick her outa bed.'

'It's more than that, Biddie. Please, Biddie, tell her I want
to see her.'

'She's goin' to be bilin' mad, Mister Maxwell.' Somewhat
grudgingly she opened the door and motioned him inside,
indicating Mother's reception room, which smelled of stale
cigar smoke, sweat, perfume, and whisky. The drawn curtains
blocked out all the light and when Biddie opened one of them,
the harsh morning sunshine made everything look tawdry.

'Not when she hears what I want to talk to her about.'
Drum had suddenly made up his mind to do something.

He sat gingerly on Mother's chaise longue, listening to
Biddie's heavy footsteps go up the stairs, then to a knock on a
door and the opening and closing of the door. In a few moments Biddie was back.

'It's herself a-saying that if you'll give her ten minutes,
she'll let you come up.'

Drum nodded in agreement. 'And Rosalie?' he asked.

'Dead to the world. All the girls had a hard night last night.
Portugee freighter just in yesterday and them poor bastards
four weeks at sea. You can imagine. By the time the last one
was finished, the first one was already to start in again. What
with the Madeiry wine they brought and taking over the house
for the night, them girls worked like drayhorses.'

'Go and wake her up anyway. Tell her I'll be wanting to see
her as soon as I finish talking with Mother.'

Biddie drew down the corners of her mouth and then pursed
her lips in reproach. 'You mean you're looking for something
at *this* hour of the morning. Jesus, Mary, and Joseph,
boy, there's a time for everything and night's the time for
that.'

'Not with me, Biddie, especially if I didn't get it last night.
Morning, noon, or night or in between with me, Biddie. When
a fellow's hair-triggered like me, all he has to do is think about
it and it's up, ready for action.'

She snickered at him, and the tip of her tongue wetted the

circle of her lips obscenely. 'You're a case, Mister Maxwell, but if you're needing it as bad as that, I'll see that you get it.' Once again she was off, only to return in a few moments and beckon for him to follow her upstairs. This time the door to Mother Carey's room was open and Biddie ushered him in. Mother was sitting up in an elaborate carved and canopied rosewood bed, propped up by fat pillows, her brassy hair hidden under a lace and sequinned cap and a fuzzy soiled marabou bed jacket wrapped around her.

'Drum, darling boy,' she said, retreating a little farther into the shadows of the canopy. 'Mother's happy to see her own dear boy even at this ungodly hour. Biddie'll be bringing up a cup of coffee for you – Irish coffee, laced with whisky. Now, tell me, dear boy, why is Mother so fortunate as to be favoured by this early morning call? My God, it's the middle of the night.'

'It's the middle of the morning, Mother, and all honest people are up and about their work.' He drew a chair up beside the bed and sat down in it. 'But, thank God, we're not honest people, are we, Mother?'

She rummaged among the sheets and drew out a thick roll of greenbacks, which she tossed to Drum, waiting for him to heft the roll before he tossed it back to her. 'That's honest money, Drum. They's some what might not think so, but it's been worked for and earned.' She pointed a pudgy, ringless finger at him. 'I ain't never cheated a person out of a cent in my life. Never! My girls all give good service for what they're paid for. And I treat them right too. They always get their fair percentage.'

Drum waited to answer while Biddie came in, drew up a small table for him, and placed a steaming cup of black coffee on it that gave off a strong aroma of whisky. She handed another cup to Mother Carey, who sipped it with a spoon.

'I agree' – Drum savoured his coffee – 'and it's about one of your girls that I've come to see you this morning.'

'Rosalie, I bet. You've taken quite a yen to her, haven't you.'

'I've already asked Biddie to wake her up. I'm needing her

this morning but not just for an hour or half an hour. I think I'll be needing her for quite a spell. The fact is, Mother, I intend to marry Rosalie.'

'Good God in Heaven!' She screamed as the hot coffee spilled from the cup, upset by her violent reaction. The scream brought Biddie and for a moment they were both occupied in sopping up the coffee from the counterpane. Then Mother turned to Drum. This time there was no facetiousness in her manner of speaking. She was dead serious.

'Now, you look here, Drum Maxwell, I've known you a long time. I've practically wet-nursed you from the first time you were here, just a horny little bastard that didn't know what to do or how to do it. Why, I remember that first time you were over and done with in five minutes until I got my girls to teach you how a man does things. I've always liked you and we've always been friends. Now, what in the holy name of hell do you want to marry a whore for?'

'I've heard tell that whores make the best wives.'

'I'll not deny it. I've known girls from my own house that got married and made goddam good wives. But they marry poor men, Drum. Then they can love them, work for them, and raise their children for them and nobody's the wiser as to who or what they've been. But if Drum Maxwell marries a whore out of Mother Carey's house and takes her to Beacon Street, what's going to happen?'

'I'll not be taking her to Beacon Street. I'm going to take her to New Orleans and from there on to my own home in Alabama. Mother, it's true what that New Orleans slut said. I've just found out that I am part coloured. Soon it will be all over Boston. I can't stay here and face it. That's why I'm leaving.'

'You, Drum Maxwell! You part nigger?'

'So they tell me, Mother – my aunt and uncle both. I'm really not related to them at all. They brought me up from the South and reared me, but it's true.'

'I can't believe it, but let me say this. It doesn't make a goddam bit of difference in the way I feel towards you. You're still my own dear, darling Drum.'

58

'Thank you, Mother. It's hard for me to believe it, too, but the fact is that I'm a nigger. Call it "mulatto" or "quadroon" or "coloured man" or what you will. It all boils down to one thing – I'm a nigger.'

'Shut your mouth! You ain't. Maybe there's just a smidgeon of coloured blood in you and it don't amount to a pisshole in the snow. So that's why you want to marry Rosalie. Well, it ain't a good enough reason.'

'But don't you see' – Drum was pleading now – 'I can't marry a coloured girl and no other white girl would have me. The idea of my marrying a coloured girl would be as loathsome to me as it was to the parents of a certain girl up on Commonwealth Avenue last night when I asked her to marry me and told her the truth about myself.'

'Probably some long-faced, flat-breasted, hoity-toity bitch anyway.' Mother turned up her nose. 'Most of them society girls look as if they wouldn't know how to give a man a good time in bed. Maybe you're lucky.'

Drum shrugged his shoulders and took another sip of his coffee. It was hot and invigorating and the whisky settled in a warm ball in his stomach.

'But don't you see, Mother, I'm not one thing or another. If I were black, I wouldn't mind sleeping with a black girl. My servant Mede doesn't. If I were white, I'd have no problem. I've never had any before. But with Rosalie I'd have a white woman and one that I like in a way.'

' "In a way" ain't enough.' Mother Carey settled back in her pillows and stared up at the dusty brocade of the canopy over her bed. She was not altogether unprepared for Drum's confession about his background. She had not, despite her promise to Drum, sent Gigi packing the other night but had called her in and questioned her after Drum had left. Although she had been unwilling to believe it and was not, even yet, thoroughly convinced, she realized that there was some basis in Gigi's words. She stared at Drum now. Yes, there was something faintly Negroid about his face if one looked closely enough, although she had never noticed it before. However, it did not in the least detract from his good looks, nor did it in any way diminish her fondness for him. Suddenly she sat bolt upright in bed.

'Now, look here, Drum Maxwell! You've been hurt to the quick and you're running around in circles looking for a way to stop the pain. Never make decisions when you're mad or when you're sad. They'll never be the right ones. You think your life has suddenly come to an end because you've got a smidgeon of coloured blood in your veins. Well, it ain't. Don't go fighting the world and marrying up with a whore just because you're mad. Look, you'd never have thought of marrying Rosalie a week ago. Why do you do it now?'

Drum gulped a swallow of coffee. 'Because she's white and I want a white wife.'

'Shit! That ain't an elegant word, but I'm not elegant either and it's the best word I can think of. There's more to a wife than white skin. Outside of that, what has Rosalie got that you want?'

The very thought of what Rosalie had that he wanted very much excited Drum. 'I've always enjoyed her in bed,' he said.

'And so have you enjoyed a hundred others.'

'Yes, but Rosalie the most.'

'Hell, boy, that's because I personally taught her a few tricks that men like. Remember this! She pleased those Portugee sailors last night just as much as she pleases you. That's her business. But, Drum boy, that ain't enough. There's more to getting married than hopping into bed every five minutes. After a month you'd get sick of it and Rosalie's white skin wouldn't be worth it. Not by a damned sight! She's a good enough girl, Rosalie is, but let me tell you this – she's as stupid as hell. She'd bore you to death. All she can talk about is the goddam cows up on that farm in Vermont where she came from. Besides, just take a look at her. She's slim and pretty now, but in another five years she'll be nothing but a fat slob. That kind always go to flesh.'

What she was saying to him made truth. He nodded his head slightly in agreement.

'Please, Drum, don't rush into anything this morning just because your little world suddenly fell apart at the seams.'

He regarded her long and searchingly, knowing that this woman, worldly wise as she was, was giving him good advice. There was not only sense in her words but love and affection, too. He was acting hastily. He knew now in his own heart that he didn't want to marry Rosalie, but he did want her. God! How he wanted her. He wanted her so badly that he could feel the tight constriction of the broadcloth of his trousers. Putting his hand into his pocket to ease himself into a more comfortable and less apparent position, his hand encountered the little morocco box that he had intended taking back to Shreve's. He pulled it from his pocket, snapped open the lid, and took out the diamond. Reaching for Mother Carey's hand, he slipped it on her finger.

'For me, Drum?' She held up her hand to see the play of light on the stone. 'It's too much. I know how much a ring like that costs.'

'If it cost double, it wouldn't be good enough for you. I didn't buy it for you, Mother. It was for that girl up on Commonwealth Avenue that I told you about, but she didn't want it. It's second-hand, Mother, but will you take it and remember me when you look at it?' He stood up, depositing the coffee cup and coming nearer the bed.

'I'll never forget you, Drum, and it isn't just this ring that will make me remember you. Good God! I wish I were younger. I'd go to New Orleans with you and you wouldn't have to marry me to get me to go.' She let her hand with the glittering diamond on it remain for one moment on his thigh. 'Look, Drum, you're a lucky fellow. If you've got some nigger grandpappy to thank for that, just be glad. I think you're lucky, even luckier than that Swede Olaf that comes here. Remember this, you'll always be able to make some woman happy. Now, skedaddle. It will take Rosalie to cure that.'

'How can I thank you, Mother? You've done a lot for me this morning.'

'Pshaw, Drum, I ain't done nothing and look what I got.' She waved her hand with the ring on it. 'Remember this, Drum Maxwell. I never had a son of my own, but if I did have one, I'd like him to be just like you. Yes, Drum boy, you're a fine fellow. Keep yourself so. Bend over. I'd like to kiss you goodbye.'

He leaned over to kiss the raddled cheek and felt the pressure of her hands on his shoulders.

'Maybe a blessing from an old whorehouse bawd like me won't mean much, Drum, but I want to say "God bless you" and if you ever need a friend, come to Mother.'

He felt tears coming in his eyes. There were no words he could say to her just now; only the pressure of his hands on her shoulders could speak for him. He turned from her and started towards the door. 'God bless you too, Mother.'

'God isn't bothering with any old bawd like me. Now, skedaddle! Go and show Rosalie what a real man is. And know this – I envy her.'

He was able to smile at her as he left the room.

CHAPTER SEVEN

WHEN DRUM AWOKE in his own bed on that morning on which he was to sail, it was hard for him to realize that this would probably be the last morning he would ever open his eyes in these familiar surroundings. This had been his room and this had been his life for as long as he could remember. It had always been a pleasant, sheltered life with Uncle Chris and Aunt Mary. Now he was leaving them for something unknown and he wanted nothing more than to turn over and go back to sleep, knowing that it was all just a bad dream and that his life would go on as usual.

What had changed? He threw down the bedclothes to see if it was he who had changed. No, he was the same Drum Maxwell who had occupied this room, yet he was different. Everything was different. Even Uncle Chris and Aunt Mary had changed, although their love for him must be the same, because they had always known what he was and their love had not been predicated on his whiteness or his blackness. It was only he who had not known it. Now that very knowledge placed an impenetrable barrier between them. They were white and he was not. They were safe in their established position; he had suddenly been dismissed from it. Even were he to remain here with them, the breach would widen day by day until finally there would be nothing in common for any of them except the love they had for one another. That would not be enough to fill his life. He would become an outcast, cut off from all his friends because he knew that none of them, not even those whom he considered his best friends, would tolerate him as he was now.

As he was now! He stared at his body again, his skin a glowing olive against the white sheets of the bed. He had always loved his own body, not only from the pleasure he had derived from it but from the pleasure he knew it had given to others. Just where might those few drops of coloured blood be? Were they separate from his other blood or did they mingle with it? Were they responsible for the tightly curling hair on his head and the mat of hair on his groin? Were they what made his body glabrous instead of hairy like so many of his friends? And were they, as that French bitch and even Mother Carey had intimated, responsible for his size and his grandeur? Why did those few drops of Negro blood, mingling with that of white blood, set him apart from other people? They alone were responsible for the step he was being forced to take.

But that step he was taking was the best one. He had become a different man; let him seek a different environment. A clean separation from the life he had always known was better than a gradual drifting away, harassed by one unpleasant happening after another – a snub here, another there, until finally he would not want to show his face in Boston. At least he was not making the break alone. Mede was going with him and Mede was what? His uncle? Ridiculous! Yet it was true. His own grandmother was Mede's mother and Mede must be a brother or at least a half-brother to his father.

Now he almost regretted that he was not taking Rosalie with

him. He need not have married her. She would have gone with him anyway. He would have had a white woman and that would have proved that he was not entirely a nigger. No nigger ever had a white woman. Damn it! He did want a white woman. He'd never settle for any kinky-haired, thick-lipped, wide-nosed wench. Once again he carefully scrutinized his own body. Thinking of women had made a change in it that was altogether apparent. He wished he could go to Mother Carey's just once more before he left. All those days on shipboard! Alone! What would he do? He lifted his right hand and regarded it disparagingly. Well, it was a poor substitute.

Getting out of bed, he rang for Mede, bathed and dressed and descended the stairs to a difficult breakfast, featuring his Aunt Mary's tears and his Uncle Chris' over-solicitude about the voyage and certain remedies for seasickness, among which the most heartily recommended was champagne. Then came the gathering together of the luggage, the donning of wraps, the getting into the carriage, and the drive to the pier. All the way Aunt Mary held his hand and he welcomed the pressure of her gloved fingers against his own. He discovered now, at this very last moment, how much he cared for these two people. They were all the family he had, unless, of course, this black grandmother, who was also Mede's mother, was still alive.

Aunt Mary talked little, but Uncle Chris babbled on about money being transferred to New Orleans banks; about how he had written on to reserve a room for Drum in the St Charles Hotel in New Orleans; about Sylvester, the overseer of Falconhurst; about the cotton crop and various workings of the plantation that Drum should know of. He told him about the village of New Quarters, just across from the mansion house of Falconhurst, which was now a real village, populated by former Falconhurst slaves. He told how he had written on to have the big house opened up and prepared for Drum's arrival, along with countless trivia, which Drum paid little or no attention to. The carriage rattled over the Boston cobblestones, through the business section of the city, down to the wharves, every turn of its wheels bringing their separation nearer.

The *Delaware* was a new steamship, shining in its paint of black and resplendent with white paintwork and polished brass. From its single narrow funnel a cloud of black smoke soared upward, smudging the clear blue of the sky. The pier was crowded with the usual throng of people – those who were leaving and those who had come to bid them bon voyage. Once on board, Chris Holbrook took Drum up on to the captain's bridge and introduced him as his nephew, which elicited the response that everything possible would be done to make the nephew of such an illustrious man as comfortable as possible.

They descended to the first-class quarters, whose main salon ran the length of the ship. It was carpeted in Turkey red with white panelling all around, interspersed with doors, each with a shining brass number. One end of the salon was decorated with plush chairs. The other end held the dining tables. Ornate chandeliers supported oil lamps and an immense skylight gave illumination. There was a profusion of ornamentation from the elaborate upholstery of the chairs to the carved frames of the mirrors, which were interspersed between the stateroom doors. White-jacketed Negro stewards stood around at attention, ready to fetch luggage, open stateroom doors, or run minor errands for the oncoming passengers.

Drum located his cabin, which was larger than he had expected, with an ingeniously contrived upper and lower berth, a mahogany wardrobe, and a washbowl and pitcher under a mirrored towel rack. A little door under the washstand, which Aunt Mary opened in her tour of inspection, disclosed a white chamber pot and there was a painted metal slop bucket beside the washstand. The porthole looked out on to the narrow promenade deck, although there was no outside entrance to the cabin – its only door was the one off the main salon.

A similar cabin, but much smaller, opened into Drum's by means of a narrow door that was a part of the panelling. This was for Mede.

Now that he was on board, Drum was anxious to get started and dreaded the tearful farewells between himself and his aunt and uncle. It was even more difficult than he had expected, so difficult that he welcomed the deep blast of the whistle signalling for 'all ashore'. Surprisingly, most of the crowd in the salon departed and there were only a few people left, which omened a small list of passengers. Caught up in the surge that was passing out on deck, he leaned over the rail, waving down to the figures of his aunt and uncle on the pier. Now that the separation had become actual, he welcomed the fact that he was alone – alone for the first time in his life. He had a strange feeling that, as much as he loved them, he never wanted to see them again. Their part of his life was past. A new life was beginning. He walked back into the salon, noticing the paucity of people, and across the red carpet to the door of his stateroom. A Negro youth, his jacket freshly ironed and starched, produced a long brass key and unlocked the door for Drum.

'Yes, suh, Mista Maxwell suh,' he said, bowing low.

The thick gumbo of his Southern accent attracted Drum and he looked at the fellow. He was probably in his late teens or very early twenties and, although his skin was black, his features were not Negroid, nor was his hair, which fell to his shoulders. There was a certain prettiness about his face that belied his masculinity – full pouting red lips, long-lashed eyes – and his mannerisms were as much feminine as masculine.

'How did you know my name?' Drum asked.

'Yo' Mista Maxwell suh. Been a-talkin' to that fine young buck what's yore servant, name o' Mede. He shore a handsome buck, that boy.'

Something about the way the fellow drawled the words made Drum look at him again. Damn it! He spoke more like some schoolgirl in love than a man. When he took Drum's elbow to assist him over the high threshold, Drum was torn between a desire to punch the fellow on his pretty nose or to cup his pointed chin in his hand and kiss him. He'd never seen a person before who so combined the male and female. Put him in women's clothes and he'd make a pretty girl.

'I'se yore stateroom steward,' the fellow said. 'My name's Lucifer, but mostly they calls me Lucy. You'll find everything ready, suh. They's drinkin' water in the pitcher, they's clean

towels, 'n' yore buck Mede he's unpackin' yore valises, suh.'
He stepped back into the cabin behind Drum and pointed to a
dangling cord. 'If'n yo' a-wantin' me, yo' jes' ring. Don' be
skeerful 'bout ringin'. It a pleasure to serve yo', suh' – he
fluttered his eyelashes at Drum – ' 'n' yore buck too. 'N' less'n
I forget it, the captain he a-sendin' word he a-wishin' the
honour o' yore company at his table in de dinin' salong.'

'Where's my boy Mede going to eat?'

'That all fixed up, Mista Maxwell suh. Mede he a-eatin'
'longside o' me in de pantry. He goin' to eat white folks' food
'n' not steerage food. I takin' care o' Mede real good, suh.'
Once again he glanced sidelong at Drum and glided out of the
cabin, closing the door behind him.

Drum stood alone in the cabin – really alone for the first
time in his life and, contrary to his expectations, he was not
unhappy. He raised his arms over his head in a gesture of
victory, took a long breath, and called out, 'Mede!'

The little door between the rooms opened and Mede
entered. He was grinning, his even teeth making an island of
white in his face.

'Yes, Mista Drum.'

'Help me get ready for lunch. I'm to sit at the captain's
table, so that means a clean shirt at least.'

While Mede took a clean shirt from the drawers of the
wardrobe, Drum looked at the upper berth.

'This is going to be a lonesome trip in a way, boy. Just you
and me alone in these two rooms. From what little I saw of the
passengers, there's not much to choose from. Guess it's going
to be a bachelors' hall for the next two weeks.'

'Ain' so bad's all that, Mista Drum.' Mede grinned sheep-
ishly. 'Went 'n' got something lined up for myself.'

'You mean there are black wenches on board?'

'Didn't say nothing 'bout no black wenches, Mista Drum.'

'Well, no white woman will let you at her. Keep away from
white women, Mede.'

'Didn' say nothing 'bout no white wenches neither. Got me
something which ain' a wench but it jest as good. Got me that
Lucy boy all lined up.'

67

'You mean—?'

'Why not, Mista Drum? Why not? That Lucy boy he mighty pretty and he right willing. I know 'cause he been foolin' 'round in my stateroom. Yes sir, Mista Drum, he right willin'. Mayhap yo'd care to try him?'

'You goddam black bastard!' Drum's fist shot out and caught Mede a glancing blow. 'Do you think for one minute I'd do anything like that?'

'Better'n nothing, Mista Drum. Damn sight better'n nothing.'

'Well, you're welcome to it. In the old days when black boys like you were slaves, I could have had you strung up and whipped, but today things are different. Guess there's not much I can do about it. It's your own business. If that's what you want, you're welcome to it.'

'Yes sir, Mista Drum. I'm welcome to it and I'm damn well going to have it.'

'Enough. I don't want to hear any more about it. Now, jump to it. Help me get ready for lunch.'

CHAPTER EIGHT

THERE WAS A very small passenger list in the first class and, although Drum had been especially invited to sit at the captain's table, he found no special distinction in that honour because all the passengers were seated at the same long table, bunched up together at the captain's end. Besides Drum there were a middle-aged couple from Dorchester who were going down to New Orleans to visit a daughter; a slate salesman from Vermont – slate was beginning to replace tiles on New Orleans' roofs; an elderly lady from the western part of Massachusetts who passed herself off as an author and said she was going south for local atmosphere; and two fluttery sisters between thirty and forty who never did make clear what their reason for taking the trip might be – Drum thought it was probably to snare a man. At least they were overly attentive to him, as a single man.

He was glad there were no people from the South on board. If, as that Gigi had said, Southerners had a sixth sense that detected the slightest trace of coloured blood, he might have been discovered and some unpleasant scene could well have ensued. However, nobody seemed to suspect that the tall blond young man in first class, travelling with his own servant, was anything other than he presumed to be. His position was even more firmly established when it was discovered that he was the nephew of Christopher Holbrook of Boston and Drum was somewhat surprised that so many people had heard of his uncle. As a result he was accepted without question. Although he was far too young to be considered a suitable mate for either of the fluttery Misses Sanborn, he was, nevertheless, a man and an extremely handsome one. It was evident that the Misses Sanborn intended to take full advantage of the fact that he was unattached.

After luncheon was over, he discovered that there was little for him to do. He walked aimlessly around the deck, taking particular notice of where the Misses Sanborn had placed their deck chairs so that he might avoid being near them, and finally chose a secluded position aft of the first-class promenade where he could look down on the steerage passengers on the deck below.

In contrast to the paucity of the first-class passengers, the steerage was overcrowded. As there were no chairs, the passengers sat on the deck and he noted that there was a preponderance of blacks among them, although Negro and white seemed to mingle without any restrictions. He bundled himself into his steamer rug and tried to get interested in a book, although he had never been a great reader. It failed to interest him, so he devoted his attention to the milling crowd on the steerage deck beneath him. There was a constant going back and forth, new people appearing and others disappearing into the crowded steerage dining-room, which also doubled as a salon.

69

He espied Mede down among them and then Lucy in his white jacket and black pantaloons. Evidently they had pre-arranged their meeting, for they waved to each other across the crowded deck and then went aft to lean over the rail and look at the wake of the steamer while they talked. Drum could see that their talk was animated and Mede was as assiduously attentive as a lover courting a lass, while Lucy had become coy and feminine, like a young girl being wooed. This sickened Drum, yet he was so fascinated that he continued to watch them, noting that occasionally and surreptitiously their hands met on the deck rail. Finally they too left, Mede going in one direction and Lucy in another. The sky had become overcast and the wind chilly, so Drum decided to quit the deck for his own cabin. At least he could sleep. He had been up early and a nap seemed to be in order.

Mede was not in the adjoining cabin when Drum entered, so he slipped out of his clothes himself, turned down the coarse cotton sheets, and climbed into the lower berth. How long he slept he did not know, but he was awakened by the sound of muted voices in Mede's cabin. Although the walls appeared solid, they were nevertheless of some thin panelling that allowed the sound to come through, if not the actual words. Drum suspected that it was Lucy with Mede. He got up out of bed, tiptoed across the cabin, and tried the door that led into Mede's cabin. It was bolted on the other side. He thought of rapping and disturbing what he was pretty sure might be going on in there but decided to let matters take their course. After all, it was nothing to him.

About an hour later, however, the door between the cabins opened and Mede entered, acting as if nothing had happened. 'Thought you might be wantin' to wash yourself before dinner, Mista Drum. Sent that Lucy boy for hot water and a bathtub. Thought mayhap I could help you, seeing as how this's a pretty small place.'

'You kind of like that Lucy boy, don't you, Mede?'

'He's a nice kid. Mighty glad I met up with him. There's some nigger wenches down in the steerage, though, and may-hap I get to know one 'fore the voyage is over. Just now Lucy he comes along all by himself, so don't need no looking 'round nor worrying to see if'n I find myself a wench. Lucy has to be mighty careful, though. He's got a friend, one of the sailors, who is powerful jealous of him. He don' want Lucy going out with nobody else.'

'The eternal triangle,' Drum said, laughing.

'Don't know about no triangle, Mista Drum, but Lucy he pointed out that red-headed sailor to me and I'm sure going to keep out o' his way. Big brute, he is. Lucy say he gettin' awful sick of him. He so jealous he won' let Lucy look at no one else. How come, Mista Drum, they's boys like Lucy?'

Drum detected a slight change in Mede's speech – the adoption of a thicker Southern accent – and he wondered if perhaps it had been his contact with Lucy. When Mede had come as a child to Boston, he had had that same broad accent, but during his years in Boston he had lost most of it. Now it seemed to be returning. Drum spread his hands in a gesture of ignorance.

'That's something I don't know anything about, so I can't tell you. But there are some fellows like that. We had one or two when I was going to school. None of the other fellows would have anything to do with them. They were—'

He was interrupted by a knock on the door and Lucy entered, wheeling a small tin washtub with a can of hot water and a can of cold water in it. Glancing meaningfully at Mede and then admiringly at Drum, he waited, closing the cabin door behind him.

'If'n I kin be of any help?' he volunteered rather lamely.

Drum shook his head.

'They's clean towels on the rack' – Lucy indicated the towel rack over the bowl and pitcher on the washstand – ''n' when yo' finish, yo' jes' ring the bell 'n' I come 'n' take it away. Mayhap yore boy he like to use the water after yo' gits through?' His statement was more of a question. 'It salt water 'n' it don' lather much less'n yo' got special soap. Wantin' I should get yo' some soap?'

'Can you?'

71

'Shore kin, Mista Maxwell. Anything yo' want, yo' jes' ask Lucy for it. Lucy kin git yo' anything yo' wants.'

'What I'm wanting now, you can't get me, I'm afraid.'

'What yo' wantin'?' Lucy was at least willing to try.

'Well, I'd like a pretty girl, young and preferably dark-haired.'

'Yo' a-meanin' a white gal?'

Drum nodded.

'Cain' git yo' no white gals, Mista Maxwell. They's two or three down in the steerage, but they's papas 'n' mamas with them 'n' 'sides I'm a-thinkin' they ain' never been split, they's so young and countrified. How yo' likin' a nice black wench?'

'Not now.' Drum shook his head. 'That's probably all I'll get at Falconhurst.'

'Yo' say "Falconhurst", Mista Maxwell. Yo' a-goin' to Falconhurst?'

Drum stared at Lucy, wondering at the excitement in the boy's words. 'What do you know about Falconhurst?'

'I'se a Falconhurst boy, Mista Maxwell. Born 'n' raised there till I 'bout thirteen.' Suddenly Lucy looked at Drum in a new light. 'Yo' Mista Maxwell! Yo' the owner of Falconhurst. Yo're Mista Drum Maxwell! I knows yo', Mista Drum. Ain' never seen you afore, but I knows yo'. Been thinking all 'long yo' a purentee white man, Mista Drum, but yo' ain'. Ever'one at Falconhurst they knows about the sucker that ol' Miz Sophie had by Drummage 'n' he tooken the name o' Maxwell. Yo' that sucker, Mista Drum. Yore pappy he Mista Drummage Maxwell what was kilt by the Klan. Yo' the sucker them folks tooken up North. This Mede he a Falconhurst buck too?'

'Shore am,' Mede answered. 'My mammy she called Big Pearl 'n' my pappy he Zanzibar.'

'Knows 'em, I do. Big Pearl she a-gittin' on now. She old woman 'n' Zanzibar he daid. Everyone sort o' fearful o' Big Pearl. She the big woman o' New Quarters 'n' she a right powerful conjure woman.'

It was difficult for Drum to realize that the woman Lucy was talking about was his own grandmother. His grandmother

– a Negro crone! A conjure woman! He had a vision of bleached skulls and a white-haired hag stirring a cauldron. Then, with the knowledge that Lucy knew about him, he became frightened.

'I suppose you're going to tell everyone on the ship about me?' he asked, wondering what might happen if the first-class passengers found out he was a mulatto. He'd have to go down into the steerage with the rest of the Negroes.

'Laws no, Mista Drum. Why yo' thinkin' I a-goin' tell? Ain' aimin' to tell nobody. We all Falconhurst boys – we'll stick together. Yo' 'n' Mede 'n' me – Falconhurst boys. Proud to meet up with yo', heard so much 'bout yo'. My pappy 'n' yore pappy good friends onc't. Ain' nobody on this ship a-goin' to know 'bout yo'.'

'But you do.' Drum still doubted Lucy's good faith.

Lucy came closer and studied Drum for a long minute. He inventoried the angles of his face, the close set of his small ears, the tight curls of his blond hair, the dark eyes, the sensitive nostrils, and the almost-too-full lips.

'Kin see it if'n I look close. Yes, now I kin see it, Mista Drum. Kin see it right clearly, but never suspected it afore, yo' travellin' here in first class with yore own buck 'n' everythin'. Kin see that yo' a mustee.'

'What's that?' Drum had never heard the word before.

'A mustee's a white nigger. Oft-times he so white yo' cain' tell if'n he got a teeny drop o' nigger blood in him. Lots o' mustees in New Orleans 'n' in the South. Many of them a-tryin' to pass for white folks today, but ain' many a-gittin' away with it 'cause they's always somethin' that tells. But I'se thinkin' yo' kin git away with it 'n' pass for a white man. Cain' figure out how yo' so white like, though. Big Pearl she Drummage's mama, she purentee black. She a Mandingo. Never hear but what Drummage Maxwell he mos' black too. Leastwise never heard he much white. Cain' never tell. Jes' cain' never tell. Sometimes two bright skins git together 'n' git theyselves a black sucker. Sometimes two bright skins git together 'n' git theyselves a white one. Ain' no way o' tellin'. But yo' white. Awful hard to see where yo' niggery, but mos'

73

folks in the South they kin tell. They al'ays lookin'.' Lucy stared at Drum as though to corroborate his statements. 'But yo' rest easy on one thing, Mista Drum. Ain' a-goin' to tell nobody that yo' a mustee. Ain' nobody's business. It a secret 'tween yo' 'n' Mede 'n' me.'

Drum reached in his pocket and took out a gold eagle, which he offered to Lucy.

Lucy reached out his hand to take the money, letting the shiny gold piece lie in his pink palm. 'That a lot of money, Mista Drum. That more money'n I ever saw in my hand at one time afore. What yo' a-wantin' me to do with it?'

'It's for you, so you won't mention anything about me.'

Lucy's eyes smouldered with resentment. 'Yo' a-thinkin' money a-goin' to keep me from talkin'? Ain'! It a lot o' money 'n' I'd like to have it but ain' 'ceptin' it, Mista Drum. I likes yo' 'n' I likes Mede too. Here, take back yore money.' He proffered the coin to Drum. 'Shore I takes money from men sometimes. It usually two bits, but onc't a man gave me a dollar. Steals money from 'em sometimes too, but I ain' takin' yore money jes' to keep my mouth shut. Yo' don' have to buy me, Mista Drum. Yo' cain'. I yore frien' – that is, if'n yo' wants a nigger boy what is like me for a frien'. I know what I am. Mede he a-knowin' what I am 'n' reckon yo' knows too. But jes' 'cause I'm like that don' mean I cain' be yore frien'. Kin, Mista Drum, kin be.'

Drum took the money back and pocketed it. His gesture in offering it to Lucy had, he realized now, been nothing but a bribe. Lucy could well have accepted it and Drum would have thought nothing more about it. Now, regardless of what Lucy's peculiar morals might be, Drum felt that there was a lot more to him than the simpering queen he pretended to be. He put out his hand.

'Let's shake on it, Lucy. We'll be friends.'

'Yo' 'n' me 'n' Mede, huh?' Lucy grinned. 'We all Falconhurst bucks, huh?'

So that's what he was, Drum thought. A Falconhurst buck. It was a category that he did not particularly want to be in, but it was true. It was inevitable.

74

' 'N' 'bout that wench yo' a-wantin', Mista Drum.' Lucy put his hand on the latch of the door. 'Yo' ain' a-goin' to want none of them scrawny white gals. Yo' ain' a-goin' to want no stenchy nigger wench neither. But we got us one bright skin down in the steerage. She pretty too. She from N'Orleans 'n' she a-sayin' that she Spanish 'n' that she a dancer 'n' she jes' a-comin' back from Canada, where she been a-dancin'. Thinkin' myself she nothin' but a little nigger whore, though she got two black bucks with her that play the gee-tar for her to dance. Shore she ain' havin' no truck with them, though, 'cause she too uppity to take on a nigger buck. Mede he tried 'n' she wouldn't have no truck with him. Thinkin' mayhap I tell her they's a handsome white man up'n first class what likin' her.'

Drum tossed the gold eagle up in his hand and then pocketed it. 'No, Lucy, but thanks anyway.'

'Yo' could have me.' Lucy was all too anxious to volunteer.

'Never tried it, Lucy, and don't have any idea I ever want to.'

'Neither did Mede, but he a-likin' it. But if'n yo'd rather I do pimpin' for yo', Mista Drum, shore goin' to try hard to earn that gold eagle. Ain' goin' to be easy, though. Ain' no place yo' kin come down in steerage 'n' it goin' to be hard to git her up here, but I kin do it.' Lucy closed one long-lashed eye provocatively, lifted the door latch, and backed out.

Drum looked at Mede, spreading his hands in a gesture of helplessness.

'Falconhurst bucks, eh?'

'Seems like that what we are, Mista Drum.'

'Niggers.'

'Why yo' take on so, Mista Drum? I ain' never foun' it so bad being a nigger. 'Joys my life jes' so much as you. You've been living a white life, Mista Drum, 'n' you've been a-likin' it. Cain' say as how I blames you. Now yo're a-goin' to see what it like havin' a black life. Mayhap yo' 'joys that too.'

'Not if I can help it, Mede. I'm going to stay white. By God, I am. I'm not going to turn into a Negro. I'm not. Understand? I'm going to stay white come hell or high water.'

'Yes, suh, Mista Drum. You just do that. You just do that, but 'member one thing. Ain' many men like you. You can stay white if you want o' you can be black if you wants. You can have white gals o' black gals. You can do anything you want. Thinking you're a mighty lucky man, Mista Drum.'

Drum shook his head sadly. Whatever prospect Mede was offering him did not appeal to him. He wanted only one thing. He wanted to be back in Boston and be white.

'I think I'm the most miserable man in the world, Mede.'

CHAPTER NINE

As THE DAYS on shipboard passed, Drum found himself depending more and more on Mede and, strangely enough, on Lucy for companionship. He had managed to elude the Sanborn sisters to the point where they had ceased to pursue him and even the spectacle of the steerage passengers, which he viewed from his deck chair, soon lost its fascination for him. As a result, he spent more and more time in his stateroom, conversing with Mede, who was not only a tie to his old life but a connexion with the life he was about to lead, the life at Falconhurst. Lucy stole every minute that he could from his duties, which were not onerous, as he had little to do except make up the beds, clean the cabins, and answer the bell. As Drum and Mede were the only occupants of staterooms in his particular section, his work was soon over and he spent most of his free hours in Mede's cabin, with the result that when Mede was in Drum's cabin, Lucy was invariably there too.

Drum had recovered from his initial dislike – nay, even repulsion – for the boy. He ceased to blame Lucy for what he was and he realized that the boy had some fine qualities. His story was an interesting if somewhat sordid one. He was the youngest son of Brutus, usually called Brute, who had, for many years since the death of Drum's father, been the leading Negro at New Quarters. Brute had sired him on an attractive wench named Helena, who was part Cherokee Indian, a fact that accounted for Lucy's long black hair. Helena herself was not a Falconhurst woman. She had arrived there with a group of itinerant Negroes who were seeking sanctuary after the war, remained at New Quarters after giving birth to Lucifer for about thirteen years, then, taking her child with her, she had drifted off with a ne'er-do-well mulatto journeyman tinsmith who had abandoned her and Lucifer in Mobile. Seeking work, she had found it in a sailor's tavern on the waterfront, drab work that included prostituting herself to the demands of the seamen. Lucy had started along with her, serving corn whisky to the tavern's waterfront clientele.

He had developed into a pretty, graceful youth with a feminine appearance, which quite belied his masculinity. The owner of the tavern, finding him one night seated in a sailor's lap and being fondled by the man, was quick to recognize the appeal the boy had for many of the rough sailors who frequented the tavern. He dressed Lucy in girl's clothes, tied ribbons in his hair, relieved him of his job of serving, and trained him to pander to his clients' perverted tastes. All of which, of course, made Lucy profitable to the tavern owner but put no money in either his pockets or his mother's. Lucy did not resent the new job that had been forced upon him. He was an apt pupil and he adopted the role of prostitute willingly, revelling in the attention that was paid to him by the men who pursued him.

There was, however, one sailor who had singled the boy out for his own and whenever his ship was in port, he gladly paid for all of Lucy's time, refusing to share him with anyone else. This was a young red-headed Irish giant by the name of O'Brien – even Lucy did not know his first name – about whom Mede had spoken to Drum. It was this same O'Brien who had persuaded Lucy to run away with him to New Orleans and got him the job on the same ship on which he was a seaman – the *Delaware*. Lucy had now made several trips on the ship and rather enjoyed his work. It was clean work and the money he earned from his small salary and his tips was his own. The only thing that galled him, however, was the almost insanely possessive attachment that O'Brien had for him. The man watched Lucy like a hawk and, especially when he was drinking, he was jealous of the slightest attention that Lucy paid to anyone else. He would beat up the boy, punish him unmercifully, and then relent and plead for the boy's forgiveness. Fortunately, at least while on board ship, O'Brien could not indulge openly in his liking for corn whisky and Lucy's life became almost bearable, particularly as he was forced to spend his working time in the first-class section of the ship, while O'Brien was only a deckhand. But even in his moments of freedom Lucy knew that O'Brien's eyes were always watching him.

The boy longed to be back at Falconhurst. He remembered his early years there as free from the near slavery he had been subjected to in the tavern and the possessive attitude of O'Brien. His childhood years at Falconhurst had been the happiest of his life. His father, Brutus Biggs, had allotted a small cabin to his mother and while his mother worked in the fields with the other Falconhurst hands Lucy ran wild with the children of New Quarters. His one dream was to return there. He was willing to exchange his comparatively easy duties on board ship to get back to the plantation and work as a field hand – anything to get away from O'Brien.

It did not take Mede long to tire of Lucy's ministrations, which were only a stopgap for his concupiscence. He discovered an unattached wench in the steerage who appealed to him far more than Lucy, but, strangely enough, he did not abandon Lucy. There was something about the boy that Mede liked and the longer he knew him, the better he liked him. Drum also came to appreciate the boy. Despite the sordidness of his background and the life he had been compelled to lead, Lucy was surprisingly and inherently good. He had a keen mind, a ready wit, and a gift for loyal and devoted friendship. Each day he insinuated himself more and more into Drum's good graces. And, despite the fact that Mede made it quite apparent he was no longer interested in Lucy other than as a friend, Lucy continued to court him assiduously and sometimes successfully because Mede could not always resist his blandishments.

There was something about the big black fellow that appealed to Lucy. Perhaps the fact that Mede was younger and stronger than O'Brien gave Lucy a sense of protection. As for Drum, Lucy idolized him, although he doubted that he would ever be able to indulge himself with Drum as he had with Mede. He did not, however, entirely give up hope; and after he had lingered in Drum's cabin one day, while Mede was giving his master a bath, he was all the more determined that eventually he would persuade Drum to accede to his demands.

One afternoon, two days before their arrival in New Orleans, Drum, Mede, and Lucy were together in Drum's cabin, during the quiet of the after-lunch siesta in which most of the passengers indulged. There was little for them to talk about and Drum listened idly, lying on the berth while Mede sat in the cabin's one chair with Lucy on the floor in front of him. Although they had all left Falconhurst as children, they had been comparing such vague memories as they had of the place. Most of their conversation consisted of 'Do-you-remember's', and both Drum and Mede were interested in the few recollections that Lucy had of Big Pearl.

'She a purentee Mandingo wench,' Lucy explained, ' 'n' afore the war a purentee Mandingo bring the highest price of any nigger. She 'normous woman too, but she pretty 'n' kin see that onc't she might have been goddam pretty. Lot o' talk 'mongst the folkses at New Quarters 'bout Big Pearl. Seems like'n she had a brother named Mede—'

'He the one I named after, though he not her brother, he her husband,' Mede interrupted.

'He her brother an' her husband,' Lucy said nodding his head wisely. 'Ol' Masta Hammond Maxwell, him who had Falconhurst, was set on gettin' a purentee Mandingo buck, so he put Mede to Big Pearl, his own sister. Got one too, but he sort o' half-witted. But this Mede, not this one' – Lucy reached up and patted Mede's knee – 'but t'other one, he got into right bad trouble. He got to beddin' hisself with Masta Hammond Maxwell's white wife 'n' she got knocked up 'n' gave birth to a nigger sucker. Ol' Masta Hammond Maxwell he so mad he kilt Mede. B'iled him up'n kittel, so they say. Anyway that the end of that Mede. Not the end o' Big Pearl, though. She take up with a New Orleans buck named Drumson, which'n Masta Hammond Maxwell buy in New Orleans, 'n' her sucker was Drummage Maxwell. Drummage Maxwell he marry up with Miz Sophie what ol' Masta Hammond Maxwell's daughter. She purentee white, but she likin' black bucks jes' like her mammy did.'

It still seemed strange to Drum that some Negro woman far away on an Alabama plantation could actually be his grandmother and some New Orleans slave his grandfather. He was also aghast at the talk of buying and selling Negroes, of breeding them, and of murdering them. What kind of a life was he going into? Surely some traces of this must linger in the present generation.

Lucy had told all he knew about Big Pearl and a long silence ensued, during which Lucy tried in vain to arouse Mede, but Mede would have none of it, so Lucy came over and sat on the edge of Drum's berth. After so many days of continence, Drum was tempted to stroke the boy's smooth cheek or let his fingers play in his long hair, but the temptation was conquered by his very disgust for such a thing. Yet, despite his mental denials, the physical need still existed. He was glad that Mede was there; otherwise, he felt, he might have succumbed. At one time he was sorely tempted to dismiss Mede, but he resisted the temptation.

'Yo' a-goin' to be out on deck tonight, Mista Drum?' Lucy asked.

Drum noticed that he had ceased to be 'Mista Maxwell' and had now become 'Mista Drum'. He didn't know whether to object to such intimacy or not. As a matter of fact, how could he, with Lucy sitting beside him? He did not answer the question, merely shrugged his shoulders. The question was far from important and he felt that Lucy was merely trying to make conversation.

'Yo' a-goin' to be settin' in yore deck chair, so's yo' kin see down into the steerage?'

Again Drum paid no attention to the question.

'Thinkin' yo'd better,' Lucy persisted. ' 'Member what I a-sayin' to yo' 'bout that wench what claimin' she Spanish 'n' she travellin' with two nigger bucks what plays the gee-tar?'

Drum recalled the conversation and nodded.

'Well, she ain' Spanish 'tall. She call herself Lola, what is a Spanish name, but them two black bucks is her brothers 'n' they ain' Spanish. That Lola she jes' a bright-skin nigger wench from New Orleans. Thinkin' her pappy ain' the same as them bucks' pappy. She say she one good dancer, though. Sayin's how she travel all over with them two gee-tar playin' bucks, dancin' one place or 'nother. Thinkin' she dancin' mostly in whorehouses, though she a-sayin' she dance in the big theatres. She a-lyin', though. She nothin' but a cheap trollop, but she mighty pretty, she is.'

'So what's this Lola got to do with my being out on deck tonight?' Drum could find no connexion between the two things.

'She a-goin' to dance down on the steerage deck. She say she a-goin' to git herself all dressed up 'n' her two bucks a-goin' to play the gee-tar 'n' she a-goin' to dance. Then she a-goin' to take up a collection from the steerage passengers. She say she ain' got no money 'n' that a good way to git some.'

Lucy's hand crept slowly and surreptitiously up Drum's leg to his pocket, where the outline of the coins was imprinted against the light linen of his trousers. Drum did not push his hand away, although he could see that Mede was aware of what was going on and was looking at him strangely.

' 'Member that gol' piece what yo' said yo'd give me?' Lucy's finger outlined the contour of a coin in Drum's pocket, then abandoned the coin to slide further up Drum's thigh. ' 'Member yo' said that if'n I do some pimpin' for yo' 'n' git yo' a wench, yo' a-goin' to give it to me?' His hand ascended a little higher. 'My, my, Mista Drum, seemin' like'n yo' need someone pimpin' for yo' right off fast. Um-um!'

'I said a white wench, didn't I?'

'Why yo' wantin' only a white wench, Mista Drum?'

'Because I'm white, that's why. No nigger wenches for me.'

Lucy hesitated a long time before he spoke. 'Yo' shore goin' to git mad at me, Mista Drum, but jes' gotta say it. Yo' ain' white – that is, not purentee white. Look, Mista Drum, if'n yo' never pestered nothin' but white gals, yo' don' know what fun pesterin' kin be.'

'Pestering?' Drum dashed Lucy's hand away. He did not relish the warmth of it through the thin material of his trousers. It was altogether too provocative. 'That's a word I never heard before. What does it mean?'

'Jes' that – pesterin'. Some calls it pleasurin', but mostly we calls it pesterin'. It's when a man beds hisself with a woman.'

Drum laughed and Lucy, his hand forcibly removed, sat up straight. 'What do you know about pestering a white wench or a black one, Lucy boy? Bet you've never pestered either one.'

'Ain',' Lucy admitted without compunction. 'Ain' never, but I knows. I knows this, that if'n yo' got only a smichin' o' black blood in yo', yo' ain' never goin' to 'joy no white woman. Black blood calls to black. Tha's why I like Mede better'n O'Brien. Tha's why yo' a-goin' to like a coloured wench better'n a white one. Ain' meanin' no purentee black wench. Meanin' one like that Lola what dances. She yaller 'n' she right pretty 'n' she right willin' too. I tol' her 'bout yo' 'n' she seen yo' walkin' 'roun' up here. She a-sayin' she shore admire yore hair – a-sayin' it look like gold.' Lucy's hand crept back to finger the coin in Drum's pocket.

Drum considered it for a long moment that seemed to stretch the silence in the cabin.

'Why'n't yo' do it, Mista Drum?' Mede said, breaking the silence. 'Lookin' like yo' a-goin' to git nothin' but black wenches at Falconhurst. Might's well git used to them now.' Mede's talk was becoming more and more slurred and Southern.

Drum still could not make up his mind, but the pressure of Lucy's hand and his wandering fingers on his thigh eventually brought about the decision.

'Why not?' he asked them both but most of all himself. 'Why not?'

'Then, yo'll do it, Mista Drum?' Lucy was enthusiastic but whether more over the prospects of getting the gold eagle than providing pleasure for Drum was uncertain. Still, the sincerity of his voice belied the supposition that his interest was wholly commercial.

'I'll do it.'

'Tonight?'

'Tonight.'

'Let me fix it up for yo'. Don' be surprised, Mista Drum. May take a little figurin' on my part, but I'll do it.'

Drum reached in his pocket and withdrew the gold eagle. He handed it to Lucy, who took it without enthusiasm and then handed it back for the second time to Drum. 'Ain' goin' to charge yo' nothin', Mista Drum. We's friends 'n' it jes' a favour for yo'. 'Sides, yo'll have to pay that Lola wench 'n' she not cheap neither. Cain' take it, Mista Drum, much's I'd like to. That money might git me off the ship 'n' 'way from O'Brien when we land in N'Orleans. Might git me back to Falconhurst, but much's I'd like to go, ain' a-takin' yore money.'

'If it's that important to you to get back to Falconhurst, perhaps we can arrange it,' Drum said, pocketing the coin. 'We'll think about it, Lucy. Now, what do you want me to do?'

'Wants that yo' go out on deck tonight 'n' watch this Lola gal dance. 'N' after she dancin', yo' stay there. I 'range everythin'.' Lucy got up and beckoned to Mede to follow him. 'We a-goin' down in the steerage now' – he looked up at Mede – 'that is, if'n Mede willin'.'

'Might's well.' Mede raised himself from the chair and followed after Lucy. Lucy stopped him.

'Ain' wantin' that O'Brien see yo' 'n' me together. He suspectin' somethin'. Gettin' awful mad 'n' pent up, he is. I go first 'n' yo' come later.' Lucy opened the door, winking at Drum. 'Yo' shore goin' to be surprised, Mista Drum.'

'Time I was,' Drum answered. For about five minutes Mede remained in the stateroom; then he too left, leaving Drum alone.

Drum lay back on the berth, stretching out his legs and

pillowing his head under his hands. The prospects that Lucy had offered him excited and at the same time repelled him. He realized it was a step he had never taken before and he didn't know whether it was a step upward or downward, but he rather suspected the latter. Well, did it matter? Did anything matter now except the throbbing demands of his own body? He bethought himself of the case of champagne that his uncle had had delivered aboard as a specific for seasickness. It was in Mede's cabin. Getting up from the berth, he went to the other cabin and located it. He had no corkscrew and was unable to get the cork out, so he knocked the top of the bottle on the corner of the washstand and broke it. The wine frothed out and he caught it in a thick glass. It was warm and insipid, but it was what he needed. He decided that if he got drunk enough, he'd not know whether the woman was black or white. After all, he didn't know whether he was himself – black or white – so what difference did it make?

CHAPTER TEN

FOLLOWING LUCY'S instructions, Drum pleaded a headache after dinner that night. The captain had scheduled a ship's concert after what was supposed to be a gala dinner – at least there were paper hats at every plate – and those of the few first-class passengers who were in any way talented were to perform. The middle-aged couple from Dorchester had agreed to tell jokes in the style of a minstrel show; the lady writer was to read some of her poetry; and one of the Misses Sanborn was to sing while the other accompanied her on the mandolin. That in itself was sufficient for Drum to excuse himself, but the prospects of what Lucy had offered were far more exciting than listening to the lady's poetry or to either one of the Sanborn sisters warbling.

At about ten o'clock, which was the time Lucy had told him to be in his deck chair aft, Drum went out on deck. The chill of the northern April had vanished and it was so warm outside he took off his light jacket and hung it on the back of his chair. Once seated, he looked down on the steerage deck to see that a place had been cleared in the centre and that a bull's-eye lantern, fastened to a mast, spilled a circle of yellow light on the deck. Evidently this was to be a gala night for the steerage passengers too. Seated in the shadows around the pool of light, their conversation came up to him in an excited hum. They seemed to be expecting something unusual.

The strings of a guitar were swept by an unseen hand, followed by another. The music was Latin, probably Cuban because it had a seductive beat that embodied the rhythm of the Tropics in it. The two guitars became louder and suddenly there appeared in the circle of yellow light, the figure of a girl. Drum wondered why he had not singled her out before because she was so beautiful he certainly could not have missed her. Her long black hair was loose, veiling and unveiling her face as she moved slowly in tune to the music. Whether it was the yellow light or the powder on her face, she seemed to be made of burnished gold – her bare arms, her full breasts, which were only partly covered by the gold satin of her dress, and even her long, expressive fingers, which snapped out a staccato accompaniment to the rhythm of the guitars. A burst of applause greeted her and she stopped her dancing for a brief moment to acknowledge it. Then, picking up the rhythm, she began to dance again.

It was one of those flashy, heel-tapping, Spanish dances and Drum was forced to admit that though she had little talent as a dancer, she had such a glorious body that one could scarcely quibble at the ineptitude of her talent. Her long, full skirts whirled about her, her raised arms gleamed in the light of the lantern, and her snapping fingers became a part of the music itself. Now, beyond her in the darkness, he could dimly distinguish the seated figures of the two Negro guitar players. They too were dressed in pseudo-Spanish costumes – black pantaloons and white shirts with full sleeves. Occasionally one of them would lift his voice in a few notes of song – not words but high-pitched encouragements to the dancing girl.

To Drum the dance seemed overlong and repetitive, but he was fascinated by the girl herself. Her dress concealed no detail of her figure and he could see that she was long-legged, narrow-waisted, and wide-hipped, with full, provocative breasts that threatened to break the confines of her dress. There was a certain voluptuous movement to her body that promised much – so much in fact that he became excited watching her and, although he was bored with her stamping and finger snapping, he regretted the moment when the music stopped and she disappeared into the shadows. Then it was the turn for the men who had accompanied her to step out into the circle of light. Each of them held a hat and passed it around to the figures in the darkness, but she, stepping out once again into the light, shielded her eyes with her hands and peered up to where Drum was standing alone at the rail. She had evidently been briefed as to just where to look, for as soon as she had spotted him, she started picking her way among the seated forms until she reached the bottom of the narrow stairs that led to the upper deck where he was standing. A locked metal grating at the top of the stairs barred the entrance of the steerage passengers to the upper deck, but, as she slowly walked up the stairs, Drum walked over to the gate, waiting for her to come up to it.

She was panting slightly from the exertion of the dance and he noticed now, even in the dim light, with her hair brushed away from her face, that she was beautiful in a savage way. There was something exotic about her, something almost cat-like. She was darker than he had thought her to be. He could see where the light powder on her face was runnelled with perspiration and the dark colour of her skin showed through the maquillage.

She was direct with her words. There was nothing coy or evasive about her.

'Yo' the gen'leman that li'l Lucy boy been a-tellin' me 'bout? Yo' the man what wantin' to git dreaned?'

The expression struck him as unusual. He had never thought

of it in those words before, but he could see how direct and appropriate they were.

'I expect I am.'

' 'N' yo' a-wantin' to git dreaned tonight?'

'Right.'

'He a-sayin' as how yo're a rich man 'n' that yo' got a twenty-dollar gol' piece for me.'

Drum reached in his pocket and took out the coin, holding it up for her to see. At the same time her hand reached through the grating to stroke his thigh.

'Uh-uh!' She clutched at him with her hand. 'This a-goin' to be the easiest twenty dollars I ever got. Yo' shore a-wantin' it, mista, 'n' I the gal what kin give it to yo'.'

'When?' Drum clasped her hand tightly with his own, pressing it even harder against himself, welcoming the warmth of it through his thin trousers.

'Lucy he a-goin' to 'range that.' She allowed him to push her hand away, realizing the danger he was in if it remained. 'He say to go back to yore stateroom now. 'Bout half 'n' hour, if'n yo' kin hol' out that long, yo' rings the bell. Don' be surprised. Lucy he'll come. Gotta go now. Gotta see how much they took up in the collection but don' think it goin' to be much. Them folkses ain' got more'n nickels 'n' pennies. Ain' got nothin' like'n that twenty-dollar gol' piece what yo' got in yore pants. M-m! That shore is a double eagle, if'n yo' knows what I mean.'

'Think you can earn it?' Drum had a feeling that the girl would willingly give full value for every dollar he paid her.

'Listen, man! If'n I cain' ain' nobody else what kin.' She nodded her head vigorously in affirmation. 'Gotta go now. See you later. Don' fergit to ring the bell.'

He strolled along the deck, which was dimly lighted by occasional lanterns, into the main salon, where the big chandelier had been extinguished and only a few bracket lamps gave any light. Once in his room, Drum took off his clothes and lay down on the berth. It was hot in the cabin; he got up and blew out the lamp, then stretched himself out, feeling his body respond to that which he so ardently anticipated. It had been

87

so long – longer, he thought, than he had ever gone before in his life, far longer than any man should go. Damn it! He had even responded to Lucy's hand on his leg today. Was he getting as low as that? Could this be Drummond Maxwell, lying here now, waiting for a coloured wench to come to him? And the worst part of it was that he was excited over the prospect of this coloured girl. She was not a full Negro, he told himself, not with that long hair. No, he would not think of her as Negro, he would think of her as he was himself.

He had been lying there about half an hour, which was the time mentioned by the girl – what was her name? Lola? – and now, according to her instructions, it was time to pull the bell cord. He reached up, lifting himself by one elbow to reach it, gave it a few yanks, and then sank back on the bed again. He had not long to wait. There was a rap at the door. He had not bolted it from the inside, so he murmured a soft 'Come in' and the door opened, letting in some of the light from the dimly lighted salon outside.

The figure silhouetted in the doorway certainly wasn't Lola, instead it was only Lucy in his white jacket and pantaloons. Drum could even see the little silver badge with the word *steward* on it, pinned on Lucy's coat. He entered the stateroom, closing the door and bolting it behind him, and came over to sit on the edge of Drum's berth. His face lowered to that of Drum's and his lips sought Drum's, but Drum pushed him away.

'Goddam you, Lucy! What are you doing here?'

'I not Lucy.' The voice was Lola's. 'Jes' dressed up in Lucy's clothes so's I kin git up here 'thout nobody askin' any questions. Look!' She unbuttoned the jacket, took his hand, and placed it on her bare breast under the jacket. 'Lucy he ain' got nothin' like'n them, he ain'.' She had proved to him that she certainly was not Lucy and now, standing up, she unbuttoned the black pantaloons and let them slide to the floor, shucking off the white jacket and lowering herself beside Drum. For a moment they lay there, their bodies barely touching and then, his desire for her uncontrollable, he pulled her to him, so that their lips met. Suddenly all thought of black or

88

white had vanished from his mind and he felt only the soft, warm flesh of a woman under him. The pent-up desires of the last few days vanished all too quickly and he lay panting beside her. She allowed him to caress her, snuggling up in the hollow of his arm, her head on his chest, while her fingers traced exciting patterns on his body. Her hair was flung across his face and he moved his hand to brush it away, clutching at it and lifting it from his face so he could breathe. He felt her struggle in his arms and then he felt the long hair that he held in his hand became a separate thing, something entirely unconnected with the girl beside him.

'Damn you!' She slipped out from under his arm and clutched at the wig he was holding in his hand. 'Damn you!'

His hand released his clutch on the long hair and she snatched at it, but he would not release her from his arms. Instead his hand reached over to stroke the head from which he had removed the wig to find it covered with a close wiry mat of wool.

'Yo' foun' me out.' She was trying to keep the tinge of anger from her voice. 'Now yo' a-knowin' jes' what I am.'

'Just a nigger wench.' He felt a sudden revulsion for her.

'Yes, jes' a nigger wench,' she admitted. 'Tha's all I am. But jes' a minute ago yo' a-likin' me. What difference it a-makin' if'n I got long hair o' not? Jes' the same's I was five minutes ago. Kin pleasure yo' jes's much, kin make yo' jes's happy, kin earn that gold eagle jes's well.' Her hands grasped at him, invigorating him once more. He yielded. Somehow nothing seemed to make any difference at that moment except her softness and her nearness. Having made this decision, he determined to enjoy her. This time he did. It was no quick indulgence merely to relieve himself but a studied act in which she met every response of his and he reacted to every nuance of her tempting hands and lips and body. He was lost in the absolute sensuality of her, a wildness he had never encountered in a woman before, and when it was over, he was too exhausted to move.

After a few moments of breathlessness on her part she propped herself up on one elbow. The dim light through the porthole showed the arabesques of long black hair on the pillow and she adjusted the wig on her head, then slipped out of bed and into Lucy's pantaloons and jacket, winding the hair around her head so that it looked like Lucy's.

'Yo' a-goin' to give me that twenty dollars?' she asked.

'It's there on the washstand.' He had had the foresight to remove it from his pocket.

'Thank yo', mista. Hope I earned it. Hope yo' don' min' if'n I ain' got long hair like'n yo' tho't I had. Ain' Spanish. Jes' pertend to be. Them two bucks is my brothers 'n' it easy to see they ain' Spanish. Sorry yo' foun' me out. 'Spects yo' didn' like it too much, a-findin' out.'

'Maybe I liked it even better.' Drum was reluctant to admit it, but he had enjoyed it. Maybe it was right what he had heard about the more primitive passions of coloured girls.

She walked to the washstand, felt around in the dark for the gold piece, and then after kissing him lightly on the lips, she left, closing the door quietly behind her.

Drum, completely satiated, got up and opened the porthole, letting in the clean breeze of the sea. The room was filled with a muskiness that he suddenly realized was distasteful to him. He sniffed his own armpits, amazed that the muskiness came from him as well as from the girl who had lain there. Without lighting the lamp, he poured water from the bowl and scrubbed at himself until he was certain the odour had disappeared. Then he smoothed the tumbled sheets and stretched himself out on them. All the tension was gone from his body and he felt at ease.

He was just drifting off to sleep when the door between his cabin and Mede's burst open. Mede stumbled over the threshold, speaking with a voice hoarse with fear. 'Mista Drum, oh, Mista Drum!' He came over to Drum's berth and shook his arm, thinking he was asleep. 'Somethin' terrible's happened.'

'My God, what now?' Drum was out of the berth and on to his feet.

'It Lucy.'

'What's happened to him?'

'He nearly kilt, Mista Drum.'

'How do you know? What's happened?'

'Saw it myself, I did. Whilst yo' had that Lola wench up here in yore cabin, I was with Lucy. He got a place in the storeroom off'n the steerage pantry. Got a door on it what he kin bolt. We down there together. When we git through, he says, "Yo' let me go on first 'n' yo' follow me in 'bout five minutes. Don' trust that O'Brien. He been a-spyin' on me but thinkin' it safe 'cause he a-sleepin' up in the fo' castle. He don' sleep down with the stewards."

'So Lucy he leave 'n' I sit 'n' wait a few minutes. When I come out on deck, I see Lucy talkin' with that O'Brien. They arguin'. Could hear 'em. O'Brien he a-sayin' that Lucy he been up here in yore stateroom 'n' Lucy a-tellin' him he ain'. O'Brien sayin' he knows it 'cause he saw Lucy go in your stateroom 'n' he waited on deck for him to come out 'bout 'n' hour later. Say he followed Lucy down to the steerage 'n' then Lucy he went into the women's cabin 'n' he los' him, but O'Brien he waited up on deck. Then he see Lucy a-comin' out'n the steerage pantry. Say he cain' figure out how Lucy got from the women's cabin inter the steerage pantry, but he foun' him 'n' he a-goin' to teach Lucy a lesson. He start maulin' Lucy 'n' Lucy tryin' to hit him back, but Lucy no match for that man. Then Lucy take a knife outa his pocket 'n' try to slash O'Brien, but O'Brien take the knife away from Lucy 'n' he stab him 'n' Lucy sink down on the deck. Then O'Brien run. Lucy still 'live 'cause I went to him 'n' his heart beatin'. What we goin' to do, Mista Drum? It goin' to go bad for us. They goin' to find out that Lucy sent that Lola wench up here 'n' they goin' to find out that I bin with Lucy. We in trouble, Mista Drum.'

Drum tried to quiet the frightened fellow. 'We're in no great trouble, Mede. After all, we've done nothing very wrong. It's no serious crime to smuggle a wench into one's stateroom and as to what you and Lucy have been doing, well, it isn't the first time it's been done on board ship, from what I've heard. Is Lucy still there?'

'He still there, less'n someone foun' him, Mista Drum.'

'Then we'd better see what we can do.' Drum slipped into his pants and drew on a shirt. 'We're going out for a walk on deck. Remember now, just what I tell you. I couldn't sleep, so we decided to walk around the deck. Remember that?'

'Yes suh, Mista Drum.'

Together they crossed the salon and stepped out on deck. It was cool and there was a path of moonlight across the sea. In the full light of the moon, everything was sharply etched in black and white.

As they passed along the side and made their way aft to where Drum's chair was, they could look down on the steerage deck. It was deserted except for a single figure, prone on the deck. They could see that it was Lucy, dressed as usual.

Drum, followed by Mede, jumped over the gate and ran down the stairs leading to the steerage deck. He leaned over Lucy. There was a wet spot, black in the moonlight, on Lucy's white jacket, and Drum felt the warm stickiness of blood on his fingers, but he could feel Lucy's heartbeat and knew that the boy was still alive.

Cupping his hands around his lips, Drum screamed for help and he was aware that he could hear his own screams sounding time after time. From the upper deck several officers of the ship appeared, struggling into their shirts. In a few seconds there was a ring of people around Lucy's inert body. Finally after what seemed an interminable period, the captain arrived, half dressed himself.

Drum explained to him what had happened – that he had been unable to sleep, so he had awakened Mede and they were taking a turn around the deck. They had seen a body on the steerage deck and had come down to investigate, only to discover that it was their own cabin steward, lying in a pool of blood.

'I know the culprit,' the captain said. 'I've been expecting something like this for a long time.' He nodded to two of his seamen, who lifted Lucy.

'Where are you taking the boy?' Drum asked.

'We've neither hospital nor doctor on board, Mr Maxwell, but I'll try to make him comfortable in his quarters. He's lost a lot of blood and we've not much to work with here, but perhaps we can save him.'

'He's my own cabin steward,' Drum said. 'I've grown rather fond of the boy because I learned that he's from my own plantation. As a matter of fact, I had intended taking him with me when we arrived in New Orleans, as he is anxious to get back to his home. I suppose it would be against the rules of your ship if he were to occupy the small cabin beside mine where my servant now sleeps. We'd be glad to look after him.'

'What you are asking is certainly something out of the ordinary.' The captain regarded Drum closely in the light one of the seamen held. 'However, I do know the boy was originally from Falconhurst Plantation, which I understand is yours. That is what he put down on his papers when he signed up. It can well account for your interest in him. If you and your man are willing to nurse him for the two days before we reach New Orleans, I can see no objections. Nobody else on the ship will have time to do it and he would be more comfortable in your cabin than in the dormitory where the stewards sleep. It's most unusual, Mr Maxwell, but for you I think it could be arranged.' He turned to the two seamen who were carrying Lucy. 'Take this boy to Mr Maxwell's cabin. Then' – he looked around to see if the person he was about to mention were present – 'go to the forecastle and rout out O'Brien. If he's guilty of this, I'll arrest him and keep him in the brig for the remainder of the voyage.'

CHAPTER ELEVEN

NEITHER DRUM NOR Mede had had any experience in nursing but, drawing on the captain's medicine chest for such meagre supplies as laudanum and carbolic acid, they managed to make poor Lucy at least more comfortable than he would have been in the steaming confines of the stewards' dormitory. Mede relinquished his berth and together they managed to undress Lucy and get him into it. The wound was deep, but it was in the fleshier part of the shoulder and had not penetrated either his heart or his lungs. Drum made a solution of carbolic acid and sea water, washed out the wound, packed it with lint that he had soaked in the solution, covered it with wet cloths wrung out of sea water, and then administered a dose of laudanum to make Lucy sleep. Soon his breathing was regular; and Mede and Drum felt they had done all they could to make him comfortable.

Drum could still detect a certain muskiness about his sheets that was so distasteful to him that he sought refuge in the upper berth, but he did not sleep much that night. It had become hot and humid, the coarse cotton sheets stuck to his body, and now that the thrill of Lola's physical nearness had passed, Drum castigated himself for having slept with a coloured girl. Other men did it, he thought, trying to ease his conscience. That was the reason why the South was populated with people of such a variety of colours, ranging from almost pure white down through all the tones of gold and sepia. Southern men, so he had been told, preferred coloured girls. Well, why not? Certainly he had never enjoyed an encounter more than the one he had just experienced. Even Rosalie, who had so pleased him, had not compared to the primitive fire and unleashed savagery of this girl called Lola. Despite all his attempts at justifying himself, however, he felt soiled and guilty. He had stepped down a rung in the ladder of his own self-esteem and he wondered how many more rungs he would descend.

And yet, with all his self-castigation, he found that he was already looking forward to another bout of the same sort. With Lucy unable to help him, he doubted if he could arrange to get Lola up in his stateroom again, but in two days – no, only one now – they would be in New Orleans. He would stay in the city for a while and now he had a good excuse. If he were taking Lucy with them, he could not travel until Lucy was fully recovered. Yes, he would enjoy New Orleans. Damn it all, he would! There would be more opportunities for him to explore this delightful study of miscegenation. But no, it was hardly that. A meeting between himself and a coloured wench was not in that category because he was coloured himself. Between white and white or black and black there was no such a thing as a miscegenation. He suddenly realized that all the experiences he had had with women before were just that. This last one was the first that was not. Despite the drain that Lola had made on his body, he found himself responding to the fantasy of more such experiences. Damn it! Was this hot-bloodedness also an inheritance from his father along with the fact that he was hung like a stallion? Well, so be it. At least he could look forward to a lot of pleasure and he should thank his father. He had bequeathed more to him than a plantation and some money: he had bequeathed a zest for life. He rolled over on his stomach to quiet the throbbing of his loins and eventually went to sleep, but his dreams were peopled with dark-coloured forms whose soft flesh and smooth skin tantalized him.

In the morning he discovered that Lucy had recovered from the effects of the laudanum and, although he appeared to be in considerable pain, he was able to talk with Drum. It seemed that O'Brien, always suspicious, had seen Lola, dressed in Lucy's clothes, go to Drum's stateroom. He had waited out on deck for her to leave and followed her down to the steerage. Then when Lucy had mysteriously reappeared, quite in the opposite direction from which O'Brien had seen him disappear, O'Brien, his mind befuddled with drink, had assaulted Lucy in a fit of uncontrolled jealousy. That O'Brien had stabbed him Lucy admitted was his own fault. He could have assuaged the man's anger by granting him the favours he requested. Instead, thinking to defend himself, he had pulled a knife on him. O'Brien had stabbed him with his own knife. However, now that it had happened, Lucy admitted that he was glad. It would serve to sever the relationship between him and O'Brien and he could leave the ship in New Orleans and get away from him. When Drum told him that O'Brien was securely locked in the brig, Lucy even consented to let Mede spoon some breakfast into him.

Later in the morning the captain sent a seaman who, he said, was versed in binding up wounds. He was the unofficial doctor of the ship. Grudgingly he approved the way Drum had treated the wound; he repacked it with fresh lint and then bandaged Lucy's entire shoulder so that he could not move it and dislodge the packing. After that, Lucy was able to sit up in his berth, propped up by several pillows, and during the next day he continued to improve. When Drum informed him that he had had a talk with the captain and that he had given permission for Lucy to leave the ship, Lucy was even more jubilant over the return to Falconhurst. The new steward that had been assigned to their staterooms packed Lucy's poor belongings in a ragged kerchief and brought them up to Mede's cabin while Mede was busy packing Drum's and his own valises.

They docked at New Orleans early in the morning, in a damp stickiness of heat that to Drum, coming from the fresh April of New England, seemed unbearable. He saw nothing in the waterfront of the southern city to remind him of Boston. Most of the people around the levees were Negroes and the noise they made was deafening. It was a pandemonium of shouting, swearing, sweating stevedores; of high-wheeled carts and cursing drivers; of hawkers of coffee, fruits, and pralines. Yet with all its noise and confusion, everything seemed to move with a certain lethargy that was brought on by the heat.

Drum made his formal farewells to his fellow passengers, agreeing to look them up at the various addresses they handed him, even while he had no idea of ever wanting to see them again. He thanked the captain for his kindness during the voyage and for his cooperation in regard to Lucy; super-intended Mede's carrying the luggage ashore; and engaged two seamen to lift Lucy from his berth and carry him ashore, depositing him on the levee alongside their pile of luggage. He sent Mede off to find a conveyance of some sort and after what seemed to be an overlong period of waiting, as he stood in the hot sun in his warm northern clothes, Mede returned with a decrepit barouche driven by a gangly young Negro in soiled red and white candy-striped pants and a vivid, though dirty, yellow shirt.

'The Hotel Saint Charles,' Drum said to the fellow, who looked at him rather stupidly and then shrugged his shoulders as though it were no concern of his where anyone wanted to go. The sway-backed nag that pulled the vehicle could do no more than walk and they made their leisurely way through the narrow cobbled streets under overhanging balconies of wrought iron. Away from the confusion of the waterfront, New Orleans presented a more attractive appearance. The houses were mostly of stucco with tall windows and the inevitable iron balconies on the second and third floors. They passed a pleasant square with a cathedral at one end, then went on through other narrow streets to an imposing hotel.

'This yeah's the Sain' Charles Hotel,' the candy-striped driver informed them. 'This yeah where yo'-all a-wantin' to go?' His accent was so gumbo-thick that Drum had difficulty in understanding him, but the sign outside informed him that this was indeed the Saint Charles, so, bidding Mede and Lucy wait in the carriage, he jumped down and went into the tall, pillared doorway. Inside it was cool and semi-dark with thick carpets, white marble, potted palms, and ornate furnishings. He breathed a sigh of relief. Once again he felt on familiar ground. All the colour and unfamiliarity of the city had vanished and he felt at home in surroundings he could understand. Now all he wanted was to get upstairs into a cool, dark room, strip off his sweat-soaked clothing, and lie on a wide, white-sheeted bed. It would be a relief after the narrow confines of his berth aboard ship and the constricting cabin.

Allowing a moment for his eyes to adjust to the dim coolness of the hotel lobby, he walked across the carpeted floor to a long mahogany counter where a young man, immaculate in a black suit and white linen and smelling of bergamot, looked up from the ledger he was writing in, smiled the usual formal smile of welcome, and asked the usual question as to what he could do for Drum.

Drum smiled in return. 'You have reservations here for Drummond Maxwell of Boston. They were made by my uncle

97

Christopher Holbrook and should have arrived some time before now.'

The clerk took a long and studied look at Drum, then turned to a pigeon-holed stand and thumbed through several letters shaking his head in negation as he looked at each one.

'Just a moment.' Once again he inventoried Drum with an insolence that seemed entirely out of keeping with his initial professional courtesy. 'I do not seem to have the reservation here. Will you please wait until I see if the manager has received it?'

There was nothing for Drum to do but wait. Seconds passed into minutes and the minutes mounted up to ten before the fellow came back accompanied this time by a stout man with a full beard. They conferred at some little distance from Drum, then both came to the counter together. The bearded man was evidently the manager, for it was he who spoke.

'No such reservation has been received.' His tone was brusque and his words lacked civility. 'Unfortunately without having received the reservation, we cannot accommodate you. Every room in the hotel is taken.'

'That seems impossible,' Drum said hoping to placate the man in some way. 'I could not help but notice the size of the hotel as I drove up. I will accept even a small room for the present. I have a sick servant with me who badly needs a doctor's attention.'

The bearded man shook his head. 'Again I must say we have no rooms.'

'Then, will you see if you can make reservations for me in some other hotel? I am a stranger in New Orleans and this is the only place I know about.'

A guarded look passed between the bearded man and the bergamot-scented young fellow.

'We would recommend the Hotel de Trouville. It is located on Rampart Street and has a very good reputation among its own particular clientele.'

'Its own particular clientele?' Drum caught a hint of double meaning in the words. 'May I ask, sir, just what that clientele is?'

'The Hotel de Trouville happens to cater to a well-to-do class of people of colour. We do not here at the Saint Charles. Need I offer any further explanations as to why our rooms are taken?'

Drum was too humiliated, perhaps even too angry, to answer. He turned and made his way across the carpeted floors, through the pillared doorway, and out into the sunshine. Mede and Lucy were still sitting in the cab and Mede was fanning Lucy with a piece of newspaper.

'Lucy he a-gittin' pretty tired, Mista Drum suh. Kin we go in now?'

Drum shook his head and instead of answering Mede he addressed the cabbie.

'Do you know where the Hotel de Trouville is?'

'Sho' do, masta suh. It over on Rampart Street.' He made an encircling gesture with his whip that might have included all New Orleans.

'Then take us there.'

'Could of tol' yo' that fust off, masta suh. The Sain' Charles it don' 'low no coloured folkses in it. Mighty perticular at the Sain' Charles. Yo' a-goin' to like the Trouville better anyhow. Madame Helene, she set the bes' table in New Orleans. Nice folkses there too.'

'Well, take us there.' Drum would have willingly gone anywhere to get away from the Saint Charles.

After another seemingly interminable drive through similar narrow streets with similar lace-balconied houses they came out on to a wider street of small white houses, surrounded by opulent gardens. Stopping before a building of pistache green stucco, which was flush with the sidewalk, the driver pulled up his nag with a 'Here we is'.

It was an older building than the others on the street and had a high gabled roof of ancient pink tiles, which descended to make a gallery on the second floor. A wide doorway with a wrought iron gate set in the solid masonry of the first storey faced the street.

'This yeah's the Hotel Trouville,' Peppermint Pants announced, with a certain amount of pride in his voice.

Its plain and rather discouraging exterior did little to comfort Drum except for the fact that it appeared freshly painted, gay with flowering boxes on the balcony, and apparently clean. It had no similarity to any hotel he had ever seen before and except for the sign in faded gold lettering over the door it might well have been a private home, although it was considerably larger than any other house in the street. A boy in his early teens, light brown in colour, came rushing to the gate and opened it with a sweeping gesture that combined a low bow with his swinging of the gate.

'Yes suh, masta suh.'

'I'd like to get a room here, provided there is one.' Drum accepted the gesture that the boy made and walked through a cool, damp masonry-walled entrance hall into a brilliant courtyard ablaze with flowers and shaded by tropical trees.

'Yo' a-wantin' to see Madame Helene, then,' the boy said, gesturing again for Drum to follow him. He led him across the courtyard, past a small fountain that sprayed a rainbow-hued jet of water into a blue-tiled basin, then up a flight of wooden stairs to an inside gallery. The door at the head of the stairs was open, but the boy rapped on the doorpost, waiting for a voice from inside.

'Yes? That you, Clarence?'

'Yes, ma'am. This's Clarence 'n' got me a gen'leman here what wantin' to know if'n yo' got a room for him.'

'Then, ask the gentleman to come in.' The voice was low and had a slight French accent, although it lacked the typical slurring that Drum had come to associate with Southern speech.

Drum stepped into the room, which was dimmed by jalousied windows and smelled faintly of lavender and camphor. A distinguished-looking woman with an aureole of white hair was sitting in a high-backed chair. She had been sewing – embroidering, rather – and carefully put her needle into the square of lawn, stretched on a hoop, on which she had been working. She looked up and smiled at Drum and at the warmth of her smile he felt for the first time since he had arrived in New Orleans that he had found a friend.

'Drummond Maxwell of Boston, madame,' he introduced himself. 'My uncle had made reservations for me at the Saint Charles Hotel, but when I presented myself there, I was told that there were no rooms available and they suggested that I come here.'

'Come closer, young man.' She beckoned him with the embroidery hoop and when he neared her chair, she indicated a spot on the polished floor where the sun shone through the jalousies in a series of brilliant stripes. Fussing for a moment among the laces of her dress, she produced a gold lorgnette on a thin chain, flicked it open, and examined him.

'You might almost have gotten away with it, young man. Almost, I say. Just almost. Because it is apparent if one looks closely. If you had gone to a hotel in New York or Chicago or any northern city, I doubt if it would have been noticed, but we Southerners—'

'Yes, I know.' Drum felt he could smile about it to this understanding woman. 'You Southerners have a sixth sense—'

'. . . which tells us. I hope you were not badly treated at the Saint Charles. I always resent such treatment when it is meted out to others. As for myself, I try never to mingle with whites so I never receive such treatment. But to answer your question – yes, I have a room for you, a most comfortable room.'

'And I shall need accommodations for my two servants, one of whom is badly ill.'

'Not with an infectious disease, I hope.'

Drum shook his head. 'He was wounded, madame, through no fault of his own. Have no fear, he is nothing more than a boy and not a contentious sort, but the fact that he is still sitting outside in the carriage in the hot sun worries me.'

'I can accommodate your two servants in the *garçonnière*, unless, of course, you are accustomed to having one or both of them sleep on a trundle bed in your room. Many of my gentlemen who bring their body servants with them prefer that.'

'No, they can be accommodated in the . . . what did you call it?'

'*Garçonnière*. If you are familiar with French, you will recognize the word as a place for boys. In the old days – and I say this without blushing, for it was an acknowledged custom of the times – when a boy reached his teens, he was moved from the main house to the smaller house in the back of the courtyard. It was here that the servants slept, but there were also special apartments for the sons of the house. Here each one was allotted a female servant who was called, even openly, a bed wench. That is one of the reasons why you see so many people like yourself and myself. At one time you and I would have been referred to as having a goodly percentage of human blood. You see, in slave times, the Negro was considered animal and not human. But regardless of the high percentage of this so-called human blood, it could never make a man white. Therefore he was neither white nor free but remained an animal. Oh, how I take up your precious time while your wounded servant languishes in the sun.' She clapped her hands and the boy who brought Drum to her room appeared in the doorway. 'Clarence, get Obadiah and Lucius and have them get this gentleman's luggage out of the hack. Pay off the driver and add it to Mr Maxwell's bill. Put Mr Maxwell in Number Seven room and put his two servants in the *garçonnière* in the room that Madame LeClerc's maids just vacated. There are two beds there.'

'Thank you, Madame Helene,' Drum said, relieved. He had finally found a place to stay. 'May I pay you now?'

'Pay?' Madame Helene nearly tossed the embroidery hoop in the air. 'We never mention money here, Mr Maxwell. You will receive a bill every week, which will include your meals and lodging and that of your servants. It will be fair, I assure you.'

'Thank you again. And now, with your permission, I shall go to my room.'

'You have not my permission, Mr Maxwell. I would talk with you a little further. Everything will be attended to by Clarence and Obadiah and Lucius. Your name interests me, Mr Maxwell.'

'My name? Drummond Maxwell?'

'Yes, because I once knew a Mr Drummage Maxwell and there is, you must admit, a certain similarity between the names. I met him in Mobile while he was attending a Republican convention there. He was about to run for Congress before he was murdered.'

'And he was from Falconhurst Plantation, I presume.'

She nodded again, peering at him through her lorgnette but shaking her head as she scanned his features.

'He was my father, I believe.'

'A wonderful man, Mr Maxwell. He was a father to be proud of, but strangely enough I see little resemblance to him in you.' Again she raised her lorgnette and stared at him. '*Mais oui!* But I do. You have his size and there is a trace of his nobility in you.'

'My mother was white.' At her words of praise Drum stood a little straighter. 'Actually I know very little about my antecedents. I was raised in Boston by adoptive parents. As a matter of fact, until about a month ago I was unaware that I was coloured.'

'It is nothing to be ashamed of' – she reached out a thin, parchment-coloured hand to him – 'nothing at all to be ashamed of. It is rather a difficult cross to bear at times, but it is certainly not your fault. Yet, Mr Maxwell, being coloured as you and I are does carry with it certain responsibilities.'

'Yes?'

'Yes, indeed. We must so conduct ourselves that nobody, least of all a white person, can in any way find fault with our behaviour. That, Mr Maxwell, is our responsibility. It is a big one.'

CHAPTER TWELVE

IT SEEMED AN interminable time, after Drum left the friendliness of Madame Helene's room, before everything settled into some semblance of order. Lucy was carried across the courtyard and installed in the small room of the *garçonnière*. Mede began unpacking all the valises and hanging up Drum's clothes. A doctor was summoned by Madame Helene for Lucy. At length Drum had a chance to look around and appraise the big room in which he was so comfortably installed. It was cool, with full-length jalousied windows that looked out on the courtyard. Even the door was nothing but a louvered shutter. The plain white walls, relieved only by a small wooden crucifix hanging over the bed, added to the coolness and the sparse furnishings and, along with the highly polished wood floor, gave it an air of uncluttered spaciousness. He dismissed Mede and sat down in one of the high-backed chairs – evidently a remnant from some Spanish don. It was good to relax in this dim coolness, even though his clothes were wringing wet.

A knock on the door introduced Clarence with a cup of chicory-flavoured coffee served along with a crusty croissant and a jam tart whose taste Drum was unable to identify.

'Yo'-all wantin' to wash yo'self all over?' Clarence lingered after pouring the coffee.

'You bringing the bathtub and the water?' Drum asked, wondering if he should ring for Mede to pour the water over him.

'Ain' no need.' Clarence stood first on one foot and then the other, regarding Drum. 'We got us a place here. Jes' shuck down outa them sweaty clothes 'n' wrap a sheet 'roun' yo' if'n yo' ain' got no nightshirt o' dressin' robe like'n some folks have, 'n' I'll show yo'. He'p yo' too, if'n yo' wants. Ain' no need for sendin' for that Mede. He a-takin' care o' his Lucy boy.'

Drum was about to dismiss Clarence but realized he would need him as a guide for this mysterious bathing place. He crossed to the armoire to get his silk robe, noticing that Clarence's eyes followed him about the room, and when he returned to undress, Clarence was beside him, helping him off with his clothes, folding the soggy trousers, and hanging the coat on the back of a chair.

'Yo' shore wet, Mista Maxwell suh.' Clarence let one hand slide across Drum's wet back. 'An' yo' shore a damn purty man. Yo' even purtier'n the other man – that Mr Brantome what we got here. He ain' got no body servant with him, so I undresses him if'n his wife not there. He right purty, that M'sieur Brantome, but ain' so purty nor so biglike, like yo'.'

Drum felt that the compliments were only a venture on Clarence's part for the picayune tip he hoped to get, so he slipped into his robe and motioned for the boy to lead the way.

Clarence conducted him out on to the balcony, down the stairs, and across the courtyard to the bathing place, a lattice-screened corner of the courtyard that was hidden by vines. A little white flag on the door was turned down and Clarence explained that when the flag was turned up, the bath was occupied but, being turned down, it was free now. Inside Drum found a most ingenious arrangement far different from the usual tub he had been accustomed to. A tank on the roof into which water was pumped daily was exposed to the heat of the sun, which gave it a pleasant tepidity. All Drum had to do, so Clarence informed him, was to stand under a perforated nozzle, pull a chain, and the water would shower down over him. Clarence produced a cake of hard-milled French soap from his trousers pocket – evidently he had anticipated Drum's bath – and told him he would wait outside with towels to dry Drum when he had finished. Following Clarence's instructions, Drum pulled the chain, felt the warm water enveloping him, scrubbed himself clean with the sweet-smelling soap, and then summoned Clarence with the towels. It was, Drum decided, the most delightful bath he had ever taken, although he was annoyed by Clarence's too intimate method of drying his body. He did not wish to rebuke the boy on his first day at the hotel, but he decided that from now on he would have Mede attend him.

Back in his room he dismissed Clarence, who had seemed disposed to linger, spread down the linen sheet of the bed, and soon fell asleep, not even hearing the gong that rang for luncheon. When he awoke in the late afternoon, he decided on another of those delightful shower baths and was happy to note that the white flag was not up. This time he bathed and dried himself alone, then returned to his room and pulled the bell cord.

Clarence answered. 'What kin I do for yo', masta suh?' He noted the drops of water in Drum's hair. 'Yo' been a-washin' yo'self all over 'gain. Whyn't yo' call for me? I likes to help yo'.'

'Run over and get Mede for me.'

'Kin do whatever yo' want better'n Mede.'

Drum took the boy by the shoulders and propelled him towards the door. 'Now, look here, Clarence! If you and I are going to get along here, let's remember something. I'm not interested in you and you are not in me. Right?'

Clarence took the rebuke without speaking. It was evidently not the first time he had been so reproved and he left the room. In a few moments Mede appeared.

'How's Lucy?' Drum asked Mede.

'The doctor he 'lows as to how Lucy a-goin' to be all right,' Mede said. 'He say yo' fixed him up purty good. No 'fection, if'n yo' knows what that is. 'Bout a week, Lucy a-goin' to be all right again.'

The thickness of Mede's accent annoyed Drum, but he did not criticize him. Instead he wondered why he felt so relieved about Lucy, for whom he had always felt the same repugnance he had recently felt for Clarence. But now that he had taken Lucy under his protection, he really was concerned about him and he was glad he was doing all right. He attributed his concern to the fact that, as Lucy had said, they were all from Falconhurst. Therefore it seemed right that the boy should seek Drum's protection. It was, Drum decided, a certain seignorial feeling, a certain sense of ownership, and he wondered if this was the way white masters had felt towards their Negro slaves before the war. While he considered Mede a friend as well as a servant, he felt almost fatherly towards Lucy, even though he did not actually like the boy.

Mede continued to talk as he helped Drum to dress. 'Cain' understan' somethin', Mista Drum. Jes' cain' understand why I a-likin' that Lucy so. Ain' lookin' for no wench now that Lucy he 'roun'.'

'You'll get over it. Wait till you get to Falconhurst. There'll probably be a lot of wenches there. You'll forget all about Lucy.'

'Don' know, Mista Drum. Don' know. Finds myself a-lookin' at that Clarence boy now. Wonderin' if'n he like Lucy too.'

Drum reached out and landed a cuff on Mede's ear. 'Better keep away from Clarence. He's too young for you, but I can tell you this. He and Lucy had better get together. They're two of a kind. The boy was only too willing while I was taking my bath. Don't get mixed up with him. Lucy's enough for the time being.' He could see, however, that his words had little effect on Mede.

'That Clarence boy shore wearin' his britches mighty tight.'

'Well, you keep your hands off his tight britches and for God's sake stop talking like a goddam nigger.'

'Lucy he a-sayin' that the way to talk, 'n' after all, I am a nigger, Mista Drum. Got to do like'n the others do. Ain' wantin' to be different. Bein' a nigger in Boston different 'n bein' a nigger here. In Boston ain' many, here they's lots, so I a-goin' to be like'n the rest. Whar yo' a-goin', Mista Drum, now that yo' all dressed up?'

Drum thought the matter over. Actually he had no place to go. He knew nobody and outside of his two trips to the bathing place, he did not know much about the hotel. He had no means of conveyance and had no particular desire to go out on the street. There seemed to be nothing for him to do but sit in his room and he was tired of that. He'd go himself to see Lucy and see how he was getting along. It was the only place he could think of to go.

'We'll go across and see Lucy. Want to see how he's coming along. Go ahead and show me the way.'

They found Lucy half sitting up in bed, propped up on pillows. He had a professional-looking bandage on his chest, the white contrasting with the darkness of his skin. Lucy smiled out a welcome and Drum stayed long enough to encourage him and promise him that they would be taking him to Falconhurst with them. Somehow off the ship and minus his steward's jacket, Lucy looked younger and handsomer, but, Drum decided, he must be shorn of his long hair. Without that he would look more like a man than a girl. Drum issued an order. Either short hair or Lucy would have to remain in New Orleans. Lucy let his fingers stray through his long locks as if he regretted parting with them, then, with an impatient gesture, threw them back over his head, smoothing them down with his hand.

'Think mayhap yo're right, Mista Drum. Ain' wishin' to look like a slut no more. Ain' a-sayin' as to how I kin change my ways, but kin change my looks. Been a-thinkin' since I a-lyin' here. Goin' to be right happy to git myself back to Falconhurst. Co'se my mammy she ain' there now, but Mista Brute, what's my pappy, he a-goin' to be glad to see me an' I come home lookin' like a boy 'n' not a gal.'

Leaving Lucy, Drum made his way down the narrow stairs of the *garçonnière* and back across the courtyard. While he was crossing it he heard the dinner gong and saw several people descending the steps from the second floor gallery to the ground floor. He waited, until they had all come down, for Madame Helene, who with the aid of a tall, silver-topped, rosewood stick descended the stairs alone and last. Going over to her, he offered his arm to her and together they passed through a tall double door into the hotel's dining-room.

A long mahogany table glistened under the flickering lights of two candelabra. Lights were necessary, even though it was daylight outside, because the only aperture in the room was the wide doorway into the courtyard – the other walls were solid masonry. The room was cool but had a faint odour of damp plaster. By the time Drum and Madame Helene entered, the rest of the guests were seated at the table, but they all rose at Madame Helene's entrance and she made a slow circuit of the table on Drum's arm, introducing him to each of the guests. He did not remember all their names in the quick introductions, but there were a middle-aged couple from an upstate plantation, an elderly man with a white imperial, who was introduced as a historian and author, a family of father and mother and three adolescent girls, and then a young couple.

The latter were so attractive that Drum took particular care to catch their name.

'M'sieur Brantome and his wife,' Madame said. 'Please meet M'sieur Maxwell of Boston and Falconhurst Plantation.'

The young man, who seemed a bit too handsome to suit Drum's taste, extended a hand the colour of old ivory. Only when it came in contact with Drum's own, could he notice that the fellow's skin was just a shade darker than his own. He grasped the slender, ringed fingers with their elaborately manicured nails and glanced up at the fellow's face. Yes, he was altogether too handsome, Drum felt. Carefully curled and pomaded hair, arching eyebrows, a perfect nose, and lips that held no hint of any Negroid ancestor were all combined in a face that was too perfect. Yet there was nothing effeminate about the face, only that it seemed too handsome to be true. It lacked that one small defect that might have made it believable. The man himself was tall, slender, and carried himself well despite his conspicuous clothes. He wore a smartly tailored white linen jacket, whose effect was somewhat spoiled by the fact that it had been worn for some time since laundering and was wrinkled, fawn-coloured trousers, an overly frilled shirt, and a black satin stock, which sported a flashing red stone surrounded by diamonds.

'My pleasure,' the young man said, bowing low over Drum's hand.

This must, Drum considered, be the Mr Brantome Clarence had mentioned, but why any man would be interested in Clarence when he had such a beautiful wife was beyond Drum's imagination. Madame Brantome, Drum could see, in contrast to the showy good looks of her husband, was a real beauty. She was tall, almost as tall as her husband, and her skin was a shade lighter in colour than his, approximating Drum's own. Her hair, instead of being curly like his, was straight, parted in the middle to show a white line of her scalp, and then arranged in an oversized chignon at the back. There was a marked resemblance between the two, but whereas the husband only approximated an aristocrat in his looks, the wife really was one.

She had an oval face with rather high cheekbones, which gave it an exotic look of mystery. Brows that were perfect black stencils swept back like swallow's wings. Under them were large, expressive brown eyes, framed in sooty lashes. Unlike her husband's nose, which was straight and Grecian, hers was just a trifle *retroussé* but only enough to add a look of piquancy to counteract the exoticism of the angular cheekbones and soften her face, preparing one, as it were, for the soft, red fullness of her lips.

Drum was so absorbed in her face that he did not notice that the lace on her dress of white sprigged lawn had been mended, that the pearls she wore were not genuine, or that her earrings were only plain gold hoops. Nor had he noticed that the flashing red stone in her husband's cravat was only glass or that the cuffs of his linen jacket were slightly frayed.

'Madame,' Drum said, bowing low over her proffered hand, and kissed it, noticing the faint odour of Muguet du Bois.

'M'sieur Maxwell' – she acknowledged the greeting – 'but, as *la bonne Madame Helene* has placed us next to each other at the table with my husband across from us, would it not be better if I told you my name is Claire and that my husband's name is Narcisse so that we may not have to stand on too much formality?'

'And mine is Drum, which is short for Drummond.' He pulled out the chair she indicated and seated her, taking the one next to her for himself.

Narcisse smiled at him across the table, displaying a row of extremely white teeth. 'At last we are to have a guest here at the hotel of our own age. My wife and I' – he nodded in her direction – 'have missed such companionship since we came here several months ago. It is nice to welcome you . . . Drum?' He made the name into a question, as if asking permission.

It was a delicious meal, even though Drum had never been initiated into the delights of Creole cookery. The crawfish bisque was flavoured with a hint of sherry, the rice was fluffy, and the gumbo rich with flavour. There was a salad of crisp greens with just a suggestion of garlic and a torte that was a fitting accompaniment to the delicious coffee. During the meal

Madame Helene herself directed the conversation, throwing the verbal ball back and forth from one guest to another, so that everyone was included and nobody felt neglected. She seemed to know everything about everyone at the table, what interested them and what they were doing. From her conversation with Narcisse and Claire, Drum gathered that they had but recently sold their plantation north of New Orleans on one of the numerous bayous and moved to the city. Madame Helene made references to incidents in the past and from these Drum gathered that they were more or less permanent guests.

Once during the dinner his knee came in contact with Claire's under the damask tablecloth. For one slight moment he felt the warmth of her flesh against his. Looking at her sideways after she had withdrawn her knee from contact with his, he saw a red flush on her cheeks and she dropped her napkin, making quite a to-do about Clarence's recovering it for her. By then the blush had disappeared and she appeared quite natural. It was such a trifling incident, yet it caused Drum to wonder if this glorious creature were really happy with her husband, handsome though he might be.

It was only after dinner, when those at the table arose and went up the gallery stairs to the drawing-room on the second floor, that Drum had a chance to talk with Claire and Narcisse alone. They had allowed the older people to precede them and as they stood waiting at the bottom of the stairs Claire turned to her husband.

'It's such a lovely evening, Narcisse' – she opened and closed her fan nervously – 'why don't we invite Drum out for a drive, that is if you are not busy tonight? This is his first day in New Orleans and he has seen so little of our lovely city. It's much cooler now and he will enjoy it.'

'A most entrancing idea, dear Claire. And I have no appointments this evening.' Narcisse laid a restraining hand on her as she started up the stairs. 'Provided, of course, we can find any sort of decent conveyance to take Drum in.' He spread his hands apologetically in Drum's direction. 'Unfortunately we sold our horses and carriages when we disposed of our plantation and as a result we must depend on hired *fiacres* these days. Most of them are miserable things.'

'I know,' Drum admitted, 'I rode in one this morning. But tell me, is there not a livery stable near here? I have had in mind hiring a carriage for my stay here in the city.' He looked to Narcisse for a reply.

'A very poor one' – Narcisse shook his head and pursed his lips in complete disparagement – 'but,' he added more cheerfully, 'over in Dumaine Street there is an excellent stable with really fine carriages for hire.'

'Which they usually use for funerals,' Claire added. The little pout and the fullness of her lower lip added to her attraction for Drum.

'Then, why don't we go there and see if I can hire one and' – he laughed – 'I can assure you it will not be used for a funeral.'

'Would you mind putting off your ride until tomorrow?' Narcisse asked his wife. 'By the time we get to Dumaine Street and see if there is anything there that Drum wants, it will be too late for you to go out.'

'But it was her suggestion,' Drum interrupted. He was far more anxious for her company than her husband's.

She smiled at them both. 'What difference will one day make? Naturally I do not mind putting it off until tomorrow, when we shall all ride in style with our friend Drum rather than mope along in some hired *fiacre*. Besides' – she winked at Drum – 'I know my husband is just waiting for a chance to get away from me.'

Narcisse didn't deny it. With Drum who, he was certain, had well-lined pockets, Narcisse felt he would be able to suggest certain activities and Drum would pay for them. Drum, on the other hand, was scarcely interested in Narcisse's company. He would much have preferred to have Claire go along. He could at least admire her, if nothing else, and he cursed himself for the desire he felt for her. Why was it that every time he looked at a beautiful woman, he wanted her. Were all men like that? Or was it the curse or possibly the blessing of his father's blood?

However, a contretemps had arisen and it seemed better to

follow Narcisse's suggestion, particularly as Drum had had in mind hiring a suitable conveyance anyway. His evening with Claire would come later. Perhaps during his stay in New Orleans he might manage to find some few moments alone with her. He had a feeling that she might enjoy being alone with him too. Why, he did not know, but there was a certain something, a certain barely perceptible touching of each other's soul, that told him this was true.

Drum excused himself for a moment to go to his room. He did not know how much the carriage hire would be and he needed more money. As he turned the corner of the gallery he looked down. Narcisse and Claire were in a heated conversation and, although Drum could not hear them, Narcisse seemed to be angry with her. Could he have sensed that certain something that Drum had felt between himself and Claire? Narcisse in his excitement even pointed an admonishing finger at Claire and his words were accompanied by a scowl. Her slight nod of acquiescence, however, seemed to reassure her husband and, his anger passed, he smiled at her.

When Drum came down, they were still standing at the foot of the stairs.

'Please, M'sieur Drum, it is quite unimportant that I do not go with you this evening. Shall we make it for tomorrow evening, when you have your so-grand carriage?' She stepped a little closer to him, so that he could again smell the Muguet du Bois.

'A pleasure that I shall anticipate.' Drum in turn stepped a little closer to her. She did not back away from him but held out her hand. For the second time that evening he took it and kissed it, moving his lips a little distance up the back of her hand. She made no effort to remove her hand. Drum stood up and looked at her. He found that they were alone – Narcisse was running up the stairs.

'My husband went up to get his hat,' she explained. There seemed to be an invitation in her eyes, but Drum could not be sure of what it said. For the first time in his life he was baffled by a woman, although, truth to tell, it was not the first time he had been interested in a married woman. But even with her suggestion of an invitation, there was a certain reserve in her manner that kept him away from her.

Narcisse came running down the stairs, his hat in his hand. Drum stepped away from Claire and she waited for her husband to come down and then put a hand on each of their arms.

'At least,' she said, smiling at them both, 'if I cannot accompany you both this evening, I can go as far as the gate with you.'

'And that is as far as you will go?' Drum could not resist saying it, even with her husband present.

'For tonight, M'sieur Drum, for tonight.'

CHAPTER THIRTEEN

USUALLY THERE WAS a cab standing in front of the hotel – so Narcisse explained – but this evening the length of Rampart Street was empty and Narcisse asked Drum if he would mind walking. It was really not far and a sufficiently cool evening, so they set out along the narrow banquettes, as Drum learned sidewalks were called in New Orleans. Walking through the narrow streets – the same that he had driven through that morning – gave Drum a more intimate acquaintance with the city, which he found entirely different from either Boston or New York, the only two cities he was familiar with. He missed the smug red brick and bay windows of Boston. There was a semi-tropical European look about New Orleans, which Drum supposed was because of its mixed French and Spanish ancestry. He decided that it was really not an attractive city, although the flowers and plants everywhere did much to enliven it. It reminded him of a grande dame who was not too much addicted to cleanliness but covered her face with powder to hide the grime, and her body with perfume to kill the odour of accumulated sweat.

While they walked along, Narcisse delivered an uninterrupted monologue, and, as Drum was anxious to gather whatever information he could about the couple, he did not interrupt.

Narcisse was, so he informed Drum, the son of one Aristides Brantome but – and Narcisse had no hesitation in telling Drum – born on the wrong side of the blanket because his mother was coloured. His mother had been a slave of Brantome's, purchased at one of the great octoroon balls in New Orleans where exotic hybrids were sold to the highest bidder. However, his father was madly in love with her and had, after the war, legitimized their union by a legal marriage, so Narcisse had become his father's legal heir. With the change in laws after the war that made it possible for both Negroes and coloured people to hold property, the vast plantation had become the property of Narcisse.

'And your wife?' Drum was far more interested in Claire's history than in Narcisse's.

About his wife, Narcisse was rather vague and disinclined to talk. She was, he said after a few moments' hesitation, similar in antecedents to himself and born on a neighbouring plantation. They had known each other all their lives and on the death of her parents, it was only natural that they should marry and, as there were legitimate heirs to her home, she had come to live at Mon Plaisir with Narcisse. Once again, in describing his home, Narcisse became eloquent. His plantation was known throughout Louisiana for the elegance of its big house, the extent of its acres, the faithful colony of Negroes – former slaves who lived there – and its hospitality. But – and here Narcisse shrugged his shoulders as much as to say that even Eden might have had its drawbacks – both he and Claire had become bored with life on a plantation. They were completely isolated from the rest of the community and had no dealings with anyone except the Negroes who worked for them. So they had decided to sell Mon Plaisir and come to New Orleans to live, where they would be in some contact with people of their own kind, where they could go to the opera (even if they did have to sit in a special section) and have some social life.

But as far as managing a plantation, Narcisse boasted, there was nothing he did not know about the intricacies of such a venture. He had learned the management of Mon Plaisir from his father, who had been an astute businessman. Was Drum, he asked, familiar with the management of a cotton plantation?

And here Drum had to shake his head and tell Narcisse that he had actually never seen a plantation, although he had heard about Falconhurst all his life.

'I remember now that Madame Helene introduced you as the owner of Falconhurst Plantation. Isn't that in Alabama?'

Drum nodded.

'It might be interesting to you to know, *mon ami*, that although I have never been there, I am not entirely unacquainted with this Falconhurst of yours. It is a name to conjure with here in the South. You see, before the war Falconhurst was almost a household word. Everyone had heard about it.'

Drum did not interrupt but looked to Narcisse for an explanation.

'Falconhurst Negroes were the finest in the South. If one wanted a fine Negro stud for his plantation or a wench for breeding, one bought it from Falconhurst. Yes, Falconhurst was a slave-breeding plantation and its Negroes were its pride. Before the war a fine Falconhurst buck would bring two or three thousand dollars or even more. Usually they were pure Negro. Falconhurst did not specialize in fancies – only in handsome, big black or occasionally light-coloured bucks and wenches. The more exotic specimens were for the more specialized slave dealers in New Orleans.'

He looked at Drum, inspecting him closely. 'You, I can truthfully say, would have been a real fancy. You might have sold for around five thousand and I rate myself as high in value as you. We would have been purchased, probably, by some wealthy widow, ostensibly as her butler or coachman, but her real reason for purchasing us would be to use us for her pleasure.'

'I can't imagine a worse life.' Drum could not but be thankful he had not lived fifty years earlier.

'I can,' Narcisse said vehemently. 'On a cane plantation a buck purchased at the age of twenty was usually dead before thirty. It was gruelling work and even the strongest could not last long. These field hands, however, were seldom used for breeding. As a matter of fact, we had several Negroes at Mon Plaisir who were of the Falconhurst strain. These were the ones my father used for breeding when breeding slaves was a mania all over the South. The cotton crop might fail, the plantation might be plastered with mortgages, but a man looked to his slaves for his prestige and reputation.'

And, Narcisse went on to say in a tone that revealed a mixture of pride and shame, there was actually Falconhurst blood in himself. His own grandmother, his mother's mother, had been a Falconhurst slave, probably a quadroon, so he had been told. Slaves had been proud of their Falconhurst ancestry and it had been handed down from generation to generation. There was little for a slave to be proud of and he treasured anything that set him apart from the rest.

'I must say I do not treasure my Falconhurst ancestry. I would much prefer to be white.'

'Why?' Narcisse asked. 'If one stays with one's own kind, one never gets involved with questions of colour, although of course the whiter one is, the more it is to be desired. There is no stigma attached to it among our own, although it is considered as lowering oneself in the social ladder if one marries a person darker than oneself. We mulattos – and I use the word in its general meaning, because we are really not mulattos, who are the result of a mating of white and black – look down on the Negroes as much as the whites look down on us. But among ourselves, as you have already seen at Madame Helene's, we are not without resources. We are educated, cultured, and able to take our places in the world. Actually many of us feel that we are better than most whites because some of the most aristocratic blood in the South is ours for the claiming. Look at me, Drum! Look at me! The Brantomes were one of the really old and aristocratic Creole families.' Drum felt he was listening to a man forcing himself to believe what he said.

Narcisse took Drum's elbow and turned him at the corner

of a street. Looking up to the weathered street sign, Drum could make out the faded letters DUMAINE STREET.

'Here's where the stable is.' Narcisse pointed down the street, the direction of his finger changing. 'See that house over there?'

Drum looked across the street at a house that was older than the others and wondered what in particular there might be about it to command either his or Narcisse's attention.

'There's quite a story about that house,' Narcisse said. 'It's almost a legend in New Orleans. That house used to belong to the most famous madam in New Orleans. I've heard my father tell about it and he got the story from his father and grandfather. Seems that this Madame Alix was a real French countess who landed here in New Orleans by way of St Domingue and Cuba. And' – he looked curiously at Drum – 'she had a nigger fighter and whorehouse stud by the name of Drum, the same as yours. Might have been some ancestor of yours because it is said that his son was sold to Falconhurst. Well, anyway, it came out after the old lady died that this Drum was really her son, sired on her by some Negro stud the lady had taken a fancy to. Anyway, this Drum was black or nearly so and she was white, so it must have been a full-blooded Negro who sired him.'

'And his name was Drum?' Drum asked. 'That, you know, is my real name. I felt when I went to college that it seemed so different and so *outré* that I changed it to Drummond, which is a good old English name. But my name still remains Drum. It's an unusual name.'

'Almost too unusual to be a coincidence.'

'You say this Drum's son was sold to Falconhurst?'

Again Narcisse nodded.

'Then, there may be something in what you say,' Drum agreed. 'My father's name was Drummage, which is also an unusual name. His father's name, so the boy Lucy who is with me informed me, was Drumson. Yes, there may be a connexion.' Drum looked at the weatherbeaten house with renewed interest. It had both a second and a third upper balcony with wooden railings, whereas the ground floor, flush with the banquette, presented a blank appearance to the street, as it was without windows and of solid masonry very much like the Hotel de Trouville. Apparently both houses had been built before the vogue for ornamental ironwork had struck New Orleans. It was evidently no longer a private home or a bawdy house, because there were sundry signs nailed on the wall and on the balconies. It now housed a tailor, a harness maker, and a dealer in medicinal herbs.

Drum considered the house carefully. If this legendary Drum who had once lived there was his ancestor, the man would be his great-grandfather. Well, it could be. Drum rather hoped it might be. The similarity of names might prove something. At least, having a French countess who was also a bawdy house keeper seemed rather in line with what his antecedents should be. He wished that he might be transported back through the years and see the place in its heyday, even to visit there to take advantage of its occupants and to see his great-grandfather.

So the place was formerly a whorehouse. Drum wished that it still might be. The thought of having a woman entered his head – in fact it had been there ever since he had kissed Claire's hand.

'Too bad the place isn't open for business now as it was in those days. I'd turn right in the doorway.'

'You feeling that way?' Narcisse asked.

'Always do,' Drum said grinning.

'It seems to be a common failing among us coloured boys. Oh yes, we try to cover it up and to appear as cold-blooded as our white brethren, but we can't. We've all got one thing on our minds. It's that bit of primitive blood in us that makes us so randy all the time. I'm feeling that way myself.'

'Then, why don't we do something about?'

Narcisse allowed himself a deprecatory shrug of his shoulders. 'As much as I would like to, I can't tonight. I find I have come out without my *porte-monnaie*. I haven't a picayune with me.'

'Then, allow me.' Drum was more than willing to accommodate Narcisse. 'It's only a fair exchange. You show me where to go. I'll pay for the entertainment.'

'Then, wait until we get the carriage. It would be some distance to walk.' Narcisse pointed down the street to where a gilded horseshoe hung over a wide doorway.

The manager of the livery stable, although a white man, was nothing loath to rent one of his rigs to Drum, although Drum felt that the man was charging him a higher price than he would ordinarily have charged. For the seemingly enormous sum of $10 a day, Drum could have the use of a fairly present-able barouche with a black coachman to go with it. The carriage would come to the hotel every morning after breakfast and Drum could then give the orders for the day. He would have the carriage at his disposal all day and as far into the night as he cared to use it. Both Narcisse and Drum tried without success to drive a better bargain; in fact Narcisse even felt he might do better in bargaining with the owner than Drum, and excused himself, taking the man aside and whispering with him, but in the end he returned saying that the fellow was adamant and insisted that Drum would have to pay that amount unless he could furnish his own coachman. As neither Mede nor Lucy had ever driven a horse, Drum accepted the price, although the sum of $70 a week for a carriage seemed exorbitant to him. However, there was nothing else he could do, at least for tonight, so he agreed.

He was, however, somewhat surprised when the same peppermint-striped youth who had driven him that morning appeared and announced that he was to be Drum's coachman. His name, so he said, was Ciceron. He recalled driving Drum to the Trouville and at Drum's affirmative nod, which closed the deal, the boy went to harness the horses.

It was, at least, a more fashionable turnout than the one he had driven that morning, although Ciceron himself, with his soiled clothes, added nothing to its smartness.

'Where to?' he asked, as Drum and Narcisse climbed up into the carriage.

'Perhaps you'd like to see the cribs?' Narcisse suggested.

'Cribs?' The word meant nothing to Drum, but Ciceron forced his own observations upon them.

'Yo' boys a-plannin' to git yo'selves dreaned tonight?'

Ciceron asked. 'If'n so, them cribs ain' no place for gen'lemen like'n yo'. Them cribs is jes' two-bit whores. All clapped up too, they be, every one o' 'em a fireship. I kin take yo' to a better place.'

'We're just going to look, that's all.' Narcisse silenced Ciceron with the tone of authority in his voice. 'We have in mind a better place than the cribs.'

'Do you mean Belle LaBelle's?' Drum recalled the name that Mother Carey had mentioned.

'Hell, no!' Narcisse spat on the floor in contempt. 'Belle would take one look at us and have her bouncer throw us out. She's just for white folks. I have in mind taking you to Hermione's, where I am known.'

Ciceron, still undaunted, spoke up. 'Tha's the place.' He winked one big brown eye knowingly. 'Tha's the place where all you rich young high-colour boys go. But she's jes's fussy's old Belle. Won't let no brown skin like me inside her goddam doors. No matter how much money I got, she say, "Nigger, get to hell outa here." She don' wan' nothing but lightskins. A-sayin' her gals too good for niggers. Nigger boy like'n me gits to go to the cribs 'n' tha's all.'

'Why don't you keep that big mouth of yours shut?' Narcisse was exasperated with the fellow.

'Kin talk if'n I wants. Yo' two ain' white mastas. Yo's jes's niggery's I on'y yo' thinkin' 'cause yo' mustees, yo' better'n me.'

'And so we are.' Narcisse would have slapped the fellow had not Drum intervened.

'Let's try Hermione's.' Drum was willing to go anywhere now.

Ciceron, angry over Narcisse's attempt to slap him, stepped up and eyed Narcisse carefully. 'I see yo' before. Yo' the fellow what's always a-hangin' 'roun' Hermione's. Yo' tryin' to be so high 'n' mighty. Yo'—'

This time Narcisse did strike him, but instead of striking back, Ciceron, who was larger than Narcisse, merely started to blubber.

'One more word out of you and you lose this job. Understand?' Narcisse was speaking with white authority, which Ciceron evidently recognized. 'If you'd rather be a coachman for Mr Maxwell here than drift along all day through the streets trying to pick up a fare, you'd better keep still.' He turned to Drum, half apologetically, laughing to minimize his words. 'The fellow's right in a way. I am one of Hermione's best patrons, but let me warn you of one thing, Drum, before we go. She charges five dollars.'

Drum remembered Mother's usual rate of two dollars and wondered in what way these girls might be superior. Certainly they could not exceed Rosalie. He got into the carriage, noting the deference with which Ciceron assisted Narcisse to enter. The fellow's mood had changed with the slap that Narcisse had given him. Now he acted almost craven in Narcisse's presence. After they had started, Drum spoke to Narcisse about it.

'The only way to handle a nigger is to let him know who's master at once. Never let them get intimate with you or they'll run all over you. Now that they are free, they think they are just as good as we are, but once they feel the touch of authority, they creep back into their place. It's a lesson you will have to learn, Drum. Don't you be too familiar with your own black boy.'

'With Mede?' Drum laughed the matter off. 'Mede and I grew up together. We're friends.'

Narcisse shook his head. 'Never be friends with a black man. They cannot be trusted. Choose your friends from your own kind. We are a race apart, Drum. These niggers are ignorant black bastards. They are barely human. We have more human than Negro blood in us, therefore we are human beings.'

'And what are the Negroes?' Drum asked.

'Baboons! Animals! That's what they've always been and that's what they are now, regardless of what Lincoln said.'

'Then, there's a little of the baboon in each of us.'

'I'm not always proud of it, yet I have to live with it.' Narcisse was bitter. 'If there's one person in the world I hate, it's that black wench who polluted my blood. Yet, sometimes I am glad I have that blood in me, strange as it may seem.

Just having it there makes me feel superior to white men. Regardless of how much I hate that black wench, I know that some white man preferred her to his pure-white lady. I know that he enjoyed her more and that he came back to her again and again. She had something his white lady didn't have and she passed it on to me. Yes, Drum, I hate her, but in between hating her I have sort of a love for her. But, goddam it, if it had not been for her, I would be white. Every door in New Orleans would be open to me because I would be a white Narcisse Brantome. We could go to Belle's instead of Hermione's. White men would call us "mister". We could take a drink at the Saint Charles bar or the Old Absinthe House. But, no! To a white man I'm as much a nigger as that black baboon up on the box, but I'm not, Drum, I'm not.'

Drum could see how pride was trying to conquer fear and frustration in Narcisse and for a moment he felt sorry for him until he realized that he too had the same problem. Then he began to feel sorry for himself, but lest the mood of depression keep him from enjoying himself, he asked about the cribs.

Narcisse instructed Ciceron to drive through the street so Drum could see it, admonishing Drum not to be tempted to stop.

'If you've never had a nigger wench, one of those crib women would be too much for you. There's no better pestering in the world than a black wench, but they are strenuous, boy, strenuous!'

'I know, I've already had one.' Drum enjoyed the turn the conversation had taken.

'One?' Narcisse laughed and slapped Drum on the knee. 'One? Only one? You've never lived. You mean to say you've only had one?'

'One black one,' Drum admitted, 'but I cannot count the white ones.'

'I've never had a white one,' Narcisse admitted. 'Somehow I never wanted one.'

It was a narrow but brightly lighted street. Ciceron, with a pride of ownership, flourished his whip. 'Here they be. Ain' no other city in the world got anything like'n this.'

Drum gazed in never-ending wonder as they traversed the street. Each tiny house boasted a door and a barred window. Each was brilliantly lighted from inside and sitting in the window like merchandise on display was a woman. There were all kinds, but all of them were black. Some were dressed in tawdry ball gowns, some in almost transparent dresses, but all stood up as the barouche drove down the street. Some of the houses had windows that were dark and these, Narcisse explained, were the ones whose occupants were busy. Others that were dark had a line of men waiting in front of the door, which attested to that particular inmate's popularity. At one door Drum counted six men, lined up against the wall, each patiently awaiting his turn.

'They gits only fifteen minutes for their money,' Ciceron explained. 'Tha's why they like a gal what kin drean 'em quick-like. Ain' much fun a-pesterin' if'n yo' know yo' ain' goin' to make it 'fore the time comes.'

They passed along the street, accompanied by a constant stream of importunings.

'Here I is, man. Jes' come in here.'

'Oh, yo' pretty boys. Kin make yo' happy, I kin.'

'Ciceron, yo' knows me. Bring them boys in here.'

'Want to learn some new tricks, man?'

'Ciceron, whar yo' been? Ain' seen yo' in a coon's age!'

Ciceron did not stop and after the first block Drum told him to turn off. He was sickened by so much flesh so blatantly exposed. All he could think of was a butcher's shop with meat piled high on the counter.

Ciceron did turn off from the brightly lighted street into a narrow dark one. With three or four more turns, he drew up before a fairly decent house, its balconies filled with girls and a flickering red light over the doorway.

'This Hermione's,' he announced. 'Wantin' I should wait?'

'Of course,' Drum answered.

Ciceron slithered down from the box to the sidewalk. 'Men usually gives me two bits if'n I waits.' He held up a pink-palmed hand. 'Ain' nothing for me to do but jes' sit here 'n' wait whilst yo' boys a-pesterin' inside. Ain' much fun jes' sittin' here, wishin' I was yo'. But if'n I git two bits, I kin git back to the cribs 'n' git my fun too. Then it don' make me no neverminds how long I got to wait.'

Drum threw him the two bits. He already had a feeling that all of New Orleans was out to get the last penny in his pocket. He even began to wonder about Narcisse and his excuse that he had left his wallet at home. But Narcisse was halfway across the banquette, so Drum followed him. As Narcisse pulled the bell cord Drum wondered why he was not as excited as he had hoped to be. Then he knew. The image of Claire's face came to him and he realized that he would rather be sitting with her in the courtyard of the Trouville than entering this rather run-down bawdy house. But it was too late to turn back and he realized that just looking at Claire's face would not give him the release his body was now demanding.

The door opened and the brilliant light from the inside hall outlined a light-skinned mulattress in a tight red satin dress, trimmed with jet passementerie. Her black hair was piled high on her head and adorned with an ornament of white aigrettes. For a fleeting second Drum wondered if it were her own hair or a wig like the one Lola had worn. She seemed to know Narcisse well and greeted him effusively, but the warmth of her greeting for Narcisse was as nothing compared to the way she greeted Drum.

'My, oh my! What a pretty man yo' done brung us, Narcisse. He the handsomest man ever to step through these doors, I do say. M-m-m! My gals jes' goin' to be crazy 'bout this man. They a-goin' to claw each other ter git him. Come right in, gen'lemen, 'n' set yo'selves in the salong. Yes, suh, we goin' to see that this young mister not goin' to be a stranger long at Hermione's. Yes, suh.'

She ushered them into another brilliantly lit room furnished with French gilt armchairs and a dubious oil painting of a nude woman in a wide gold frame. He and Narcisse took the chairs Hermione indicated and she immediately called a maid and instructed her to bring iced champagne for both of them.

'Now le's see.' She ticked off the names of her girls on her fingers. 'Bessie she busy 'n' so's Imogene. Agnes ain' for this handsome man 'n' neither is Beulah. Thinkin' I'd better give him Coralie. What yo' thinkin', Narcisse? Coralie the one for him?'

'If he wants to spend the money you ask for her.'

'What's money to a rich young man like'n this young mista? He a-wantin' the best 'n' that none too good for him. Coralie she the best in New Orleans, the best in the South. She kin do everything – ain' nothin' Coralie cain' do. No, suh, ain' no other gal here what kin give him such a good time's my Coralie. I go fetch her.'

Drum downed a glass of the icy champagne and poured himself another before Hermione came back with Coralie. Much to Drum's surprise, she was an enormous woman, not obese but tall and well formed, with breasts that strained at the white satin of her ball gown. There was something primitive and regal in her appearance, even savage, despite the fact that she was almost as light in colour as Drum himself. He had never bedded himself with such a giantess and he felt that the experience might be novel and entertaining.

It was. Coralie had been well trained, but she was exhausting. Drum acquitted himself well but was unable to respond to her efforts to revive him. Instead he complimented her on her prowess and promised that the next time he came, he would be in a better mood. He already felt satiated but certainly not satisfied. He had thrilled to the trained manipulations of her fingers and the abandon of her body, but she had not comforted him as Rosalie had. Now he had only one desire – to be quit of her.

He found Narcisse already dressed and waiting for him in the ornate salon. He was alone.

'We were both quick tonight' – Narcisse looked up at him and smiled – 'and I was quicker than you, but that's a way that Hermione's girls have. No man can last long with any of them, particularly Coralie. What did you think of her?'

Drum lied. 'She was wonderful.'

He paid the bill for Narcisse and himself, astonished at its size, for every item had been listed on it – the women for himself and Narcisse, the champagne, even tips for the maids. It came to nearly thirty dollars and he noticed a moment's hesitation on Hermione's part when she held the money in her hand.

'Yo' a-comin' tomorrow, Narcisse?' she asked.

He nodded in reply.

All the way home Drum wondered how a man as lucky as Narcisse with Claire for a wife would frequent such a place daily, as seemed to be his habit.

CHAPTER FOURTEEN

THE NEXT MORNING after Drum, in company with Narcisse and Claire, had finished a late breakfast on the gallery, Mede came rushing up the stairs to announce that there was a carriage outside waiting for Drum. As Drum had had no previous opportunity to tell Mede that he had hired the carriage and as Mede had recognized Ciceron as the driver of the day before, he was unable to explain the presence of the carriage, but a few words from Drum set him straight. He told Mede to go outside and tell the fellow to wait, because he would require his services later.

He had found the summer suits he had brought from Boston altogether too heavy for the New Orleans heat and now, seeing the dark splotches of sweat around Mede's armpits, he realized that his servant was also in need of cooler clothes. And what about Lucy? His clothes, although cool enough for the climate, were certainly not suitable for his position as a servant to Drummond Maxwell. He turned to Narcisse.

'I have in mind making some purchases this morning,' he announced, 'and if you could tell me the best place to go, I would appreciate it. I am interested in finding a tailor and one who can do things quickly. I find that all of my suits, and my servants' too, are far too heavy and uncomfortable for this climate.'

'Even better than telling you, *mon cher* Drum' – Narcisse was certainly most affable this morning – 'I shall go with you and take you to the best tailor in New Orleans, that is' – he drew down the corners of his mouth with a slight disgust for the situation – 'the best tailor that caters to our kind. I doubt if M'sieur Alain, who is considered the best tailor in the city, would be interested in making clothes for either of us. Now, our own M'sieur Fabre is an excellent tailor and would be happy to serve you, although whether or not you could persuade him to make suits for your servants, I do not know. He does not as a rule do work for Negroes.'

There were, Drum was beginning to discover, many intricate ramifications to this question of coloured blood. There were no longer two divisions – black and white – but three, actually, and within that third one countless more minor classifications. Blacks, and that included all Negroes and even those with enough white blood to keep them from being the prune-black of Africa; Coloured, as they preferred to call themselves rather than *mulatto*, which the white world applied to them indiscriminately; and White, who considered themselves as far above the mulattos as the mulattos did above the blacks. To be sure, there were far more whites and blacks than there were of this rare strain of near white, but these latter formed a close little society of their own, rarely mixing with the blacks unless in the role of master and servant and avoiding the whites because they did not wish to be snubbed.

The restrictions irked Drum. In Boston he had gone to the best tailors and they had been only too glad to see him. Now he felt his world growing smaller and smaller, yet, looking down into the courtyard of Madame Helene's, he had to admit he had never been more comfortably situated in his life. Lifting his eyes to look across the table at Narcisse and Claire, he realized she was the most beautiful girl he had ever seen and, despite his first intuitive dislike of Narcisse, he was, in truth, a handsome fellow and after last night, Drum was forced to admit, an engaging companion.

'But again we shall have to leave Madame at home' – Drum inclined his head towards Claire – 'and I think she should really go along with us to christen the new carriage.'

'From the lateness of the hour at which you two returned last night, I would consider it already christened.' She seemed to feel no rancour towards her husband for staying out all night and, knowing him, she must have suspected where he was and what he was doing.

Drum, however, felt the colour mounting to his face. It seemed difficult to reconcile the riotous abandon of their evening before with this poised and beautiful woman.

'But not formally,' Drum managed to say. 'It will never be formally christened until you go with us.'

'*Hélas!*' – she made a charming moue – 'we cannot have the carriage go unchristened. So I must needs accompany you, but as M'sieur Fabre's is not far from my milliner's, I shall go along with you.'

'Not a new bonnet, my dear.' There was a tone of caution in Narcisse's words.

Claire sought to set him at ease. 'I am only having the ribbons freshened on my pink bonnet,' she said.

This little gesture of economy seemed entirely out of place with the splendours of the plantation that Narcisse had described as just having been sold. Perhaps the money had not come through yet, Drum thought, trying to explain the matter away. Then he remembered Narcisse's all-too-patent excuse that he had left his wallet behind last night and this too seemed hardly compatible with the picture he had painted. Something was wrong.

'Then, we shall all go and we shall really christen the carriage,' Drum answered after too long an interval. 'I am somewhat at a loss to know how to christen a carriage. With boats it is done with a bottle of champagne but with carriages—'

'It should be done with a bottle of perfume,' Claire said, laughing, 'particularly with hired carriages, as they often have a disagreeable odour about them from the so many people who have ridden in them.'

'Then, I shall buy you a bottle of perfume,' Drum added, 'but we shall not break it against the carriage. You will wear it. Muguet du Bois. Am I right?'

'You are discerning, M'sieur, or rather I should say, Drum. *Mais oui*, it is my favourite perfume and I used the last of my bottle yesterday. And now I must needs fetch my bonnet and my reticule and you, Drum, must get your hat and so must Narcisse, so we shall all meet at the gate in five minutes, yes?'

'In five minutes.' Drum separated from them and walked to his own room, pulling the bell to summon Clarence and send him running across the courtyard with instructions for Mede to meet them at the gateway. Once again he had to replenish his wallet and he reminded himself that he must make contact with the bank in New Orleans where Uncle Chris had deposited his funds. He had a feeling that if he were to continue with the pleasure of the Brantomes' company, he would have to foot all the bills. But it would be worth it. It was certainly far better to be with them than to be alone with Mede and just being able to look at Claire would recompense him for anything he would have to spend.

Mede was waiting for him in the courtyard and while they were waiting for the Brantomes to appear, Drum inquired about Lucy.

'He a-feelin' fine, Mista Drum.' Mede was grinning broadly. 'He a-sayin' he a-gittin' right musky not havin' had a wash all over 'n' asking me to do it, but when yo' called, he say it all right, that he kin git Clarence to do it. Lucy he been a-noticin' them tight britches, too. Funny thing, though, Mista Drum, much's I like Lucy, I ain' never jealous o' him. Ain' like havin' a wench. Boy git in love with a wench, he right jealous if'n another boy look at her. But don' min' what Lucy do so long as he there when I a-wantin' him. But ain' needin' him so much now. They's a light-skin wench in the kitchen what says she like dark-skin boys.' He winked at Drum. 'She like 'em a-right. She shore do, so ain' needin' Lucy like'n I did.'

'Yo' won' be wantin' him if'n we gits ourselves to Falconhurst.' Drum found it easy to mimic Mede's jargon. 'Onc't we gits there, a-goin' to turn yo' out to stud.'

130

'What's that yo' a-goin' to do to me?'

Drum nodded in the direction from which the Brantomes were approaching. 'I'll tell you later. It was just a joke anyway. Just now I want you to come along with us. You can sit up with Ciceron. Got to get you some decent clothes to wear here and some for Lucy too. Think we can get them to fit him even if Lucy doesn't go along?'

'Lucy he a-goin' to like new clothes now that he gotten his hair cut like'n a boy. He goin' to look more like'n a man 'n a wench,' Mede assured Drum, falling behind him when he approached the Brantomes.

The barouche waiting in front of the door was a far better carriage than the one Drum had arrived in the day before. The only jarring note was Ciceron, who looked as soiled and dishevelled as ever, despite the fact that he had added an old beaver hat with a cockade of red, white, and blue feathers on one side. Narcisse assisted Claire into the carriage and then obligingly sat with his back to Ciceron so that Drum could occupy the seat beside Claire. Mede climbed up beside Ciceron and they started. The springs on the new barouche were far better than those on the fiacre that Ciceron had driven the day before, the horses were younger and able to proceed at a trot, so the ride was not only more comfortable but enlivened for Drum by Claire's presence beside him.

Her very nearness excited him. It seemed, even though their bodies were not touching, that he could feel the warmth of her flesh and once when she opened her reticule, took out her fan, and fanned herself, and then laid the fan on the cushions between herself and Drum, he felt the merest grazing of her hand along his thigh. It was such a quick motion and apparently so accidental that he did not credit it with being voluntary, but in his imagination he tried to make it seem that she had done it on purpose. He looked across at Narcisse, who, he was sure, had seen the movement, but he saw only a look of satisfaction on his face. Could it be that Narcisse was deliberately throwing Claire at him? That Narcisse was not overwhelmingly in love with his wife was quite apparent. They seemed to be merely good friends, nothing more, or else why should Narcisse have been so anxious to go to Hermione's last night? Or was it merely because Narcisse, being of the same blood as Drum himself, had also inherited this same fire and passion, so that no one woman would ever be sufficient for him?

One woman! Drum was glad now that he had not brought Rosalie with him. Mother Carey's advice had been good and now he thanked her for it. After having seen Claire, he wondered why a white woman had been so important to him. Claire was indeed more beautiful than any other woman he had ever seen and not only was she beautiful, but she was a charming companion. Yet . . . just one woman? Could he devote his whole life to one woman any more than Narcisse was doing, even provided she was, as in the case of Claire, the most beautiful woman he had ever seen? He wondered.

Ciceron drove up with a flourish of his whip to a small tailor shop. *Fabre, Tailleur*, the sign over the door proclaimed. Ciceron cramped the wheels of the carriage so there would be room to alight and Mede, although entirely unversed in the duties of a footman, was on the banquette ready to help them out. Claire pointed down the street to a small window filled with bonnets and assured them she would wait there for them. Drum started to walk across the banquette with Narcisse but, halting and placing a confidential hand on Drum's shoulder, Narcisse said, 'There is really no use for you to come in, *mon ami*, if the good M'sieur Fabre is so filled up with work he cannot accommodate you, because I know you want something quickly before you perish in your Boston broadcloth. Just let me run in and see if he can help you, and, if not, I know of another tailor's shop to which we can go. I'll only be a second.'

It seemed a logical and kindly gesture on Narcisse's part, although the second that he had promised turned out to be some five minutes, during which Drum got up and sat in the carriage. He was tempted to go in and get the information first-hand, but at length Narcisse came out and informed Drum that although M. Fabre was, as he had suspected, extremely busy, were Drum to pay an extra two dollars on each suit, M. Fabre would stop what he was doing and work for Drum. Once again Drum felt that everyone in New Orleans had designs on his money, but, he also reminded himself, he was anxious to get the clothes, so he went with Narcisse into the shop.

Once inside, he found a wide selection of fabrics and from the suits that Fabre had finished and that hung from the walls Drum estimated that the man was a good tailor. He thought he preferred linen for his white jackets until M. Fabre convinced him that white drill was better in that it didn't wrinkle and it laundered more easily. With the jackets he purchased several pairs of pantaloons in shiny black mohair, lightweight fawn-coloured, and white. Then he called Mede over to be measured and ordered two suits of black alpaca for him with an equal number for Lucy, whose measurements both he and Mede tried to explain to the tailor.

When Drum had finished his business, Narcisse decided to order a suit for himself. He disdained the idea of a white jacket and thumbed through the bolts of materials until he found a coffee brown mohair, which he selected and which M. Fabre promised would be ready, along with Drum's suits, in a fortnight. He informed them that he would have to call in his two nephews, both of whom were tailors, but that the suits would be finished and entirely to Drum's satisfaction, even if it was necessary for them all to work day and night to accomplish this.

Claire was waiting for them in the barouche, shaded by a black lace parasol that was so tiny it scarcely kept the sun from her face. She had changed bonnets and the one she now wore, of pink straw with bows of rose and mauve ribbons, was, Drum thought, even more becoming than the one she had had on earlier. Again in settling themselves in the carriage he felt the brush of her hand against his and this time he was sure it was no accident. Her hand lingered and even when he moved his knee a little closer, it was not taken away. He thought he intercepted a quick glance between Claire and Narcisse. It was almost as if Narcisse was encouraging her.

The bank, it seemed, was not too far away, and when Drum arrived there, he went in alone. Much to his surprise he found he was treated with courtesy and when he entered the bank manager's office, he was even offered a chair, although he noticed that the man did not address him as 'mister'. Evidently, however, the prestige of Christopher Holbrook's name was known and acknowledged in New Orleans. The money that had been deposited there for Drum's account was turned over to him, but he did not care to take such a large amount of cash with him, so he took only five hundred dollars, leaving the rest on deposit.

'I am glad you came.' The banker almost said 'Mr Maxwell' and then caught himself in time. 'We have a letter for you from your uncle and I was wondering just how we could reach you. He had told us you would be at the Saint Charles Hotel but—'

'Perhaps you are now aware why that is not possible.' Drum looked straight at the man and could see a red blush spread over his face. 'I was denied entrance at the Saint Charles and am at the Trouville over on Rampart Street.'

'I understand.' The banker seemed unable to relieve himself of his embarrassment. 'If you would care to remain here while you read your letter, I am sure it would be more comfortable than out on the street in the hot sun.'

It was the first charitable gesture that Drum had received from a white person in New Orleans. He sank back in his chair, slit open the envelope, and read the letter, which had been dictated to one of his uncle's clerks and was written in a copperplate hand in decided contrast to Christopher Holbrook's scrawled signature at the bottom.

MY DEAR DRUM,

First let me say that your Aunt Mary and I both miss you. The house in Boston seems lonely and quiet now that you are gone and I do hope that things are going well with you in New Orleans. Although I have not been South for years, I know you will be well taken care of at the Saint Charles; I am sure the rooms, food, and service are as good as ever.

I want to urge you to go to Falconhurst as soon as possible. A most regrettable affair has just occurred there. I wrote Mr Sylvester, the capable overseer in whom I had the utmost confidence, that you were coming and have just received a reply from him that he has quit the job, so Falconhurst is, at present, without a head. I urge you to go there as soon as possible and take over the reins yourself. I do not know if Sylvester planted any cotton – he did not say. Although I am aware that you know nothing about plantation management, I suggest that you rely on Brutus, a friend of your father's and a most capable man. He lives in the village of New Quarters and has always been connected with Falconhurst.

This is your inheritance, Drum, and I want you to prove yourself in maintaining it. I cannot send you any more money now but you will have enough to last you until fall. I have made some well-planned investments for you and do not want to disturb them, so try to make do with the money you have in New Orleans and an additional five thousand I am sending to the bank in Benson.

Your Aunt Mary sends her love, in which I join her. I wish it were possible for us to come down and help you get started. But I have a sincere conviction that you will be able to take over and make a go of it. Oh yes, as to why we cannot get away, we are sailing for Europe with the Higginsons and plan to be away for about six months.

My best wishes always,
Your affectionate uncle,
CHRISTOPHER HOLBROOK

Drum folded the letter and put it back in the envelope. Well here he was with a big cotton plantation on his hands and he didn't even know what a cotton plant looked like. Out in the carriage again he read the letter aloud to Narcisse and Claire.

'The goddam polecat of a stinking white bastard.' Narcisse immediately begged Claire's pardon for his profanity but added, 'That's what he is. You know, of course, why he left?'

Drum shook his head.

'Because he was too high and mighty to work for a coloured man. He evidently knew who you are.'

If Lucy had known all about him, it seemed entirely logical to Drum that everyone at Falconhurst and in the town of New

Quarters must know that he was the son of Drummage Maxwell and therefore not white.

'But there's one thing you do not have to worry about.' Narcisse leaned forward and placed his hand on Drum's knee. 'Claire and I will help you out.'

Drum looked first at Narcisse and then at Claire, reassured by their smiles.

'I know how to run a plantation, *mon ami*, and Claire knows how to run a plantation house. We'll go with you. There is nothing to keep us here in New Orleans and we shall be bored to death at Madame Helene's after you have gone.'

'Yes, Drum, do let us help you out of your difficulties.' Claire laid her hand on top of Narcisse's. 'It is true Narcisse does know a lot about running a plantation and handling Negroes and I can easily take care of the house for you. So, won't you let us help you?'

Drum laid his hand on top of theirs. 'How good of you both.' He was jubilant. 'I've put off going because I dreaded going there and being alone. Now I shall have you both with me.'

Again he thought he saw a glance pass between Narcisse and Claire, but he was so pleased over the prospect of having them accompany him that he failed to pay any attention to it. He was too happy.

CHAPTER FIFTEEN

DESPITE THE URGENCY of his uncle's letter, Drum dallied in New Orleans for another month. Having always lived in a city, he dreaded the isolation of Falconhurst and could see nothing but a dreary succession of days spent alone in the country. Now, with Narcisse and Claire going with him, he had considerably more to anticipate than if he were to go alone with

Mede and Lucy. Yet he invented many excuses to delay setting out for the plantation. There were the clothes he had ordered, which had to be delivered; there was Lucy's wound, which had to heal, although after the first week Lucy was up and about and showed little effects of his accident. He, Mede, and Clarence were off somewhere every evening – where, Drum did not know or question, but they seemed to be having a good time, although Mede appeared rather bleary-eyed each morning when he came to help Drum dress.

Then, too, time passed happily at the Hotel de Trouville. Madame Helene had the knack of making her guests feel at home and she was always organizing small social affairs for them. Madame did not limit her guests at these functions to those at her hotel and through her teas, soirées, and dinners Drum was able to meet others of the coloured aristocracy of the city. They were well educated and could discuss books, music, and paintings, especially those who had been educated in France and who made occasional trips to Europe. All in all, he was delighted with them, although he made no close friends among them, devoting all his time to Narcisse and Claire. He wondered if Narcisse sensed his growing interest in Claire and hers in him. Certainly it must be apparent, although Narcisse seemed never to notice it.

In addition to the social life at the Trouville, there were picnics and drives out of the city with Ciceron seated up on the driver's seat and more often than not either Mede or Lucy or both of them along to carry the lunch basket, spread the cloth on the ground, and wait on them. Narcisse ignored Mede's presence as much as possible, but it was easy to see that Lucy was his favourite and even Claire seemed to make much of the boy. With his hair cut and his new clothes, he presented a far different appearance from the Lucy they had met on shipboard.

With Narcisse and Claire, Drum attended services at the cathedral and he went to the opera, although he resented the small section that was reserved for coloured people. After becoming better acquainted with the city, he began to appreciate it. It did have charm and the more he came to know it, the more it reminded him of Boston. Both were old cities and both had storied backgrounds – the one English and the other a combination of French and Spanish.

He and Narcisse had worked out a business agreement by which Narcisse agreed to take twenty-five per cent of the earnings for his duties as overseer. One quarter of the proceeds seemed rather high to Drum, but he was helpless. He knew nothing about running the plantation himself and it appeared that he would have difficulties in getting a white overseer to work for him. However, when Narcisse presented him with a legal document for him to sign, he felt that his having to sign it not only was unnecessary but also impugned his trustworthiness. He also noticed that in the document it stated that Madame Brantome was to receive a salary of $10 a month for being housekeeper.

There had been a constant drain on Drum's resources since he had arrived in New Orleans and he was well aware of the fact that during the month he had been there he had been paying all expenses except the actual cost of room and board for the Brantomes. The substantial amount that his uncle had deposited in the bank was fast dwindling and, although Drum knew that he could eventually call on his uncle for more money, it was this ebbing bank account that finally precipitated his leaving New Orleans. His uncle had written that there were five thousand dollars waiting for him in the bank at Benson, which was the nearest white community to Falconhurst. The presence of the money there, with such a small balance in New Orleans, decided him to leave while he still had enough money to pay the railroad fares for himself and his entourage. How it had grown! He had started out with only Mede; then he had taken on Lucy; and now he had Narcisse and Claire. He had a faculty, he felt, for attracting dependents.

Getting to Falconhurst posed a problem. It would be necessary for them to go by train and the journey would consume an entire day and the better part of two nights. First they would have to go by train to Mobile, then change trains and go to a small town called Westminster, which was the nearest railroad station to Falconhurst. Drum wrote on to the

Brutus his uncle had mentioned in his letter and who happened to be Lucy's father, asking that some conveyance be waiting at the station at Westminster and that there be food and servants in the big house at Falconhurst on the day of their arrival.

On the trips he had made back in Boston, whenever he had travelled by train, he had always ridden in the new and elaborate parlour cars, with their comfortable chairs, plush draperies, mahogany panelling, and mirrors. Now he found he would have no such opportunity. He and his whole party would be compelled to travel by day coach, and a special coach at that, reserved for Negroes. It galled him to think of his being accorded so little civility, but both Narcisse and Claire assured him that there were no distinctions on trains for coloured people. There was a place for whites and a place for blacks and no in-between. Because they were, in the eyes of the railroad, as black as the blackest African, they must, perforce, travel with the Negroes. But – and Claire tried to allay his resentment over the fact – it would not be for long, just the two nights and a day, and once they were at Falconhurst, he would forget about it.

The night before they were to leave, Narcisse excused himself, saying that he had some business deal he wanted to conclude before leaving and, although Drum offered to go with him, he diplomatically turned Drum off, suggesting that he remain behind as company for Claire. He did. After dinner he sat with Claire in the courtyard and remained there until long after the other guests in the hotel had gone to bed. He saw Mede and Lucy come in, accompanied by a giggling Clarence, and he wondered where they had been as they walked across the courtyard on the way to the *garçonnière*.

They had talked, Drum and Claire, about trivialities – about their coming life at Falconhurst, about the journey, about the various places they had been in the city; and finally they had run out of words and sat, side by side on the uncomfortable iron chairs, which were screened by a hanging vine from one lantern that did little to illuminate the courtyard.

Claire yawned, covering it daintily with her hand, and stood up, reaching down to touch Drum on the hand. 'Come, it's getting late and there is no longer any need for us to sit up for Narcisse. He will be very late.'

Drum looked at his watch, angling it to catch the reflection of the lantern. It was already half past eleven. He had an idea that Narcisse might be at Hermione's for one last fling before leaving for the country, but why he had gone without asking Drum to accompany him was a mystery. Each time they had gone, and it had been frequently, Drum had paid. He arose from his chair, stretching himself and holding back the vines to make a passageway for Claire, and as they passed through them their bodies brushed against each other. Suddenly, without any thought of the consequences, he had her in his arms and his lips sought hers.

He was surprised that she made no resistance. Her body melted against his own and her lips were as avid for his as his were for hers. For a long moment they stood there, completely enraptured, and then she removed her lips from his and took her hands from around his waist and placed them on his chest, pushing him away.

'We must not, Drum.'

'Why not?' He knew now what he had been wanting for so long, but a mere taste was not enough.

'Need you ask me that? Need you?'

'But you don't love Narcisse.' He was insistent. 'You love me.'

'You have no reason to say that, just because I yielded to one little temptation. Ah, Drum, it is a romantic night, you are a handsome man, I am a weak woman. That is all. What makes you think I do not love Narcisse?'

'If you did, you would not relinquish him so easily. A wife who loved her husband would not permit him to go to the places he goes to enjoy the love of other women.'

'There is much you do not know about Narcisse, Drum. I knew a long time ago that no one woman would ever satisfy him.'

'Possibly no *woman* ever will satisfy him.' Drum was merely hinting, remembering what Clarence had said.

'Oh, you are quite wrong.' Evidently Claire had understood the *double-entendre*. 'Listen, Drum, Narcisse is what he is and we cannot change that. He is a sensualist and he makes that his life, but I can tell you one thing truthfully. Narcisse loves me. And as for tonight, he is not, as you say, enjoying other women. He was telling the truth when he said he had to go out on business. Oh, Drum, I must confess one thing to you. The position we have been trying to maintain here is entirely false. Regardless of what Narcisse might have told you, we did not sell Mon Plaisir. We left because it had fallen into ruin. We have nothing. We have sponged too long on your generosity. But there was one thing Narcisse could not bring himself to do and that was to ask for a loan to pay our bill here at Madame Helene's. He had to go out and collect some money that was due to him so that we might pay her and walk out of here with our heads erect, owing nobody. I have confessed this to you and you must promise never to mention the matter to Narcisse. He is proud. Leave him his pride. No, I do not worry about his absence. It is necessary.'

Drum held out his arms to her, wanting to comfort her. He took a step forward, but she retreated.

'You would be a wonderful man to love, Drum Maxwell.' She held her hands outstretched before her, ready to repulse him. 'I envy the woman who marries you. I could so very easily fall in love with you in spite of Narcisse, but this is neither the time nor the place for it. Perhaps someday I shall and if I do, I shall tell you. There is much I would like to say to you tonight, but I will not. We must all go on a little longer, playing a very strange game, but tonight because I am weak and because I am a woman and because you are so extremely handsome with the light shining on the gold of your hair, I shall relent in one little thing. You may kiss me again.'

He pulled her to him savagely and his lips sought hers. His hands discovered the softness and the warmth of her body under the thin material of her dress. His fingers fumbled with the buttons of her tight bodice and sought entrance among the laces to the firm flesh beneath. From her lips his own lips traced a path down her neck to her breasts and he heard her little, almost inaudible moans. Holding her so closely he knew she must be conscious of his rising desire for her, but apparently she did not resent it and for a brief moment she accommodated her body to him, meeting his movements with her own. Then for the second time she pushed him away.

'Thank you, Drum' – she managed a little laugh – 'perhaps that one kiss has repaid you for all you have done for Narcisse and me while you have been here. I am all too aware of what you have done and I appreciate it, although I have felt like a beggar in accepting it. Now, perhaps, I have repaid you a little for all the happiness you have brought into my life. But no! I am wrong! I have not repaid you, because your kiss gave me as much pleasure as I hope it did to you, so now I am deeper than ever in your debt.'

He reached out his arms for her again, but she turned away. 'No, Drum, let me go to my room and do not try to follow me. I might be tempted to let you do more than kiss me. Wait here until I have found the strength to go up those stairs alone and bolt the door of my room.' She turned and left him, running across the little pebbled path of the courtyard.

His first impulse was to run after her. If he did, he knew what might happen – what would indeed happen. He would follow her through the door of her room and in his present mood he did not dare trust himself. Better to wait here and let her go than to have Narcisse come home and burst into the room to discover them. He listened for her light footsteps on the stairs and then heard her running down the gallery. The door of her room opened and closed and a few seconds later he saw streaks of light coming through the louvers of the door.

'Damn!' He slipped his hand down under the waistband of his trousers the better to accommodate himself to their constricting tightness. Damn, damn, damn! There was only one answer to his present need. Either the cribs or Hermione's. No, he couldn't demean himself by a quarter-of-an-hour, two-bit release in the cribs. He would go to Hermione's. Without going to his room to fetch his hat, he ran out the gate and stumbled over Clarence, who was sleeping in the hallway. Clarence pulled himself up, using Drum's leg for support.

'Mista Maxwell suh, yo' a-goin' somewhere at this time of night?'

'Yes, is there a cab outside?'

Clarence peered through the iron gate. 'They's one a-waitin' down at Madame Roland's house. Thinkin' she got company perhaps.'

'Then, run down and get it for me. Tell him I'll pay him double if he'll get me to Hermione's quick.'

Clarence's hand caressed Drum's leg. 'My, my, Mista Maxwell, yo' shore a-needin' a wench, ain't yo'? But ain' no need for a wench. Clarence kin fix yo' up right here.'

Drum pushed the boy away from him, angered by his implication. 'Go get that cab. Go, or I'll knock the shit out of you.'

'Ain' no need for yo' to git mad, Mista Maxwell. Jes' tryin' to he'p yo'. Now, you take that Mista Brantome what's here—'

'You take him. Start running.'

He waited outside on the banquette, watching Clarence run down the street to the faint light of a streetlamp. He saw the boy speak to the driver, then climb up in the cab, and the driver turned around and headed back. As soon as the hack reached the hotel, Drum jumped in.

'To Hermione's,' he said, 'and quick.'

The old man who was driving roared with laughter. 'Ain' no need to hurry, masta suh. Show ain' a-goin' to start at Hermione's till 'bout one o'clock. I knows, I do, 'cause I'se got to pick up one or two boys what's a-goin' there.'

'I'm not going to Hermione's to see any show. I'm goin' to see one of her girls.'

'Guess yo' must be a-needin' one right bad' – the driver roared out his laughter again – 'but if'n yo' a-wantin' one now, yo' a-goin' to have to wait till after the show 'n' then yo' a-goin' to want her more'n yo' does now. Everyone a-sayin' this the last show she a-goin' to put on for some time with Harlequin.'

'Harlequin?' Drum leaned forward to make himself heard over the clatter of the wheels on the cobbles. 'Who's Harlequin?'

'Yo' must be a stranger in town, masta suh, if'n yo' ain''

never heard o' Harlequin. He Miss Hermione's show boy, he is. He jes' the handsomest, best-lookin', heaviest-hung, pretty coloured boy in all New Orleans. Miss Hermione she have special shows with this Harlequin boy. Even white mens come to see it. Ain' like'n the circuses other who'houses have. This special. Lots o' men go to see it 'n' most stay on at Miss Hermione's after it finish so they kin git one o' her gals. Ain' never seen it myself 'cause I too black to git in but heard 'bout it. Costive, though. Miss Hermione she a-chargin' a gol' eagle jes' for lookin'.'

When Drum arrived at the flickering red light that marked the entrance to Hermione's house, he was surprised to see the street lined with carriages and hacks. There was a festive air about the place with all the drivers lined up on the sidewalks, the music of a pianoforte coming through the jalousied windows, and the laughter of *vendeuses* on the outside and that of girls coming through the louvered windows.

He paid off the hack driver, who said he would wait around for an extra two bits to take Drum back to the hotel, walked up the steps, and jangled the bell. One of the maids at Hermione's, a black girl in stiffly starched white, let him in.

'Miz Hermione's she right busy jes' now,' the girl volunteered, 'but yo' kin pay yore money to that gal there.' She pointed to the giantess who had accommodated Drum on his first night there. He drew out a gold piece from his pocket and paid the girl, whereupon she gave him a piece of cardboard with a lewd picture printed on it. The salon was filled with men – Drum estimated that there must be some twenty there, but there were only three girls in evidence and they were busy serving iced champagne at a dollar a glass. Two white men stood in one corner, aloof from all the rest, most of whom were young mulattos with a few older men. Drum ordered a glass of champagne from the maid, but as there was no place for him to sit down, he leaned against the wall to drink it. A young fellow whom Drum had met at one of Madame Helene's dinners came over and spoke to him.

'I'm Jean Duroc,' he introduced himself, 'and I met you at the Trouville one evening. Aren't you Drum Maxwell?'

Drum acknowledged the boy's greeting, glad to find someone to talk to.

The fellow sighed. 'What a pity we are losing Harlequin. *Mon Dieu!* For New Orleans it will be like losing the Opera House or the Cabildo. Harlequin is one of the sights of New Orleans. Look' – he nodded his head in the direction of the two white men – 'even the *blancs* condescend to mix with us just to see Harlequin. *Quel homme!* I've seen him every time Hermione has put on her show and every time he is better than before. Six tonight, they say, but I cannot believe. The last time I came, a friend of mine from Cuba was with me. He was astonished. Said they had nothing to compare with it in Havana.'

Drum wondered why Narcisse had never told him about this event, which was, apparently, so phenomenal. During his moments of speculation Hermione herself appeared in the doorway. Tonight she was dressed in lilac taffeta with a garniture of amethysts. The coq feathers in her hair had been dyed to match her gown.

She clapped her hands for attention. 'Everything's ready, gentlemen. The show's about to start. Please give your tickets to Mariette' – she indicated the maid in starched white who stood in the doorway – 'and follow me.'

She led them down through the hall to a large, well-lighted room where chairs were arranged in rows facing a curtain of some dark stuff. The walls had been frescoed by a painter of some ability with lewd paintings, intended to increase the mood of concupiscence that most of the men already seemed to be in merely through anticipation.

With Duroc's elbow guiding him, Drum managed to find a seat in the front row of chairs, only a few feet away from the curtain. There was a clash of cymbals and the curtains were drawn apart to disclose a scene that was evidently intended to represent an Oriental seraglio. Three mattresses on the floor were covered with coloured silks and on them six of Hermione's most beautiful girls were indulging in erotic play with each other and seemingly enjoying it. There was a great slithering of arms and legs and a display of ardent affection that was

145

rather disgusting to Drum. He had always been as unable to understand how women could find gratification with each other as he was to comprehend Mede's liking for Lucy or Clarence's trying to tempt him. If this was all that the widely touted circus of Hermione was to consist of, he was ready to leave.

The cymbals crashed again and a stark-naked man leaped into the centre of the floor. His tall, strongly muscled body was painted with the multicoloured diamonds of a Harlequin suit and he wore a close-fitting cap that came down over his face with only two holes for his eyes, making it impossible to identify him. The perspiration running down his body had already started to streak the colours on his skin. Drum could see why he had been chosen for the part. The fellow was indeed a stallion, almost disgusting in his oversized display of masculinity. He folded his arms across his chest and slipped his feet, spread wide apart, into wide leather straps that were nailed to the floor. For a long moment he stood there, displaying himself by moving his hips slightly.

'Nobody knows who he is,' Duroc whispered to Drum. 'Some say he's a wealthy boy who does this just for fun. I often look at my friends and wonder if one of them might be Harlequin.'

'With such a distinguishing feature as that,' Drum said, pointing to the fellow, 'it should not be hard to identify him.'

Duroc laughed. 'Ah, that is a not too uncommon characteristic among us coloured boys. There are many of my friends who could almost qualify, even I and undoubtedly you yourself.'

The cymbals crashed again and now the women on the mattresses appeared to notice the man for the first time. They left off their dalliances and began to crawl towards him, crowding around him. The displays of kisses and affection had vanished and they began screaming and snarling at each other, pulling each other's hair, scratching and biting to see who could get to him first. He stood still, his legs spread apart, his arms folded across his chest. Drum could picture a sardonic smile under the mask.

'It's true,' Duroc whispered again, 'there are six of them.

Impossible, but they say he takes some kind of a drug to keep him potent.'

From the mêlée of struggling women, one clawed her way to the man. Her mouth slavered over his legs, smudging the paint diamonds. But her victory was only for the moment. Another of the women got a fistful of the successful one's hair and yanked her back, pulling her to the floor and climbing over her to gain the man while he stood stock still, unperturbed by the screaming, biting, clawing mass at his feet. Now one girl, more successful than the rest, was able to stay with him long enough to accomplish her purpose. Of this Drum was sure, because no man could have been a good enough actor to pretend the climax that he reached. It appeared altogether genuine, but it did not daunt him, for he still stood there until one by one the girls accomplished their purpose. After the sixth one had finished with him, Drum was sure that the man was a phenomenon, because he still appeared as virile and erect as before they had started. Surely no man could endure for so long a period, but this one had. Drum's eyes had witnessed the performance.

The women crawled back to the mattresses while the curtains were slowly pulled together. Just as they almost met, there was a hitch that interrupted their slow closing. Then there was a yank and the curtains closed. But during that one fleeting second Drum saw the man relax from the rigid position he had held. He unfolded his arms and let them drop to his sides. The paint had almost disappeared from his body and Drum could see that there were two tiny tattoos on his chest – two flying birds that were poised over the copper pennies of his paps.

'You're going to stay?' Duroc asked.

Drum could not picture bedding himself with any of the girls who had slavered over the man. He shook his head, anxious now to get out of the house. He bid a quick goodnight to Duroc and got out of the door as quickly as possible. The old man who had driven him saw him come out and walked up to him.

'Ain' a-stayin', mista?'

Drum climbed into the carriage.

'Has to wait a long time for a gal at Hermione's after one o' her shows. I a-knowin' a nice clean gal at the cribs. She jes' started this week. She young 'n' pretty 'n' she clean, too.'

'Take me to her.' Drum needed something, but he wanted it so impersonal and so mechanical that he would achieve only physical relief, nothing more.

CHAPTER SIXTEEN

MADAME HELENE WEPT over their departure like a mother about to lose her entire family. She averred that Claire was closer to her than a daughter and that Drum and Narcisse were both as dear to her as her own sons. She would be desolate without them. Of course, they must plan to return as soon as possible to the Trouville. Plantation life was barbarous – no opera, no friends, and no entertaining, especially for coloured people. They must promise to come back to the Trouville every few months. She embraced them all but broke into a fit of weeping and had to leave the room.

Up in his room, superintending Mede's packing, Drum received an envelope delivered on a silver tray by Clarence. It was addressed in Madame's spidery handwriting and inside he found his bill, so meticulously itemized that he knew every item must be correct without his having to check them. He inserted the money in the same envelope and placed it at Madame's place at the table at their last luncheon. He noted that Narcisse did the same. Evidently the business deal he had had the night before had paid off because he was paying his own bill without asking Drum for a loan, which Drum had somehow anticipated.

Late that afternoon Mede and Lucy appeared, dressed in

their new suits, which fitted them perfectly. When Drum came down wearing one of his new white jackets, Madame prevailed on him to change. 'The trains, *mon cher* Drum' – she threw up her hands in horror. 'Ten minutes after you leave New Orleans, your fine white jacket would be jet black. Do put on something of a darker colour.' Evidently Narcisse and Claire had had experience with Southern trains, for they were both in dark clothes and Claire was without the usual white lace at neck and cuffs. They were astonished, however, when Ciceron arrived to drive them to the station. Instead of waiting outside with the carriage, he walked into the courtyard. For the first time since they had met him, he had abandoned the peppermint-striped pantaloons. Instead he was dressed in dark trousers with a decent grey shirt and was carrying a small bundle tied in a bandana. He went to Drum and, reaching in his pocket, he drew out a crumpled wad of bills, together with a handful of change.

'If'n yo' don' mind, Mista Drum suh, I'se a-goin' wid yo'. Been a-workin' here all my life 'n' ain' never had 'nough money to git me a steady gal. Sick o' goin' to them cribs alla time. My mammy say go 'long with that nice gen'leman yo' a-likin' so much. She say he a-goin' to need a coachman wherever that plantation o' his be 'n' ain' no better coachman 'n yo'. I been 'roun' horses since I a pickaninny, Masta Drum suh. Knows 'em, I do. Been a-drivin' here in the city for three, four years. My pappy 'n' my mammy 'n' all my uncles 'n' aunties they git together 'n' give me this yere money. Don' know if'n it 'nough to pay my train, but if'n it ain', reckon I kin work it out. Please, Mista Drum.'

'But why do you want to go with me?' Drum had felt that Ciceron was as much a part of New Orleans as the cast-iron grillwork. For a boy who had been raised in the city to want to go to the country seemed strange.

'Likes yo', I do. Likes Missus Brantome, too. Likes Mede 'n' I likes Lucy if'n he don' pester me. Ain' never had such a good time's I had wid yo'-all. Yo' treat me fine. Take me on a picnic, yo' gives me yore food to eat. Yo' ain' never cussed nor swore at me. Feels sorta like yo'-all my kinfolk. Oh, kin I go,

Mista Drum suh? Yo' a-knowin' that I a good coachman. Kin drive for yo' better'n anyone else. Please Mista Drum.'

Drum could see that it was mighty important to Ciceron to go. He suspected – and rightly so – that Ciceron with his city background intended to cut a wide swath among the wenches at Falconhurst. Perhaps the boy actually did want to have a woman of his own. The evidence of the money Ciceron had given him was one of good faith. He was not trying to take advantage; he was willing to pay his own way.

Drum reached out a hand and took the warm, sweaty one of Ciceron's. 'If you want to go as much as all that, boy, you can come along. You keep this. I'll pay the fare.' He handed the wad of bills and change back to Ciceron.

While Ciceron was trying to express his thanks, Drum looked around the courtyard. He had started out from Boston with Mede, then he had taken on Lucy, then the Brantomes, and now Ciceron. He seemed to have a faculty for attracting people to him. It might be his affluence that had attracted them. But not altogether, unless possibly for Narcisse, whom Drum liked but could not seem to trust. Narcisse had a charming personality, but there was still an unknown something about him that kept Drum on his guard. As for Lucy, he merely wanted to get back to Falconhurst, but Drum could feel a certain respect and friendliness in Lucy. Claire he had wanted and he welcomed her company and – yes, he had to admit it – he was glad Narcisse was coming also because without him Drum could not have had Claire. And now poor Ciceron. Whatever motive he had had for coming was not entirely selfish. Drum knew the fellow liked him.

Somehow, as he surveyed the little group, he could not but feel that he was transported back fifty years into the time of slavery. He would be the rich plantation owner of Falconhurst with an entourage of slaves. But no, the Brantomes would not have been slaves. But yes, they would have been and, the awful thought struck him, so would he. He would have been a Falconhurst slave, a chattel, an animal to be disposed of as his white grandfather saw fit. He would be here in New Orleans to be sold. Oh, forget it! That was years ago. He was a free man – but was he free? Dammit, no! Although he could not be bought and sold like in the old days, he was still a slave. Here in the South slavery had never ended. But it had. It had! So once again forget it and get started. He began giving orders for the transportation of the valises.

Among Ciceron, Mede, and Lucy and with the help of Clarence, who was also wiping away tears from his eyes, they got the baggage out on to the banquette. Madame Helene came along with them, refusing to part with them until they were actually in the carriage. Drum had to smile as he looked up on the box and saw the familiar peppermint-striped pants and yellow shirt being worn by the driver.

'He my brother Jodey,' Ciceron explained. 'He a-goin' to take my job, so I gave him my trogs, seein' as how everybody in N'Orleans knowin' them pants o' mine.'

Madame Helene waved them out of sight and at the last minute Drum had a desire to tell Ciceron's brother to turn around and go back. He felt he would be far happier in returning to the Trouville and taking up the pleasant life he had had with Claire and Narcisse. He was a bit frightened at his venture into the unknown. But what the hell! Falconhurst was his and as it looked now, it was all he had. It was the only home he could claim and he'd better look after it.

When they arrived at the New Orleans depot, they were driven around to the side where a dingy sign over the door said COLOURED. Drum wondered for a moment if he had been misinformed and that the trains did, after all, have special cars for the coloured gentry like the Brantomes and himself, but he was immediately disillusioned when he saw a drunken Negro stagger out of the door. The sign should have said – and more truthfully – NIGGERS. Inside it was dark and gloomy, barely more than a shed, lighted by one hanging oil lamp in the centre and another on the wall by the ticket seller's window. Drum purchased the six tickets for Mobile from a surly red-faced man who evidently felt that the grating between him and his customers set him apart from the rest. From the card tacked on the wall Drum could see that the fare for blacks was the same as for whites, although the whites, he was sure, had far superior accommodation. Fortunately they did not have long to wait on the plank benches of the waiting-room, as the train for Mobile was leaving within the hour.

Although Drum had certainly not expected the luxury of a parlour car, he was totally unprepared for the extreme discomfort he found in the segregated car. Plain wooden benches with straight wooden backs were the only accommodation. Each bench, which seated two, was beside an open window, but even the open windows could not take away the stench from the car, accumulated from the thousands of unwashed bodies who had sweated in it and the rank odour of urine from the one primitive toilet that served both men and women. Having to tote their baggage the long distance to the train, they were late in arriving and found that there were no double seats left, so they had to share seats with others and Drum was relieved when he saw Claire sit beside an elderly coloured man whose black coat and Roman collar proclaimed him a cleric. Lucy slid into the seat beside a flashily dressed young buck, then got up and relinquished his seat when Narcisse demanded it. Mede, Lucy, and Ciceron were scattered up and down the aisle. Drum at last found a seat for himself beside an enormous Negress whose buxom bare arms were the same dark brown as her dress. She smiled up at him while he was contemplating the seat, evidently approving of him, because she hitched over closer to the window to make more room.

'Yo' jes' set yo'self here 'side o' Mammy Morn 'n' that's short for Mornin' Star if'n yo' wants to call me by my full name.' She swept her skirts aside to make room for him. 'Plenty of room, masta suh.' Although the smoky oil lamps gave but little light, she appraised him carefully. 'What a fine gen'leman like'n yo' a-doin' here in de nigger car?'

Her white-toothed grin was infectious and, mimicking her accent, he replied, 'Jes' 'cause I nigger too, Mammy.'

'Go on wid yo', Mista Man wid de yaller hair. I too black ter mammy yo'. All my chilluns they come blacker'n me 'cause my man he de blackest nigger I ever did see. Yes suh, Mista Man, that man he blacker'n coal, but he a good man. Widdered me twenty years 'go 'n' lef' me 'lone wid six chillun. Brang 'em all up, I did, a-cookin' for white folks. Now my chillun all lef' me, but I still known as de bes' cook in N'Orleans. People come to a house where I a-workin' 'n' they take one taste of the vittles 'n' they say to the mist'ess, "M-m-m! Yo' a lucky woman. Yo' got Mornin' Star a-cookin' fo' yo'.'"

Drum rather welcomed the loquacity of the old woman and encouraged her to go on talking about herself, telling him her whole history. She had, he found out, lost the daughter she was living with in New Orleans and was now on her way to Mobile in search of another daughter. This daughter had been married and the old lady (for so Drum thought of her, although she was probably no more than sixty) was going to Mobile to search for her. She seemed quite unperturbed over the fact that she had spent all her money on the railroad ticket and that she knew neither where the daughter lived nor what her name now was. Nothing daunted her. She had overcome one difficulty after another during her lifetime and she felt that all she had to do was ask for her daughter and she would be found.

Once she had finished her long discourse, she bade Drum reach up in the luggage rack above and take down a large market basket. With it on her lap, she handed him a worn white napkin and took out one for herself. Then she proceeded to ply him with food and cold coffee, which she poured into a tin cup for him, drinking her own out of the bottle. He found he was hungry and enjoyed the sandwiches of white bread with thinly cut ham, cold hard-boiled eggs, which he dipped in her little paper packet of salt, and a slice of pound cake, which was even better than Madame Helene's. Thinking of Madame Helene reminded him that she also had packed a basket of food for them, so he called down the aisle for Mede to get it and pass it around. He had no desire for any more food, feeling replete with the collation that Morning Star had spread before him.

Then it was his turn to tell about himself. She was as good a listener as she was a talker and said that she had recognized him at once as quality. The hours passed and the fresh air, coming in through the windows, drove out some of the stench from the car. He began to feel sleepy and tried to find some comfortable position on the hard bench. Morning Star noted his fidgeting and told him to reach up in the rack again, directing him to a certain string-tied bundle. This she opened, smoothing out the paper and carefully rolling up the string, and produced a quilt, which she folded for him, making a cushion both for the back and for the seat.

'Don't need it myself,' she said. 'I so fat don' feel them boards 'tall, but yo' shore a-needin' it. Nothing fat-assed 'bout yo.'

He agreed with her. The hard boards felt more comfortable and he soon fell asleep. Some time during the night a stop at one of the numerous depots awakened him and he was lying against her, his head on her soft, capacious bosom and her arm around him. He started to sit up, but she patted his head and whispered to him to go back to sleep. He did not need any urging. He felt complete protection and security on the bosom of this unknown woman. She was the mother; he was the little boy. She was the eternal woman who had mothered all blacks and whites and all the earth and everything in it. Despite the hard seat and the motion of the train, he slept contentedly, not awaking again until they had reached Mobile and the sun was shining.

They were all glad to be quit of the train and to Drum's astonishment both Narcisse and Claire looked as black as Ciceron and Morning Star. Looking down at his own hands, Drum realized that they were as black as the others. His face was gritty with soot and cinders and he wondered just how the railroad official would ever be able to separate the sheep from the goats – the blacks from the whites – if all were black.

The coloured waiting-room at Mobile presented an even more depressing appearance than the one at New Orleans. Just the thought of sitting there for four hours, bedraggled as they were, was unthinkable. Sitting on the hard benches after the long night on the train would be difficult enough, but sitting there without a chance to wash the grime off one's face was even worse. It was Ciceron who solved the problem. His long experience as a driver in New Orleans led him to leave them and go out in front of the depot and fraternize with the drivers there. He was soon back.

'Better us gits all that baggage together. We's a-goin' somewhar whar t'ain't so bad's here 'n' whar we kin git ourselfs washed up.' He pointed to Morning Star. 'She a-goin' alongst wid us? If'n she do, we'se a-goin' to need two carriages, she such a gyrascutus.'

'Shet yore mouth, nigger, 'n' don' insult yore betters.' Morning Star collected her various bundles, baskets, and paper bags. 'I a-startin' out to fin' my daughter. Everyone a-goin' to know her 'n' I fin' her right soon. Goin' to say goodbye to yo', Mista Drum. Yo' a right fine man 'n' I hopes to see yo' 'gain. Goodbye, boy.' She clasped him in her arms, then gathered up her bundles and waddled off.

'Glad she ain' a-goin'.' Ciceron watched her leave the shed. 'We jes' got one carriage 'n' it a-goin' to be hard to take all of us 'n' that baggage too.'

The hack driver had evidently settled their destination with Ciceron, because they started off through the cobbled streets without any directions being given. They had only driven a few blocks when the driver pulled up to a narrow three-storey building with the grand name of THE WASHINGTON HOTEL stretching from one side to another.

'Bes' hotel for coloured folkses in Mobile,' Ciceron announced proudly. 'Ain' so good's the Trouville in N'Orleans, but it good 'nough for the li'l time we's here.' In a whispered aside to Drum he announced, 'It kinda a who'house too, but don' tell Miz Brantome.' Once again they had to tote all the luggage inside. The small lobby was bare, with only a zinc-covered counter and a fat Negro behind it. The most conspicuous thing about him was the glassy stone that glittered in his collar button. After a careful consideration of the pigeon-holed rack with keys hanging from it, he allowed as to how he could give them three rooms, but that he would have to charge them a whole day's rate for each of them. By this time any refuge from the heat of the city and the hard benches at the depot would have been worth any amount to Drum, so he engaged the rooms, allotting one to Narcisse and Claire, one to Ciceron and Lucy, and one to Mede and himself. Before following the bejewelled man up the stairs, he ordered that each room be supplied with hot and cold water, a bathtub, and soap and towels.

The bathtubs turned out to be nothing but tin dishpans and there was only a meagre pitcher of hot water with a pail of cold. These along with a supply of coarse towels were delivered to Drum's room by two giggling Negro girls in loosely hung wrappers that they had to clutch about themselves to hide their nudity, because it was apparent that they had nothing on under the thin garments.

'Yo' fine handsome gen'lemen a-wantin' us gals to help yo' wash up?' one of the girls asked, letting her wrapper slip to reveal a pair of enormous breasts. 'Kin wash yore backs for yo'.' She stroked her breasts with both hands, lifting them up for Drum's inspection. 'Ain' I well tittied out?'

'Kin wash more'n yore backs, yo' both such handsome boys.' The other girl let her wrapper fall to the floor and sidled over to Drum, letting her hand caress his thigh. 'Kin jes' do that better'n yo' ever had it done afore.'

Tired as he was, Drum's response was automatic, but there was no desire behind it, even when the girl's fingers started their frantic manipulations. He saw the other girl fondling Mede, who was responding, but Drum pushed his own girl away, picking up her dress from the floor and handing it to her. All he wanted to do was to get clean and eat a substantial breakfast. Possibly he might have been tempted had the girls been cleaner and prettier, but they were both flat-nosed and wide-lipped with peppercorn hair.

Merely shaking his head, he pushed the girl away. Mede was disappointed, but Drum insisted on the girls leaving, pushing them out into the hall and closing the door behind them. No sooner had he closed the door than it opened and the big-titted one stuck her head in, sticking out her tongue.

'Reckon as how yo' two jes' like that fancy boy what yo' bro't along wid yo'. Yo' not a-wantin' no wenches. But they's one real man wid yo' 'n' we a-goin' to him.' She slammed the door behind her, but Drum was too dog-tired to retaliate. He merely sat down in the one straight-backed chair in the room and stretched out his legs for Mede to remove his shoes.

Almost immediately there was a knock on the door and Lucy entered, crying and holding on to his face where a purple bruise was beginning to show. 'Kin I come in wid yo'-all. Damn that Ciceron! I just bein' nice to him 'n' he hit me 'n' then he grab that wench when she came with water 'n' kicked me out. Kin I, Mista Drum? Yo' my folks. That Ciceron he nothin' but a dirty cab-driver. He made a dive for that wench 'n' he tell me to get t'hell out. He a-goin' to do things 'n' he don' want me watchin'. Kin I come in wid yo', Mista Drum?'

'If you behave yourself. I just kicked those two wenches out and I'll kick you out if you start any funny business. Help Mede. I want to get this black washed off me and get into clean clothes.'

It was over an hour or more before they were all assembled in the hotel dining-room, where they had a surprisingly good meal of fried ham, eggs, grits, and hot coffee. The same two girls who had carried the water waited on them and, although they were most polite and solicitous over Narcisse and Claire, and fussed over Ciceron, they completely ignored Drum, Mede, and Lucy.

Everyone had been refreshed by their baths, however, and the breakfast with the hot coffee had revived their spirits. They would willingly have gone upstairs again to lie down, but Claire warned them that she had inspected the beds and found bedbugs. So once again it was Ciceron who solved the problem of how to pass the time. He went out and found another carriage and for an hour or more they drove around the city, which Drum found far less interesting than New Orleans, ending up a few moments before train time at the railroad depot.

When they entered the Negro waiting-room, Drum was surprised to see Morning Star, seated on one of the benches surrounded by her paraphernalia. She was a figure of woe. Tears were running down her cheeks and she was moaning, but when she saw Drum come in, she sat up straight, wiping the tears from her eyes with the corner of her skirt.

'Oh, praises be, Mista Drum! It's a happy day now jes' a-seein' yo'. Should never have left N'Orleans 'n' come to this place. Been a-walkin' alla mornin' tryin' ter fin' my gal. Ain' no one never heard o' her. Don' know what I a-goin' to do now. Ain' nobody here in Mobile know 'bout Mornin' Star's cookin'. Mista Drum, yo' shore a-goin' to need a good cook in that place yo' goin'. Take Mammy Morn with yo'. Please, Mista Drum, take Mammy Morn.' Her arms encircled his legs and she gazed up at him, pleading with her eyes.

Obviously he could not abandon the poor woman. Of course he could pay her fare back to New Orleans and give her a little money, but that would not make her happy. She had left New Orleans because of loneliness and sending her back there would not help that. She was right. He would need a cook at Falconhurst. That was obvious and he was sure she was a good cook. He liked her too. After last night he felt very close to her. She was the mother he had never had. Not that Aunt Mary had not been a mother to him, but now he felt closer to this old Negress than he had ever felt to Aunt Mary.

'You bet I'll take you.' He reached down and patted her on the shoulder. 'I can still taste that ham and that pound cake.' He looked to Claire for confirmation. 'She's a wonderful cook and we're going to need one at Falconhurst. I've decided to take her along. We'll arrive with a whole staff – you, dear Claire, as my hostess and housekeeper, you, Narcisse, as my overseer, you, Mede, as my body servant, you, Lucy, as our butler, and you, Ciceron, as our coachman. What more could we want?'

Narcisse's reply had an edge of sarcasm. 'You could go back to the hotel and get those two wenches there for parlour maids.' He laughed, trying to make a joke out of his words, despite the bitterness of his tone.

'No, Drum.' Claire was quick to take exception to her husband's words. 'We'll have plenty of girls to choose from at Falconhurst, but a good cook is a jewel.' She came over and patted Morning Star's shoulder. 'And so is a good coachman. Now I'm sure we have the best of both.' She waggled a finger at the grinning Ciceron. 'From this moment on we're all one family and we might as well start now.' Again she looked at Morning Star. 'Welcome to Falconhurst, Morning Star.'

'I'se Mammy Morn to yo'-all now. Jes' a-goin' to take every one o' yo' as my own chillun, my own flesh 'n' blood, even yo', mista, though I a-thinkin' yo' don' like me.'

'Of course I do, Mammy Morn.' Narcisse became his usual congenial self.

They did not have long to wait for the train that was to take them to Westminster. If they had bewailed their fate at having to travel in the car provided for them from New Orleans to Mobile, they were appalled at the baggage car in which they had to ride to Westminster. It was dirty, with only one small window, and did not even have the luxury of benches. They were forced either to stand or sit on the floor, but Mammy Morn showed her resourcefulness. By propping some of the valises against the wall of the car and putting various quilts, shawls, and blankets on the floor, she made some attempt to better their conditions. She herself sat in the corner, patting a place for Drum to sit beside her, then Claire and Narcisse, Lucy and Mede, and last of all Ciceron. It was a ten-hour ride, but Mammy Morn's basket was not depleted of good things to eat; and at one stop Ciceron was able to persuade the brakeman to get them a big tin can of hot coffee, which he proudly paid for with his own money.

The daylight faded from the small window and a smoky lamp was lighted in the baggage car, but it did little to dispel the gloom. They were all exhausted but could not sleep and finally even conversation became difficult, so they rode on silently through the darkness. Drum again found some rest with Mammy Morn's arm behind his head. He discovered Claire's hand between her and himself and he held it, feeling somehow that the mother he had never known and the wife he had never had were both with him. Narcisse's head was in Lucy's lap, while Mede and Ciceron, nearest to the lamp, played with a greasy pack of cards that Ciceron had brought along in his pocket. Around midnight the brakeman came in and told them that Westminster would be the next station. By the time they had repacked their quilts and blankets, they were there. The train wheezed to a stop and they got out the wide door, the men having to help Claire and Morning Star down to the ground. Then the train left and they were alone, stranded in the darkness. There was no moon, but they could see the dim outline of the roof of a depot. Holding hands, they stumbled across the tracks to it, sending the boys back for the luggage.

While they were standing there a pinpoint of light appeared; then it grew into the faint gleam of a lantern. A voice from behind the lantern called out.

'That yo', Mista Drum?'

'Right here,' Drum answered.

'Wait there, I a-comin'.'

The moving lantern revealed a middle-aged Negro, his hair white but his strong figure neither bent nor his steps faltering.

'I'se Brute,' he explained. 'Been a-waitin' here since sun-down 'cause I didn't want to miss yo'-all.'

'That's my pappy,' Lucy called out of the darkness.

'Who I pappy to?' Brute turned in the direction of the voice.

'I'se Lucifer. 'Member me, Pappy? Done lef' here long time 'go with my mammy. Mista Drum a-bringin' me back now.' Lucy rushed out of the darkness and embraced his father, who held the lantern up to his face.

'Never tho't I'd be layin' eyes on yo' again, son, but yo' welcome. Ain' much at Falconhurst to offer yo'. Lean days come to Falconhurst, Mista Drum. Lean days! Ain' never seen nothin' like it. Hopin' yo' kin help us. Talk 'bout it later. Better we git started. Got us a long drive ahead o' us. Won' git there till 'mos' daybreak. So many o' yo' had to bring a farm wagon. Ol' barouche ain' too good no mo'.'

'There's more of us than I wrote you – seven of us now.' Drum once again realized how his following had grown.

Brutus flashed his lantern at the group. 'With all that baggage, boys got to take turns a-walkin'. Yo' there' – he pointed to Mede – ' 'n' yo'' – he pointed to Ciceron – ' 'n' this boy o' mine. Got to take turns walkin' 'n' I take turns too. Goin' to slow us a little but not much. These horses cain' go too fast nohow.'

They got in the wagon and seated themselves on the floor. This was different from the stuffy trains. The night air was warm and clean and there were bright stars in the sky. On the ground there was a chirping of insects; points of light flashing in the blackness came from fireflies. Drum had the feeling that he was nearly home at last. Brute clucked to the horses and slapped them with the reins. The wagon started moving towards Falconhurst. Ciceron, who was walking in back with Mede and Lucy, started to sing. It was a song of the New Orleans streets, bawdy and filled with obscene words, but it had a good marching tune. Soon the others picked it up, all except Claire, while Mammy Morn's deep alto voice rose above all the others.

CHAPTER SEVENTEEN

SITTING ON THE hard boards, hearing the clop-clop of the horses' shoes as they pulled the lumbering wagon, passing from the absolute blackness of the over-hanging trees into the now moon-drenched countryside, Drum felt that they would never arrive at Falconhurst. The two nights of weary travel on the train, the dirt and sweat and cinders, the disgraceful discomfort of the baggage car, and now this tumbledown farm wagon. He was too exhausted to talk to Brutus, too tired to join in the singing, and unable even to think as they made their snail-like progress through the hot night. At intervals Brute would stop and those who had been walking would ride and those who had been riding would plod wearily along. It was not even suggested that Drum or Claire walk and they did not volunteer.

It seemed an eternity of passing darkened houses, shuttered cabins, and lonely fields until they reached a pair of brick gate-posts that supported rusty opened gates that led to a long avenue of trees. Drum knew without being told that he was home. He was glad to be there. He would have been glad to arrive at any destination after the trip from New Orleans.

'We'se here!' It was almost the first words that Brute had spoken. 'Reckon yo' folks a-wantin' somethin' to eat, so bro't over what food we could spare from New Quarters. 'Tain't much, but it the best we could do. Lean days at Falconhurst, Mista Drum, lean days.'

Drum was too stupefied with fatigue to understand Brute's words. He and the others dumbly followed the bobbing lantern up a flight of wide steps, under a pillared portico, and into the house. Drum saw soaring white pillars on the outside, felt the texture of brick as he steadied himself against the wall and, once inside, caught a glimpse of a wide, curving staircase in the light of the lantern that Brutus put down on the floor. He entered through a wide, pillared doorway at the right into another room and lighted a single candle, whose feeble light did little to illuminate the vast drawing-room with a big segment of plaster fallen in the middle of the floor. From there they proceeded into a magnificent dining-room, where the big fan over the table hung by one hinge, and then through a butler's pantry into the kitchen.

'Better we go into the kitchen tonight. Brought over Matilda from New Quarters 'n' she got a fire a-goin' 'n' goin' to git yo'-all somethin' to eat.' Brute ushered them into a large room that seemed warm and cosy after the desolation of the rest of the house. There was a fire burning in the big black range, which stood before an immense brick fireplace, the tea-kettle was singing on the stove, and the loud tick of a clock gave some semblance of life to the room. A number of candles illuminated it and Drum saw a tall, angular, and gaunt-faced woman in a much-mended dress standing by the table. A startling white headcloth served only to make the dead prune black of her face with its high cheekbones and sunken cheeks even blacker.

'How de do, masta.' She bobbed a curtsy. 'Ain' much ter eat 'n' didn't dare cook it till yo'-all got here 'cause cain' waste it.' She pulled out a straight-backed kitchen chair from the table and Drum dropped into it, letting the others, even Claire, find their own places. They all sat down except Mammy Morn, who bustled over to the stove.

'What yo'-all got to eat, woman?' she demanded with authority.

' 'Tain't much. Got some white flour 'n' saleratus for biscuits. Got us three slices o' ham 'n' ten eggs – no got us fo'teen eggs 'cause Beulah give' us four mo' – 'n' some lard 'n' got us 'mos' a pound o' coffee what we been a-savin' up over to New Quarters.'

'Well, then, le's move our stumps 'n' git to cookin' it.' Mammy Morn seemed to shed her fatigue at the sight of a stove. 'I a-goin' to stir up the biscuits 'n' soon's I git them in the oven, we'll fry the ham 'n' eggs. Break an egg into the coffee pot' – she stopped momentarily and counted heads. 'No, if'n we only got fo'teen eggs, that is two apiece 'n' we won' waste one on the coffee, though 'tain' much good 'thout'n it. Git me a bowl to stir up them biscuits, Matilda, if'n that how they call yo'.'

'Ain' had much to work with,' Mammy Morn informed them as they sat down at the kitchen table a half hour later, but the biscuits were tender and hot and smelled slightly of saleratus; the ham was cooked just right with the fat a golden brown; and the eggs were white and gold. There was unsalted butter, fresh cream, and a big pitcher of milk, cold from the springhouse.

When they had finished, Mammy Morn pushed back her plate. 'Ain' one for leavin' dishes, but a-goin' to die if'n I don' git my head on a piller.'

'Servants' quarters up two flights,' Brute said, opening a door that disclosed a flight of stairs. 'Matilda'll go with yo' 'n' show yo' the rooms. Plenty up there to pick from. Matilda'll git yo' blankets 'n' sech.'

' 'N' sheets,' Mammy Morn was positive. 'I ain' no wench 'n' I like sheets.'

'Plenty o' them.' Matilda nodded. ' 'N' all real beds too – ain' jes' pallets for the servants.' She took the candle stubs in the brass candlesticks and handed one to Mammy Morn, another to Mede, and a third to Ciceron. 'That boy Lucy he a-goin' with us?'

'A-stayin' here, Pappy' – Lucy spoke to his father – ' 'n' ain' no use makin' up a bed for me. A-sleepin' wid Mede, I am.'

'Ain' a-sleepin' wid me, that's shore,' Ciceron said, starting up the stairs.

Brute fitted more candles into tarnished silver candlesticks and led the way out through a side kitchen door, then through a room that appeared to have been used as an office or study, as it contained a desk, and finally up a narrow flight of stairs to the second floor through a bedroom and out into a long hall. He opened a door on to a large bedroom. 'This for yo', Mista 'n' Miz Brantome.' He deposited the candlestick on a table beside the bed and motioned to Drum to follow. Drum's goodnight to the Brantomes was scarcely audible; he was far too sleepy to observe the amenities, and followed Brute across the hall to another door.

'This yere's yore room, Mista Drum. Same one yore pappy had.' He handed Drum the candlestick, but did not go into the room with him. Instead he departed down the curving staircase.

Drum pushed open the door of his room. The dim light of his candle showed a high four-poster bed with the covers turned down. A naked black girl stirred on the bed, waking up with the light. Scarcely believing his eyes, he walked over to the bed, watching her sit up and yawn. There was a pleasant odour from her body from the lemon verbena leaves she had rubbed her skin with.

'Are you real?' he asked, wondering if he in his extreme fatigue might be dreaming. Holding the candle down to her face, he could see that she was fine-featured, although dark. He wondered as he saw the long curly hair that covered her shoulders if this too might be a wig. 'Who are you?' Drum had suddenly lost his drowsiness and felt awake. He touched one of the girl's breasts with his finger, feeling the warmness of her flesh, then cupped it in his hand, pinching the nipple in his fingers.

'I Debbie.' She tried to smile but spoiled it with a yawn.

'Brute he a-sayin' yo' a-needin' a bed wench 'n' he picked me. If'n yo' don' want me, mista, I sleep on the flo', but don' send me back to New Quarters. Big Pearl she puts ha'nts on the road to New Quarters 'n' I skeered.'

'Stay!' Drum unbuttoned his clothes and let them fall to the floor. He was tired – damn tired from lack of sleep – but as he walked towards the bed he saw the girl stretch out, black against the white sheets, and he knew that his need for her was greater than his need for sleep.

'I been busted,' she confessed, 'but yo' so big I kinda skeered.'

'Don't have to be afraid of me. I won't hurt you tonight and the next time we'll take it slow and easy so I won't hurt you at all. What's your name again?'

'Debbie,' she whispered, as he blew out the candle and stumbled in the darkness across the floor to the bed. He fell on to the mattress and it was a moment before he could get the strength to pull his legs up on to the bed. For a few minutes they were both still – he too tired to move a finger to touch her, despite his desire, and she too frightened to move without his permission.

'Well, how about it, Debbie?' he asked. 'Let's get this over with before I fall asleep.'

'Yo' meanin' yo' not wantin' to do nothin' 'n' yo' wantin' me to do it to yo'.'

'It's all yours, Debbie,' he said, yawning.

With his hands behind his head, he relaxed on the pillow, stretching his long legs out until they touched the footboard of the bed. Tonight he was content to let her be the aggressor. She had never been with a man who played the passive partner before. This was entirely different from the stolen moments she had passed in the weeds or in some of the abandoned buildings with the bucks. She knew enough not to kiss his lips. She had heard that white men never kissed a nigger wench on the lips. Of course, he was not white – everyone said he was just a mustee – but she had seen that his skin was white and to her he was a white man, the only white man she had ever been with.

Although scarcely awake, he could feel, in that delicious borderland between waking and sleeping, her lips touching his neck, and then the trail of her darting tongue down over his chest. With her lips she caressed his paps, letting her tongue circumscribe them slowly and then faster until she fastened her teeth delicately into them. Her lips moved over his body and now her hands started to roam over him, clutching at him with warm, grasping fingers that excited him so much he had to make the effort to unclasp them. Now he could relax a small second, his body rigid. Again he felt the warmth of her lips and the darting movements of her tongue that caused his body to arch, caused him to fill his lungs with quick draughts of air, and made him grab a handful of her hair and pull her away from him. He was glad that it was over and now he wanted to get away from her. She sensed his wishes and moved to the very edge of the bed. Still sprawled on his back, he fell asleep immediately. Once during the night he half awakened, his body tense and stimulated by her hands. He was powerless to stop her until she had finished. Then again he managed to push her away and fall asleep.

When he awoke in the same position in which he had dropped off to sleep, the girl was gone and the room was flooded with sunshine as well as with flies, which had poured in through two of the windows that had been propped open with sticks. There was a fullness in his bladder that demanded immediate attention. Fortunately he found a chamber pot under the bed; otherwise he would have had to use one of the opened windows, displaying himself for anyone to see. Now, having satisfied that pressing need, he sank down on to the bed again, putting one pillow on top of the other and sitting up to survey his immediate surroundings.

The room was large and architecturally fine, with a white painted wainscot that extended up to the chair rail and the rest of the wall papered with a faded French wallpaper that showed bunches of roses tied with blue ribbons. A fireplace, with a Greek temple motif, reminded him of the glimpse he had had last night of tall white pillars outside the house and the pillared entrance to the drawing-room. Paint was scaling from the woodwork and one long sheet of wallpaper had become dislodged, curving over itself in a long flap on to the floor, revealing stained plaster on the wall. The windowsills were covered with dead wasps, and streamers of cobwebs floated from the dusty tester over the bed. Although the furniture in the room was old-fashioned, it was as elegant and in as good taste as that in his former home in Boston. Two finely carved Chippendale chairs were upholstered in dusty rose damask; a large carved armoire reached from floor to ceiling; a capacious chest of drawers supported an eagle-carved mahogany mirror; and the bed he was on had tall fluted columns that reached nearly to the ceiling and supported a tester of the same rose damask that was on the chairs. It was elegance gone to decay. Despite the opened windows, there was a close smell in the room, an odour of dust and mustiness, of old wood and dead insects. It had been a long time since his Uncle Chris had been here and he remembered now that on his last visit he had slept in the overseer's house.

The heap of sweaty, dirty clothing on the floor offered no temptation to get up and dress and, although he rang the bell cord beside his bed several times, Mede did not appear. Drum had no idea where his valises were. He slipped into his trousers, disdaining the soiled drawers and the sooty white shirt, and barefooted he tiptoed over the dusty carpet and opened the door. The door to Narcisse's and Claire's room was open. He peeked in, noting that the bed was empty and also that there were the same fine furnishings and evidence of neglect he had found in his own room. He walked along the dusty floor of the hall, where his bare feet left damp imprints, and descended the curving staircase to the hall below. He turned through the big doorway at his left and again crossed the long drawing-room, feeling the gritty plaster under his feet. But as he passed through the door into the dining-room he saw a somewhat different picture.

The big mahogany table had been dusted and was set for three people with fine china and silver. A tall silver coffee urn, still black with tarnish, stood at the farther end of the table. The curtains were open and sunlight streamed through the room, giving it light and cheerfulness, despite the disorder and neglect. Hearing voices in the kitchen, he passed through the butler's pantry with its tall glass-doored shelves and came out into the big, light kitchen, where Mede, Lucy, and Ciceron were eating at the long kitchen table. Claire, her skirts tucked up around her waist to disclose her white petticoats, was standing at the stove beside Mammy Morn.

'Here come my boy Drum.' Mammy Morn beamed at him. 'My, my, but he even prettier 'thout'n his shirt than with it.'

'Just couldn't face those clothes I wore yesterday. If I could get some hot water to wash my face, I'd have Mede get me a shirt to put on.'

'Got clean clotheses here, Mista Drum' – Mede pointed to the back of a chair where a complete outfit of clean clothes were hanging – 'but didn' want to wake yo' up. Knowed yo' was tired.'

Mammy Morn lifted a heavy iron tea-kettle from the stove and poured some water into a tin basin. Claire had evidently brought down a bar of her own French soap and there was a clean but yellowed towel. 'Your bath will have to wait. I don't even know what facilities there are for bathing, but wash your face and slip into a shirt and for heaven's sake put on some shoes. It isn't safe to walk around these floors barefooted. Narcisse will be in in a moment. He just stepped out the back door to look around—'

'And it's a pretty depressing sight.' Narcisse had caught her words as he opened the back door. 'Everything's grown up to weeds or tumbled down to nothing. How about breakfast?'

'There's not much but eggs that we found in a basket at the back door, a little dab of grits, and some coffee, but there's milk and clabber if you want it. We had a mysterious donation during the night.'

' 'N' thank the dear Lord for it.' Mammy Morn sighed as she looked at the pans on the stove. 'A-wishin' we had flour for biscuits though. Used it all up las' night.'

'It seems that they are on short rations here,' Claire said. 'Outside of what the folks at New Quarters have been able to raise, they have nothing. Brutus is waiting to talk to you after

168

you eat. Perhaps he can explain things.' Claire sent Mammy Morn into the dining-room to get the coffee urn and poured the hot brew into it. Mammy Morn transferred the fried eggs on to a Sèvres platter. From a pan she measured out scant spoonfuls of grits on to another platter.

'Ain' much like'n the meals they useter serve here in the big house,' Matilda moaned. 'Never did see 'em, but my frien' Marguerite she tell me 'bout 'em afore she die. She been the cook here at the big house.'

'That's enough, Matilda.' Claire silenced her volubility kindly but effectively. 'Now we'll all go into the dining-room and you, Lucy, wipe the egg off your mouth and come in and serve us. Although we've only hominy grits and fried eggs, we're going to eat them in style.' She linked one arm in Drum's and one in Narcisse's and led them into the dining-room. Pausing for a moment on the threshold, she surveyed the room. 'This must have been a truly gorgeous home once.'

'Almost as good as our own,' Narcisse interrupted, looking to her for confirmation. But she did not answer him.

'And it can be again, Drum, believe me. There must be plenty of women over in this place called New Quarters, where the Negroes live, and we'll put them to work. In a few days you won't know the place.'

They sat down to eat their meagre breakfast and, despite the forlorn room, Claire's presence at the table made the miserable meal almost happy. When they had finished and Lucy was ready to clear away the table, Mede entered.

'Foun' yo' a bathtub, Mista Drum, 'n' Lucy he a-sayin' he help yo'. Wantin' to run 'cross 'n' see my mammy. She live right near 'cause she ain' never moved to New Quarters.'

Before Drum could reply, Narcisse stood up, staring at Mede across the table. 'Who the hell do you think you are, boy, coming in here and telling us what you're going to do?'

Claire pulled Narcisse's coat sleeve and, although he shook her hand off angrily, he did resume his seat.

'What Narcisse means, Mede, is that it's your job to help your master. Lucy is needed down here. You are Mr Drum's servant, not Lucy, and it is up to you to attend to him. If we are going to accomplish anything here at all, we must have a certain amount of discipline. I believe that once your job is finished, Mr Drum will permit you to visit your mother. But now your job comes first. Go upstairs with Mr Drum. Help him bathe and dress. Bring his soiled clothes down and put them in that big hamper beside the sink so that they can be laundered.'

'And keep a respectful tongue in your head or I'll see to it that you do,' Narcisse added.

Mede stood looking at the Brantomes, his mouth agape. He recognized the authority in Claire's voice as well as the rancour in Narcisse's. He had almost forgotten the master-servant relationship between Drum and himself since they had left Boston. Now it was about to return. He returned meekly to the kitchen and in a few moments they could hear his footsteps going up the stairs.

Claire levelled a warning finger at Drum. 'You're in the South now. There are only two categories here – white and black, master and servant. Mede must look up to you and respect you as a white man and his master. Between whites and Negroes there is no equality. Neither can there be between coloured people like ourselves and our black servants. They must be kept in their place. You'll have to use discipline. It need not be unjust, but it must be stern. You would have let Mede go to visit his mother, but that would have disrupted the household. It would have taken Lucy away from his duties here. It would have set a bad precedent. Mede is here to serve you, not to attend to his own wishes first. Now I'm going to give you an order, Drum.'

'Yes ma'am, Miz Claire ma'am.' Drum grinned.

'Go upstairs and get dressed. Dress up in your best clothes. If you are going to be Master of Falconhurst, you've not only got to look the part but act it.'

Drum was able to see her reasoning. He had fraternized far too much with both Mede and Lucy. Now it was necessary for the gap to widen between them. He was, as Claire had just said, Master of Falconhurst and although at present it looked like damn little to be master of, he was still master of that little.

A rather disgruntled Mede awaited him upstairs, but Drum paid no attention to his surliness. He discovered, however, that Mede was more efficient and took more pains than he had been taking lately. It was more like the old days in Boston, when there was a wide gulf between them. When Mede had finished and Drum had donned one of his new white jackets, a clean white shirt with a high black stock, and one of the new pairs of black breeches, Mede asked, 'Kin I go 'n' see my mammy now?'

'After you take these things downstairs and put them where Miss Claire told you.'

'How come she a-givin' me orders?' Mede's wide lower lip stood out in a pout. 'She ain' mist'ess here. I ain' her boy. She cain' order me 'roun', 'n' that Narcisse neither. 'Sides, they niggers too.'

Drum turned and slapped him sharply across the face. 'We don't use that word here. Miss Claire is mistress of this house now. You do as she says. If you don't, I'm going to trounce you and you know I can do it.'

Mede suddenly became humble. 'Yes suh, Mista Drum. I do jes' that, but I gotta take orders from Mista Narcisse too?'

'To a certain extent, yes. You must be respectful to him, but if Narcisse asks you to do anything you don't think is right, you can say, "I'll have to ask Mista Drum first."'

'Yes suh, 'n' after I cleans up here, kin I go to see my mammy?'

'When your work is finished.' Drum rather enjoyed the feeling of authority. 'You can ask Miss Claire after you have finished. Tell her I said you could go, but be sure to ask her first. And' – he paused for a moment and smiled at Mede – 'tell your mammy that her grandson is also coming to see her.'

Claire was waiting for him as he descended the stairs. She made a low bow. 'Behold the Master of Falconhurst.' She smiled up at him and took his arm, leading him out on to the portico where, much to his surprise, he found Brutus waiting for him, along with Narcisse, who was mounted on a horse. Brutus was holding a horse for Drum and held out the stirrup for Drum to mount.

Now that it was daylight, Drum could see the man much better. He judged him to be somewhere between forty and fifty, lean, spare, and muscular, with a thick head of grey hair. He was a good-looking man with intelligent eyes and when he came close to Drum, he looked directly up at him. There was no subservience in his look, rather one of respect, nay, almost adoration.

'Goin' to be nice to have a real masta at Falconhurst onc't more,' he said. 'Goin' to be real good. Been a-needin' one ever since your pappy got kilt. Drummage he a real man, he was. Bit too hot after the wenches' – he winked at Drum – ' 'specially when he a young buck, but he a smart man. Seemin' good to have yo' here. We a-needin' yo' bad. We in bad trouble here.'

'Tell me about it, Brutus.'

'Calls me Brute, they do, Mista Drum.'

'Then, tell me about it as we ride along. Where are we going?'

'Jes' a-goin' to show yo' what's left o' Falconhurst 'n' how badly we a-needin' yo'. Kin yo' save us, Mista Drum? We come on hard times. Hard times, Mista Drum.'

CHAPTER EIGHTEEN

DRUM MOUNTED THE horse, the saddle feeling strangely hard and wide because he had not ridden for over a year. Narcisse started to trot down the driveway that encircled the mansion, but Drum halted him. This was his first opportunity to see the big house at Falconhurst by daylight and he wanted to look at it. It was, as he had imagined from the size of the rooms inside, a fine, big house, made of bricks that had turned a rose colour over the years. It was a high house of two storeys with a third storey behind the dormer windows of the roof.

His impression of the tall white pillars on the portico was

correct. There were four of them, but they were not as white by daylight as they had been at night. The white paint was scaling and in many places had completely disappeared. Birds had nested at the tops of the Ionic columns and droppings soiled the capitals. One of the bases of the columns had rotted and it had been propped up by boards, but it still listed dangerously towards the house. The wrought-iron balconies that circled the long windows of the first floor were red with rust and the shutters were askew or missing. Added to the ruin of the house was the rank garden, which had grown in such profusion of weeds and creepers that it presented the appearance of a jungle. A long double row of trees bordered the drive, now grass grown, that led to the main road and looking down them, Drum could see the gateposts and gates, which he dimly remembered seeing the night before.

There had been great beauty here. Could he restore it? It would take a lot of work and money, but, he consoled himself, labour was cheap and he had five thousand dollars in the bank at Benson. It would go a lot further here than it would up north. He was ready to start his ride now and he slapped his reins against the horse's neck. The animal was nothing but a work-horse, as was the one that Narcisse was riding. Their coats were long and unkempt. Neither had ever seen a curry comb or brush. Brute was mounted on a mule and as he rode up to Drum and Narcisse with the intention of riding alongside them to point out different parts of the plantation, Narcisse turned on him.

'They call you Brutus, boy?'

'My name Brutus 'n' mos' people calls me Brute.' There was pride in his voice as he mentioned his name and he seemed proud of his nickname also, but there was resentment in his voice when he added, ' 'N' I not a boy no longer, Mista Brantome.'

'All niggers are boys. That's the way we always called them on my plantation and that's the way I'll call them here. And by the way, boy' – he stressed the word – 'it's "masta" and not "mister". Remember that and be sure to add the word *sir*. If there's one thing we're going to have here, it's discipline. Mr

Maxwell has appointed me overseer of this plantation. From now on you will take orders from me.'

Brute looked to Drum, who nodded his head in confirmation. 'Mr Brantome is my new overseer, Brute. It's true, you will take orders from him because, I must confess, I know nothing about running a plantation.'

'Yes suh, Masta Maxwell, suh.' The words reminded him of those long-gone days when he was serving another Master Maxwell. Well, those had been good days, prosperous days, even though he was a servant for life. If calling Drummage's son 'masta' would bring prosperity back to Falconhurst, he'd be willing to do it.

'Follow behind us, not alongside us.' Narcisse in authority was quite a different personality than Drum had ever known before. There was a touch of superiority in his voice and a curve of cruelty to his lips.

'But Brute is taking us on a tour and he wants to explain things to us as we go along,' Drum insisted.

'He can tell us from half a length behind us just as well as beside us. There's one thing you've got to learn, Drum. Niggers have got to be kept in their place. Just like Claire pointed out this morning with Mede. You can't put yourself on a level with them or they will cease to respect you. Before you know it, they'll be out of hand. Niggers are a lazy lot. They don't like to work and they'll get out of it at every chance. There's only one thing that will make a nigger work and that's a whip. Punishment too! You've got to put fear in their hearts or you won't get anything out of them and you've also got to remember that you are better than they are. Never identify yourself with them. We're not black. We've got to keep a distance between us.' He turned back to speak to Brute. 'Where are we heading now, boy?'

Brute raised his head and glanced at Drum again; but, receiving no encouragement from him, he answered Narcisse respectfully. 'To the barns, Masta Brantome suh. Is yo' a-wantin' to git down 'n' go in o' jes' look at 'em 'n' go on?'

'We'll have plenty of time to inspect them later. Today we'll just look at the outside of things.'

The barns and the outbuildings had once been proudly painted white, but there was scarcely a fleck of paint left on them. Doors were missing, windowlights broken, and one building had a sway-backed roof that looked ready to collapse at any minute. Drum listened as Brute catalogued the various buildings, noting that he used the past tense in describing them. It was not 'This is the stables', but 'That was the stables'. The stable was nearest the house, its doors flanked by pilasters instead of pillars and, originally, it had been adorned with a pillared cupola that was now a splintered mass of wood on the ground. Behind it was a long cattle barn, a large henhouse, and a pigsty. Near the latter was a small building that had collapsed and had been, Brute explained, the corncrib from which the cows had been fed. A roofed structure, its roof level with the ground, except on one side where a flight of brick steps led down, was the springhouse, where food was kept cold; and another small classical building with two entrances turned out to be the privy. Drum felt the desire to urinate, so he got down off his horse and entered one of the doors of this building. It was as elaborate inside as the house itself, with a wooden wainscoting, remnants of wallpaper, and privy holes that were disguised as chairs, with upholstered backs. He noticed a sign on the floor whose dim lettering announced LADIES and he wondered about the hoop-skirted females who had so long ago used this place. Seated on their chairs, their voluminous skirts around them, they were as presentable as in a drawing-room. Some strange sense of perversity prompted him to stand before one of these bottom-less chairs and unbutton his breeches. While he relieved himself he wondered if he might be the first coloured man to defile this sacred precinct of white femininity. He could almost hear all those delicate females screaming in terror over the very idea that a coloured man had pissed there. Well, he had and to hell with the ghosts of those ante-bellum women. Buttoning his pants, he stepped into the adjoining room. Here, evidently, the men had congregated, for the room was decorated in a masculine style with one old hunting print hanging at a crazy angle on the wall. From now on he'd use this side. But, he was sure, the ghosts of the white men who had stared at the hunting print would equally resent his presence here.

Back on his horse again, he rode alongside Narcisse as Brute pointed out a row of small buildings that he identified as a cobbler's shop, a carpenter's shop, and a harness maker's shop. A larger building through the windows of which Drum could see looms and spinning wheels was the weaving house. It was evident that at one time Falconhurst was a good-sized village in itself. At the very end of a grass-grown road there was a small building of heavy planks with a grated window high in one wall. 'The calaboose,' Brute explained. 'Mista Sylvester kept the fellows there what he was a-goin' to whop.'

'Whipping? Now?' Drum had always thought that whipping had ended with the war.

'Mista Sylvester he shore a whopper,' Brute admitted.

Drum stared at the building but said nothing.

'That there's the new house.' Brute pointed back to the mansion and then, pointing across a wooded ravine to another group of buildings, he said, 'Old house over there burned down. Mos' of the slave quarters over there onc't.' He directed them down a path that led through a copse of trees to a narrow stream. A ruined gothic summerhouse and a small fancy bridge were both in ruins.

Crossing the river, they went up a steep embankment at the top of which four large live oaks marked the four corners of a burial plot. Drum dismounted a second time and climbed over the fallen stone wall. Pulling away the creepers and the bindweed, he uncovered the white marble stones. Two of them bore the names Warren Maxwell and Sophie Maxwell, his wife. An insignificant stone carried only the name Blanche. Beside it there was a tall finger of marble, partly eroded, which had on its base another single name – Drumson. A short distance from this was a very elaborate stone that had supported a buxom angel, now fallen into the weeds. The base of this, larger by far than any of the others, bore the name of Apollon Beauchair with the words 'Beloved Husband of Sophie Beauchair'; and beside this there were two stones that said 'Sophie Maxwell' and 'Drummage Maxwell', and Drum figured this must be his mother and father, but he was interested to know who the others might be. He called to Brute, who dismounted and came to stand beside him.

'Tell me, Brute, who all these people are and how they are related to me.'

Brute removed the straw hat he was wearing and scratched his head. 'Well, that there Warren Maxwell, he the gran'pappy o' Miz Sophie, what was named after her grandmammy.'

'How many Sophies were there?'

'Jes' two, Masta Maxwell suh. They's Masta Warren's wife what was Sophie 'n' Miz Sophie what was yore mammy.'

'Then, who is this?' Drum pointed to the base of the fallen angel. 'This Sophie Beauchair?'

'She yore mammy too. Fust she Sophie Maxwell 'n' then she married up wid an Englishman, but disremember his name. Then 'long comed this Apollon Beauchair what Miz Sophie married up with 'n' he got kilt 'n' last Miz Sophie married up wid Drummage, who tooken the name o' Maxwell, 'n' so she Miz Sophie Maxwell 'gain.'

'But what about Hammond Maxwell, who was my grandfather?'

Brute shook his head. 'Masta Hammond, he not here nor Miz 'Gusta neither. Masta Hammond he died in de war 'n' Miz 'Gusta she went to nurse him up someplace long ways 'way afore he died. Miz 'Gusta she die too, so she ain' here neither. Fine man, Masta Hammond, 'n' fine woman, Miz' Gusta. Miz 'Gusta Masta Hammond's second wife. First wife that Blanche there' – Brute pointed to the little broken stone. 'She yore grandmammy 'cause she Miz Sophie's mama, but Miz Sophie she never see her mama. She died the same time Mede died. Sayin' as how Mede – he Big Pearl's brother – he raped Miz Blanche 'n' she had a nigger sucker. Big Pearl she kin tell yo' all 'bout it. She kin 'member Masta Warren Maxwell 'n' Masta Hammond Maxwell what busted her 'n' Masta 'Pollon 'n' all. But don' know now if'n she remember rightly. She all spirits 'n' Obeah now. Her mammy Ol' Lucy tol' her 'bout them. Mede he Ol' Lucy's son, but he mated up to Big Pearl 'n' she bein' his sister 'n' Ol' Lucy too, she bein' his mama. They

177

all Mandingos 'n' Masta Hammond he set on having Mandingos. This boy Mede what yo' have, he named after that Mede what raped Miz Blanche.'

Drum was so confused now by the genealogy of the Maxwell family that he felt he knew even less than before. Evidently his mother had been married three times and his grandmother had been raped by a nigger buck named Mede, who was his grandmother's brother. It was all too complicated.

'We'll sit down and talk about it sometime, Brutus.'

'Cain' sit down with yo', Masta Maxwell suh. Masta Brantome he not a-goin' to like it if'n I sit with yo'. Kin stand up 'n' talk with yo'.'

Drum laid a reassuring hand on Brute's shoulder. 'You're going to be working with Mr Brantome, Brute, but remember, Falconhurst is mine. Anytime you want to talk with me, you come to me. Remember, you take orders from Mr Brantome, but I'm still the head man 'round here. Brantome is just my overseer.'

'So was that Mr Sylvester 'n' he a bad man, Masta Drum suh. He ruint this place. He al'ays a-writin' letters to Cap'n Holbrook 'n' sendin' him a little money from cotton, but things never been good here since Mista Sylvester comed. He didn' do nothin' but work us to death 'n' we never got no money. Ran a store over to New Quarters, he did, 'n' we never got outa the book. He never spent nothin' to keep the big house fixed up 'n' de barns 'n' sechlike. Soon's he hear yo' a-comin', he sol' off all the horses, all the cattle, all the pigs, 'n hens. He skedaddled with all the money. Us'ns over to New Quarters ain' got two bits between us. Only one 'roun' here what got anything is Big Pearl 'n' she get it from Obeah. All I got is them two horses yo' 'n' Masta Brantome a-ridin'. This ol' mule belong to another man at New Quarters.'

'We'll talk about it, Brute. We're going to put Falconhurst back to what it used to be.'

'Bless yo', Mista Drum. Do anythin' I kin. Falconhurst always so proud-like. Give me a misery to see it like this.'

They had reached the horses and Drum remounted. 'Been

learning my family history,' he said by way of apology to Narcisse, who had been waiting under the shade of a tree.

Once again they started down a grass-grown trail where ruins of slave cabins, barns, and outbuildings were a mass of weather-worn boards and stumps of chimneys. Brute pointed to some creeper-covered masonry stubs that he said were the foundations of the old house, which had burned after the present Falconhurst had been built. At the far end of the road was a large building, still standing, with what looked like a belfry on top. This, Brute said, had once been the chapel, but it had later been used to house young studs.

As they rode along, Brute noticed a movement of the high weeds. He was off his mule in a leap that sent him running through the high growth. Lashing out with the whip he was carrying, he whipped away at the weeds. Drum heard a terrified scream and saw a naked boy in his teens stand up, trying to ward off the blows of the whip with one hand while he rubbed an angry red welt on his thin buttocks with the other.

'Who that wench with yo'?' Brute continued to lash at the boy.

A girl stood up, younger and smaller than the boy, covering her face with her dress.

'Ain' I tol' yo' a hundred times, ain' havin' no pesterin' in the weeds. Declare yo' younguns like animals only worst.' Brute let his whip tickle the girl's legs. 'This place a-goin' to rack 'n' ruin. Ain' even 'spectful no more. Git yo'self back to New Quarters 'n' I'll fix yo' both tonight.'

The two started to run. The boy ducked down to pick up his ragged pants, but he did not wait to put them on. As he passed Narcisse on his horse Narcisse stopped him, stared at him in his nakedness, and smiled.

'What's your name, boy?' he asked indulgently, as though humouring the boy to take away the sting of Brute's lashes.

The boy stopped and Drum could see that he was trembling all over. He kept his head bowed, not daring to look up at Narcisse.

'Look up at me' – Narcisse was not quite so indulgent – 'and tell me your name.'

'I'se Abel.' He managed to get the words out while he looked up briefly at Narcisse.

Narcisse started to laugh. 'Abel? That's a good one. You certainly should be, hung like that. *Mon Dieu!* Drum! Look at him! Behold a phenomenon. The little buck's no more than sixteen and he's hung like a jackass.'

' 'N' he a-goin' to git whopped like one, onc't I git to New Quarters.' Brute had just ridden up.

'You'll do nothing of the kind.' Narcisse turned on Brute. 'Any whipping to be done around here, I'll attend to. Look up at me, Abel.' Once again his tone became indulgent and he waited for the boy to lift his head. Drum noticed that he was not bad-looking, even though he was black. He had a nice face and although his skinny shanks and arms needed filling out, he was well built, with good shoulders.

'Yassuh, masta suh.' Abel had no idea what was going to happen to him.

'I'm going to need a boy for a body servant. How'd you like to be that?'

It was too much for poor Abel to comprehend, but he did manage a 'Thank yo', masta suh.'

'Well, then, go home and get yourself all washed over good and come to the overseer's cottage this afternoon. Wait for me there. I'll have you trained as a body servant by Lucy, one of the boys at the big house.'

'He a good boy, but he awful randy,' Brute said, mollifying his opinion of the lad in the face of Narcisse's favouritism.

'When I want your opinion, I'll ask for it.' Narcisse closed the matter with Brute but turned to Drum. 'You don't mind if I have a body servant too? I used Clarence back at Madame Helene's and miss having one here.'

'Why not?' Drum knew how he would miss Mede, but he wondered why Narcisse had not asked him first and even more why he had chosen this untrained boy.

'Lucy can train him, if you don't mind, and I'll keep him down at the cottage.'

'Isn't that a matter for Claire to decide? She's running the house?'

'Claire does as I tell her. Besides, Drum, this boy's going to be a star attraction here at Falconhurst when we start entertaining.'

'Another Harlequin?' Drum asked.

The blood mounted to Narcisse's face. 'Where did you hear about him?'

'I not only heard about him, I saw him.'

Narcisse bit his lips, then laughed. 'Never did see him myself, but he must have been quite a sight. Always seemed to miss his performances.' Then, as though wanting to change the subject, he pointed to an extraordinary structure set somewhat back from the ruins of slave cabins. Drum followed his finger. It was indeed a strange-looking place. Originally it might have started out as a slave cabin to which another had been added, but the most incongruous thing about it was the four peeled tree trunks that had been added to the front porch and whitewashed in imitation of the pillars at the big house. The garden around it was carefully tended. A cow grazed at the back (the first live beast Drum had seen at Falconhurst). There was a large pigsty and a flock of hens; and a rooster pecked around the front yard.

'That there's Big Pearl's,' Brute explained. 'She the oldest woman 'round here. She a Mandingo – a purentee Mandingo – 'n' Masta Hammond he right proud o' his Mandingos. That boy o' yourn – that Mede – he half purentee Mandingo. His papa was Zanzibar, but he daid now. 'N' yo' part Mandingo, Masta Maxwell suh. Yore grandpappy he Drumson what got the big white stone over in the buryin' groun' 'n' he sired yore pappy Drummage on Big Pearl. Kin see to look at yo', Masta Maxwell suh, that yo' part Mandingo, yo' so big 'n' powerful 'n' if'n yo' not white, yo' look like yore pappy. He shore a handsome man, Drummage.'

They rode over towards the house, but Mede had evidently seen them coming because he was out on the rickety porch, waving to them.

'Mista Drum, oh, Mista Drum. Come 'n' meet my mammy. She a-wantin' to lay eyes on yo'. She a-sayin' she a-seen yo' comin' in the fire for more'n a month. She a-sayin' she want to see the boy what her Drummage had.'

Narcisse smiled. 'Look, Drum! Go over and talk with the old lady. It's sort of a family reunion and you won't want strangers standing around. I'll go down and look at the cotton, which would only bore you, as you said you didn't even know what a cotton plant looked like.'

Drum was glad to leave. He had been curious about Big Pearl, of whom he had heard so much – his black grandmother. When he arrived at her house, Mede held his horse and helped him down. Together they walked up the sagging steps to the house. All the shutters were closed to keep out the sun and when Drum entered, it took him a moment to adjust his eyes to the darkness. The tallest and biggest woman he had ever seen stood at the far end of the room. She was dark in colour, with pure white hair, but her skin was smooth as a girl's. His first thought was that he would have liked to have known her when she was younger. What a majestic girl she must have been and what a truly majestic figure she was now. She was dressed in a long white dress that hung straight from her shoulders and she was barefoot. Crossing the room without making any noise, she walked up to him and laid her hands on his shoulders, her eyes on a level with his own.

'Yo're my boy too.' She smiled at him, showing a row of teeth that were white and perfect. 'Conjure been a-tellin' me in the fire that I a-goin' to see my own boy 'gain. But each time conjure a-tellin' me 'bout my own boy, he tellin' me 'bout another boy what mine too, but he younger'n my own boy by 'bout a month. Yo' the son o' Drummage, ain' yo'?'

'And you're my grandmother.' He kissed her cheek.

'Drummage,' she said, lost in a reverie. 'His pappy Mede. No, not Mede, he Drumson. It all so long ago, but spirits a-tellin' me. What yore name, boy?'

'Drum.'

'Drumson tell me onc't that his pappy's name. Yore pappy's name Drummage. Wa'n't really, though. Masta Hammond he called him Drum Major, but we all call him Drummage. Got somethin' 'portant for yo'.'

She dropped her hands from his shoulders and went over to a small table by the fireplace. Carefully unfolding a clean white napkin, she took something from it. It appeared to be a small bag, not much larger than Drum's thumb, but it sported a cockade of black, white, and red hen feathers. Carefully and reverently she came towards Drum with it in the palm of her hand, then opened Drum's pocket and put it inside.

'Don' lose it,' she warned him. 'It strong Obeah. Took me long time to make it. Already had one made for Mede, but when conjure tol' me yo' comin', made one for yo' too. I th' only conjure woman 'roun' 'n' I strong conjure. My mammy learned me. She high conjure woman too. Even white mens come to me – men from Benson – if'n they want real conjure. Glad to see yo', boy. Yo' set.'

Mede brought Drum an old gilded French chair whose missing leg had been supplanted by a broomstick. Drum sat down, wondering what he would say to this strange woman. It was difficult for him to think of her as his grandmother, although he knew that she was and now, having seen her, he felt rather proud of her. 'They tell me you are pure Mandingo.' At least it was something to talk about.

She raised her head proudly. 'I'se purentee Mandingo, son. My mammy 'n' Mede, the one that Masta Hammond kilt because he raped his wife Blanche, though it wa'n't no fault o' Mede's – we all Mandingo. Mede the handsomest man I ever did see, but I don' think he so handsome as yo'. Yo' got yella hair like yore mammy, Miz Sophie, but yo' ain' gootch-eyed like'n her. Yo' mos' white lookin', but yo' still part Mandingo 'n' that the best thing on earth to be. Masta Hammond right proud that he had three purentee Mandingos, me 'n' my maw 'n' Mede. Then when Mede pestered me, we had Ol' Mista Wilson 'n' he Mandingo too, but he died. Now, this boy here' – she patted Mede's shoulder – 'he only half Mandingo, but he right proud o' that.'

It seemed to be a favourite subject of hers and Drum reminded himself to find out more about this mysterious African tribe, for such he supposed it to be. He could think of nothing more to say but remembered the little pompom of chicken feathers that his grandmother had put in his pocket. He reached in for it, but she screamed out a warning to him.

'Mus'n't touch it less'n yo' have to. That Obeah jes' for yo'. Keep yo' safe. Give yo' money. Make yo' strong wid the wenches. Took me long time to make it 'cause I had to get so many things to put in it. Powerful conjure, it is. It work all yore life, but if'n yo' needin' anythin' special, yo' come to me.'

As much as Drum admired the old woman, he was uneasy in her company. Now he was anxious to get away from this mysterious aura that hovered over the house. 'Better get going. Got a lot to do. You'd better come along with me, Mede.'

'Goin' to lose both my boys' – she started to cry – 'but yo' a-comin' back to see Big Pearl.'

'We a-comin',' Mede answered, and when he got down off the porch and a little way from the cabin, he turned to Drum. 'She kinda crazy, my mammy, but I guess she quite a woman 'roun' here. She say everyone else a-starvin' but her. She got hens 'n' pigs 'n' a cow 'n' everythin'. Gits it conjurin'. Some niggers give their last penny jes' to git a conjure. She a-sayin' things bad here at Falconhurst.'

'They are.' Drum shook his head. 'It's nothing but an empty shell and a lot of starving Negroes. Guess Uncle Chris didn't look after the place much. Seems that Sylvester, the caretaker, let things go to ruin. He's been sending Uncle Chris enough money each year to pay for the cotton crop, but that's all. He's never spent a cent on the place and let it all run down. There isn't an animal here, not a horse, not a mule, not a cow or a pig or even a chicken. The houses and barns are falling to pieces. The folks in New Quarters are starving and I don't know if we'll have anything for dinner. This place is hopeless.' He stopped, kicking at the weeds with his foot. 'Guess we'd better go back to New Orleans.'

' 'N' take that ride in them steam cars 'gain. No, Mista Drum, le's stay. I know I'm not supposed to talk to yo' like'n this after what Miz Claire said this mornin'. Yo' the masta. I nothin' but a servant, but with Mammy conjurin' we kin do it. Yes we kin, Mista Drum.'

'You think so, Mede?'

'I knows it. Wait here, Mista Drum. Forgot somethin' back at Mammy's.' He turned and ran back to the cabin, only to reappear a few moments later with a heavy basket. 'Mammy pack this up for us – got us a ham 'n' two chickens 'n' some white flour 'n' lard 'n' melon rind pickles 'n' okra 'n' Mammy say when yo' a-wantin' somethin' more, yo' jes' let her know.'

Drum picked up one side of the basket and together the two walked along the grassy road, past the cemetery with its white marble slabs and its fallen angel, and down to the little stream, which they crossed on the fallen bridge.

Mede was right. They would stay. There was nothing but the five thousand dollars in the bank, but that was enough to give them a start. That afternoon he would go into Benson and get some money. It would be a beginning. He looked at Mede, dimly remembering that long ago when they had been children, they had played here at Falconhurst. There was little he could remember, but Mede had always been with him. Why not fraternize with Negroes? Who was Narcisse to forbid him? He had just seen his own grandmother and she was black and, he reminded himself – absurd though it might seem – Mede was actually his uncle. And what was that other thing he was trying to think of – yes, he was a quarter Mandingo and whatever that might be, he was proud of it.

CHAPTER NINETEEN

MAMMY MORN'S ECSTATIC whoops welcomed the basket of food that Drum and Mede toted into the kitchen. She had grudgingly retained Matilda in the kitchen as a helper and, although Matilda professed to be a good cook herself, Mammy Morn allowed her to cook only the most unimportant things and even these she managed to find fault with.

Although she had professed to have nothing in the house to cook for dinner, she had food waiting for them. 'Ain' fittin' fer a dog,' she said, disdaining the meal, but the little there was

tasted good. It was only clabber, cold milk, corn pone without butter, and the remainder of Mammy Morn's pound
cake.

'Ain' a thing in this house ter eat 'n' nothin' to cook with
'cept a little smidgein o' salt I foun' in the pantry. We got to git
food in, Mista Drum, o' we a-goin' to starve. Matilda here she
a-sayin' they ain' got nothin' to eat over in New Quarters but
some collard greens 'n' sech 'n' no fatback to cook it with. Ain'
nothin' in the store at New Quarters to buy 'n' the man what
has the store in Benson he won' sell less'n he gits hard cash in
his hand. Them po' folkses over there a-starvin' to death 'n'
lookin' like we a-goin' to here.'

Claire appeared in the kitchen. She was wearing a dark
calico dress and had her head bound up in a piece of madras.
Her hands were black and she went to the sink, asking Matilda
to pour some water in the washbasin from the tea-kettle.

'There's more to do here than I reckoned on,' she said, as
she soaped her hands and rinsed them off. 'Everything needs
attention. I've just been cleaning some of the silver, but there's
so much of it and it's so black, I'll never get through. But,' she
sighed, 'I don't know what good it will do to have clean silver
if we've nothing to eat.'

Drum pointed to the basket of provisions.

'Where did all that lovely looking food come from?' Claire
ran over to the basket and lovingly patted the ham.

'From my grandmother, or perhaps I had better say my
grandmammy. She's a purentee Mandingo, whatever that is,
and she's also a conjure woman and she gave me this thing
made out of chicken feathers.' He took the charm from his
pocket, but Mammy Morn's shriek caused him to put it back.

'An Obeah woman here?' Mammy Morn gathered the
corners of her apron and flung it over her head as though to
protect herself from some occult damnation. 'O, Sweet Jesus,
help us! No wonder this place like'n it is.'

'But she's my grandmammy,' Drum repeated, 'and she says
she's going to help us.'

'Then, that good.' Mammy Morn lowered her apron.
'Obeah woman kin be right helpful if'n she on yore side, but

if'n she ain', the Good Lord better help yo'. Better yo' be daid. Yo' a-sayin' she a Mandingo – a purentee Mandingo?'

Drum nodded.

'Wa'n't never many Mandingos.' Mammy Morn seemed to feel that Falconhurst had some claim to distinction if it had a real Mandingo. 'They scarce, them Mandingos, 'n' always mighty uppity. Best-lookin' bucks I ever did see. Handsome they was. Always wanted me a Mandingo buck but never did have one. Wenches handsome too. Mandingos big 'n' strong but gentle's kittens, but they always Obeah like'n Dahomeys. They got a big green snake what they calls Damballah. He kin do anythin' for 'em. Al'ays keep 'n Obeah woman on yore side, Mista Drum. Skeered o' 'em, I am.'

'Now, Mammy Morn, that's all foolishness. There's nothing to Obeah, nothing at all.' Claire dismissed the matter while Mammy Morn shook her head dolefully. 'Look, Drum, I found out from Matilda that there's a village about five miles from here called Benson. There's a store there and I suggest that Mammy Morn and I make up a list of things we need. It will be a long one because there isn't a thing in this house to eat and, as Matilda says, nothing in the village of New Quarters either. You'll have to go in the wagon with Brute because I guess that's the only transportation we have. Anyway, you'll need a wagon to bring all the stuff back.'

'And I must visit the bank there to get some money. What I brought from New Orleans is almost gone. Here come Brute and Narcisse now. They've been looking at the cotton fields while I was visiting my Mandingo-Obeah grandmammy.' He winked at Mammy Morn, who crossed herself to ward off any evil that the mention of Obeah might bring.

Narcisse seemed jubilant as he stepped into the house, followed by Brute. They had made a circuit of all the cotton fields and regardless of the disrepair of the house and the barns and the lack of food, he insisted that one part of Falconhurst was flourishing – the cotton fields. Although he did not compliment Brute on the excellent care he had taken of them, he did seem to have a certain respect for the man's ability.

'Tell Masta Drum what you told me, Brute.'

'Masta Drum suh' – Brute was becoming indoctrinated – 'shore glad I got a masta 'gain. Things was better when we servants for life 'n' had mastas. Yes, Masta Drum suh. We planted this spring. Ol' Mista Gassaway, what was a friend o' Masta Hammond's, he guv us the seed. Men at New Quarters 'n' I we planted and chopped weeds. We a-thinkin' that if'n no one come, we git 'nough from the cotton to git us some store things for the winter. It good cotton 'n' Masta Brantome he say so, too. Now if'n we kin just live till pickin' time.'

'We'll live,' Drum assured him. 'You and I are going into Benson this afternoon. We're taking the wagon and I'm going to get enough groceries for the big house and some for New Quarters too. Then I've got to go to the bank and get some money. When we get back from Benson, Brute, we're all going over to New Quarters. We're going to need more help in the house and in the barns. Going to need carpenters and painters, if you've got any men who know how to do that.'

'Got 'em,' Brute said.

' 'N' we a-goin' to need horses 'n' mules 'n' a kerridge.' Ciceron spoke for the first time. 'Been out'n the barn 'n' foun' jes' one ol' kerridge out there. It ain' safe for to ride in, Mista Drum. It so ol' 'n' weak. Goin' to need us a buckboard too 'n' saddle horses for yo' 'n' Mista Brantome.'

'Goin' to need cows 'n' pigs too, Masta Drum suh,' Brute added. ' 'N' like'n that boy say' – he pointed to Ciceron – 'needs us workhorses 'n' mules. Used those two o' mine 'n' the mule for ploughin', but they not 'nough. Men 'n' boys they rigged up harnesses for to plough with. Used our own ploughs too. Mista Sylvester he sol' all those here. But it mighty hard for men to plough 'thout'n any meat in their bellies – jes' a mess o' greens.'

'You did well.' Drum was willing to compliment Brute even if Narcisse did not. 'I'm going to make you head man under Mr Brantome – that is, with your permission, Narcisse.'

'That boy knows a lot about cotton.' Narcisse waved grudgingly in Brute's direction. 'He can work for me, but he's giving no orders unless they come from me. Understand, Brute?'

'Yes suh, Masta Brantome suh.' Brute was sufficiently servile even for Narcisse, but there was a slightly different tone in his voice when he added, 'O' less'n they come from Masta Drum.'

Suspense hung in the air for an awkward second until Narcisse confirmed Brute's words. Again there was a silence until Drum asked, 'How come this man Sylvester was able to strip the plantation but did not come into the house? There are a lot of valuable things here.'

'He mighty 'fraid o' Obeah, Masta Drum. Mista Sylvester he born in the bayou country 'n' he know Obeah well. Big Pearl, she skeered him. She say if'n he come nigh the big house, she kill him with Obeah. She show him a li'l man she made up outa clay. She say tha's him 'n' if'n he touch the big house, she a-goin' to stick red-hot nails in it to give him a burnin' fire in his guts. Big Pearl she say nothin' goin' to hurt the big house 'cause it belong to her boys. She right smart, Big Pearl is.'

He went on to tell them how Sylvester had systematically robbed the plantation, working the people at New Quarters from early morning until after dusk. He knew cotton, Sylvester did, and he managed a bumper crop each year. Cotton was king! The northern mills were hungry for more and more of it and England was hungry too, so Sylvester got good prices, but Brute suspected, although of course he didn't know, that Sylvester did not send any more to Chris Holbrook than he had always sent. He paid the folks at New Quarters poor wages, but they never got any of them.

'Why?' Drum asked.

Brute continued his story. Sylvester had taken over the store at New Quarters and all the people who lived there had to buy from him. He kept a book for each family and everything they bought was entered into the book. They never had any money because they were always in debt to the store. After he heard that Drum was coming he sold off things at Falconhurst – horses, cattle, and mules, everything he could get his hands on. He took everything from the store at New Quarters. During the years he had been overseer, he had never spent a penny on the upkeep of barns, outbuildings, or the big house itself. Rumour was that Sylvester had retired from Falconhurst a rich man and that he had gone back to the bayou country and bought himself a place of his own.

Consequently the people at New Quarters had nothing to buy and no money to buy it with anyway. The Benson store would not sell on credit. Outside of what they raised themselves or traded, they had nothing. Gradually their livestock was traded off to get the barest of staples and when spring had come, the women picked greens and that was about all they had to live on until the seeds they had saved were planted, but as soon as they were up and ready to eat, they ate the produce, not saving any seed for next year. One by one they had killed off the laying hens, so that there were few eggs; and now they were planning to kill off the few remaining cows. After that, they would starve to death unless they were able to shoot some game. Often they had eaten woodchucks whenever they could kill one.

So this was the Falconhurst that Drum's uncle had sent him to, thinking it was a working plantation with satisfied, well-fed workers and a big house in perfect condition. It was far from it – merely a shell. Drum wondered how far the five thousand dollars and the little he had left from New Orleans would go. If it would only last until Uncle Chris' return. Well, he had enough to keep them all from starving now. He'd go into Benson and get the money and he'd start stocking up the place and repairing the big house. He'd get food in the store for the people at New Quarters.

Suddenly he felt ambitious. There was a lot to be done and it all depended on him. Falconhurst had, at one time, been a prosperous place. He'd re-establish it. He'd make it like it was before. For a moment he wished that the old times were back, when Falconhurst had been a breeding farm for slaves. No wonder it had prospered, when every black buck was worth from two to three thousand dollars and when every black wench could produce a pickaninny a year that would develop into a saleable buck or wench. Those must have been wonderful times for the owners, yet he shuddered to think of what they might have been for him. Once again he saw the old auction block in the Cabildo in New Orleans and saw himself mounting it, perhaps stripped naked so that the buyers would know what they were getting.

No, it was better the way it was. At least he was free and even if he weren't white, he was Master of Falconhurst, empty as that title might be right now. By God! He'd make it a real title. He'd be a real master.

Narcisse interrupted his thoughts. His smile was always engaging when he wanted something. 'Drum, I've been thinking. There's nobody in the overseer's house. There's a lot of paper work to be done on a place this size. Why don't I take it over for an office. Of course,' he added, 'I'll continue to sleep here, but it will be easier for me if I keep all the books and records down there and pay off the help from down there. No use in having a stream of sweaty field hands passing through the house each month. There's a desk in the old office off the kitchen and I could probably find a few chairs and take one of the beds from the servants' quarters upstairs in case I wanted to catch a short nap.'

Drum could see no reason to disagree. Narcisse always seemed to think of everything. He gave his approval.

Claire and Mammy Morn had been busy at the kitchen table and finally Claire produced a long list. 'I'm afraid you'll be frightened, Drum, but these are the things we are going to need for the house and the folks in New Quarters should have some things too. Actually there isn't a thing in the house to cook with. We've kept the list to a minimum and I've told Mammy Morn we can't have luxuries like citron and white raisins and sherry, no matter how much she wants them.'

'But we can have a bit of corn whisky.' Narcisse proudly laid two dollars down on the table. 'You'd better get a jug for the house and I'll keep one down in the overseer's house. We aren't going to be able to buy champagne here, but there's nothing wrong with good corn. I say it's better than champagne any day.'

Drum took the two dollars and put it in his pocket. He'd get Narcisse's corn, but suddenly he had lost all desire for liquor himself. He had too many plans going around in his mind. Wheels grated through the gravel out in back and he looked out the window to see Brute with the same two horses hitched to the farm wagon.

'Anyone want to go to this place called Benson?' Drum called out.

Claire pointed to the silver coffee urn that she was starting to clean with pulverized wood ashes. 'Too much to do here, Drum.'

Narcisse declined also. 'That Abel boy is coming and I'm going to teach him how to keep the other house clean.'

'Got all your clothes to unpack, Mista Drum.' Mede had never volunteered for work before.

' 'N' I a-goin' to help him.' Lucy had suddenly become as industrious as Mede.

'If'n yo' don' mind, Mista Drum' – Ciceron stood up from the table – 'I reckon as to how I'd like to go. Whilst yo' a-doin' business, wantin' to look 'round 'n' see if'n they any horses for sale. We a-goin' to need horses bad.'

'Know anything about cows or pigs?' Drum asked.

'Never saw one 'live in my life.'

'Well, come along, then.' Drum left with Ciceron and once more he felt the hard board of the wagon seat beneath him. On the long, slow miles that took them into Benson, Brute pointed out the various houses that they passed. Most of them, Drum thought, looked worse than Falconhurst. Former pretentious mansions had fallen into ruin and their once wide acres had been divided up into small farms where red-necked farmers had a few fields of cotton, a few cows, a couple of mules, but always a lot of children.

Benson too was a disappointment to Drum. He had not expected a metropolis but rather one of those neat, tidy New England villages. This place looked about as down-at-the-heels as some of the places they had passed. It boasted one fairly substantial three-storey building, which, Brute explained, was the courthouse, as Benson was now the county seat. Of course there was a general store. It sported a faded sign that said HICKS & SON over it and a long porch that was filled with churns, washtubs, and ploughs. Ciceron pointed out a livery stable as a possible supply of horses and, with Drum's permission, jumped down from the wagon and walked over there. They passed a tavern, a milliner's shop with some dusty bonnets in the window, and a hotel, which was a fairly new building. Beside it was a bank made of brick with a false front to make it appear two storeys high. One street had shade trees and a few well-kept homes, but the rest of the town was a conglomeration of slab-sided cabins and, in a special section, the Negro cabins, which were nearly as dilapidated as those at Falconhurst.

Brute pointed out the store. 'That where yo' goin' fust, Masta Drum suh?'

'Had thought of going to the bank first, Brute, but I suppose they could be getting this order together and loading it in the wagon while I'm in the bank. Yes, I'll go to the store first.'

'Watch out for Ol' Man Hicks. He's a mean varmint. Cheat the eyeteeth out'n yo'. My wife a-sayin' she needed a poun' o' lard. Didn't have no money, but we did have a good new scythe. Scythe worth 'bout three dollars, but Ol' Hicks took the scythe 'n' gave me 'bout a half pound o' lard. Watch out for him.'

Drum walked up the wide wooden steps that led to the store. There were several men sitting on the veranda, their feet dangling over the edge. All were dressed more or less alike – wide straw hats and butternut clothing that was begrimed and bepatched. Everyone stared at him and he wished now that he had changed his clothes, because he still had on those he had dressed in that morning. The men kept quiet but continued to stare as he walked across the porch and into the store. When he stepped across the threshold, he heard a loud guffaw of laughter that rose above the snickerings. Then there was a hoot of derision.

Somebody asked, 'That the nigger what comin' to live at Falconhurst?'

'That's him all right.'

'Nat Sylvester certainly fixed that bastard.'

'Shore did. Good for Nat.'

'Nat a right smart fella.'

'Always says anything yo' kin git 'way from a nigger's good. Nat sure stripped that plantation.'

'Damn glad he did. Ain' got no use for them uppity mustees.'

Drum walked out of range of hearing any more remarks as he crossed the store to a zinc-covered counter where a stout man in a striped bed-tick apron regarded him with tiny eyes, deep set in the fat of his cheeks.

'Yo' a-wantin' somethin'?' There was a note of belligerence in his voice as he thrust forth a small pointed chin that protruded from under his fat cheeks. 'Yo' that Falconhurst nigger what jes' came?'

Short as the time he had been there was, news evidently travelled fast in Benson. Drum decided that there was no use arguing with the man. He supposed that in the eyes of the men on the porch and also of this man, whom he supposed to be Hicks, he was 'that Falconhurst nigger'. These men, he thought, were as ignorant as the Negroes except that they could probably read and figure. He nodded his head in answer to the question.

'Cash on the barrelhead, boy! Hard cash! Ain' trustin' no nigger, even if he white-lookin' like yo'. Don' know what the Maxwells would of said, seein' yo' the owner of Falconhurst. Remember Ham Maxwell, I do. I nothin' more'n a saplin' an' he went off to war. Fine man. Quality folks, the Maxwells. Never tho't there'd be a nigger bastard runnin' Falconhurst. Well, what yo' a-wantin'?'

Drum realized that if they were to eat, he'd have to swallow the insults and stand there like any other Negro, servile and humiliated.

'I have a list of things here I'd like to buy.' Drum's voice trembled as he tried to control it and his fingers itched to squeeze the man's fat neck between them. Only by making himself feel superior to this ignorant lout could he deal with him, but he realized he must not let this sense of superiority show. 'Let's see! It starts off with twenty hams, twenty pieces of side meat, a barrel of white flour, a barrel of corn meal, a barrel of hominy, ten gallons of molasses, a barrel of white sugar, ten dozen eggs—'

'Whoa, there, boy.' Hicks held up a protesting hand, fat, pudgy, and grimy. 'All that's a-goin' to cost yo' money. Yo' got money to pay for it? Ain' a-gittin' no credit here. No credit never to no niggers whatsoever.'

'If I haven't got it here' – Drum took out his wallet – 'I've got it on the other side of the street in the bank.'

'Then, yo' jes' go 'head 'n' read off that list o' better still, yo' give it to me 'n' I'll tot it up for yo'. I ain' a-puttin' nothin' in that wagon less'n I gits paid for it.'

He took the long list that Drum handed him and with the stub of a pencil, which he kept wetting with his lips, he priced each item.

'And two gallons of corn whisky,' Drum added.

Hicks did not look up but kept on figuring. Drum wondered how a man who looked so stupid could keep all the prices in his head and suspected he wasn't being too careful about what he was being charged.

'Vaniller!' Hicks came across an item. 'We ain' got that. 'Magine! Vaniller in a nigger's house.'

'We have an excellent cook.' Drum felt he had to retaliate in some way, show some superiority, make some effort towards being recognized as something besides a field hand. 'I brought her from New Orleans.'

Hicks looked up at him, thrusting out his chin even more belligerently, but kept on with his work. When he had finished, he began adding up the long column.

'Figures as how yo' owe me perzactly two hundred two dollars and thirty-eight cents. Yes, boy, that's how it is 'n' don' ask me to make it an even two hundred. Ain' a-doin' business that way. Ain' takin' off a cent. Yo' pay me two hundred two dollars and thirty-eight cents 'n' I'll have your boy put it in the wagon. Even give yo' both a peppermint drop, 'cause that's what I gives a nigger what orders more'n a dollar's wuth. Ain' a-cheatin' yo'. Gives yo' back the list so's yo' kin check it off onc't yo' gits to Falconhurst. Honest, I am. Ain' cheatin' nobody. Well, boy, whereat's the money?'

Drum was aware that he had only about $175 in his wallet along with the two that Narcisse had given him. He had not expected a bill for groceries to come to more than a hundred dollars, but it was a long list with a lot of big things in it. Mammy Morn had not stinted herself.

'I'll pay you a hundred seventy-five dollars now and the rest when I come back from the bank.'

'Loads a hundred seventy-five dollars wuth o' stuff into the wagon. No credit, 'member? Yo' a-comin' back from the bank with the money 'n' I fills the rest o' the order, but yo' a-goin' to git what yo' pay for 'n' not a goddam red cent more.'

'My uncle, Christopher Holbrook of Boston, has sent money on to me at the bank. Don't worry, you'll get your pay.' Suddenly Boston seemed another world, another planet.

' 'Members him. High cockalorum Union cap'n round here during the war. 'Member him 'n' his nigger boy Drummage what called himself Maxwell. Ain' no one in Benson got no use for that Holbrook. Cheated everyone outa their farms. Kept Falconhurst for hisself, though.'

There was no use in arguing with the man. Drum was aware that Hicks held all the cards. He consoled himself with anticipating the pleasure he would have when he returned and slapped the money down on Hicks' dirty counter. Without answering him, he went out the door to tell Brute to go in and help Hicks load as much as he was willing.

'Look at 'em stovepipe pantaloons.' The derision on the porch started again.

'Never did see a nigger afore with yella hair.'

'Goddam bastard, he right white-like.'

'He jes' 'nother damn mustee.'

'Hates mustees. Give me a black nigger every time. Knows their place. These mustees too uppity. Thinks they as good's a white man anytime.'

'He a pretty boy, though. Better lock yore wimmen up o' they a-goin' to git raped. Yore ol' lady a-gittin' raped by this mustee, Newt, ain' never a-goin' to want yo' 'gain.'

'Sayin's as how a white woman a-gittin' raped by a nigger ain' never got no use for white man's pleasurin'.'

196

'He a-rapin' any white woman, he a-goin' to git hisself hung.'

'He well hung anyway. He a nigger, ain' he?'

Drum pretended not to hear the remarks as he made his way across the dusty street to the bank. Passing the granite statue of the Confederate Soldier in front of the courthouse with its cannon and pyramid of cannon balls, he wished he could aim it at the store and blow the whole damn place to hell and gone. Damn ignorant red-necks! No wonder their plantations were run-down, when they sat all day on Hicks' porch. No wonder they were so poor. He was walking so fast, he could feel the sweat channelling down his spine and he hoped he wouldn't smell of it when he got in the bank. To him it already seemed that he could detect a certain musk from his body. Ridiculous! He was just imagining it.

The bank was a small but substantial building, although its false second storey fooled nobody. It did, however, boast a screen door – a mere framework of laths covered with mosquito netting, but it gave Drum an idea for Falconhurst. Why not have some lath frames made for each window and door to keep the hordes of flies out of the house? He examined the door carefully, noting its construction, before he opened it and walked in.

Through a brass grillwork a man peered out at him. Drum knew he elicited more than the usual amount of curiosity, being a stranger. He walked over to the man, a florid-faced individual with bushy iron-grey whiskers, and inquired for the manager of the bank. The teller pointed to a door that Drum noticed bore a brass plaque that said PRESIDENT.

'He's alone, but better knock afore yo' goes in.' The bushy whiskers parted to show a red mouth. 'Sometimes he don' like it, bein' disturbed.'

Drum did as he was instructed, knocking, waiting to hear the words 'Come in,' turning the knob, and entering the room. The bank president whisked a glass from his desk, turned in his chair, and challenged Drum with a stare that immediately catalogued him for who and what he was.

'Name's Jenkins. What yo' a-wantin'?'

Drum was glad that he was not addressed as 'boy', which he had come to discover applied to any Negro, regardless of his age. He noticed the chair beside Jenkins' rolltop desk and deliberately sat down without being asked, wondering if Jenkins would insist on his standing, but nothing was said. Drum felt a little more comfortable.

'I am Drummond Maxwell and my uncle in Boston, Christopher Holbrook, has written me that he has transferred some funds here for me – five thousand dollars to be exact.'

Mr Jenkins fitted his fingers deliberately together, one after another, and peered at Drum over his steel-rimmed spectacles. 'Yo' a-sayin' yo' Drummond Maxwell. Yo' must be the nigger what came to Falconhurst last night. Yo're a-sayin' it, but that don' mean I a-believin' it. How I know yo' this Drummond Maxwell? 'N' if yo' are, don' yo' know better'n to sit yo'self down 'thout'n I say so? Yo' ain' a-thinkin' yo' a white man, be yo'? Ain' thinkin' yo' a-comin' here to Benson to put on airs? Well, not by a damn sight. Here in Alabama a nigger's a nigger, no matter how white-lookin' he is. Stan' up!'

Drum stood. As much as he resented the command, he stood. He was becoming inured to this sort of treatment. But he did not stand humbly; he stood straight and tall.

Now Jenkins had to look up at him and he removed his glasses. 'Yes, we got us five thousand dollars here what was sent us by a bank in Boston 'n' by a Mista Holbrook. Got it right there.' He half turned in his chair and pointed to the big safe behind him, which was decorated with a medallion showing a pastoral scene of cows grazing in a lush meadow while a train sped by in one direction and a steamboat came down the river in another. 'That five thousand dollars is right in that safe a-waitin' for this Drummond Maxwell whenever he come.'

'Well, here I am.'

Again Jenkins inventoried Drum. 'That's what yo're a-sayin', but yore sayin' it ain' makin' me believe it. How I know some fancy-dressed nigger ain' jes' a-comin' in here 'n' a-sayin' he this Drummond Maxwell 'n' gittin' the money in his hand 'n' skippin' out. Then a week later another dressed-up mustee a-comin' in and he a-sayin' he Drummond Maxwell 'n' askin' for five thousand dollars. How I a-goin' to know which un's the right un? Ain' handin' out no money less'n I know yo're he. Yo' got anyone to identify yo'?'

'Mr Brantome is my overseer at Falconhurst. I can bring him in. He can identify me.'

' 'N' if'n yo' a nigger, he mus' be one too. Ain' no white man a-goin' to oversee for a nigger. His word ain' no better'n yourn. All I know he might be in cahoots with yo'. That money a-goin' to stay right there' – he pointed over his shoulder to the safe – 'till the real Drummond Maxwell come in here with a white man who I a-knowin' tha's a-goin' to say it the right one. That's the way it is, boy. That's the way it a-goin' to be. If'n yo're the fellow, yo' go git yourself someone to come in with yo' 'n' yo' kin have the money. Till then, don' bother me to come in 'gain.'

'But the bank in New Orleans did not question me.'

'They slack, those city banks. We ain' slack. Got to pertect our depositors. Five thousand dollars a lot o' money to pass out to the fust mustee what comes along a-sayin' it's his'n.'

'My uncle in Boston is—'

'Whoa, there. He ain' yore uncle. Knows all 'bout yo'. Yore pappy he Drummage Maxwell, though he never had no right to the Maxwell name. Yore mammy she Miz Sophie Maxwell what this Drummage raped. But that Cap'n Holbrook he married 'em up legal-like 'n' then he produce a will what gave Falconhurst to this boy Drum under him's trustee. That time Union soldiers here 'n' it passed the courts 'n' now the Federal Gov'ment say anything which pass through a Union Court got to stand. Ain' a-goin' to dispute yore right to the land such as it is. If'n yo' this Maxwell, yo' kin have it.'

'After a white overseer ruined it.'

'Now, now!' Jenkins pointed an accusing finger at Drum. 'He a right honest man 'n' 'spected 'round here. Sent a draft to Mista Holbrook in Boston every year right through this bank. He right honest, Mr Sylvester.'

Drum was about to speak when Jenkins held up his hand.

'Ain' disputin' that yo're Maxwell, though yo' don' have no right to the name. Maxwells was quality folks 'round here 'n' never suspected a nigger a-goin' to bear that name. No, ain' disputin' yore right to Falconhurst but could if'n I wanted to. Could have the sheriff keep yo' off'n the property till yo' identified yo'self. Ain' my business. My business's bankin'. If yo' kin prove who yo' are, yo' kin have the money quick's a wink, but till yo' prove it, yo' cain' touch a goddam cent. Guess that's final 'nough, ain' it, 'n' there's the door.'

Why carry on the pointless argument further? Drum realized the futility of anything he might say. Jenkins had a solid foundation for his refusal – a cleverly thought-out one. Evidently the whole village had conspired against Drum. Certainly there was no white man in the vicinity who could identify him or would if he could. For the first time in his life he was penniless. After paying Hicks, he'd not have a cent left. All he would have was enough food to last them a few weeks and a roof over their heads. He wondered if Mammy Morn knew anything about picking greens – that might be all they would have to live on, with an occasional woodchuck. He smiled in remembrance of the shooting lessons he had once taken. Was it as easy to hit a woodchuck as a bull's-eye?

Dragging his feet through the dust, he walked back to Hicks' store and this time he did not even hear the snickering and the remarks from the front porch loiterers. Brute had the wagon loaded and he saw Ciceron running up the street from the livery stable.

He walked in and laid his last $175 down on the counter.

'That is all I'll take today.' He avoided looking at Hicks, keeping his head down. He felt like a proper nigger not daring to look at a white man.

'Thought so,' Hicks sniggered. 'Hank Jenkins ain' no fool. He been a-talkin' 'roun' town that when this-yere Maxwell nigger turned up he ain' jes' goin' to walk in 'n' snatch his money. Nosiree! Not by a damn sight. But they's one hunerd 'n' seventy-five dollars o' groceries 'n' sech 'n' two gallons o' corn liquor in yore wagon 'n' here's yore bill. Matter of fact, it come to only a hundred seventy-three 'n' seventy-five cents, a dollar 'n' two bits in change.' He laid the money down on the counter and reached in a glass showcase, taking out two red and white striped peppermint balls. 'Them's for yo' 'n' yore boy.'

Drum pocketed the dollar bill, the two dimes, and the nickel. He looked at the two peppermint candies, then finally picked them up. He jiggled them in his hand a moment, feeling their stickiness on his moist palm. He handed them to Hicks, who automatically put out his hand to take them.

'I think you need these more than I do, Mr Hicks.' For the first time Drum smiled. 'With these you might even be a man.' Hicks' face grew red and he started sputtering like a wet fire-cracker while Drum turned and walked out of the store.

'Oh, Mista Drum!' Ciceron was so excited he was dancing an absurd shuffle. 'They got some spankin' fine horses down to de livery stable. Wantin' yo' should see 'em. Nice team of greys I'd admire to drive 'n' some good saddle horses 'n' bout ten workhorses 'n' some mules. Betta come right now, Mista Drum.'

Drum thanked Ciceron and shook his head, hating to take away the fellow's pleasure at having discovered horses for him. He motioned to Ciceron to climb up on to the load and they started back towards Falconhurst. He was going home to a ruined house on a ruined plantation. His only assets were a load of groceries, one dollar and a quarter in his pocket, and five thousand dollars in the bank, which he couldn't touch.

Well, he consoled himself, he could go back to New Orleans and take the place that Harlequin had left vacant. That would be one way of earning a living. Yet he doubted if he would be able to do it. One, perhaps two, but never six. Never! So that was out too.

CHAPTER TWENTY

THE ARRIVAL OF the wagon brought Mammy Morn flying out of the back door. She exclaimed over the barrels and the hams and the bundles wrapped in newspaper with even more ecstatic whoops than she had earlier greeted the lone basket from Big Pearl. Drum knew that there would be some things missing and she would be disappointed, but at least they had enough to eat for a while, although he would be able to do little for the starving folks at New Quarters. When he came in through the back door, he found Claire sitting at the kitchen table surrounded by a bevy of black women and he heard female voices in other parts of the house. Two of the women were carrying dishes from the butler's pantry to the sink, washing and drying them and carrying them back. She waved to him and then got up and walked him through the pantry into the dining-room.

He was amazed at the transformation in the room. Although it was still shabby, it was clean, with shining silver on the long mahogany sideboard, the table polished like a mirror, and even the big fan over the table once more hung solidly on its two hinges. Sounds of work came from the others parts of the house and while she led him through the drawing-room out into the hall, he saw other women in patched osnaburg dresses, working away with brooms and dustpans, dusters and wet rags. From the drawing-room, she led him across the hall into what must have been a parlour, because it was even more elaborately furnished than the drawing-room, with Belter chairs and sofas, each one a maze of hand-carved rosewood.

'There are more changes upstairs.' She gestured towards the curving staircase, which gleamed in the dim light. 'I caught a girl this morning trying to sneak out the back door' – she looked at Drum accusingly – 'who said her name was Debbie.' She waited a moment to see if Drum would make any confession, but he tried to look unconcerned, although he felt the flush mounting to his cheeks.

He wanted to confess, yet he did not dare to. There should not, he felt, be any secrets between Claire and himself. He was in love with Claire, of that he was sure, but Claire, sleeping with Narcisse, could not solve his immediate problems for him. Debbie could and he realized somewhere back in his mind that he was already anticipating tonight, when he would not lie passive as a log of wood but would be the aggressor. Try as he may, he could not put the thought from his mind while he looked at Claire, anxious to know what she might say next.

She too had hoped that he would say something about it, but when he didn't, she continued, her voice as casual as before. 'She told me she was from New Quarters, so I told her to get back there as quickly as possible – run if she had to – and see if she could round up twenty women who would like to earn two bits for a day's work. They arrived in about half an hour, marching like an army, shouldering brooms and mops, carrying pails and even a precious can of soft soap. Mammy Morn discovered an old bottle of lemon oil, which is the best furniture polish in the world, and we've been at it ever since you left. At least the house is clean, but, oh, Drum dear, there is so much that has to be done, so very much.'

He opened the heavy front door, noticing how the brass knob and hinges had been shined, and led her out on to the wide veranda, glancing up at the soaring columns, then dropping his eyes. For a long moment he surveyed the rank, overgrown garden, the noble avenue of trees, and turned again to look at the house itself. Slowly, as though admitting defeat, he explained what had happened in Benson – the insults he had received at the grocery store, the inability to get his money from the bank; then, reaching his hand in his pocket, he drew out the dollar and the pitiful amount of change.

'That, my dear, is all I have to my name right at this moment. That, this ruined house' – he kicked at the scaling paint on the base of a column – 'and some food on the wagon out in back. I can't even pay these poor women, can't pay you or Narcisse or Mammy Morn or even poor Ciceron. I don't know when if ever I shall be able to get the money out of the bank or what we are going to do for food when these groceries run out.'

She tried to console him with words that she knew were empty. He could get the money. Of course he could. It belonged to him. He must write immediately to Boston; he must write to his bank in New Orleans. Who was the man Brute had said had given him the cottonseed? He must find out and go to him. Surely if he were kind enough to give Brute the cottonseed, he would help Drum. Oh, there were a million things to do to get the money and now he must not worry any longer.

'The girl Debbie' – her encouragement and the feeling that she loved him as much as he loved her had made him contrite and now he wanted to confess – 'I didn't know about her. Really, Claire. She was already in my bed when I went into the room. And, you'll find it hard to believe, I didn't do anything to her.' He neglected to say that she didn't do anything to him. 'Forgive me, dear, I wasn't being unfaithful to you. I've been so in love with you for so long and it's all become so hopeless.'

'Naturally I am jealous of her' – Claire clutched his arm – 'and naturally I hate her because she is free to have what I cannot have. Oh, Drum, my very darling, there is so much I want to say to you, but I cannot. So much, dear. I do love you but I love Narcisse too. I don't know how the whole thing is going to turn out, but you'll end up by hating me.'

'Never,' he assured her, squeezing her hand. 'I'm too much in love with you.'

'But you will.' Her fingers gripped his arm through the thin linen of his coat sleeve. 'As for Debbie, I shall not allow myself to be jealous and I shall not hate her. It's an old Southern custom, held over from slave days, you know. A bed wench! There was one for every unmarried man on the plantation – for every white man, I mean. Even for the boys, and some of them started having bed wenches at the age of thirteen or fourteen. Of course it was purely a physical relationship. There was never any thought of love between these white men and their black bed wenches. So I know you will never love this Debbie and we'll keep her on here as parlourmaid and you shall have her nights. I can stand it. Every Southern woman always has had to share the man she loved with a nigger wench. Otherwise you and I would not be here. Some black woman had to give herself to a white man—'

'It was the other way around in my case.' Drum remembered the marble gravestones across the brook. 'A white woman gave herself to a black man. That may account for all the animosity I met with today. Then, too, everyone seems to hate the name of Holbrook around here. I thought the war was over, but they still hate Northerners and Uncle Chris in particular. So it's no wonder they hate me. I'm everything they detest – coloured blood, a Northerner, and they probably think I have more money than they have.'

Claire held up a warning finger, then placed it on his lips. 'Sh-h-h! We've talked enough. Let's not discuss this question of black and white any longer. There is nothing we can do about it, so let's face it. I always say, "Fight what you can change, but accept what you cannot."' She allowed him to kiss her finger, then took it away but without reproaching him. 'Look, Drum dear, we can't make our blood white, but right this minute you can go in and eat a scrumptious dinner that Mammy Morn is going to fix for you from the new supplies. She's a treasure, she is. I'm so glad we found her.'

'But I can't pay her or those women from Falconhurst.'

'Right at this moment it doesn't matter.' She opened the big front door and led him into the semidarkness of the hall. Reaching her arms up around his neck, she pulled his face down to hers and kissed him. 'Now does my Drum feel better? Just promise me one thing, Drum. No, two things,' she added.

'Anything, Claire.'

'First' – she held up a finger, then snatched it away as he tried to touch it with his lips – 'you will not tell anyone, least of all Narcisse, that you didn't get the money at the bank today.'

'But why?' He could not understand her reasoning. Surely if she could bear his bad news, Narcisse could too. 'Sooner or later he will have to know. We need so much. Barns to be fixed, horses and livestock to be purchased, and men to work for us and—'

'None of which you could do today even if you had the money. So promise.'

'If you say so.' He nodded his head.

'Now, your second promise. It may not as be as easy as the first.'

'If it's for you, it will be.'

'Then, you must promise me that you will never kiss Debbie.'

'I have no desire to.'

'I'm glad. It's another old Southern custom that a white man never kissed his bed wench. Silly as it may seem, it was just not done. Everything else was considered quite blameless except kissing. Now I understand why. Kissing is a token of love. The rest is just a meeting of bodies.'

'Again I promise.' It seemed a small thing to acquiesce to when he had no desire to kiss the girl anyway. Although he was, even now, aroused and in one part of his mind he was looking forward to his night with Debbie, he was willing to surrender her if it would make Claire happy. 'Send her away, dear, if it will make you any happier.'

She shook her head knowingly. 'A man's a man, Drum, and certain things are as necessary to him as food and water. I'd not deny you that, but I must be reassured that there is no love – no real love – mixed up in it.'

'Can you imagine me falling in love with Debbie?' he asked.

'Hardly.' She smiled back at him, moving close to him again, so that their bodies touched. She lingered there only a moment, then stepped back. He noticed her eyes dropping and this time he was not ashamed. After all, his condition was a compliment to her and he felt she recognized this fact. He did not realize how much she gloried in it.

'Now let's go out into the kitchen.' There was a forced gaiety in her words, which told him she had much rather stay than go. 'I want to see all the wonderful things you brought back from Benson. I'm so excited and I know Mammy Morn is. Just wait and see what she cooks for dinner tonight. I'm getting hungry already.'

'And so am I but not for food.'

She ignored his words and took his arm and led him through the clean rooms into the kitchen, where Mammy Morn had Mede, Lucy, and Ciceron all rolling in barrels and stowing them wherever she thought they would be most convenient.

'My, my, Mista Drum' – she stopped directing the boys long enough to beam at him – 'we shore a-goin' to eat now.'

He held up a warning finger. 'Cook what you want, Mammy, but no waste. This has got to last us a long time.'

She regarded him as though he were not very bright. 'Me waste food? Ain' never wasted a scrap in my life. Good cook knows how to use all the scraps – makin' soups 'n' things. Yo' never know today what yo' a-eatin' that was lef' over from yisterday. Many's the time I thinks it better second day than the fust. Yo' leave that to me, Mista Drum.'

Mede stopped his work, wiping the sweat from his forehead. 'This ain' no job for a body servant,' he grumbled to Drum. 'Ain' never tooken no one's bidding but yourn 'n' now Mammy Morn she a-comin' 'long 'n' a-sayin', "H'ist that barrel o' sugar in here, boy," 'n' if'n I say no, she a-sayin' she goin' to give me a swipe o' her han'.' He came over closer to Drum and whispered, ' 'N' another thing, Mista Drum, my mammy, Big Pearl, she say to come over to her house with me right 'way. She got something mighty 'portant to tell you.'

Drum nodded absently, thinking that whatever Big Pearl might have to tell him could not be of any particular importance. The only important thing now was money and how to get it.

'We all got to pitch in and help, Mede. But just now I need you more as a body servant. Get a bath ready for me and some clean clothes.' Drum was amused at the alacrity with which Mede dropped the bundle he was carrying on to the kitchen table and went to the stove to pour out a can of hot water from the iron tea-kettle.

After his bath Drum felt a little better and, as it was cooler, he invited Claire to take a little walk with him. Once again they came out on the front portico and made their way by means of an unkempt path around the house and by the abandoned barns to a road not entirely overgrown with weeds, which led down a slope to the overseer's house. When they got there, Narcisse was just closing the front door, oblivious to the screams of terror that were coming from within.

'Bedding that boy Abel down here,' he winked at them as though to apologize for the screams. 'Got to get him used to it. Little bastard says he's afraid of haunts, staying there all alone, but a couple of good swipes with this' – he flipped the belt he was about to buckle around his waist – 'gave him something to think about besides haunts. He'll stay. I found some old spancels in the barn and he's got to stay.'

'Spancels?' The word was unfamiliar to Drum.

'Leg irons. Found an old pair in one of the barns – in fact, a whole heap of them. Used to use them a lot in slave times but not much now or Sylvester would have taken them.' Narcisse started to walk back to the house with them, but Drum stopped.

'You chained him up and beat him and intend to leave him there all alone?'

'Sure, why not? Remember what I said? You've got to discipline these niggers. They've been running wild too long.'

Drum hesitated. He did not approve of Narcisse's actions; on the other hand, he could not discredit Narcisse's authority by intervening. Authority and discipline were necessary, Drum knew, to handle the field hands and get work out of them. If he discredited Narcisse before this young lad, word would soon spread that any man or boy having a grievance could go over Narcisse's head and appeal to Drum. No, this was not the time to interfere, but he would have a talk with Narcisse later. Despite the shrieks of terror from within the house, Drum decided not to act. He wanted to go inside and let the boy loose, but he merely inquired, 'Anything for him to sleep on in there?'

'Nigger sleeps on the floor. That's good enough for him.'

'I'll send Matilda down later with some supper for the boy

and a couple of blankets.' Claire seemed vexed with Narcisse.

'Slave days are over, Narcisse.' Drum's anger increased. 'These people have had it hard enough as it is.'

Narcisse laughed at them both. 'You're new to niggers, Drum. You've got to make them afraid of you first off. No nigger's going to respect you unless he fears you. You use a whip on a horse, you use a whip on a nigger. It's all the same.' He put one arm around Claire's waist and the other around Drum's shoulders.

'But no whippings,' Drum said, resenting the weight of Narcisse's arm around his shoulder.

'Not unless you say so.' Narcisse was his own charming self, completely unperturbed. 'Did you get the money in Benson, Drum?'

Claire answered before Drum had a chance to open his mouth. 'You should see the dinner Mammy Morn's getting for us. That will answer your question. As the Negroes say, "We're living high on the hog now."'

'And I'm hungry too,' Narcisse admitted. 'Been working that Abel boy all the afternoon. Hope you don't mind, Drum, but we toted a bed from the servants' quarters down there, along with some tables and chairs. When I work late, keeping records, I might not want to come back to the house to sleep. Come on, let's go!' He quickened his pace until they were nearly running. 'Let's eat!'

What a dinner it turned out to be! Mammy Morn, who would not have ordinarily quitted her place in the kitchen, stood in the doorway of the butler's pantry while she watched them enjoy the supper of baked ham, candied yams, spoon bread, and all the other items she had concocted out of the new groceries. The big silver coffee urn shone, the silver knives and forks were agleam, and even Mede and Lucy stood straighter, while a lad recruited from New Quarters remained out in the pantry and pulled the big fan over the table slowly back and forth to keep off the flies and cool the air. Drum told them of the screened doors and windows at the bank and everyone became enthusiastic over them, including Drum himself, until he realized he had no money to pay for them.

After dinner they sat a long time at the table. One extravagance Drum had permitted himself at Hicks' was a box of cigars and, although they were far from being Havanas, they were satisfying. Lacking brandy, Mammy Morn brought in a tray of steaming hot toddies made with the corn whisky that Narcisse had contributed. With a well-filled stomach, the smoke of a cigar in his nostrils, and the sharp, sweet tang of the toddies in his mouth, Drum almost forgot his troubles. The candlelight hid the shabbiness of the room and he felt he had travelled years back in time to the era when Falconhurst was functioning as a slave-breeding plantation with plenty of money behind it.

Mede reached down to flick away a few ashes from the tablecloth with his napkin. 'Gittin' dark outside,' he whispered so low that Drum could hardly hear him. 'Mammy 'spectin' us.'

Drum was so contented that he was in no mood to leave the candlelight and Claire's face, which appeared among the flames of the big candelabrum, but there was an urgency in Mede's voice. With a request to the others to excuse him, he followed Mede out into the kitchen.

'Mammy say come, we'd better come. She ain' no triflin' nigger. She a conjure woman 'n' we'd better do's she say.'

Conjure woman or not, she was Drum's grandmother and he supposed the least he could do was to humour her. Probably she wanted to hang another bunch of chicken feathers around his neck. He'd go back to the table and make a real excuse this time, but what would he say? Could he tell them the truth – that he was going to visit his grandmother, who was a conjure woman? Both Claire and Narcisse would think him even more ignorant than he thought himself to be. What would be his excuse? Something to do with Mede? No, Mede was only a servant. Some question Brute might want to ask him? Brute was a servant too, but he did have some standing. That was it. He went back into the dining-room and told Claire and Narcisse that Brute had asked to talk with him over at New Quarters and that he would be back later. They excused him, although he noted a look of disappointment on Claire's face.

It was dark outside, with no moon, but Mede seemed to know the path that led down the ravine, across the ruined bridge, and up the other hill. Drum shivered as they passed the burial plot, where the marble stones made ghostly patches of dim white in the night. They both hurried along until they could see the light from Big Pearl's cabin. She had evidently heard them coming, because she was standing in the doorway, silhouetted against the light from inside. Tonight her greeting was more exuberant than it had been that morning and she flung open her huge arms, enveloping them both and drawing them into the cabin. Closing the door carefully, she pulled in the latchstring and tested the big wooden latch to see that it was secure. Drum noticed that all the shutters were closed with crossbar pieces of wood to keep them securely locked.

'Ain' wantin' nobody a-lookin' in nor listenin' 'roun'.' She indicated the closed door with a majestic wave of her arm without taking her eyes from Drum and Mede. Clapping her hands together in almost childlike ecstasy, she came over to them, stroking their faces and letting her hands slide down over their arms. 'My, oh, my! What pretty boys I'se got. Mede he so big 'n' tall 'n' pretty 'n' black, 'n' Drum he so nice 'n' pretty 'n' big 'n' white. Cain' tell which un the prettiest. Jes' cain'.' Lowering her voice, she whispered to Drum. 'Yo' a-needin' money, boy?'

'Needin' it bad, Grandmammy,' It seemed natural for him to reply to her in her own dialect. 'But how yo' a-knowin' that?'

She took her hands from his shoulders and nodded knowingly, as though loath to give away her secret. 'If'n yo' wa'nt my own boy, I'd say it 'cause I conjure. Conjure do a lot o' things, but conjure didn' do this. Stonewall Jackson Lee, he the boy what sweep out the bank, come a-ridin' out to see me this afternoon after the bank close. Stonewall he in love with a married woman what won' pay no 'tention to him, so I made up an Obeah charm for him. If'n he kin git it under her pillow, she a-goin' to git such an itch she cain' live 'thout'n him. He a-tellin' me he hear Ol' Man Jenkins talkin' 'bout yo'. He a-sayin' yo' ain' gittin' no money outa him till hell freeze over.

He a-sayin' 'tain' right for no coloured boy to have that money 'n' git biggity 'n' fix up Falconhurst. Don' wan' no biggity yaller boy 'roun' Benson.'

'It's my money. I'll find some way to get it.' Drum realized as he said it how futile his efforts might be.

'Yo' don' need it.' Big Pearl slowly lowered herself into a big wooden chair and leaned forward to put her hands on her knees. 'Don' need it 'tall. Yo' got plenty. More'n in that piddlin' bank. Reckon as how I'll put a curse on that Jenkins anyway. Goin' to put a fire in his belly. Buts I was a-sayin', yo' got plenty o' money right here at Falconhurst.'

Drum studied his grandmother's face, wondering if perhaps she might be more than a little crazy. Money at Falconhurst? That was impossible. He glanced at Mede, who was looking at Big Pearl, slack-mouthed in wonderment and absolute belief.

'Kin git it for yo', I kin' – she emphasized each word with a nod of her head – 'but they's some things I gotta talk 'bout first. Might's well set, boys.'

They both took straight-backed chairs and she motioned to them to draw them up to her as close as possible. She seemed intrigued with their appearance, looking at them again long and searchingly.

'Kin see yore pappy in yo', Drum. He the bes'-looking boy I ever did see. His pappy, Drumson, lighter in colour 'n' mighty handsome but not so fine-lookin's Drummage. That 'cause Drummage he half Mandingo 'n' lookin' like Mede – not this yere Mede but my Mandingo Mede, who sired Ol' Man Wilson on me.'

She turned to study Mede. 'Yo' a-lookin' like purentee Mandingo, boy, jes' like'n the fust Mede. Yore pappy Zanzibar he a right powerful man. He was a-studdin' Miz Sophie regular-like whilst she married to that 'Pollon man.' She sighed and held out a hand to both of them. 'Guess I a-gittin' ol'. Tol' yo' all that afore. Cain' always 'member what I says but knowin' what I want to say now.'

There was a long silence during which Drum watched a moth circling around one of the candles. Its wings finally touched the flame and it was consumed in a tiny burst of fire before its charred body fell to the table. Mede shuffled his feet and sucked his thumb, not daring to break the silence, until at length Big Pearl spoke again.

'Kin git money for yo', boy.' She nodded in Drum's direction. ''Nough to git Falconhurst goin' 'gain. It yore money, boy, but I the only one what knows 'bout it. It comes from Masta Warren Maxwell what was pappy to Masta Hammond Maxwell what was pappy to Miz Sophie. Nobody a-knowin' 'bout that money but me. I ain' never been usin' but jes' a li'l of it 'n' ain' been lettin' none of them worthless niggers at New Quarters know 'bout it. It all safe 'n' soun'.'

Drum was now convinced that his grandmother's mind was wandering, but he continued to listen, if only out of politeness to the old lady.

'But afore I gives yo' that money, yo' got to make me a promise, Drum. I got to git me a sacred promise afore I gives yo' that money.'

'I'll promise.' He was in the mood to humour her.

Her eyes met his and he felt the intensity of their gaze. She was probing his consciousness to know if he was telling the truth. Evidently she was satisfied that he was.

She placed her hand on Mede's knee. 'Now, Mede here, he my own boy – the onliest one I got now that Ol' Man Wilson 'n' Drummage is daid. Po' Mede he's black 'n' he ain' nothin' but a servant 'n' never will be. He ain' got no chance. He ain' like'n yo'. Yo' my boy too, but yo're white o' mos' white. Yo' got everything – Falconhurst 'n' Mede 'n' all the servants yo' want. But my Mede he got to have somethin' too. Ain' fittin' that he be nothin' but a servant. My boy Drummage he live in the big house 'n' he not a-sleepin' in the servants' rooms. He sleepin' in the big room right 'longside Miz Sophie. 'N' now yo', Drum, yo' a-livin' in the big house, but yo' ain' sleepin' in no servant's room, but Mede he is. I wants it changed. Mede he jes' so good's yo', Drum, though he blacker. Gotta make me a promise, Drum, that Mede he ain' goin' to be a servant no more.'

'I'll be glad to,' Drum acceded. If she wanted Mede to

transfer his bed from the third floor to the second, it would be very little to ask.

' 'N' Mede he kin eat his vittles in the dinin'-room 'longside that mustee boy 'n' girl what yo' have.' It was a statement, not a question.

Drum nodded assent.

'Mede he a-goin' to have good trogs too – jes' so good's yo'.'

'Can't promise that until we go to New Orleans again. No tailor here would make clothes for a black boy.'

'Then, he kin use some o' yourn. Yo' both of a size.'

'I'll give him some.'

'Mede he a-goin' to git ten dollars every week jes' for hisself.'

Drum laughed. 'If I've got ten dollars to pay him, he'll get it.'

'Mede he a-goin' to have a voice in Falconhurst too. It ain' his'n, but he a-goin' to have a voice.'

'All right, Grandmammy, we'll all work together.'

Big Pearl seemed satisfied. The tip of her tongue showed between her teeth as she nodded her head vigorously. Suddenly she turned to Mede.

'Now it's yore turn to promise something, Mede boy, 'fore yo' gits what Drum a-goin' to give you. Ain' havin' yo' beddin' yo'self with that fancy boy what yo' been beddin' with. Yo' got to git yo'self a wench. Marry up with her if'n yo' wants o' jes' git yo'self a bed wench, but git that Lucy boy outa yore bed. Un'erstand?'

Mede bowed his head, ashamed to look his mother in the face, while Drum wondered how Big Pearl could possibly know about such a thing. News, it seemed, travelled fast at Falconhurst.

'Ain' nacheral,' she continued, ' 'n' ain' right. Yo' a-goin' to promise me?'

'Yo' got my word, Mammy,' Mede said, not lifting his head.

' 'Member that I a conjure woman. Don' want to conjure 'gainst my own kinfolk but kin if'n I have to. Kin set a fire in yore guts jes' like'n I kin in ol' man Jenkins o' that other ol' Mista Sylvester.' She took a little clay image out of her pocket and showed it to them. It had been broken in two where a nail had entered it. 'He daid now,' she said, pursing her lips in satisfaction.

'I've promised and Mede's promised and now tell us how do we get the money?' Drum leaned forward in his chair expectantly, for the moment almost believing his grand-mother.

She reached into another pocket and took out a gold eagle, which she flipped towards Drum. He caught it in mid-air.

'More'n yo' kin shake a stick at where that one comed from.' She reached over and took it away from him. 'Needed money, I did, 'n' he'ped myself to ten o' 'em. This the last one, but knowin' I ain' goin' to need no more with my two boys here a-runnin' Falconhurst. Now listen! Open up them ears o' yourn 'n' listen. Come midnight yo' both comes back here. Don' let nobody see yo'. Don' bring no lantern 'cause be moon-up then. Jes' be here, tha's all.'

They both stood up and for some reason that he could not understand, Drum leaned down and kissed her. She was his grandmother. Now he knew it. He could feel a love that he had never felt before between himself and this old black woman.

She pushed him away playfully. 'My, my, wishin' I jes' a young wench. Don' know which 'un I'd take first, yo' both so pretty-lookin'.'

CHAPTER TWENTY-ONE

IT WAS ABOUT nine o'clock when Drum and Mede returned to the big house. A dim light burned in the kitchen, just one candle that had almost burned itself out, so evidently Mammy Morn, Ciceron, and Lucy had all gone to bed. There was little to sit up for in the evening and, like the Negroes, plantation owners also retired early, although, as they had neared the house, Drum and Mede had noticed a light down in the overseer's cottage and this seemed unusual to Drum because Narcisse had left the boy Abel there alone and it was most unlikely that Narcisse went back and left a light to dispel the boy's fear of haunts.

Mede went first to the big table, where there was a pitcher of water, covered by a clean dish towel. A glass tumbler and a tin cup sat beside it. He poured himself a drink, but instead of using the tin cup that was for servants he poured the water into the glass tumbler and drank it, peering up from under his eyelids at Drum to see if there might be any comment forthcoming. Drum did not censure him as he might have done the previous night.

'Mammy a-sayin' I ain' no servant no more,' Mede half apologized for using the glass. 'I a-sleepin' in the bedroom tonight o' still sleepin' up with Lucy?'

Drum shrugged his shoulders. 'Better make it one more night with Lucy. Too late now to make up a bed for you. Tomorrow you can take the rear chamber, which opens off my room, the one that has the stairs going down to the office. Tomorrow will be time enough. Better come up with me, though, and wait with me.'

'Don' make me no neverminds if'n I not sleepin' with Lucy no more. Mammy's right. Gittin' tired o' Lucy anyway, but it fun for a while 'n' now's the time to go back to wenches. What we a-goin' to do till midnight? Mammy say come back then.'

Drum held up his hand for silence. He heard footsteps coming in from the drawing-room and while he waited the door of the pantry opened and Claire stood there with a candle in her hand.

'Thought I'd wait up for you.' She placed the candle on the table beside the other. 'I've been trying to pass the time by mending a tablecloth, but candlelight is so poor to work by. Some day we must get oil lamps here, Drum. Candles give almost no light at all.' She shivered as though a cold hand had touched her. 'It's lonely staying in the big house all alone. Mammy Morn and Matilda are in bed. Narcisse discovered that Lucy can read and write, so he took him down to the overseer's house to set up some account books. That left me here all alone and I was just thinking about bed when I heard you come in.' She looked at Drum and the unnatural brightness of her eyes showed them to be glazed with tears. 'No, I should not say I am alone exactly. Debbie is up in your room.'

He did not know what to say. The mention of Debbie started the hot blood surging in his loins. He knew he really didn't want her, but at least it would be a release. He wanted Claire and only Claire. Swiftly he gathered her into his arms, oblivious of Mede, who was watching them.

'Darling, something strange is about to happen tonight. I don't know what it is, but I do have faith in it. Do you trust me?'

'Of course, one always trusts the one she loves.'

'Then, go up to bed. When will Narcisse be back?'

She shook her head, unable to answer his question in words but knowing that words were necessary. She could only tell him that she really did not know. He had told her that he might not come back at all that night. He might be working late and there was no use in disturbing her, so he would stay over at the overseer's cottage.

He could not imagine what work would keep Narcisse away all night, but the mention of Lucy gave him a clue. He remembered Clarence back at Madame Helene's and then he remembered the admiration Narcisse had expressed for Abel. But for a man like Narcisse with a wife like Claire! Surely there could be no truth in his supposition. Minimizing what was going through his mind, he laughed. 'Well, at least poor Abel won't be afraid of haunts.'

'But I am afraid, Drum, and not of haunts. I seem to sense that something is going to happen and that is what frightens me.'

'Then, tell me about it.' He drew her closer to him. 'If anything frightens you, you always feel better when you talk it over with someone, especially someone who loves you.'

She shook her head sadly. 'I think you mean it when you say you love me, Drum, but the fact remains that I really do love Narcisse. Not the way I love you but in a different way and, I am afraid to say it, perhaps even more than I love you. Oh, Drum darling, there is so much I would like to tell you, but I can't, I can't, I can't. How silly for us to be standing here talking in riddles.' She wiped her eyes with her handkerchief and forced a smile. 'Come on, Drum, let's all go up together. It's getting late and we should get up early. There's so much to do. Mammy Morn said breakfast at half past seven.' She placed her arm in his and picked up the candle. 'Take the other one up with you, Mede.'

'Going to need Mede tonight.' Drum yawned and blew out the candle. 'Too tired to get undressed alone. Come along, boy.'

With Claire and Drum leading the way, Mede followed them through the downstairs rooms and up the stairs. Stopping at Claire's bedroom door, Drum took her in his arms and kissed her goodnight. He wanted to follow her inside and he sensed that she wanted him, but she was too frightened. Narcisse might return at any moment, she warned him. He pleaded with her, telling her he would post Mede at the head of the stairs and if he heard a door open, there would be time for him to get back into his room. With her body pressed so close to his own, he knew she was aware of his urgency. Taking her hand by force, he pushed it down between them, but she withdrew it.

'Don't torture me, Drum. Oh, please, please, please.' She withdrew from his arms and pushed open the door, slipping through it. He thought he could hear the bolt being pushed and then her voice, strangled with tears. 'Oh, Drum, I love you so much, so very much, darling. Don't tempt me any more.'

He waited, hoping she might relent and open the door, but there was no movement inside. For a moment he was tempted to crash his fist into the panel of the door, but Mede reached up and grabbed his hand. 'Yo' better do some thinkin' with yore head, Drum.'

Drum lowered his hand and allowed Mede to guide him across the hall to his own room. A flood of light followed the opening of the door. Debbie was not asleep tonight. The room was brilliantly lighted by candles and she was sitting in a chair, fully clothed.

'Yo' a-wantin' me tonight, Masta suh? Been a-waitin' a long time.' Her hands stroked her body, cupping her breasts and thrusting them towards him.

God, how he wanted her, just the woman flesh of her; yet he did not want her. With Claire so recently in his arms, his need for Debbie was not enough to make him forget his desire for Claire. Better think with his head, as Mede had said. Were he to take Debbie now and then rout her out of bed in time to keep his rendezvous with Big Pearl, she would think it unusual. She would wonder at his getting up and getting dressed and leaving the house. By tomorrow it would be all over Falconhurst, and New Quarters too, that he had dressed and gone out at midnight.

'You got a room upstairs in the servants' quarters?' Drum asked.

She shook her head dully and he could sense her disappointment.

'Ain' got none. Supposed to sleep here 'n' if'n yo' don' wan' me, sleeps on the floor' – she pointed to the pallet on the far side of the bed – 'case yo' wants me come mornin'.'

'You know where Mede sleeps up in the servants' quarters?' As he asked the second question he smiled to think what Lucy might say should he come in and go up to bed and find Debbie there rather than Mede.

'Ain' a-knowin' whereat he sleepin'.'

Drum pointed to the door that led from his room into the back chamber, where the stairs led to the first floor. 'Show her, Mede, and let her bed down in your room.' He handed him one of the candlesticks. 'And then come back here,' he added.

'I a-goin' to be all 'lone up there,' she wailed.

'Mammy Morn she right 'cross the hall 'n' Matilda too. Ain' nothin' to be scairt of,' Mede assured her.

'Yo' a-wantin' him tonight 'stead o' me?' Debbie pointed to Mede. 'He like'n that Lucy boy what went with Mista Narcisse tonight 'n' Big Sol over to New Quarters?'

Drum slapped her. He could see the dull purple print of his hand on her cheek. Now she was wailing from pain as well as from fear.

'Don't ever say anything like that again. Mede isn't that kind. Neither am I. Look, Debbie, I'm sorry I slapped you.' He reached in his pocket and took out the handful of change that remained to him. 'Here. Take this and buy some candy or some pretties the next time you go to Benson. Now let me ask you something.'

She took the money and stopped her blubbering.

'You know any pretty girl over at New Quarters that would like to be Mede's bed wench?'

'Got me a sister Rosanne,' Debbie said, all smiles. 'She littler'n me, but she brighter skinned.'

'If she's smaller than you, she'll never do for Mede.'

'She been busted.' Debbie held her hand on her face where Drum had slapped her but managed to grin. 'Big Sol he the biggest at New Quarters 'n' he busted her.'

With a promise to talk about it later, Drum motioned with his head for Mede to leave but advised him to leave the door open so as not to make any noise on his return. He could hear their footsteps going down the stairs and then faintly across the kitchen floor to the stairs to the servants' quarters. He wished now he hadn't sent Debbie away and yet he was glad he had. Throwing himself down on the big bed without undressing, he waited for Mede to return. It was about half an hour before he heard Mede's steps on the stairs. Knowing full well what had taken place between Mede and Debbie, Drum was ready to reprimand him when he entered, but he realized that the master-servant status between him and Mede was terminated – at least if things turned out successfully tonight.

'She right nice, that Debbie gal,' Mede announced with a sheepish grin when he came through the door. 'Jes' hopin' her sister's so good.'

'Figured out what took you so long. Hereafter you leave Debbie alone. Don't want you fooling around with her.'

'Laws, Drum, I didn't start nothing with her. Afore that wench git 'cross the kitchen, she a-fingerin' me 'n' unbuttonin' me 'n' time I got her up the stairs 'n' show her my bed, she jes' pull me down on her. What I a-goin' to do? Jes' couldn' he'p it. Won' do it 'gain, though, if'n I kin have her sister.'

Mede had already anticipated his new status. By sharing Drum's woman, he had already placed himself on Drum's level. Drum consoled himself by admitting that it really made very little difference. They had the same blood in their veins. He had promised his grandmother that they would be equals. A glance at his watch told him it was an hour and a half before midnight. He moved over on the bed.

'Come on, lie down. Might as well get a little rest. Don't blow out the candles. We can't go to sleep or we wouldn't wake up.'

Mede accepted the invitation, stretching out on the bed. He had no sooner lain down than he was asleep, but Drum managed to stay awake, wondering if this would be, after all, just some sort of fool's errand, merely some old woman's fantasy, some chimera he was chasing because it represented his last chance. But, no! He remembered the bright hardness of the twenty-dollar gold piece. That was real enough.

At a quarter to twelve he roused Mede and together they went downstairs in their stocking feet, not putting on their shoes until they were outside the back door. A light was still burning in the overseer's cottage and Drum cursed himself for parting with Claire. There would have been plenty of time.

The moon had risen, just as Big Pearl had said it would, and now it was so bright that they could see everything in sharp detail. Mede too noticed the light in the overseer's cottage and was pointing it out to Drum when the light was extinguished. They could see forms emerging from the house and hear laughter. Drum pulled Mede down into a high clump of weeds and they counted some ten men heading for the house, but as they neared it they turned and took the path alongside the house that led to the lane.

'Them boys from New Quarters,' Mede whispered, ' 'n' here come Narcisse hisself. Musta left Lucy 'n' that other boy down at the other house.'

Drum spread the weeds apart and watched as Narcisse

221

walked up to the kitchen door. He was unsteady and Drum guessed that he was drunk. Now he was glad that he had not persuaded Claire. There was nothing worse than being confronted by a drunken husband. They waited for Narcisse to open the door and go inside, then headed for Big Pearl's cabin. There was no light in her cabin, but she was standing in the doorway, scarcely distinguishable because she had changed her white dress for a black one. She came down the steps to meet them and now out in the moonlight Drum could see that she carried a spade in one hand and a slender Y-shaped withe in the other. She handed the spade to Mede but kept the slender stick in her hand.

'Don' like what's a-goin' on 'round here tonight. Smells death in the air. That mustee boy in the big house he got a lot o' boys from New Quarters over there. Don' like it. Somethin' mighty strange. Yo' cain' trust that mustee boy, Drum.'

'Why he's one of my best friends.' Drum realized he didn't entirely trust Narcisse himself, but he had no real reason not to trust him. Perhaps it was only jealousy, because now he knew that Narcisse was up in the same room with Claire.

'He ain' no frien' ' – Big Pearl was emphatic – 'but he cain' hurt us tonight. Been out drawin' me a magic circle 'n' no one kin step over it 'ceptin' yo' two.'

'See that chinaberry tree there?' She pointed to a large tree growing some little distance from her cabin. 'That where we a-goin'. That tree a gravestone for Masta Charles what was kilt here onc't. 'Members him, I do, 'cause he 'n' Masta Hammond brought Mede here long time 'go. Now they all daid but me. I the only one what 'members. That tree was nigh to the cabin my mammy 'n' I 'n' Mede lived in. Drummage he built me the new one so's I'd have somethin' better'n the others. My mammy she planted that tree so's she not forget where Masta Charles he a-buried.'

They walked on through the moonlight and Drum no longer wondered why all the people around Falconhurst were afraid of haunts. He himself expected to see some wraith-like emanation appear from the tree. Falconhurst was a place of violence. He remembered hearing how Drumson had been killed defending his master, of how his own father had been murdered by the Ku Klux Klan. Now it seemed that there had been other violent deaths at Falconhurst. The original Mede had been killed; Apollon Beauchair, whose fallen angel graced the cemetery, had also been murdered. And now this Master Charles, whoever he was, had evidently been killed and nothing but a tree marked his grave.

It did not take them long to reach the tree and once there, Big Pearl took a right-hand turn and headed for a large rock, overgrown with bindweed and creepers. Stepping up to it, she paced off about ten paces. Then, taking the Y-shaped stick in her hands so that each hand held one of the branches of the Y while the standard stood upright, she slowly started to circle the big stone. She had not taken more than ten steps when the upstanding branch started to bend down and when it touched the ground, she stopped.

'Bring the shovel 'n' dig here,' she commanded Mede.

Mede obeyed. She warned him to be careful and first to remove the sod so that it would be as little broken as possible. Then, with the sod removed, he fell to scooping out big shovelfuls of the loam. He had not dug more than three feet when there was a metallic ring as his spade hit something. Once again Big Pearl warned him to be careful and now she was at the edge of the hole, making him scoop away the dirt by handfuls rather than use the spade.

'Ain' nothin' but an ol' iron kittle,' he said, locating the bail. 'That what yo' a-wantin', Mammy?'

She whispered to him to be quiet and then told him to loosen the loam around the edges of the kettle. 'It too heavy to pull out all alone,' she said to Drum. 'Yo' got to help him.'

Between the two men, they managed to get the heavy kettle out of the ground. Drum was about to remove the rusty cover, but Big Pearl stopped him. Slowly she walked around the big stone and in the course of her short journey the withe dipped three more times.

At each place she had them dig until four rusty kettles were disinterred. Then she bade them fill the holes and replace the sod and she promised that she would be out in the morning before anyone arose to strew grass and leaves over the places where they had dug. The metal bails on the kettles had rusted through, so Drum and Mede had to tote them in their arms, heavy as they were, to Big Pearl's cabin while she remained at the big stone to guard them until the last one was carried in.

Once inside the house, she again bolted the door and lit several candles and placed them on the table. She showed them how to get the covers off with a heavy knife although two of the covers were rusted to only a paper thinness and broke before they could get them off, and one of the kettles – the one Pearl had dipped into – had no cover at all. But in each case, Drum saw that the kettles were filled with gold pieces, all gold eagles.

'All that's black money.' Big Pearl's hand swept over the kettles. 'All came from sellin' niggers. Every year Masta Warren he send off a coffle o' bucks 'n' wenches to N'Orleans o' to Natchez. Git the money 'n' he puts it in a kettle in the groun'. Masta Hammond too, though Masta Hammond not a-puttin' so much in's his papa 'cause Masta Hammond put it in the bank. Lucretia Borgia she a-knowin' 'bout it 'n' Drummage too, 'n' Drummage he a-tellin' me. Pore Drummage he kilt afore he used it all up. Mighty glad yo' comed to Falconhurst when yo' did, boy. Hopin' yo'd come afore I die so's I could tell yo'.' She seated herself at one side of the table and motioned to Drum and Mede to sit on the other.

Together they started to count the contents of one kettle. Placing the gold pieces in stacks of five each, they counted up the contents of that one kettle and came up with a little over $20,000. They did not bother to count the other kettles because all seemed to be about the same weight.

'Yo' takes what yo' wants, Drum boy. It all yourn 'n' Mede's. Yo' a-goin' to need a lotta money to git Falconhurst all fixed up like'n it was.' She brought him a basket similar to the one he had carried the food over in but a little smaller. He scooped fifty of the small piles into the basket, counting them as he listened to the clink of the coins in the basket. Strange, he thought, how iron would rust and silver tarnish, while nothing happened to gold. This had been buried for three generations.

It had been there during the lifetime of his father, Drummage, of Hammond Maxwell, and his father Warren Maxwell, yet it was as bright and brilliant as ever.

Now he had the answer to everything he needed. No, not quite everything. It would not bring Claire to him. Perhaps he should ask Big Pearl one other favour. She might make a charm that would destroy Narcisse. That was not the answer – Good God, no! He certainly did not need a charm to make Claire love him or to make himself love her. That was already accomplished. Stop thinking about Claire now. Concentrate on this glorious surprise of having all the money he needed. This was no time to think of Claire or anything else except this bright yellow gold that was in his hand. Yet, as he looked at it, he wondered how many strong black bodies it had taken to accumulate this money.

Drum placed the basket on the table and gestured to the three other kettles. 'What are we going to do with them? Where will they be safe? Shall we put the money in the bank?'

'Yo' not very bright, Drum boy.' Big Pearl leaned over ponderously to pick up one of the coins that had rolled off the table. 'Yo' got money in the bank now what yo' cain' git out. Yo' wantin' to give 'em more? Money safe right here.' She motioned to Mede to shove one of the kettles under her bed. 'Ain' nobody a-thinkin' o' findin' money in Big Pearl's house. Safe here 'n' handy too. If'n yo' wants some, yo' jes' come over 'n' git it. It yourn.' She stopped suddenly and looked up at Drum searchingly. 'Whereat Mede a-sleepin' tonight?'

'Up in his own room,' Drum answered. 'Can't rouse the folks at this hour of the night and have them get out sheets and pillows and make up a bed for him. Tomorrow night, how's that?'

She shook her head emphatically. 'Ain' havin' my boy sleep in no servant's room now on. Yo' two got to be closer. Yo're all the kin I have. Goin' to fix that up, I am, right now. Yo' both got my blood in yo'. Mede he got half my blood 'n' half Zanzibar's. Yo' got less 'cause yo' got jes' half so much's Mede has. Goin' to change that right now. Goin' to make yo' two boys brothers.'

She hoisted herself up and rummaged among the loose cutlery on a shelf, returning to her chair with a small, sharp knife. 'Cut like'n a razor, this un do,' she remarked, as she edged her chair up nearer to the table and adjusted the candles to give a better light. 'Stretch out yore arms, both of yo'! Lef' arms, 'cause the lef' arm nearest the heart. Gits the blood quicker'n the right.'

'Yo' ain' a-goin' to cut me, Mammy,' Mede said, taking his arm from the table and holding it behind his back.

' 'Course I'm a-goin' to cut yo'. Yo' a man, ain' yo', o' mayhap yo' not after sleeping wid that Lucy. Hol' out your han'.'

He placed his arm on the table and she reached over, pushing his shirtsleeve up over the glabrous black skin. Although Drum had not taken his arm away and felt a bit queasy about the proceedings, he allowed her to push his shirtsleeve up too.

'Set 'roun' sorta facin' each other.' She motioned to them to move in their chairs.

They both obeyed her and now he did not share Mede's fear. He knew that the love he felt for his grandmother transcended all sense of fear.

'Close yore hands 'n' grip 'em tight.'

They both clenched their fists and Drum could see how the veins stood out on his wrists and Mede's. He watched as the sharp knife pricked one of the veins in Mede's wrist and saw the spurt of blood. Mede had winced when the knife had touched him, but Drum did not mind the tiny cut. Placing their bleeding wrists together, she bound them tightly with an old rag. When the rag was encarmined, she removed it, standing up to press a finger on each of their arms to stanch the flow of blood. A distant look appeared on her face and she seemed to be staring through the walls of the cabin while she mumbled words of gibberish that neither Drum nor Mede could understand. Finishing the rigmarole, she seemed to return to them, took her fingers from their wrists, and nodded her head in approbation when she saw that the blood flow had stopped. She dipped a clean rag in a pail of water and washed the blood from their arms and all Drum could see was the tiny nick that the knife had made. There was no bleeding.

'My ol' mammy tellin' me 'bout this. Comed from Africa, it did. Comed from Dahomey. It the ol' ol' mystery of Africa. Never done it myself before, but it worked.

'Now yo' two's brothers, but yo' more'n brothers. Yo' got the same blood in yore veins. Done dreaned out all yore blood what ain' mine. Yo' both purentee Mandingo now. Mede ain' got none o' Zanzibar's blood 'n' Drum he ain' got none o' Miz Sophie's nor Drumson's. It all mine. 'Fore I die, I a-goin' to show yo' all my conjure so's yo' kin carry it on. Now yo' two kin never lie to each other, kin never raise a han' 'gainst one another, kin never stay 'part from one another. Ain' no more masta 'n' servant.' She reached over and shook Drum's shoulder. 'Whereat Mede a-goin' to sleep tonight, Drum?'

'If he can sleep without sheets, in the room next to me.'

'Tha's better. It gittin' light now. Better get yo'selves back to the big house. Tomorrow yo' goes to Benson. Yo' buy 'nough in Benson to start the store in New Quarters. Give all them niggers over to New Quarters some money – couple o' dollars, maybe, so's they kin buy something. Find yo'self a young buck in New Quarters name o' Joshua. Fergits his last name, but he a right smart young buck 'n' honest too. He's Drummage's git, so he a kinfolk to both o' yo'. Put Joshua in charge of the store. Yo' buy horses 'n' cows 'n' pigs 'n' chickens 'n' guinea hens. Yo' git Amos 'n' Fred to carpenter for yo'. Git 'em to fix up the barns 'n' the house. Git paint 'n' git Rex to paint – he a-knowin' how. Git Ol' Aunt Lou to seamstress for the house. Yo' got Debbie for a bed wench 'n' she right pretty too, 'n' git her sister Rosanne for Mede.'

'Joshua for the store, Amos and Fred for carpenters, Rex to paint, and Aunt Lou for seamstress.' Drum repeated the names.

''N' Rosanne for Mede. Got to git him away from that Lucy.'

'Ain' wantin' that Lucy no more nohow.' Mede remembered his brief encounter with Debbie, which had put Lucy out of his mind.

'Now, one more thing.' Big Pearl pointed an authoritative finger at Drum. 'Git yo'self all dressed up onc't yo' git some horses 'n' a good rig 'n' go over to see ol' Masta Gassaway what was a friend o' Masta Ham's. He a good man, Masta Gassaway. Onliest white man I ever trusted 'n' ain' tellin' yo' why, but he done somethin' good for yore pappy, Drummage.'

'I'll try to remember, Grandmother.'

'Ain' yore grandmother no more – I'se yore mammy, like'n I am Mede's.' She got up and put her big arms around both of them. ' 'N' send me a meal o' vittles what that Mammy Morn cooked. Wantin' to see if'n she a good cook.'

'She is,' Drum asserted, 'and I'll have her send over your dinner every night if you wish.'

Big Pearl made up a wry face. 'Cain 'bide white folkses' food nohow. Jes' wan' to taste it onc't. Now, git, both o' yo'. I'se tired.' She walked over to the bed and lay down on it making the bed ropes creak.

'Thank you for everything, Mammy.' Drum leaned over and kissed the old black face, then picked up the basket and opened the door. The sky was beginning to lighten in the east and they walked back slowly, the basket between them, through the dew-bedrenched high grass and weeds.

'Yo' glad we'se brothers now, Drum?' Mede had been wanting to ask the question but had had to summon up courage to do it.

'Guess we always were, Mede, although I didn't realize it. I can see now that I've always been closer to you than to anyone else.'

'If'n we brothers, we kin share things, huh?'

'Reckon we can.'

'Then, yo' go up to yore room 'n' I go up to mine 'n' I'll fetch that Debbie wench 'n' bring her down to yore room. Ain' goin' to need no sheets on the other bed. We share her, huh?'

'Might as well start sharing things now, I guess,' Drum answered.

CHAPTER TWENTY-TWO

THE PRESSURE OF Mede's big arm, flung carelessly across Drum's face, awoke him and he realized he had been asleep only a few minutes. Pushing away Mede's arm, he got up and walked across the room to look at his watch. Nearly seven o'clock. He did not remember what time Debbie had left, but it could not have been more than an hour ago because he remembered it was light and he had watched her dress and creep silently out the back door of the room. He had satisfied his need of her quickly, but not so Mede, who seemed to discover an entirely new pleasure in women. His own need satisfied, Drum had wanted nothing more than to turn over and go to sleep, but the strainings and groanings on the other side of the bed had kept him awake.

He returned to the bed to shake Mede awake and stared for a moment at his naked blackness on the bed. They were, he and Mede, more alike than he had ever thought they were. He'd be willing from now on to share many things with this fellow, but he made up his mind to one thing – he'd never share a bed with him again.

'Come on, get up!' He continued to shake Mede, who opened one drowsy eye only to close it again. 'Almost time for breakfast and we've got a lot of things to do today.'

Mede yawned and stretched himself, the muscles gliding under his skin. He pointed to the heap of damp clothes on the floor. 'Ain' got no trogs 'ceptin' those. Cain' put 'em on 'cause they all wet from traipsin' 'roun' in the wet grass last night.'

'Big Pearl says you're to wear my clothes anyway.' Drum splashed water from the china pitcher into the bowl and began to scrub himself. 'Get up, damn it, and get washed. You smell mighty musky anyway. Won't let you wear my clothes unless you're clean.'

Mede lifted his arms and sniffed his armpits. 'Shore am.' He swung his legs over the side of the bed, stretched again, and stood up. 'Whereat I a-goin' to eat this mornin'? In the kitchen or in the dining-room?'

After all that Big Pearl had done for him last night, it made no difference to Drum where Mede ate, but he was sure it was going to be upsetting to both Claire and Narcisse. Better get it over with as soon as possible and this morning would be as good a time as any. 'In the dining-room, but don't come down with me. Come about fifteen minutes after I do. It will be better that way.'

'What clothes I a-goin' to wear?'

'The same as I do.' Drum rubbed himself with the towel and ran a comb through his hair. 'Black pants, white shirt, string tie, and white linen jacket. Don't split my pants out, either. Come on, wash yourself and dress and be ready to come to the dining-room about fifteen minutes after I do.' Drum found his own clothes and slipped into them while Mede got up and splashed water on his face.

'Wash your goddamn stinking armpits too,' Drum commanded. 'If there's one thing the Brantomes would object to, it's having a stenchy nigger around. You've got to wash your-self twice a day from now on.' Drum finished dressing and picked up the basket with the gold pieces in it. Picking out five, he jingled them in his hand. The hundred dollars would put Narcisse in a good humour. He picked out two more for Claire. Dumping the rest of the gold into one of his boots, he hid it in the armoire. He'd have to get the rest changed into smaller money. Perhaps the bank would do it. They would have a greater respect for him now, walking in with money, than they did yesterday.

With the coins jingling in his pocket and an admonitory word to Mede to follow him soon, he walked down the stairs, through the drawing-room, and into the dining-room. Lucy was waiting on table and he stole a glance at Drum, forming the words *where's Mede* with his mouth, but Drum ignored him and walked around the table to where Narcisse sat beside Claire. Reaching in his pocket, he took out five of the gold pieces and dropped them one by one beside Narcisse's plate, then walked over and placed the other two beside Claire.

'What's this?' Narcisse scooped up the gold. 'Drum boy, you don't wait long, do you? You get the money from the bank one day and I get mine the next.' He slipped the gold pieces from one hand to the other, listening to their tinkle and smiling up at Drum.

'It's an advance on your salary, Narcisse, and on yours too, Claire.' He saw the look of surprise on her face. She alone knew that he had not received any money from the bank yesterday. 'I've got a lot of business to do in Benson today, so I'll have to hurry through breakfast. Is Brute here yet?' he asked of Lucy.

'Pappy he's a-waitin' out'n the kitchen.'

'Then, tell him I'll be going into Benson with him just as soon as I finish breakfast and, Lucy' – he called to the boy as he was halfway to the pantry door – 'set another place at the table. There will be four of us for breakfast.'

'Yes suh, Mista Drum suh.' Lucy departed, the wonderment on his face no less than that on Claire's and Narcisse's.

'A guest?' Narcisse asked.

Drum hesitated. 'Well, not exactly. Let us say my uncle.'

'Your uncle from Boston?' Claire asked. 'Did he arrive in the night?'

Drum shook his head. 'Uncle Chris is not my real uncle. This one is. Please don't ask me to explain. I cannot.' He heard Mede's footsteps on the stairs and so did the others. Claire and Narcisse stopped eating and stared at the dining-room door; even Lucy, mouth agape, stopped what he was doing to look.

Mede entered the room, immaculately dressed in some of Drum's clothes. Mede certainly was a handsome fellow, Drum thought.

'My uncle, Mede Maxwell. Yes, he is my uncle and last night, through some strange sort of alchemy, he became my brother too. I am greatly indebted to him. He has saved my life, my reputation, and my honour, although I cannot tell you how. Therefore I welcome him in my home no longer as a servant but as the brother he has turned out to be. I shall ask you both to welcome him too.'

Mede walked into the dining-room to the empty place that Lucy had set beside Claire.

'Draw out the chair,' Drum said to Lucy, 'and hereafter you will address this man as Mister Mede.'

'Good God Almighty, Drum! The fellow's nothing but a goddamn nigger.' Narcisse punctuated his words with thumps on the table that caused the dishes to jump and the cups to rattle in their saucers. 'Such effrontery! Who do you think my wife and I are? I've never sat at the table with a nigger in my life and I never shall.' He started to rise, throwing his napkin down, which caused the little pile of gold pieces to topple over.

'Please sit down, Narcisse.' Drum managed to keep his voice low and unaffected by the anger of Narcisse and the disapproval of Claire. He needed Narcisse, but he needed Claire even more and he wanted to avert any scene. 'First let me explain.'

'You can't explain my having to sit at the same table with a nigger. I'll be damned if I will.'

Drum looked from Mede to Claire and then to Narcisse. 'Yesterday when I went to the bank and when I went to the store in Benson, I was referred to as a nigger.'

'That's just a white man's opinion. You're not black, Drum.'

'According to them, I am. You were referred to as "my nigger overseer". Now you refer to Mede as a nigger.'

'But he is. He's black,' Narcisse insisted.

'Yes, he is black and so is my grandmother, the old Mandingo woman they call Big Pearl. I've made a vow, a promise, a sacred oath, or whatever you want to call it, that I shall not mention a word of something that happened last night. Call it conjure or whatever you like. I can't even believe in it myself, but I have to with the evidence before my eyes. In order to gain something very important to me, I had to promise something in return. The promise I made was that Mede was to be treated as my brother, not as my servant. I must stand by that promise.' He turned and looked at Claire so as to include her in his conversation with Narcisse.

'I want and need you both here. You are all the family I

have except Mede. But if some silly repugnance to the colour of Mede's skin, which, I assure you, is as witless as that banker's to me, keeps you from recognizing Mede as a member of the family and not as a servant, then' – Drum hesitated at the enormity of his words – 'I shall have to ask you to leave.' Drum trembled inside himself as he said the words, fearful that Narcisse might declare his willingness to go.

Claire answered at once. 'We are not going to go and, as Drum says, this discussion is witless.' She reached over one hand and laid it on her husband's coat sleeve. 'Calm yourself, Narcisse. Whether you want me to say it or not, we have no place to go. We cannot return to New Orleans.'

'Oh, yes we can.' Narcisse picked up the gold pieces and put them in his pocket.

'I'll not argue the matter with you, Narcisse' – she was near to tears – 'but you know as well as I do what that would mean. You are a good man when it comes to cotton. I know that and Drum will know it too when picking time comes along. I can take care of this house. I already feel more at home here than I did in New Orleans. It all boils down to one very simple thing – your acceptance of Mede. Mede is no field hand. He is refined and cultured. I have already accepted him and I do not feel that I have either lowered my dignity or shamed myself by sitting here beside him, any more than to have him stand behind me, waiting on me. After all, we have known him as long as we have Drum. We are not leaving, Narcisse.'

Narcisse's teeth bit his rather thick underlip. It took a long time for a smile to appear on his face, but it came at last. He gradually relaxed and then twisted his lips into the semblance of a smile. He jangled the gold in his pocket and nodded his head slowly.

'Somehow, I rather connect this' – he jingled the money purposely louder – 'with Mede's being here. I don't know how a buck like Mede could produce gold, but I have a feeling that he did. There's always money buried on these old plantations. He may have stumbled on to it. Then, again, it may have had something to do with your bank transactions yesterday, although I don't see how he could be involved, but it could be that the banker might have knocked up his old lady and suddenly felt a belated paternal affection for Mede. Whatever it is, it doesn't matter. As long as there's more money coming, it doesn't matter a hell of a lot to me if I eat with a nigger or not. Where's he going to sleep?'

Drum did not answer him but turned to Claire. 'Will you have the rear chamber that connects with mine made up for Mede?'

She nodded assent.

'I'll guarantee you'll not mind his presence after a while.' Drum began to see a peaceful settlement.

'But I'm taking no orders from him.' Narcisse was insistent.

'You won't have to. I'm still giving the orders around here.' And to prove his statement he turned to Lucy. 'Bring in Mister Mede's breakfast along with mine.'

Nobody spoke until Lucy had brought in the two plates of ham and eggs and placed them before Drum and Mede. Claire poured the coffee from the big urn and handed the cups to Drum and Mede. Her hand gently touched Narcisse's as it returned from passing the coffee to Drum. He caught the quick look that passed between them. Claire had raised her eyebrows ever so slightly and Narcisse made a scarcely perceptible nod of reassurance. Immediately after, Narcisse got to his feet and awkwardly extended his hand across the table to Mede.

'Sorry, boy – I mean Mede – that I said what I said. You're welcome to sit here, as far as I'm concerned. After all, what Drum does in his own house is none of my business.' He turned to Drum. 'Is it?'

Drum laughed and shrugged his shoulders.

'Then what I do in my house is none of your business either?' He gestured in the direction of the overseer's cottage.

Drum shifted his eyes from Narcisse and noticed that Claire was biting her lips. 'Not as long as it does not interfere with plantation business.'

'Not interfere with plantation business?' There was another trace of anger in Narcisse's words. 'Do you know what I was doing last night? I worked till about midnight. I was picking out my drivers. While you were in Benson yesterday I was over to New Quarters. Lined all the men up and picked out ten drivers. Then I had them come over to the cottage for instructions. Gave 'em all a glass of corn to get them warmed up and liking me, then laid down the law to them. Everything's fixed now. Those boys are *my* men. They'll do as I say. Each one's going to have from ten to twenty boys under him. He'll work them hard and that's what we need for a good cotton crop. Hard work and no loafing. Remember one thing – I'm as interested in getting a good crop as you are. The only way to get work out of a herd of niggers is to get good drivers, make a lot of them if you have to, but get them on *your* side. I'll be calling those boys in every night after a day's work to see how things are going. I'll be offering them a glass of corn. I'll be getting the best crop of cotton you ever saw.'

Narcisse had sat down, and now he grabbed at the molasses jug and thrust it at Mede. 'You take long sweetening in your coffee, Mede?' he asked.

Although Mede had never taken anything but sugar in his coffee, he accepted the jug and poured some into his coffee.

'Thank you.' He almost added 'Masta Narcisse suh' but caught himself in time.

'Now, Drum' – Narcisse seemed satisfied with the way he had welcomed Mede into their circle – 'what are your plans for today?'

'Got to go into Benson again. Got a lot of business to do there. Going to take Mede and Ciceron with me. Probably won't get anything to eat, as I imagine the hotel does not serve "niggers"' – he impressed the word on Narcisse – 'but I'll buy some crackers and cheese—'

'Have Mammy Morn put up a lunch for you. I'll speak to her and if she makes new coffee and puts it in a stone jug, it will still be warm when you drink it,' Claire suggested.

Drum smiled his gratitude to her. She seemed to think of everything for his comfort.

'Haven't any change, Drum' – Narcisse took out the five gold eagles from his pocket – 'but take one of these and get me five jugs of corn. Want to keep them down at the cottage. Give a nigger a glass of corn, and he'll do anything you want him to do. I'm starting the hands chopping today and want some for the drivers tonight.'

Drum accepted the coin. 'I'm going out to speak to Brute. You want to come with me, Mede?'

Mede had eaten nothing in the dining-room and now resolved to eat a full breakfast in the kitchen, where he felt more at home. He wondered just how much he was going to enjoy being a gentleman. So far it had not been too pleasant. He pushed his chair back and followed Drum out.

'You may take the coffee urn out, Lucy, and I'll ring for you when I want you to clear off the rest of the table.' Claire waited for him to go and the door to close behind him. She heard his steps go through the butler's pantry, then turned to Narcisse.

'What a fool you are, Narcisse! What an utterly stupid fool. Would you jeopardize everything we have here for the miserable existence we led in New Orleans, never knowing if we would have enough to pay Madame Helene? Look!' She held out her hand with the $40 in it. 'Do you realize that this is the first money I've had for my very own for a long time? Do you know what it means to me? I'm going to get myself a new gown with it. I'm going to write to Madame Helene and have her send me the material. It will be the first new gown I've had in years. If you knew how sick and tired I am of mending and darning and refurbishing.'

'I still don't like to eat with niggers,' he insisted.

'What of it? Many's the time we ate in the kitchen at Mon Repos with the servants.'

'Things are different now. I'm playing for high stakes.'

'Oh, Narcisse, forget all about those things! Forget them! We can live here in comfort and security. You'll be earning good money and so shall I. Why must you always want to change things?'

'Because I'm ambitious, my dear. I wasn't born to be the overseer of another man's plantation.'

'If I didn't love you so much, I'd leave you, Narcisse. I want to stay here.'

'That's because you're in love with Drum.'

'Can you blame me?'

'Not at all. I'd even like him for myself.'

'Stop it! You've nearly ruined our lives with your wild ideas.'

'It's my life.' He shrugged his shoulders.

'But I can't go through with it.' She laid her head down on the table and started to cry.

'Loving Drum as you say you do should make it a lot easier for you. Suppose he were old and ugly. That would make it even harder for you.'

'But I can't, oh, Narcisse, I can't do it.'

He reached over and grabbed one of her arms. The cruel twist of her wrist in his strong hands forced her to lift her head and look at him.

'We're going through with it as soon as the cotton is picked and I have that money safe in my pocket. Then we're going to get out of here. I don't intend to remain in this stinking hole with nothing but niggers around us. We're going to Paris, Claire. We'll be real people there. And you'll do it for me, for me, Claire.'

'Yes, Narcisse, I suppose I shall because I love you so much.'

'And you always will, Claire. You always will. There's nothing in the world that can destroy the love we have for each other. Wipe your tears away. In another year we'll be in Paris and we'll have plenty of money. Cheer up.'

He released her hand and she reached forward slowly to ring the little silver bell. Narcisse strode out of the room, the coins jingling in his pocket.

CHAPTER TWENTY-THREE

When Drum arrived in Benson, it seemed even more down-at-the-heels than it had the first time he had seen it. He stopped at the general store, then sent Ciceron off to the livery stable to look over the horses again. He told Brute to remain with the wagon and invited Mede to accompany him into Hicks' store. He felt rather proud of Mede and his new appearance. New clothes and a new role in life had changed Mede. Overnight the servant had become a gentleman.

Carrying a small leather satchel with nearly five thousand dollars in it, Drum himself felt far different from what he had felt yesterday. Now, although the remarks from the gallery of red-necks, who seemed to be a permanent fixture of the store porch, were as scurrilous as they had been before, they did not bother him. The conviction that he had more in his satchel than they would ever be able to accumulate in their lives made him feel superior to them. White they might be, but he would not change places with them and be the victim of their ignorance, their dirt, and their sterile lives. Furthermore, he felt no awe of Hicks when he entered the store. Hicks, behind his zinc-topped counter, glanced up and allowed a smirk to indent itself in the flabby flesh of his face.

'Yo' back 'gain, boy? Tho't you'd bo't all yo' had money for yisterday. Ain' no use'n yore comin' here beggin' for more. Don' do no business on credit. Ain' lettin' yo' have so much's a sliver o' cheese less'n yo' plunks down your cash.'

'That's exactly what I intend to do, Mr Hicks – plunk down my cash. But I warn you, I refuse to be overcharged, as I was yesterday. My cook went through the list of things I purchased and she informed me that I had been charged twice as much for some items as she would have paid in New Orleans.'

'Costs money for shippin', boy. Have to charge more out here in the country. Freight costs 'n' all, it's a wonder I make a cent.'

'That's no excuse for your charging me double. However, I'll continue to buy from you if you keep your prices fair. Otherwise I'll order everything from New Orleans or Mobile.' He found he was able to look Hicks in the eye and he continued to look at him until Hicks dropped his eyes and started to sweep the crumbs off the counter. 'How many barrels of flour do you have?' Drum asked abruptly.

' 'Bout ten, though cain' reckon what difference that a-makin' to yo'.'

'Then, I'll take the ten barrels.' Drum's words caused Hicks to jerk his head up.

'What yo' a-goin' to pay me with?' Again the little eyes squinted.

'Money.' Drum lifted the satchel and dropped it on the counter. 'You'll get paid for everything before it leaves your store.'

'Don' allow as to how I kin sell yo' all ten barrels. Gotta have some for my reg'lar customers.'

'Then, I'll take as many as you can sell. Eight?'

'Reckon so, if'n it for cash.'

Drum read down through the list of staples that he had had Mammy Morn dictate to him. They were merely the essentials, but they would keep the folks at New Quarters going for a time. Flour, sugar, fatback, lard, ham, and such things as soda and cream of tartar and salt. It was a long list and Hicks was kept busy running to his shelves to see how much stock he had. Whenever possible, Drum took almost his entire stock. He even ordered candy – lemon and peppermint drops – and he did not neglect to get the five jugs of corn that Narcisse had ordered. Although he had not had any desire to drink since arriving at Falconhurst, he ordered five more jugs for the big house.

Hicks was flabbergasted. He had never made such a sale in his life. Slowly and grudgingly his attitude towards Drum began to change. Not that he treated him as an equal, but he began to show a little less contempt for him. He was somewhat more polite and his politeness extended even to Mede, who was interested in the display of hunting knives and pistols. With the money Drum had given him before leaving he purchased a hunting knife for Lucy. Then he picked out a rifle for himself.

'Al'ays a good thing to have 'roun' the house,' he explained to Drum, ' 'n' I kin go huntin' 'n' shoot squirrels 'n' thin's to eat.'

'You couldn't hit a barn door, let alone a squirrel.' Drum examined the firearms. 'You can practise, but make sure I'm not anywhere around when you start shooting. What will Lucy do with a knife like that?'

239

'Lucy he al'ays carries a knife, don' yo' 'member? He a-wantin' a new one, so's I got this for him for a present. Jes' 'cause I ain' sleepin' with Lucy no more don' mean he not a frien'.'

After the purchases were all made, they had to wait awhile for Hicks to tot up his bill and Drum was surprised when the storekeeper pushed forward a straight-backed, home-made chair and suggested that he sit down while he waited. Drum accepted the chair but suggested that Mede might have the same consideration. Hicks produced another chair, although he was not as gracious about Mede's resting as he had been in offering the chair to Drum. Hicks, however, now visualized a constant money-making trade with the new owner of Falconhurst and he was pleased with the sale of the firearms and the knife to Mede. Their money was as good as anyone's. After all, the colour of a man's skin did not rub off on his money.

When the bill was totalled, it came to over two hundred dollars and then, for the first time, Drum opened his satchel and counted out the gold eagles into neat stacks of one hundred dollars each. Hicks' eyes bugged out and he surreptitiously peered into the bag to see that it was more than half full of gold pieces.

'Thank yo', suh.' The words were out of Hicks' mouth before he realized that he was addressing Drum but having said them, he did not bother to retract them. 'More stuff here'n yo' kin git in yore wagon. Yo' goin' to have to make two trips.'

'If necessary, Mr Hicks. I shall have all items checked as they are taken out of the wagon.'

'Don' need to. Don' need to 't'all. Honest, I am, whether it be with white man or nigger. Didn't find anything missin' yisterday, did yo'?'

'Nothing missing except the right prices.'

'Givin' yo' a lower price today' – Hicks became confidential in his whispering – 'seein' as how yo' bo't in quantity 'n' paid cash.' He jerked his thumb towards the door. 'Don't want that no-good white trash out'n the porch to know it, though.'

'I thought cash was your usual terms.'

'Trusts white people I do, but they ain' always good pay.

All o' them out there a-owin' me money 'n' all they does is sit on their ass 'n' chew terbaccer.'

Drum felt that no answer was necessary. He signalled to Mede to leave with him and to put his firearms in the wagon. This time when they passed the men on the porch, there were comparatively few remarks passed about them, certainly not as many as yesterday, although they were both carefully scrutinized. Drum suspected that some of them had been listening at the door and, although he was still a Negro in their eyes, he realized that he was now a Negro with money, which, while it engendered a certain amount of respect, also generated jealousy. He did not know whether it was better to be envied or ridiculed. Certainly the latter was less dangerous.

Brute was still seated in the wagon when Drum and Mede came out and Drum told him to get the wagon loaded, with instructions that all the things with but few exceptions, which he would pick out after the goods were delivered, would be taken to the store in New Quarters. At Brute's suggestion, Drum hired a Negro who was contentedly lounging against one of the wagon wheels to help him load. Once again, but this time with Mede beside him, Drum walked to the bank, pointing out to Mede the screening that he was now able to have at Falconhurst. Their entry to the bank was greeted by the same supercilious stare he had received from the bushy-whiskered teller the day before.

'Mista Jenkins he ain' in' – the teller pointed to the door marked PRESIDENT – ' 'n' ain' 'spectin' him back today neither. Ain' no use yore a-tryin' to git money here.'

'You'll do just as well as Mr Jenkins.' Drum did not forget to give the bank president the title of 'mister'. He put the satchel on the ledge under the grating, making sure that when he set it down, it gave off the sound of money. 'I merely wanted to change some money, that's all.' He opened up the bag and counted out five hundred dollars in gold, again making neat piles of the coins. 'I'd like a couple of hundred of this in silver and the rest in small bills, if possible.'

'Five hundred dollars?' The man stared first at the money and then at Drum.

'Perhaps that's too much for a small bank like this.' Drum looked around, his glance belittling the establishment.

Whiskers was not to be outdone. The status of his bank was being challenged and by a coloured man, at that. Although he was loath to be accommodating, he did not want it said that the Benson Bank could not produce $500. After considering the matter for a moment, he rang a bell beside his window and a coloured fellow, evidently the love-sick swain that Big Pearl had mentioned, dropped the polishing cloth he had been shining the brass grating with and came over. A few words of whispered conversation sent him to the inside door and when he knocked, it was opened by Jenkins himself.

At the same moment, Drum raised his voice somewhat, so that it might be heard across the room. 'I'd like to deposit another five hundred dollars here' – he started to count out more money – 'so that I shall be able to have it on hand.' He turned slightly, noticing Jenkins coming across the floor and bowed with just the sufficient hint of negligence that implied he didn't care whether he saw Jenkins or not, but his words, when he spoke, were respectful. 'Good morning, sir.'

Jenkins merely nodded. He was far more interested in peering at the gold pieces in neat piles on the teller's ledge. One could see him mentally counting the piles. One thousand dollars was a tidy sum in his estimation.

'How we a-goin' to know if'n this ain' counterfeit?' He lowered his head so that he could look at Drum over the spectacles he wore.

Now it was Drum's turn for sarcasm. 'Certainly, Mr Jenkins, if I am going to make a deposit with a banker, I trust that he will be able to tell counterfeit money from good. Isn't that one of the first things a banker has to know?'

Jenkins picked up one of the gold pieces, bit it with a long yellow tooth, and then dropped it on the counter, hearing its convincing ring.

'Jes' have to be careful, young man.' Yesterday Drum had been addressed as 'boy'; today he was 'young man'. 'It purentee gold all right. Where'd yo' git it?'

'That, Mr Jenkins, happens to be none of your business. If

242

you don't want it, I can deposit it in New Orleans, but as I intend to live here, it would seem more convenient to have money right here in Benson, however . . .' He opened the satchel with the intention of scooping the last $500 back into the bag.

'Hold on there. We'll 'commodate yo'.' Jenkins turned his back on Drum to address the teller. 'Make out a bank-book for this fellow and change his money for him. We willin' to do business with him.'

'And what about my five thousand dollars?' Drum asked.

'Hope yo' ain' thinkin' o' havin' this nigger boy identify yo'.' Jenkins regarded Mede. 'Cain' do it. We jes' pertecktin' yo', tha's all. Got to have a white man 'n' one that I know.'

'Very well,' Drum agreed. He signed for the bank-book, which had an elaborate red cover stamped in gold and started to count out the bills and change that the teller passed through the grating to him. There were two hundred dollars in well-worn dollar bills along with many rolls of dimes, quarters, and pennies. While he was stowing it away in his satchel Ciceron burst in. He was panting from running and his wet shirt was plastered to him.

'Kin yo' come, Mista Drum? Kin yo'? Got a good buy for yo'. Wants yo' should see it.'

Drum finished stuffing the money into his bag and followed Ciceron out, leaving Mr Jenkins and the teller staring at them in open-mouthed wonderment.

Between gasps for breath Ciceron told them how Brute had directed him to the bank to find them and how important it was that they hurry. A man had just driven up to the livery stable while Ciceron was there in a brand new surrey drawn by a pair of well-matched greys. He was a horse trader, so Ciceron said, and besides the surrey and the greys he had about ten horses he was leading. None of them amounted to much according to Ciceron, but the two greys on the surrey were prime examples of horseflesh. The man was willing to sell and if Drum hurried, he'd still be there.

Before they arrived at the livery stable, Drum could see the shiny black surrey and the pair of horses. Even at a distance they looked all that Ciceron claimed them to be. He hurried his steps to talk with the horse trader, who was leaning against the wheels of the surrey – a thin man of middle age, decently dressed, with a large black felt slouch hat, which sat at a jaunty angle on his head. He introduced himself as Livingood, but he did not offer to shake hands with Drum. Drum was beginning to learn not to offer his hand to strangers.

'That boy o' yourn a good judge o' horseflesh.' Livingood addressed Drum while he pointed to Ciceron. 'Cain' fool him. Knows what he's a-doin'. Yo' in'rested in buyin'?'

Drum looked the horses over. He felt he should at least give the impression that he knew something about them.

'They right good, Mista Drum,' Ciceron insisted.

'How much?' he asked Livingood.

Livingood appraised Drum. The fine clothes that both he and Mede wore, their poise, and their good looks all betokened money. 'Figures I should git me 'bout seventy-five each for the horses 'n' 'bout seventy-five for the surrey, seein' as how it 'bout new 'n' ain' been driven much.'

Ciceron, who was standing beside Drum, nudged him and almost imperceptibly shook his head.

'Two hundred and twenty-five dollars?' Drum shrugged his shoulders with an attitude of indifference but nevertheless leaned over to examine the upholstery of the surrey. He could see that it was nearly new. 'Too much,' he said, shaking his head.

'What'll yo' give?' The man did not seem at all perturbed that his first offer had not been taken.

'Hundred and fifty.' Drum had never bargained before, but he was rather enjoying the situation.

'Cain' do business at that rate.' Livingood stepped up into the surrey with all intentions of driving away, but before he clucked to the horses, he leaned down, his face almost on a level with Drum's. 'Two hundred.'

Again Drum looked at Ciceron, who shook his head.

Drum's lips set in a grim line as he shook his head also and half turned as though to walk away.

Livingood, however, sensed that he had a prospective customer and, although he took the whip from the socket and tightened the reins as though to drive away, he rather reluctantly put the whip back and slacked the reins, sitting back in the seat. For another ten minutes they bargained back and forth until a sum of $185 was reached, at which Ciceron nodded his head vigorously and Drum accepted the offer. For the third time that morning, he counted out his gold in parcels of $100 and accepted the $15 change from Livingood, along with the crudely scribbled bill of sale the man gave him.

'Yo' that Falconhurst fella, ain' yo'? The one the whole town's gassin' 'bout?'

'Yes, I'm from Falconhurst.'

'Yo' 'bout the whitest nigger I ever did see 'n' I ain' talkin' 'bout yore colour neither. Like doin' business with yo'. 'Pears like'n yo' a-goin' to be needin' some more horses if'n yo' a-goin' to work that place. Heard some scalawag overseer stripped it. Mayhap I kin help yo'. What yo' needin' there?'

Drum looked to Ciceron for a reply. It seemed that Ciceron had it all worked out. They needed twenty mules, ten workhorses, and three saddle horses – one for Drum, one for Narcisse, and one for Brute. Pointing to Mede, Drum had him make it four. But, Ciceron went on to explain, they had five good mules and two good saddle horses in the livery stable. Whereupon Livingood said that if they would give him a week, he'd have a selection of mules and horses ready for them and deliver them to Falconhurst for their approval.

'They gotta be first-class,' Ciceron emphasized. 'Don' want nothing like'n them nags what's a-trailin' yo'. Think mayhap we git the mules 'n' the two horses what they's got here 'n' we waits for yo' to bring the others.'

Just as Hicks had made the biggest sale of his life, Livingood beamed at the prospects of the sale he had just made and the one he intended to make. He relinquished the reins to Drum, jumped on one of the horses he was leading, and rode off, saluting them with a lift of his hat and a promise to be back within a week. Following Ciceron's lead, they went into the livery stable, where Drum purchased the mules and the saddle horses along with a couple of second-hand saddles to go with them. Here, also, he was treated with a modicum of respect and listened to praises of Ciceron for his expert knowledge of horses. It had been worthwhile to bring Ciceron along.

'Kin yo' drive a horse?' Ciceron asked of Drum.

'Sure.' Drum had been familiar with horses during the long summers the Holbrooks had spent on Cape Cod.

'Then, yo' 'n' Mede here drive the surrey. I'll ride one horse 'n' lead the other 'n' the mules 'n' Brute he kin drive the wagon. Like'n I tol' yo', Mista Drum, I don' know nothin' 'bout cows 'n' pigs, but Mista Higgins here, what has the livery stable, he a-sayin' that a Mista Gassaway what lives the other side o' town, he got 'em for sale. He ain' raisin' cotton no more 'cause his land all leached out, but he raisin' cattle 'n' pigs.'

Gassaway! The name was familiar to Drum. He had heard it somewhere before. Gassaway? Ah, he remembered. It was the name of the man who had given the cottonseed to Brute. He'd go to see him; he'd been wanting to thank him anyway. Higgins gave him directions to where Gassaway lived, which was only about a mile on the other side of the town from Falconhurst. Going back to the store, he saw that Brute had nearly loaded his first load. Mede got out the lunch basket that Mammy Morn had put up for them and Hicks appeared out on the porch of his store, which was now strangely vacant, as all the idlers had gone home to eat their dinners. As though he were bestowing an accolade on them, Hicks gave them permission to sit on the porch while they ate their lunch.

Mammy Morn had taken special pains with their lunch and the basket yielded ham and chicken sandwiches, cake, and buttered biscuits, while the coffee in the stone jugs was still warm.

'Ain' yo' forgot somethin'?' Hicks came out unctuously rubbing his hands.

Drum could think of nothing that he had forgotten.

'Calico,' Hicks suggested, ''n' needles 'n' thread. Yo 'a-goin' to have servants out there 'n' them wenches at New Quarters ain' hardly got a rag to cover their nekkidness. Ain' seemly to have servants in a house with theys titties hangin' out, less'n o' course yo' likes 'em that way.' Hicks was trying to be friendly, but he also had an eye out for making more money. 'Better buy 'em some bolts.'

Drum remembered Debbie's slatternly attire. Matilda's was even worse.

'Better put in about ten bolts.' Drum reached in his satchel and drew out another twenty dollars. When Hicks brought out the bolts, ugly, nondescript patterns with blacks and browns predominating, Drum had Brute put them in the wagon. These, he instructed Brute, were to be taken to the big house and given to Miss Claire. All the other stuff was to be taken to the store in New Quarters and the door padlocked (which necessitated another purchase from Hicks). Drum remembered that Big Pearl had told him to place the store in the hands of a man named Joshua, so Drum told Brute to look him up and place him in charge of things.

'He a right good boy,' Brute said in confirmation of Drum's choice. 'He akin to yo' too. He's Drummage's git.'

Drum merely lifted his eyebrows.

'Yore pappy he a great one for the wenches. Bet yo' got fifteen, twenty brothers 'n' sisters over in the New Quarters.'

' 'N' another un right here.' Mede stepped forward, his thumb pointing to his own chest. 'Only I different. I his own brother. Rest ain'.'

Drum had no desire to go into the intricacies of his relationship to the various men and women at New Quarters. Evidently his father had strewn his seed rather indiscriminately. He looked up to see Ciceron riding by on one of the horses, leading the mules. As they were now all loaded, Brute climbed up on to the driver's seat and Drum tossed two bits to the fellow who had helped Brute load. Then, with Mede, he got into the surrey and drove off in the opposite direction to see Mr Gassaway.

The houses and shacks on the road leading out of Benson were in as bad condition as those they had passed that morning, but Drum was surprised when he saw the Gassaway plantation. It had never been as imposing a place as Falconhurst but was merely a two-storey clapboard house with a long gallery along the front. The shake roof was sagging, many of the windows were broken, and there were only a few vestiges of the white paint that at one time had covered it. Seen from the road, Falconhurst still presented a good appearance, but this place was so run-down it seemed incapable of repair. He drove through the crumbling gates that supported the remains of a picket fence and up the weed-grown driveway to the house. An elderly man was sitting on a straight-backed chair smoking a pipe.

The man stood up leisurely, knocking the ashes out of his pipe; a slatternly looking Negro woman materialized in the doorway and several mulatto children appeared around the corner of the house. With one bare foot the woman lifted a squawking white hen out of the doorway and sent her flying through the air. Hitching up his worn and patched trousers and tightening the rope that he used as a belt, the man slowly descended the steps. Drum saw that he was barefoot and guessed that it had been many months since his feet had been washed, but as he looked up to the man's face he could see a welcoming smile and there was kindness in the pale blue eyes. Without speaking, the man first appraised the horses, then the surrey, and then Mede in his fine clothes. Finally his eyes rested on Drum. Pursing his lips and nodding his head as though to corroborate what he saw, he walked over to the surrey.

'What kin I do for yo'?' Although his words were slurred with the same Southern accent that Negro and white man both shared, there was a certain indefinable inflection of quality to them. 'Yo' seekin' Lew Gassaway?'

'Yes sir.' Drum looped the reins around the whip socket and jumped down. 'We're wanting to buy some livestock.'

'That's me.' Gassaway extended a work-calloused hand, which astonished Drum, but he reached out and shook it.

'I'm—' Drum started to speak.

'Don' need to tell me who yo' be. Written's plain as day on yore face. Kin see Hammond Maxwell writ all over it 'n' kin see Drummage too. Don' know yore name, but yo' shore's hell the fellow what jes' came back to Falconhurst. Know yo' anywhere.'

248

'Yes, I'm Drum Maxwell, sir. Happy to make your acquaintance and even happier that you recognized me.'

The blue eyes clouded over and the old man seemed to be looking beyond Drum into a world that had passed. 'Ham Maxwell my bes' frien'. We grew up together. Knew yore pappy too, that Drummage, 'n' knew yore grandpappy, Drumson. Yo' one o' that line, all right. Right handsome bucks they was. But, then, they was part Mandingo. No' – he shook his head – 'Drumson wa'nt. Ham bo't him in a N'Orleans whorehouse, but Drummage he Big Pearl's git.'

'That's right.'

'Well, Ham's gone 'n' Falconhurst nearly gone too. Everything gone 'roun' here.' He pointed to his own house. 'Ain' much like'n it was afore the war. Hated to see Falconhurst go to pieces. Reckon yo' didn't find much when yo' got there. That Sylvester he a no-good polecat but cain' speak bad o' him. He daid. Jes' heard t'other day. Died of a gripe in the guts.'

Drum felt his nerves twitch under his skin. More of Big Pearl's conjure, but of course it must be merely coincidence.

'But if'n I'd a'known,' Gassaway continued, 'I'da put the sheriff on to him. Didn't know it in time, though, so's I gave ol' Brute some cottonseed so's those pore folks at New Quarters could have something come pickin' time. Heard all they been livin' on's collards 'n' dock 'n' sech.'

Drum waited patiently for the old man to finish. 'Thank you, sir. I appreciate what you did for them.'

'Wa'n't much. Didn't cost me nothin'. Ben Welch over to Sparta wanted a couple o' his heifers studded by my prize bull 'n' he gave me the cottonseed for a fee. Ain' plantin' no more cotton now, so's I gave it to Brute. He a right good man, Brute is. Right knowledgeful too. Hard worker.'

Again Drum could think of nothing to say but merely added another 'Thank you.' He liked this man, who, despite his tumbledown house and his patched work clothes, was willing to extend a degree of hospitality and politeness to him.

'Come over 'n' set with me sometime when yo' ain' busy. Glad to tell yo' all about your family, but onc't I git started, cain' stop. Livin' in the past too much these days but, then, them times better'n these.' He grinned, showing a couple of yellowed tushes. 'Now, Drum, what kin I do for yo'?'

Drum explained their need for cattle both for the big house and for the people over at New Quarters and then introduced Mede.

'Mede!' Gassaway exclaimed. 'That name shore brings back a lot o' memories. Ham Maxwell was right proud of his nigger fighter Mede. That Mede purentee Mandingo what Ham bought up at ol' man Wilson's place, The Coign. Finest nigger I ever did see 'n' Ham jes' gloated over him. Kilt him in the end, though, 'n' 'most broke Ham's heart to do it. Found out he'd a-been rapin' Ham's first wife. Wa'n't Mede's fault, though. That Blanche got him to do it. Don' know how a white woman could've managed it, though. That Mede he the heaviest-hung nigger I ever did see. This boy mus' be kin to that Mede. He lookin' a lot like him. Got Mandingo blood in him, I swear.'

'Big Pearl she's my mammy.' Previously Mede would not have dared to interrupt a conversation, but his new clothes and his new status, in addition to the fact that they were talking about him, prompted him to speak.

Gassaway regarded him reflectively. 'In the ol' days I'd have had yo' strip off yore trogs so's I could finger yo'. Al'ays did like to finger a fine buck, though fingerin' wenches was better. So yo's Big Pearl's git. Ain' one myself for conjure, but I goes over to see Big Pearl onc't in a while. She 'bout the only one I kin talk 'bout old times with.' Gassaway straightened up, seeming to come back from the shadows of the past to reality. 'Come 'long' – he started – 'but be careful yo' don't step in no cow-shit, not with them fine shoes yo' fellas got on.'

Much to Drum's surprise, the barns, in contrast to the house, were in fairly good condition.

'How many cows yo' a-wantin'?' Gassaway asked. 'Mine all pure-bred Jersey.'

Drum admitted that he had no idea.

'Then, I figures yo' a-needin' 'bout four cows for the big house. That'll give yo' plenty o' milk 'n' cream 'n' clabber.

Don' know how many yo' a-wantin' for the folks at New Quarters. Cain' give a cow to every family there. That too costive, but mayhap if'n yo' buy ten o' fifteen, they kin parcel the milk out 'n' all git some. Yo'll be needin' a bull too 'n' I got a nice one. He's young 'n' I been a-savin' him to stud my new heifers, but I'll sell him to yo'. Kin show him to yo'. He right in the barn. If'n yo' want to look at the cows, have to git one of the boys to round 'em up. They all down in the pasture.'

Drum professed his ignorance and said he would have to depend on Gassaway's judgement. The nearest he had ever been to a cow was passing one in a pasture while he was driving along the road. He ordered twenty cows, along with the bull, and then inquired if Gassaway had hogs too. Yes, hogs aplenty! Thereupon Drum ordered fifty for both Falconhurst and New Quarters.

Walking back to the house, Gassaway continued to reminisce about Falconhurst. 'Ham Maxwell 'n' his papa, they right smart men. Everyone else 'roun' here was a-raisin' cotton 'n' tryin' to be quality folks whilst they plastered their plantations 'n' their niggers with mortgages. Land all leached out. Couldn't raise no more cotton nohow 'n' then the war came 'long and everybody lost everything they had. But Ham Maxwell he didn't raise cotton; he raised niggers. He wa'n't no slave trader but a nigger breeder. Got himself mighty rich.

'Falconhurst was always thrivin'. More niggers than yo' could shake a stick at 'n' every year Ham sent 'bout a hundred to N'Orleans. Good niggers worth 'bout two thousand dollars in them days. Never did know what became o' all o' Ham's money. Most o' it in Confederate bonds, I guess, 'n' they ain' worth the paper they's printed on. Reckon, howsomever, they's some Maxwell money lef'. Yo' right well dressed 'n' drivin' a good rig 'n' a-buyin' cattle. That Yankee captain what took yo' north – he a rich man too?'

'Yes, but I'm on my own now, Mr Gassaway. I want to put Falconhurst back where it was.'

'Cain' never do that. Never! Falconhurst 'thout niggers'll never be Falconhurst.'

When they arrived back at the house, Drum offered his hand to the old man, who shook it heartily.

'Been on my conscience a long time what I did to yore father. Ain' never been able to forgit it. Wrongest thing I ever done. Mayhap I kin make up a little of it to yo'. Ease me, it would.'

Drum had no idea of what the old man was talking about and as he didn't want to get involved in any more reminiscences, he got into the surrey and was unwinding the reins when a thought occurred to him.

'You didn't question the fact that I'm Drum Maxwell, did you, Mr Gassaway?'

'Hell, no! Could tell the minute I laid eyes on yo' that yo' a grandson o' Ham Maxwell's 'n' could see that yo' got Mandingo blood in yo' too. I'd swear yo're Drummage's son on a stack o' bibles. Course, if'n yo' gooch-eyed like yore mama, that even better. Miz Sophie she a bit gooch-eyed.'

'Would you be willing to identify me before Mr Jenkins down at the bank? I've got some money there, but he won't release it to me until I get a white man to identify me.'

Gassaway spit in the dust and rubbed it in with his big toe. 'That goddam Jenkins! He only been here a few years. Don't know nothin' 'bout the Maxwells. Shore, I'll tell him who yo' are. Like to take the peck-sniffin' ol' bastard down a peg o' two. Anytime yo' want.'

Drum bade the old man good-day and touched the greys with the whip. The wheels had just started when Gassaway grabbed one of the horse's bridles.

'Yo' ain' asked how much for the cattle,' he said.

'You make up a bill and bring it along when you deliver them.'

'That ain' no way to do business, young fellow. If'n yo' want to make a success outa Falconhurst, yo' always ask how much it costs afore yo' buy it. Kin git awful cheated if'n yo' don'.'

'Not when I'm dealing with you, Mr Gassaway.' Drum touched the horses again with the whip and they started away. As he turned into the main road he waved back at Gassaway.

'He a real nice white man,' Mede said. 'Wonder if'n that other Mede he hung heavier'n me.'

'Don't see how he could be.' Drum laughed. 'Bet they didn't get much work out of poor Debbie today.'

Mede started to laugh. 'Yo' jes' as much to blame for that as me. Jes' as much.'

CHAPTER TWENTY-FOUR

IT WAS DRUM'S first visit to New Quarters and when he drove off the main road into the lane that led to the collection of cabins, he was appalled at the poverty he saw. Surely these could not be human beings who were living in this squalid place? It was scarcely fit for animals; there were tumbledown shacks that had been propped up with tree trunks, crazy-looking chimneys, bare dirt yards on which only a few wilting spears of vegetables were growing. Over it hovered the putrid smell of poverty. He turned from the lane into the dusty street, which curved in an uneven line between the cabins, and saw that Brute's wagon had stopped before a rough cabin that was larger than the others and in somewhat better repair. It had a door and two windows and the logs were chinked, although the roof sagged as if it might collapse at any moment.

The arrival of Brute's wagon had attracted a throng of women, children, and old men. The women were drab, emaciated creatures except for a few who were young, but none of them had a decent dress and those that they did have were torn and patched and torn again. The children, even those in their teens, were stark naked. However, despite their woeful appearance, they all seemed happy. It was an unparalleled event for them and they were cheering Brute's arrival, pointing, shouting, and gesticulating at the marvellous barrels and boxes that were in the wagon.

As Drum drove up with the high-stepping greys and the brand-new surrey their attention was diverted and they thronged around him until he did not think he would be able to dismount from the carriage. Lean arms reached out to touch him. Women with tears in their eyes grabbed his hand to kiss and even Mede came in for his share of adulation.

'Brute he a-sayin' we a-goin' to eat 'gain.' This from a toothless old crone who was so thin she hardly cast a shadow.

'Thank yo', masta suh,' a tall, gaunt woman said.

'God bless yo', masta.'

When he dismounted and walked towards the wagon to speak with Brute, tiny babies with reedlike arms and legs and bulging bellies were thrust towards him; and children, ash-coloured under the darkness of their skins, were pushed in his path by despairing mothers.

'You're all going to eat,' Drum shouted over the turmoil, 'and you're all going to be taken care of. Don't fret yourselves any more.'

His promise seemed to console them, because the wailing and the loud keening ceased. A path was opened up for him so that he was able to get to Brute.

'Boys all a-workin' over at Falconhurst,' Brute said, hammering the padlock and hasp on the door of the cabin that had apparently been the store. Drum stepped inside, noting the empty shelves, the long counter, and the two grimy windows – the only glazed windows he had seen in the settlement. The place had been stripped clean and there was nothing to show it had ever been a store, although evidently it had been a meeting place for the men of the village because there was a rough table, its top covered with the melted stubs of tallow candles, and a few handmade chairs and stools. It smelled of mice and dust, vinegar and kerosene. Dust floated before the windows in golden motes and a papery grey wasps' nest hung from the rafters.

'Sent a boy over to fetch that there Joshua that yo' a-wantin'.' Brute continued with his hammering. 'He a-comin' any minute.'

The close, musty interior of the store was too much for Drum and he stepped out into the sunshine again.

'Have every man, woman, and child at New Quarters come over to the big house tonight.' He tested the padlock that Brute had just nailed on, wondering if the bent and rusty nails that Brute had used would hold it, but it seemed secure. 'I'll get word to Narcisse that all workers are to be excused from work an hour early.' He turned to see a young man of about his own age running down the street. 'Who's that coming?' he asked of Brute.

'Tha's Joshua, the boy yo' sen' for.'

He arrived, panting from running, the ragged remnants of his shirt sweat-plastered to his body.

'Yo' sen' for me, Brute?'

'Sent for yo', son, but now that Mista Drum here, he a-goin' to talk to yo'.'

Drum discovered a much blacker version of himself. It must be true that this fellow was his half-brother because there were certain facial characteristics they both shared that Drum could easily recognize. This Joshua's lips were thicker than his own, his nostrils broader, and his hair a kinky skullcap; yet there was a recognizable family resemblance between them. The fellow looked thin, but he had a rugged frame and needed only some good meals to fill him out. Furthermore, if appearances could be depended upon, the fellow looked honest. At least he could look Drum in the eye without hanging his head or appearing sheepish. Drum stretched forth his hand, but Joshua did not seem to understand the gesture.

'Shake hands with Mista Drum, Joshua,' Brute prompted him, and Joshua presented a damp hand for Drum to shake. At first his hand rested inertly in Drum's own but when Drum squeezed it heartily, Joshua's hand closed tighter, but he was too dumbfounded to speak.

'You know anything about storekeeping?' Drum gestured towards the load of groceries and then inclined his head towards the store.

'Helped in the store when Mista Sylvester he comed over 'n' opened it up. Helped him, I did.'

'Can you make change and write down charges?'

'Mista Sylvester he showed me. Write in de book. One poun' flour, four bits. One poun' lard, four bits. One poun' grits, four bits. Everything one pound, four bits.'

'Things will be different now. I'll come over and tell you about things. We've got to figure out fair prices. Mede and I'll help you get started. Now all you've got to do is to help Brute unload, keep the store locked up, and see that nobody here steals anything.'

'Ain' no thievin' 'roun' here. We honest people.' Brute seemed resentful that Drum might suspect anyone in New Quarters of stealing.

'Hungry people will steal even if they are honest and I would not blame them.' Drum turned from Brute to eye Joshua again. 'How did you learn to write and figure?' he asked him.

'We had a school here till that Mr Sylvester he come. Miz Leavitt, she a bright-skinned gal from down Westminster way, she taught us.' Brute was answering for Joshua. 'After Mr Sylvester come, howsomever, he ain' willin' to pay her three dollars a week for teachin', so's we had to give up the school. Some boys like Joshua here they learned to do sums 'n' read 'n' write.'

'Cain' do it well, Mista Drum.' Joshua was drawing circles in the dust with his big toe. 'Fergits, I do, but it comes back to me.' He lifted his head and smiled at Drum. 'Ain' fergot all. No, suh.'

Drum encouraged him with a wink and a slap on the back. Once again he made his way between the throngs of women and children and stepped up into the surrey. They were loath to let him go. He had appeared to them in their darkest hour and to them he was something of a god with his white skin and golden hair. He seemed to be a vision out of some other world, something for them to gaze at in wonderment, a saviour who had come to fill their empty bellies with bread and meat.

Just as he was about to turn the surrey around and head for home, a girl appeared out of the crowd, edging her way through the women that were standing there until she got up close to where Drum was seated. Sidling between the wheels, she managed to get her knee on the step and Drum did not dare start for fear of harming her.

She was much lighter than any of the others there, with a heart-shaped face and hair that hung down over her shoulders in long black waves. It was damp and Drum got the impression that while the others had been welcoming him she was bathing herself. Her dress, although patched and worn, had been freshly washed and ironed, and she herself gave off the clean odour of fresh mint. Looking closer, he could see that she had green eyes, a smooth skin somewhat the colour of café au lait, and only a vestige of Negro features. There were hollows in her cheeks and her collarbones were prominent, but she did not appear so pitifully undernourished as the others.

'I'se Rosanne.' She had a slight lisp, which slurred her words. 'I sister o' that Debbie 'n' she a-sayin' yo' a-wantin' me over to the big house. Debbie she a-sayin' he' – she pointed to Mede – 'a-wantin' a bed wench 'n' I mos' awful anxious to come over to the big house.' She lowered her eyelids, letting the long lashes make a sooty mark under her eyes, then opened them wide, with a look of such provocative sensuality that Drum felt a tightening in his groin and this increased as her eyes slowly lowered to observe it. 'Wishin', though' – she lowered her voice as she continued to stare – 'that it a-bein' yo' 'n' not him.'

Mede had overheard her. 'Yo' mine, li'l gal. Drum he got Debbie.'

'Debbie's not so purty's me. I light-skinned. Debbie she's black.' She ignored Mede, still staring at Drum, quite aware of what was happening to him.

'You'll do,' Drum said, stretching out one leg to ease himself. 'Want to come over to the big house now? Jump up in the back seat, but be careful of those parcels there.'

It was the grandest and by far the most dramatic moment in Rosanne's life. Even Victoria of England could not have entered her state coach more elegantly than Rosanne. Placing her bare foot on the step, she eased herself on to the back seat, leaned back against the soft upholstery, and surveyed the women of New Quarters with an expression of utter contempt. She was aware that each one of them knew why she was going and she also knew that each one of them envied her. She would have preferred Drum – his white skin fascinated her – but Mede was far better looking than any other boy in New Quarters and she was quite satisfied that she had been chosen for him. Even when Drum started the horses, she did not deign to look back but sat ramrod stiff against the seat quite conscious of the envy she had created.

'Hear they feeds well over to the big house. Debbie she a-tellin' me.'

Mede turned half around in the seat. 'Look, yo' pretty li'l gal, I a-goin' to feed yo' well 'n' I a-goin' to pleasure yo' well too. Yo' ain' never been pleasured till I pleasure yo'.' He laid a possessive hand on her thigh.

She relaxed from her stiff posture, slipping down on to the seat and covering Mede's big hand with one of hers. Stretching her legs out straight, she pulled up her dress, guiding Mede's hand under it. Mede's hand slid slowly upward while Rosanne closed her eyes. 'She a-goin' to be mine,' he demanded of Drum, his voice husky with desire.

'Thinkin' I'm going to bed you with Lucy again,' Drum said, shoving his elbow into Mede's stomach, all the while wishing he were not driving and that he was in Mede's seat.

'Now yo' a-knowin' what Mammy said.' Mede's petulance did not cause him to remove his hand. 'Mammy said she not a-wantin' me to bed with Lucy no more. She said we uns brothers 'n'—'

'And she also said that if we were brothers, we had to share and share alike. Well, I shared with you. You had Debbie longer than I did last night.'

'Uh-huh.' Mede had an inkling where the conversation might be leading.

'Then, if I shared Debbie with you, you can share Rosanne with me.'

'Kin, I s'pose.' It was a reluctant answer, but it did not prevent Mede from turning a little farther around in his seat.

Rosanne straightened up, although she did not push Mede's

hand away, and knelt down on the floor of the back seat, her arms on the back of the front seat and her face between Drum's and Mede's. Her darting tongue flicked against Drum's ear, making him quiver at the delicate touch. It lasted only a moment, for she turned her head and kissed Mede full on the lips while her left hand forced itself down between them, stroking the tautly stretched black cloth she encountered first on the one and then on the other. Mede grabbed at her, but she eluded him, slapping now at his questing hand, and sat back up on the seat as ramrod straight as before.

'Mighty glad yo' two's brothers.' She sighed as she slapped Mede's hand again. 'Mista Mede he mighty fine lookin' 'n' Mista Drum he white 'n' always hankered to be pestered by a white man. Behave yo'self, Mista Mede. We out'n the road now 'n' ain' decent what yo' a-doin'. 'N' button up yore pants too. White man a-comin' down the road on horseback. He a-goin' to think we'se jes' fiel'-hand niggers 'stead o' quality coloured folks.'

Mede removed his hand reluctantly and turned around to adjust his clothes, something that Drum had already accomplished. They both lifted their hats to the stranger. It was less than a mile between New Quarters and Falconhurst, so Drum concentrated on quieting himself. He knew he would never be able to get out of the carriage in his present condition. He touched the whip lightly to the greys and they trotted briskly along.

Drum was beginning to feel at home here in this country, which seemed so foreign to New England. The blazing sun, the heat, the level land, and the fields of cotton interspersed with a few fields of corn were far different from the sights his eyes had been accustomed to. Here there were no mountains, no lakes, and no seashore. He did not miss the tidy New England farms with their white houses and red barns in the burgeoning fertility of this new land. Here he was able to experience a feeling of belonging that he had never felt in New England. He seemed to be a part of this soil, this heat, this blue sky, and this blazing sun. Falconhurst was his real home, not the plush-draped stuffy drawing-rooms of Boston. Falconhurst was his and now, thank God, he had the means to bring it back to its former glories.

Its former glories! Life at Falconhurst before the war must have been a wonderful experience, at least for the owners. He fell to daydreaming of what it would have been like forty or fifty years ago and in his reverie he placed himself as the owner of Falconhurst at that time. He would be white and he would be a slave breeder. How much more interesting to grow human beings than cotton. And how much more profitable it would have been.

This fellow beside him, this Mede, and this girl in the back seat, this Rosanne, would have been his to do with as he pleased. He would have mated Mede and this Rosanne. That would not have been difficult to do because he knew, right at this moment, if he stopped the carriage and gave them leave to scramble into the bushes, they would accomplish that in a matter of minutes. And so would he, but of course as the white owner of Falconhurst in slave times, he would not have done such a thing. Yes, he would. He most definitely would. He'd have access to every wench on the plantation. What a wonderful life!

Then this Rosanne would produce a child that would grow up into a buck as handsome and as stalwart as Mede. He could sell this young buck for $2,000, maybe more. But, he remembered, by that time he would have had to sell both Mede and Rosanne and could he do it? He glanced at Mede out the corner of his eyes. Could he put him up on the slave block and let him be sold to whoever was willing to pay the highest price. In the first place he wouldn't sell Mede anyway and if he did, thinking no more about him than Livingood thought about his horses or Gassaway about his cows, he'd always wonder if he had been sold to a kind master and if he had a good home. Certainly the Maxwells who had lived at Falconhurst must have been a calloused lot. To breed a slave, raise it, and then sell it! How were they able to do it? Nevertheless, although he condemned the practice, he envied those people who had done it.

No, it was better as it was now. It was better to be Drum Maxwell, dressed in good clothes, riding along in a surrey behind two grey horses towards Falconhurst. It was better to be Drum Maxwell and not have to sell Mede or the girl on the back seat. Damn it! Right at this moment he begrudged sharing this girl with Mede. But, then, he had Claire's love, although he could not be sure of that because she said she loved Narcisse too. Then, damn Narcisse! But he couldn't do that. Narcisse was his friend. Or was he?

His thoughts about Narcisse were interrupted by Mede, who pointed out a gang of workers. Narcisse was astride a mule riding slowly up and down the rows of cotton flicking his small whip at the hands, barely touching them but just making them aware of his presence. Drum halted the team and hallooed over to him. Narcisse waved the whip he was carrying, not recognizing who it was, as he had never seen the greys or the carriage before. He carefully guided the mule down between the rows and when he came near enough to recognize them, he whipped the mule, riding up to the fence. Vaulting down, he clambered over the fence, crossed the ditch beside the road, and came up to Drum. He spent barely a moment compliment-ing Drum on his new purchase, not even deigning to inspect the horses, then looked up at Drum, his face red with anger.

'Look here, Drum.' Narcisse made no effort to control his words. 'Just who's boss around here? That's what I want to know. About an hour ago some naked pickaninny came running across the field, screaming "Joshua, Joshua," and one of my best bucks dropped his hoe like a piece of hot coal. "Brute he a-wantin' yo' over to New Quarters," the brat says, and with-out a by-your-leave this Joshua was off across the fields. He's due for a whipping, that boy.'

'Wait, wait, wait!' Drum hoped to cool him off. 'Remember, we're just getting started here. It's all my fault. I told Brute to send for the fellow. I'm putting him in charge of the store at New Quarters. He worked for Sylvester there and he knows something about storekeeping.'

'Then, just as he worked for Sylvester, he should be working for me. The overseer is always in charge of the hands' store.'

'Not here.' Drum was emphatic. 'I'm in charge of the store

here. These people are going to get a fair deal from now on. Not' – he was sufficiently apologetic to satisfy even Narcisse – 'that I think you wouldn't give them a fair deal, but it's just a hobby of mine.'

Narcisse saw a source of extra profits vanishing. It was true, most overseers were in charge of the hands' stores, keeping a book on every man and his family. It was rarely that a worker ever got his debt to the store paid up because the overseer would raise the prices so much that the hand would always be in debt. However he could not gainsay Drum, so he did not answer but merely stared at Drum sullenly.

'Furthermore' – Drum wanted to make another point – 'let's get this straight, there'll be no more whippings here.'

'You can't get any work out of a bunch of niggers without whipping.'

'These are not slave times,' Drum said softly. He didn't want an open quarrel with Narcisse.

'As far as niggers are concerned, they are. The stupid bastards don't even know they're free. It isn't like it was just after the war. The whites have got 'em licked now.' The only difference is that we can't sell 'em off and that's a disadvantage.' The anger left his voice and he made an effort to be friendly. 'I don't understand you, Drum. First this business this morning about Mede eating with us and sleeping in a bedroom, then sending for Joshua without asking my permission, and now saying that I can't ever use this' – he flung out the whip, which was coiled in his hand. 'Why don't you oversee this place yourself?'

Drum reached down from his seat and clapped Narcisse on the shoulder. 'Because I want you to do it. You handle the crops and I'll handle the folks. How's that for an even division of labour?'

'But I damn well can't handle the cotton unless I handle the people.'

'We'll both try my way for a while. If it doesn't work, I'll be the first to admit it, but I think I can do something for them that will make them more valuable to us. By the way, let them off from work an hour early today. I want them all over to

Falconhurst at half past seven. I want to talk to them and explain a few things.'

'So that means we are going to lose a whole hour's work today. They'll make up for it tomorrow, though. I'll work them twice as hard. Niggers are naturally lazy, Drum. They're shiftless. They'd rather make the motions than do the work and it doesn't make a damn bit of difference to them whether they do it right or not. Look at them now.' He turned and pointed across the field, where every one of them was leaning on his hoe, gazing at the group on the road. 'Unless I stand over them with this' – again he brandished the whip – 'I can't get a lick of work out of them.'

'Then, who planted these fields, chopped weeds, and kept them up until we arrived? You yourself said it was a good crop and well started.'

'But I'm going to make it a better one.'

'That's what I want, Narcisse. That's what I'm depending on you for, but cooperate with me. Let everyone off an hour earlier and you'll see a far different group of workers tomorrow. You wouldn't have much energy if you didn't have anything to eat in your stomach. Watch them work tomorrow after a good breakfast.'

'A couple of good flicks with a bullwhip across a man's ass makes him work harder than a good breakfast, but I'll go along with you, Drum. After all, you're the owner and you do pay in advance.' He jingled the coins in his pocket. 'See you at supper.' His anger seemed to have dissipated and he was across the fence and on to the mule, riding away and hollering at the workers, who immediately started plying their hoes.

Drum gave an extra fillip to his whip as he drove up to the front door of Falconhurst and sent Mede inside to fetch everyone in the house out on to the front portico. Because Rosanne in her present tattered garments added nothing to the smartness of the surrey and the team of greys, he told her to get out and follow Mede into the house. Soon all the others were out in front – Claire, Mammy Morn, Matilda, Debbie, and even Lucy. In the admiration and compliments that they were bestowing on the rig, Drum did not notice that neither

Mede nor Rosanne reappeared and it was not until he had driven the horses around back, where Ciceron had already arrived and had tethered the horses and mules outside the stables, that he noted their absence. It was a trifling matter, so he dismissed it, although he was pretty sure that somewhere in the house Mede and Rosanne were finishing what had been started in the carriage. He remembered his own reactions to Rosanne. How could he blame Mede? If he were not so busy, he would probably be doing the same thing himself.

Ciceron had already finished currying and brushing one horse until his coat gleamed – a far cry in appearance from the same nag Ciceron had ridden away from the livery stable. He was just starting on the second when Drum drove up. The stalls in the stable, so Ciceron informed him, were in fairly good condition and would do for the horses and there was a part of the cattle barn where he could tether the mules until they could build a barnyard for them. Again he congratulated Drum on acquiring the greys. They were, he swore, worth at least three times what Drum paid for them and the surrey itself was a fine vehicle, newer in style even than the old-fashioned barouches. Then it was Drum's turn to thank Ciceron and compliment him on his knowledge of horses. He promised him that at the first opportunity he would have a coachman's livery made for him and that seemed to be a sufficient reward for Ciceron, in addition to the gold eagle that Drum presented to him.

Lucy came rushing out of the house saying that Mede had told him about the knife he had bought for him, which was still in its paper wrapping along with the pistol and the rifle that Mede had purchased. Drum permitted Lucy to take the knife and, although he was in a hurry to get back into the house, he yielded to the boy's urging to come with him around the corner of the barn. Picking up a stone, Lucy drew a small circle on the unpainted side of the barn.

'Look, Mista Drum.' He swaggered a bit. 'Look what I kin do with a knife.' After testing the knife a moment to determine its balance and the way it fitted in his hand, he drew his arm back, squinted his eyes, and sent the knife flying through the air. It landed in the centre of the small circle Lucy had drawn. Drum's compliments to Lucy, who loved to be praised, elicited the information that a seaman had to use a knife and what he knew had been taught to him by O'Brien who, he bragged, could kill a mosquito at ten yards.

Again Drum dipped into his satchel. 'Here's your first month's pay, Lucy.' He tossed the gold eagle to the boy, who jumped up to catch it. 'And by the way,' he added, 'you won't be bedding with Mede any more. Mede's got a wench and a bedroom of his own now.'

Lucy's thick lip curled out with petulance but only momentarily. His pout changed to a smile while he regarded Drum. 'Mede he a nice boy, but wenches better for him than I am. 'Sides, Mista Narcisse he knowin' that I kin read 'n' write 'n' he askin' me kin I help him after I git through my supper work in the big house. Kin I, Mista Drum?'

'Doesn't make any difference to me what you do after your work is done, Lucy, but you'd better keep away from New Quarters. You try any of your tricks on the boys over there, and you're liable to get your head broken.'

Lucy's tongue encircled his lips. 'Ain' a-goin' over to New Quarters nohow. Likes it better here, Mista Drum, 'n' Mista Narcisse he a-wantin' me to help him.' He pointed to the house. 'They a-waitin' fo' yo' at the back door, Mista Drum.'

Just as they had all trooped out the front door, all the servants were now in the back, waiting for him, and he hurried his steps, taking the path that had now been trodden down through the weeds. As he neared the house he started to run, calling out to Mammy Morn.

'Hey, Mammy Morn, did you ever perform a miracle?'

'What yo' mean "miracle", man?' She waited for him to arrive at the door and held out a hand to hoist him up the step and into the kitchen. 'Every meal I cooks it a miracle. But if'n yo' means "miracle" ' – she accented the word carefully – 'I ain' no conjure woman. My miracles all done with food. What yo' a-wantin'? Hummin'-birds' gizzards for supper?'

He laughed, slapping her on her broad rump, which presented such an inviting expanse of taut cotton cloth. No, it was not humming-birds' gizzards he wanted, merely something good to give to two hundred hungry people who were coming over from New Quarters that night. When she threw up her hands in despair, he explained that he did not want a full meal for them, just something to pass out in the way of food – some little treat for people who had not had anything really good to eat for months.

'Pralines,' Claire suggested.

Mammy Morn negated this with the information that they had no cane syrup and no pecans.

'Ham sandwiches.' Drum thought he had contributed an idea.

She withered him with a glance that suggested he was not very bright. How could anyone roast ten hams and make all those loaves of bread in so short a time?

The old woman lowered herself into a creaking chair by the kitchen table and Drum and Claire seated themselves opposite her. For a long time nobody spoke because each was occupied in thinking of what might be cooked and served. The door opened and Ciceron came in, filled the pan in the sink with hot water, and poured in some cold. While he was scrubbing his face and hands he called out to Mammy Morn.

'Got any more o' them ginger cookies what yo' made yesterday?' He reached for the towel.

Mammy Morn snapped her fingers. 'Tha's it,' she shouted. 'Ginger cookies!' She lumbered across the kitchen and opened the door leading up to the servants' quarters. 'Matilda, h'ist yore ass down here. This ain' no time for nappin'. Got us a lot of work to do. A-goin' to bake us two hundred ginger cookies. Git a hurry on.'

'Ginger cookies all right?' she asked Drum. 'They good 'n' they somethin' niggers don' have. Give each one a ginger cookie 'n' them burr-heads think they's in heaven.' She was already bustling about the kitchen, adding more wood to the stove, setting jugs of molasses on the table, and bringing in a bucket of flour from the buttery.

'I'll help you, Mammy Morn,' Claire volunteered.

'Right kindly if'n you do, Miz Claire. I mixes 'em. Matilda

266

she bakes 'em, Miz Claire she takes 'em outa the pans 'n' ranges them on platters.' She brandished a wooden spoon at Drum. 'Yo' folks ain' a-goin' to git much for supper tonight, though. Jes' odds 'n' ends. Yo' cain' have no ginger cookies, Ciceron. If'n yo' hungry, butter yo'self a piece o' bread 'n' then yo' git to hell outa my kitchen. 'N' yo' too, Mista Drum. Ain' got no room here for menfolks a-clutterin' up the place. Shoo outa here.'

He promised he would go just as soon as he talked a few things over with Claire. He explained about the bolts of calico he had purchased that morning. Each woman was to receive a dress length of calico. Each man was to receive two dollars, which he could spend in the newly opened store. Each child was to receive some candy and everyone would get a ginger cookie. He drew the bill of sale from Hicks from his pocket and suggested that they both go over the next day and put a fair price on everything in the store, to which she assented.

Then, too, he told her, he wanted to discuss wages and hours with the people from New Quarters, along with the repairs that he wanted made at Falconhurst and the rehabilitation of New Quarters and its people.

Mammy Morn turned on Ciceron, who was still eating his slice of bread and butter. 'Ain' I a-tellin' yo' to git out o' my kitchen? Yo' all stenchy like'n a horse. 'N' yo' too, Mista Drum.'

He made a dive for her and tried to snatch the wooden spoon from her. 'Yo' mean I'se stenchy like'n a horse too?' he asked mimicking her dialect.

'Laws no, but yo' a nuisance jes' the same. Now, git – shoo fly outa here.'

'Le's go out to the barn,' Ciceron said, gulping down the last bit of his bread, 'where they ain' no sputterin' ol' jaybirds 'bout. Horses better company'n women anyway. Knows 'nough to keep theys mouth shet 'n' ain' a-blabbermouthin' alla time.' He dodged the tin cup that Mammy threw at him and grabbed Drum's coat sleeve. 'We gotta name them horses. Mista Livingood he not a-knowin' theys names.'

Claire followed them to the door, her hand on Drum's

shoulder. 'Women just don't want men around when they are busy in the kitchen. Go along with Ciceron and christen the horses.'

Drum saw that Ciceron had stabled the two greys and the two other horses and bedded them down with straw. He had found some hay up in the mow but reminded Drum that they would have to get oats and middlings too. He had combed and curried the greys until their coats were like satin; even their hooves had been polished. Drum was scarcely able to recognize the other two horses that he had bought at the livery stable. Suddenly it occurred to him that he had not seen Mede for some time and that was unusual because Mede was always around when anything was happening. He asked Ciceron if he had seen him.

Putting his finger to his mouth for silence and winking one eye suggestively, Ciceron beckoned to Drum to follow him. They walked the length of the barn to where a big box stall occupied one corner. As they approached it Ciceron started to walk on tiptoe and again silently cautioned Drum to be still.

Following Ciceron's lead, Drum peered over the shoulder-high partition of the stall. The light was dim, but Drum could see, struggling on the straw-strewn floor, the naked forms of Mede and Rosanne and he could hear the frantic gasps as Mede sucked in air, along with Rosanne's whimperings. Mede's relentless plunging and Rosanne's hands, which fluttered like bronze butterflies over his back, told Drum he had not long to wait. He noticed an old buggy whip standing beside the stall and grabbed it, reaching as far over the partition as he could. The climax was approaching and Drum raised the whip, bringing it down on Mede's buttocks just as he gave a mighty groan, which turned into a scream as the whip caught him. Drum and Ciceron both squatted behind the partition.

'Yo' shore a powerful man,' Rosanne said, recovering her breath. 'Never did hear a man yell like'n that afore.'

Drum and Ciceron slid across the floor and took refuge behind a feed bin. Peeking around the side, Drum saw Mede's head and shoulders appear over the top of the stall and from the motion of his right shoulder Drum imagined that he was stroking his backside.

'Never had that happen to me afore' – Mede could not account for what had happened to him – 'but it shore helped. Jes' wondered if'n I could make it the third time when wham – something hit me 'n' I did it.' He disappeared from view behind the partition and Drum and Ciceron tiptoed out the barn door.

'Come on, Ciceron, let's go down and look at the mules.'

They started to walk towards the other barn. Ciceron started to giggle and then let out a high-pitched whoop of laughter. 'Yo' know, Mista Drum, that grey horse he ain' the only stallion what's back there in the barn. That Mede boy right good 'n' when yo' whopped him, he shore let it go. Yes suh, Mista Drum, he sure let go 'n' bet he still a-wonderin' what happened to him.' He laughed and whooped all the way to the barn.

CHAPTER TWENTY-FIVE

SUPPER THAT NIGHT was a simple affair – merely cold ham, bread and butter, and hot coffee to wash it down. It took too much time and trouble to set the table in the dining-room and, as there was no room available on the kitchen table because of the many platters heaped high with ginger cookies, they all made sandwiches out of the bread and ham and ate them standing up in the kitchen. Lucy sliced the bread and ham and brewed the coffee. Matilda was scrubbing mixing bowls and pans in the sink while Mammy Morn sat in one of the kitchen chairs rubbing the kinks out of her arm from stirring so much batter.

Drum, who had just finished his second sandwich, insisted that everyone at the big house look their best for tonight's celebration. Mammy Morn loaned one of her voluminous starched white aprons and a white headcloth to Matilda and, although the apron was big enough to go around poor gaunt Matilda twice, it served to hide the ragged dress she was wearing. Claire donated two of her oldest dresses to Debbie and Rosanne, which, although faded and mended, were the most sumptuous gowns the girls had ever seen. Their bare brown feet appeared rather incongruous under the long skirts, but since they would be standing in the background, it would not be noticed. Narcisse, as always, appeared immaculately clad. Despite the broad-brimmed straw hat he always wore outside, his face was beginning to darken and in contrast his hands seemed strangely light, because he always wore gloves. Narcisse took pride in the lightness of his skin and did everything possible to avoid the sun.

It was necessary for Drum to loan Mede another white coat. The one he had been wearing all day had suffered too much from its being thrown so carelessly on the barn floor. Lucy, of course, had decent clothes and Ciceron had his grey pants and shirt. Drum decided on a white suit similar to what most planters wore but added a high yellow cravat and a yellow brocaded waistcoat, which made him look even more handsome than usual, as the yellow accented the colour of his hair. He was surprised when Claire joined them to see that she was wearing her most elaborate ball gown of pale blue moiré with a high, draped bustle in the back. She had even added her turquoise bracelets.

'Just to give them a little treat,' she confessed. 'They love pretty things and they see them so seldom.'

They all stepped out on to the front porch except Narcisse, who disappeared in the direction of the overseer's cottage to return with ten stalwart young men, whom he introduced to Drum as the drivers he had chosen. They were, Drum could see, all fine, tall, muscular bucks and in Narcisse's introduction, he noticed the occurrence of the name *Big*. There was Big Sol, Big Jock, and Big Ham, along with some other names that Drum did not remember. All of them appeared to be well fed, their skins smooth and glossy, with far better clothes than the rest of the folks in New Quarters. Each one possessed a grinning air of braggadocio combined with subservience and even while Drum wondered if they would be difficult to discipline, he congratulated Narcisse on their choice.

Brute, however, who had remained in the background, did not seem altogether happy about them. He was biting his lower lip and he merely nodded a 'Yes, Mista Drum suh' when Drum asked him if he considered these men a good choice for drivers. Narcisse, whose temper was always so near the surface, was about to speak, but Drum beat him to it. 'I merely asked Brute,' he said, hoping to temper Narcisse's anger, 'because he has lived with these boys and knows them.'

Narcisse turned quickly without answering and lined the ten fellows up along the rear of the porch, their backs against the brickwork of the house. In front of them, Claire arranged the house servants with Mammy Morn seated in the centre, along with Matilda, who stood beside her, and Debbie and Rosanne on the other side. Although everyone knew exactly why Debbie and Rosanne were at the big house, they were nominally parlour maids and did perform those duties during the day time. Lucy stood alone, a little before them and at one side because he considered himself superior to all the others on the household staff, both from longer association with Drum and because Drum had told him he would be the butler, the head man in the house. Ciceron, who felt he was just as important in the barns as Lucy was in the house, stood on the opposite side.

Ciceron and Lucy had previously set up a table at the front of the porch, using planks and trestles they had discovered out in the barn, and Mammy Morn had covered it with a long white damask tablecloth. The big epergne from the dining-room was filled with flowers and placed in the centre of the table, flanked by silver candlesticks whose flickering flames, protected by glass hurricane shades, gave light in the growing dusk. Four Chippendale chairs were behind the table. In front of one was a big silver bowl filled with the lemon and pepper-mint drops that Drum had bought earlier. Before the next chair was a pile of folded cloths, the dress lengths of calico. The next chair had nothing before it but a substantial-looking small mahogany chest with brass corners, while the last chair faced an enormous platter piled high with ginger cookies, some of them still warm from the oven. Drum looked around for Mede so he could seat him in the first chair behind the candies, but again Mede was nowhere to be seen. He checked to see if Rosanne was still on the porch. She was. That assured him on one count. At least Mede was not out in the stable with her, dirtying up another white coat. Claire seated herself before the dress lengths of calico. Drum took the chair behind the small mahogany chest for himself and designated the last chair, before the ginger cookies, for Narcisse. Just as they were being seated, Mede arrived with Big Pearl, and Drum regretted that he had entirely forgotten his grandmother in his plans for the evening. He thanked Mede inwardly for remembering and ordered a chair brought out from the parlour for Big Pearl and placed at one end of the table, just behind Mede. Brute stood at the end of the table, nearest Narcisse, dressed in patched but clean clothes.

When Drum opened the cover of the small mahogany chest on the table in front of him, Narcisse peeked over his shoulder. He was chagrined to see that Drum would be passing out money while he had only ginger cookies to give away. It should have been his province to give out the money. As overseer, he was paymaster. It seemed to him that Drum was constantly usurping his authority, but this time he swallowed his choler and pretended not to notice it.

They were all quiet, waiting expectantly for something to happen and their very quietness brought the sound of singing to them. It was the people from New Quarters coming down the road, their slow procession enlivened by burning pine-knot torches and paced by the music of banjos and fiddles. Their songs were plaintive ones, but as they passed the gates and started up the long tree-shaded drive to the house they all fell silent and the only sound was the shuffling of bare feet in the dust of the lane. Drum could see a long line of people and he began to doubt if he had enough of everything for everyone.

272

This certainly seemed a larger crowd than the two hundred Brute had mentioned.

Silently they grouped themselves around the porch, gazing up in wonderment at those sitting on the portico. To these simple souls of New Quarters, the well-dressed people above them seemed like denizens of another world. They gazed in awe at Claire in her ball gown and even Debbie and Rosanne in their simple dresses appeared in a new light – far different from those girls who only a few days ago had been running around New Quarters in ragged dresses. Even the ten big fellows in the rear had lost their devil-may-care grins and stood straight and tall. The people were all glad to see Brute in his position of authority near Narcisse; he was a man they had learned to trust. Big Pearl's presence also gave them confidence and they felt that her conjure was working for them, although most of them knew that she was there because she was Drum's grandmother. Slowly and silently they formed a wide semi-circle around the soaring white pillars of Falconhurst, speculating on why they had been summoned there and a bit fearful of what might be going to happen to them. Would this golden-haired, nearly white man dispossess them of the land his father had given them?

Drum waited until they had all settled down and the women had quieted the children. Looking down on them, he felt a strange and indescribable empathy flowing from all of them to himself and he knew, once and for all, that these were his own people. They were looking up at him as the Israelites of old had looked to Moses to lead them out of the bondage of Egypt. They were dependent on him and he resolved that he would not fail them. They needed him too much.

His voice, when he arose and started to speak to them, broke with emotion and he had a difficult time speaking loud enough for all of them to hear, but as he progressed he became more sure of himself and after the first few sentences he could hear his own voice loud and clear.

'Men and women of Falconhurst' – he deliberately said 'Falconhurst' rather than New Quarters – 'I want to welcome you. You are my people and I am a part of you. My father was one of you and so is my grandmother.' He turned towards Big Pearl, hearing the shouts of the crowd. 'But don't forget,' he continued, 'my mother was one of you also because Falconhurst came to me through her and she was a woman who was not ashamed to marry a coloured man.'

'Pore Miz Sophie.' 'God bless Miz Sophie.' 'God bless Drummage too.' 'He a fine man, that Drummage was.' 'Did a lot for us, Drummage did.'

Drum heard the last remark and repeated it. 'And I intend to do a lot for you too. We are all going to work together here at Falconhurst to make it the best, the happiest, and the most prosperous plantation in the whole South. To do it I shall need your help. Can I depend on it?'

'Shore can, Mista Drum suh!'

'Then, we are all going to work hard. But remember this. We are going to work together and not separately. To do that we've all got to have someone to tell us what to do and when to do it and then pitch in together and do it together. No man at Falconhurst is going to work by himself, doing things the way he wants to do them. You'll all be working under my overseer, Mr Narcisse Brantome.' Drum turned to Narcisse, who stood up to an accompaniment of cheers.

'And under Mr Narcisse, you'll be working under your old friend Brute, who is head driver here.' Drum nodded in Brute's direction and again there were cheers. 'And Mr Narcisse has chosen ten drivers to work under Brute.' He indicated the row of men at the back of the porch and, although there were a few cheers, they were rather feeble and somewhere from the darkness came the words 'Ain' working for that goddam Big Jock.'

Drum ignored the comment and continued. 'Hours of work will be from sunup till sundown, but you'll get a full hour off at noon. When it comes picking time, we'll work early and late and all hands will turn out. Every man that works gets four bits a day. When we need women and young folks, we'll pay them two bits a day. Payday will be Saturday and you'll be paid by Mr Narcisse.

'There'll be no whippings at Falconhurst. If we find a man

who does not want to work or a man who is a troublemaker, he'll have to find another place to live. This is no place for lazy folks. Mr Narcisse will report any trouble with the hands to me and I'll decide. I always want to hear both sides of the story – his and yours.'

His eyes caught a young couple who were nuzzling each other on the outer periphery and when they saw him looking at them, they immediately separated and sat bolt upright, staring at him intently.

'I know that we are going to get along all right together. It's not going to be easy. We've got to start from the bottom again and it will take time. But just as soon as I can manage it, we're going to have everything we need to work with – horses, mules, cattle, pigs, and seed for your own gardens. We need food first and decent clothes and warm, comfortable places to live in. As soon as possible I am going to build new cabins for you. We're going to have a store where you will be charged fair prices and' – he paused for a long moment – 'we are going to make Falconhurst a place where you will all be proud to work and live.'

Again there was enthusiastic cheering and he held up his hands to silence them.

'Now I want to present to you Mrs Brantome, whom you may call Miss Claire. She will be in charge of the big house here, but if any of you are sick or ailing or in trouble, I want you to come to her. She'll help you. And this' – he looked towards Big Pearl as though to assure her he was doing her bidding – 'is my brother, Mede, who will help me. If I am away, you can always come to him for advice and help.'

He surveyed them, looking into their upturned faces and feeling the confidence they had in him. Turning for a moment, he leaned down and whispered with Claire, then announced, 'We're going to need some more help in the big house. We want a laundress who is a good ironer too. We want an extra girl in the kitchen and we want a young fellow to serve in the dining-room. We'll need a boy to help take care of the horses, two boys for the cow barn, another to make us a vegetable garden, and two boys to take care of the grounds. We'll pick them out later.

'Now I want to see a man named Rex and another called Amos and another called Fred. Want to see Aunt Lou. Will all you people please come up.' Three men arose from the crowd and a stout woman stood up and walked with them to the porch. When they approached the porch, Drum beckoned to them to come up. The three men were all middle-aged, somewhat younger than Brute, and the woman looked to be in her sixties.

'You a good painter, Rex?' Drum looked from one man to another, not knowing which would answer.

'If'n I have paints and brushes, I am, Mista Drum. Ain' got neither now. Learned paintin' well, though. Even been paintin' in Benson.'

'Then, you're the painter here.' He turned to the other two men. 'Which of you is Amos and which is Fred?' He waited for them to identify themselves.

'You men good carpenters?' They admitted that they were and he had Big Pearl's word for it too.

'Then, you're hired as carpenters.' He turned his attention to the woman. 'You're Aunt Lou? How would you like to be a seamstress here at the big house?'

She was too frightened to speak, but Big Pearl spoke up for her. 'She like'n it fine if'n she kin go home nights. She got a passel o' grandchildren what needs takin' care of.' She placed her hands on the arms of her chair and stood up, searching the audience for a moment, and then pointed to a woman with a snowy white headcloth. ''N' Emmaline there, she good at washin' and ironin'.' Another woman stood up and came to take her place beside Aunt Lou.

Drum told those chosen to sit on the edge of the porch and then invited all the rest to line up and come up the steps, passing by the table one at a time. As each one appeared, Brute shouted out their names. Drum remained standing and shook hands with all the men and women, while he patted every child on its woolly head. Having seen the children run around naked at New Quarters, he was glad to see that they all had some sort of covering tonight, even though it was nothing more than a piece of sacking tied around their middle. As they

276

passed by the table Mede passed out a piece of candy to each child. Claire then handed out a length of dress material to every woman and grown-up girl, while Drum presented two dollars to every man. Finally Narcisse picked up a ginger cookie and gave it to every man, woman, and child. They were overawed by the munificence of their gifts. Some of the children popped the candy in their mouths at once, while others clutched the precious sweet in their hands. Women held up dress lengths before themselves, admiring the patterns and sometimes swapping, while the men carefully placed the bills in their shirt pockets or gave them to their wives for safekeeping. They were all eating the cookies, biting them off in small nibbles and chewing them slowly to get every last bit of flavour out of them.

Drum announced that there would be free food awaiting them in the store in the morning – a pound of bacon, grits, and fatback for each family – and that just as soon as the store was organized and the goods priced, they could buy there. He advised them that he was doing away with the book system and that all purchases would be for cash after the first week of free food.

Glancing over his shoulder, he summoned Ciceron to come forward and introduced him as the coachman and the head man of all the barns. He instructed him to go down among the folks and pick out his own assistant and the two men for the dairy barn.

Now Drum asked Mammy Morn to look for a girl to help her in the kitchen, but instead of sending Claire down to pick out the fellows she wanted for the dining-room, he himself pointed down to a young buck, sitting cross-legged in the front row, whose engaging face had been staring up at him.

'What's your name, boy?'

The fellow looked up, frightened, but Drum's smile reassured him. 'Drumstick,' the fellow answered, just as soon as he could control his voice.

'He 'nother o' Drummage's git,' Big Pearl said. 'Place's chock full o' 'em. That Drummage he pestered mos' every wench in New Quarters. He mighty powerful too. Mos' o' 'em took.'

'All right, Drumstick.' Drum beckoned to him to come up. 'You want to work here in the big house?'

Drumstick nodded his acceptance.

Brute appeared at the steps with three men – one, Buckthorn, for the kitchen garden and two others, Jemmy and Plato, all of whom, he said, knew their jobs well.

By now everything seemed to have been accomplished. Most of the ginger cookies were gone, although the platter had had to be replenished several times. Several lengths of dress material were left on the table and Drum distributed these among Debbie, Rosanne, and Matilda, with instructions for Aunt Lou to make up two dresses apiece for them and also for the new girl that would be working in the kitchen. He scooped up the few candies that were left and flung them into the group, where they were eagerly scuffled for and caught by the children. It was all over, yet he felt he had only begun.

Narcisse had kept quiet during Drum's activities, but now he stood up, holding up one hand to restrain the group from breaking up.

'All you men' – he was smiling now and when Narcisse smiled, nobody could have been more gracious – 'let your wives and children go home, but you all stop in at the overseer's cottage and I'll treat each one of you to a drink of corn and we'll settle a few things Mr Maxwell forgot to mention.' He leaned down and whispered to Drum, 'You don't need to come. I just want all these workers in a good mood to sweet-talk them a bit.' With a wave of his hand he signalled to the ten men in the back row and they followed him off the porch and down the path to the overseer's cottage. Brute also went along with them and then one by one the men from New Quarters started, leaving only those who had been picked for house servants. With the taste of ginger cookies in their mouths the women and children started down the driveway, shouting their thanks.

Mede escorted Big Pearl home. Mammy Morn and Matilda started taking things in from the porch. Ciceron came up the steps hand in hand with a tall, slender girl whom he introduced to Drum as Esther.

'Mammy Morn she a-pickin' this gal for the kitchen 'cause I asked her. She right pretty, Mista Drum.'

Drum agreed with him. There was a certain aristocratic dignity about the girl. Had Drum known, it was her Jaloff blood, which had produced some of the most beautiful Negro girls.

'She a-goin' to bed down with me out'n the barn. Mammy Morn a-sayin' it all right if'n yo' say so.'

'Let her help Mammy Morn and Matilda get these things in' – Drum recognized the urgency in Ciceron's words and noticed the way his hand stroked the girl's arms – 'then you can do what you want to.'

' 'N' yo' a-knowin' what I wan' 'n' Esther she a-wantin' it too.'

They soon had the tablecloth folded up, the candles snuffed, and everything carried into the house. Debbie and Rosanne went upstairs to turn down the beds and light candles in the bedrooms. Drum and Claire were left alone on the porch.

They sat side by side, their chairs close together, discussing the events of the evening. Drum reached for her hand and she allowed him to take it and raise it to his lips. He kissed each finger, then started his seeking mouth up her arm, touching with his lips the tender place of her throat. His hand behind her undid the hooks that held her bodice and he slipped it down, feeling the nipples of her breasts harden and swell. For a few minutes she responded to him, even seeking him with her hands, but suddenly she pushed him away at the sound of footsteps in the bushes and ran without saying a word into the house, clutching her dress with one hand. He could hear the tap of her heels on the floor of the hall and her hurrying footsteps as she ascended the stairs.

The bushes parted to reveal Mede, who stepped up on to the porch.

'You goddam clumsy bastard.' Drum could willingly have wrung his neck for appearing when he did. 'Why didn't you go in the back door?'

'Wantin' to talk with yo'. How I a-knowin' yo' a-playin' 'roun' with Miz Claire. Better button up yore britches 'n' 'listen.' He seated himself in the chair that Claire had vacated.

'What's so important?' Drum was having difficulty fitting buttons into buttonholes.

'Mammy a-sayin',' he began, 'that yo' got to watch out for them bucks which Narcisse he a-makin' drivers of. They ain' no good, Mammy a-sayin'. They got bad reputations for fightin' 'n' troublemakin'. Been a-raidin' other farms a-stealin' pigs 'n' foragin' in the fields. Been a-rapin' wenches on other farms too. They calls 'emselves the Big Ten. Tha's why every boy's name a-startin' with Big. Mammy a-sayin' that the whole place 'roun' about scared o' 'em. They wears black hoods over their heads 'n' nobody know who they are. Sheriff been a-settin' traps for 'em, but ain' never caught 'em. Mammy says for yo' to watch out for 'em. They mean as polecats.'

Drum wondered why Narcisse had picked them for drivers, but, of course, Narcisse hadn't known about their reputation. He had merely picked them because they were strong, husky brutes. And they had been hungry too. No wonder they had stolen. It took a lot of food to satisfy those big bodies.

'Perhaps, Mede, now that they are going to get enough food here at Falconhurst, they won't be out stealing. It's pretty bad to go hungry, you know. Makes a man desperate.'

'But they been a-rapin' wenches too.'

'Perhaps the wenches encouraged them. They're a rather handsome lot, all ten of them.'

'Wenches ain' 'couragin' 'em, not when they ties 'em up 'n' all ten rapes 'em. Tha's what Mammy says they been a-doin'. Kilt one wench over on Fairlea Plantation, Mammy a-sayin'.'

'I'll speak to Narcisse and warn him.' Drum got up from his chair, stretching his arms high over his head, and walked to the edge of the porch, breathing in the scented night air. There was a light still burning in the overseer's cottage and he could just make out a crowd of men around it. Narcisse must still be treating them to corn.

'Let's get upstairs, I'm tired,' Drum said, starting towards the front door, and Mede followed him. Upstairs Drum was sorely tempted to knock on Claire's door, but he resisted the temptation and followed Mede into his own room. Debbie was sitting in the chair beside Drum's bed.

'You aren't forgetting that we're brothers now, Mede?' Drum asked.

'Shore a-goin' to fergit it tonight.' Mede headed for the connecting door between their rooms. 'If'n yo' even a-thinkin' yo' a-goin' to have Rosanne, we ain' no more brothers tonight.'

Drum mimicked Mede. 'If'n we ain' brothers tonight, we ain' brothers tomorrow. 'Sides, yo' goin' to be selfish, Mede? Yo' had her onc't today. Ain' that 'nough?'

'How yo'a-knowin' I had her onc't?'

'Cause I helped yo' out. Tho't yo' wa'n't a-goin' to make it, boy, yo' a-huffin' 'n' a-puffin' so hard 'n' humpin' so fas'. Jes' teched yo' up a little 'n' that did it.'

'Yo' did that?' Mede passed his hand across his buttocks, which still smarted.

'Shore did' – Drum's thumb pointed to his chest – ' 'N' yo' ain' thanked me yet.'

'Ain' a-goin' to thank you'. Was jes' a-gettin' a little slow 'cause it the third time. Man cain' do it so easy the third time.'

'But that larrupin' shore did it.' Drum started to laugh, remembering the sound of the whip as it landed on Mede and what it had accomplished so immediately.

Drum's laughs set Mede to laughing too. He stared at Debbie and she stared back at him, then lowered her eyes. 'Ain' forgettin' last night, Mista Mede.' She giggled and lifted admiring eyes to scan them both. 'Mista Drum he mighty fine, but he no better'n yo' 'cept he white 'n' purtier.'

After all, Mede was not entirely averse to Debbie. He sighed and shrugged his shoulders. 'Cain' forgit that yo' my brother, Drum. Take Rosanne if'n yo' wants, but for God's sake stop talking like a goddam nigger. You ain't no burr-head 'n' neither am I. From now on I'm goin' to get back to talkin' the way I did in Boston. Don't mean to be no goddam Southern burr-head nigger neither.'

'Nor do I. Goodnight, Mede.' Drum motioned for Debbie to go with Mede and waited for the door to open for Rosanne to come in.

'Come on over here' – he held out his hands to her – 'and help me undress.'

She glided across to him and into his arms. 'Hope yo' a-goin' to be careful tonight, Mista Drum suh. That Mede he gotten me all sored up.'

'Guess I helped him a little.' Drum held up his arms for her to remove his shirt. She took it off and hung it on the back of the chair, then knelt down to remove Drum's shoes. While she was on her knees before him he loosened the buttons that held up his trousers, so that they fell down around his ankles. Reaching for Rosanne's hands, he had her undo the buttons of his linen drawers until they too slipped to his ankles. He pulled Rosanne to him, his body arching.

For a moment she raised her head to look at him. 'My, my. Mista Drum suh, ain' never seen nothing so splendiferous afore.'

'Not even Mede?' He grinned down at her.

'Ain' a-seein' Mede, Masta Drum, jus' a feelin' him, tha's all. But seein' yo' now shore 'nough, Masta Drum, 'n' likin' what I see.'

He drew her closer, his hand resting on her head. Then, stepping backwards while she followed him, creeping on her knees, he reached the bed and turned out the light. For the moment he had forgotten Claire.

CHAPTER TWENTY-SIX

DRUM SOON DISCOVERED that if Falconhurst were to be refurbished before the advent of the twentieth century, he would certainly need more help than the painter and the two carpenters he had recruited from New Quarters. After working a whole week, they had accomplished only one thing – the straightening and painting of the single pillar on the portico.

Drum could not complain; they had done a perfect job. The pillar was straight and true with new foundations that displaced the rotting wood. After a careful and most meticulous scraping of the Ionic capital and the fluted column, they had painted it and it now looked as immaculately new as the day it had been put there when Falconhurst was built. But if one pillar had taken a week and there were four pillars in front of the house, that would take four weeks merely to accomplish that one job, which was only a small part of what had to be done. Window sashes and balconies had to be repainted, rotting eaves replaced, windows reglazed, and bricks pointed up. At the rate they were going it would take a year to fix the exterior of the big house alone, without touching the barns or the cabins or attending to the other things that needed to be done.

True, even with one pillar replaced and painted, the house now looked better from the road. Jemmy and Plato, the gardeners, had cut down most of the heavy growth around the house, so that it did not appear engulfed in a tangle of overgrown rosebushes and creepers, but there was much more work for them to do. Drum envisioned a close-cropped green lawn like they had in New England, but he doubted if it would ever be accomplished.

Buckthorn, the kitchen gardener, had cleared a spot outside the back door of high weeds, spaded and raked it and planted neat rows of vegetables. Gassaway had delivered the cows and the bull, so now they were assured of plenty of fresh milk. Livingood had arrived with the horses and mules, along with three big farm wagons for hauling cotton, which he took a chance on selling, knowing Drum's need. So far so good! Yet, despite Drum's frantic efforts to get everything done at once, it seemed to him that they had made no headway at all.

Claire wanted all the interior of the house done over – new paint and wallpaper, along with new upholstery for the furniture, new curtains, and new draperies. Mammy Morn complained that they did not have sufficient equipment in the kitchen; the coffee grinder was worn out and scarcely usable, the old-fashioned iron stove was temperamental, and the oven did not bake well.

Ciceron said the wagons would be useless without harnesses for the horses and mules. Lucy kept insisting on a new suit so he could look the role of butler, and Drumstick, if he were going to wait on table, certainly needed clothes. His patched osnaburg pantaloons and his big bare feet lent a far from formal air to the dining-room. Then, too, Drum had promised Ciceron proper coachman's clothes and the boy reminded him of it from time to time. Even the girls who were house servants looked ill-dressed in the simple calico dresses that Aunt Lou had stitched up for them and Claire insisted that as soon as possible they be shod and have black dresses with caps and aprons along with white dresses for Mammy Morn, Matilda, and Esther, the new girl who spent her nights out in the barn with Ciceron.

It seemed that wherever Drum turned, there was work to be done and he wanted it all done in a day. He had the money. Goddamit, yes! He even had the money that had been in dispute at the Benson bank. Mr Gassaway had driven over to Falconhurst and had accompanied Drum to the bank and confronted Jenkins. Mr Jenkins, red-faced and apologetic, was completely bereft of an excuse to withhold the money any longer. Lewis Gassaway was a white man. He was known to everyone in the bank and in Benson. So when he identified Drum, there was really nothing that Jenkins could do. Drum had lived up to all Jenkins' specifications, so Jenkins was forced to turn the money over to him, but Drum, hoping to win some future favours from Jenkins, merely deposited the money to his account in the bank. Jenkins actually smiled at him when he departed. It was a thin, acidulous smile, but it was a smile nevertheless.

Actually all of Benson was regarding Drum in a different light. Of course, he was coloured and he would never be able to overstep that barrier. Yet they agreed, nodding their heads together, that a coloured man with money, especially one who was willing to spend it as freely as Drum, was something quite different and now most of the town, albeit somewhat grudgingly, was willing to deal with him.

The local dressmaker, one Mrs Twitchell, although avowing

that she had never sewn for niggers in her life, was willing, in view of Drum's offer to pay her in advance, to make uniforms for Debbie and Rosanne and for Mammy Morn, Matilda, and Esther. To give her credit, she made them well, of black cotton sateen, with lace-frilled white aprons and caps of the same material for the maids and plain white for the kitchen servants. She sighed as she handed the finished package to Drum, contrasting his youth, his strength, and the bulge in his trousers with that of the men of the town whom she discreetly entertained at times in the back room of her shop. How much more exciting it would be for him to knock on the back door late in the evening rather than Jenkins or Hicks. She sighed again, realizing that it could never happen, but did inform him that she had coaxed the local tailor to make up uniforms for all his servants, for which Drum thanked her and allowed her to straighten the folds of his cravat, feeling the desire in her fingers as she touched him.

Although the Benson tailor agreed to make clothes for the Falconhurst servants, the local shoemaker declined to make their shoes. He admitted that he would be willing to make shoes for Drum himself, which was a condescension on his part, so Drum ordered two pairs of riding boots for himself, knowing that one pair would fit Mede. When Drum came to pay for them, the old shoemaker did display a certain amount of graciousness by informing him that there was a Negro shoe-maker over on Carillon Plantation who was still living in the remains of the big house. Drum drove over, found the man living in what had been the kitchen of a once-imposing house, and brought him to Falconhurst, where he made soft black slippers for all the house servants, boots and shoes for Ciceron and Drumstick, and stayed on to make shoes for Narcisse's ten drivers and for any of the folks at New Quarters who wanted them. All of them except the children were anxious to have shoes, which, although they wore them but seldom, were a mark of status. Drum had never realized before how simply the fact of being shod moved a person a peg or two up the social ladder. Old Plato, the shoemaker, decided there was enough business in New Quarters and the big house to warrant a permanent residence and became one of the Falconhurst retainers.

But even with these minor things accomplished, there seemed to be little progress. Rex was thorough but slow. It would take him all day to scrape, reglaze, putty, and paint a window. Drum could find no fault with his work nor that of Fred and Amos, the two carpenters from New Quarters, except perhaps that they were too thorough and altogether too slow. He'd have to get more people to get the work done, but where to get them was a problem. How, he wondered, did they ever manage to get Falconhurst built in the first place? Certainly it had not been built by untrained slave labour. Then, by whom? Who had put up all the barns and the big house and kept them in repair all these years?

Finally convinced of the utter futility of three men ever being able to accomplish all that must be done, he had Ciceron drive him over to call on Lewis Gassaway one afternoon. Ciceron, in his smart new livery, was a far different looking fellow from the peppermint-striped, lackadaisical youth who had first greeted Drum in New Orleans. He was proud not only of his own appearance but of his horses, his carriage, and especially of Drum, who sat in the back seat.

Gassaway welcomed them on his front porch and when Drum had once explained his problems, Gassaway was able to solve them immediately.

Years ago, according to him, there had been a lot of building in the South. Imposing big houses and barns had been put up and each big house had been christened with some fanciful name that acted in the same way as an English title. Thus, Hammond Maxwell was not just Mr Hammond Maxwell but Mr Hammond Maxwell of Falconhurst Plantation, a title he bore with dignity.

Then came the hard years after the war, when many of the big houses had been abandoned, lost to their original owners, or destroyed. There was no money to rebuild them, for all the beautifully engraved Confederate bonds and currency were useless. Consequently the architects and builders had gradually disappeared. However – and here Gassaway waggled a hopeful finger at Drum – there was still old Adolphus Barry, who lived down in Westminster. He was the son of the famous Mobile architect who had built most of the big houses. True, Adolphus was no architect, but he was a master carpenter and had, at least the last time Gassaway had heard about him, a couple of good helpers, trained carpenters. Recently a few of the old plantation big houses had been purchased by Northerners who had had them restored and in each case it was Barry who had done it. Drum, he suggested, might ride over and talk with him.

'But would he—'

'Won' make a bit o' difference to ol' Adolphus Barry if'n yo' got a green skin o' yo' spotted like'n a houn' dog. He ain' got much work 'n' he al'ays lookin' for more. Comed here, he did, 'n' did his damndest to try to git me to fix up things here. Tol' him I had the money, but the old place would last as long as I do 'n' ain' got no kin to leave it to. It ain' much of a drive over to Westminster. Why'n't yo' go?'

This sounded as if it might be the solution to Drum's problem and he decided to go over to Westminster, of which he had no recollection except the midnight silhouette of a railroad station, to see this Adolphus Barry and if possible engage him for the rest of the work. At dinner that night he announced his intention and alerted Ciceron to be ready, telling Mammy Morn he would like an early breakfast for Mede, Ciceron, and himself.

Mede, however, although he had always been anxious for any excursion, asked if he might be excused. He had developed an interest in the cattle, which Drum was surprised at but grateful for. Mede had taken over the responsibilities of the cattle barn, supervising the two fellows who had been chosen as milkers and to care for the herd. Drum couldn't account for Mede's sudden interest in cows, but he welcomed it because Narcisse was devoting all his time to the fields. Today, Mede informed him, he had requisitioned a gang of workers from Narcisse and they were going to repair fences in the big pasture. Two of the cows had wandered away the week before and it had taken a full day to find them.

Drum would miss Mede's chatter. Mede was now trying very hard to undo his brief lapse into what he termed 'nigger talk' and get back to the way he had talked in Boston before he had met Lucy. Drum had found himself lapsing into the local vernacular at times and he had discovered that it was not, as Mede called it, merely nigger talk but the same as was spoken by white and black alike. He too was making an effort not to let his speech become infected with what he heard daily. He noticed that neither Narcisse nor Claire had any difficulty and while they did speak English with a faint French accent, it had never become corrupted by local dialects.

Drum was, however, overjoyed when Claire turned to Narcisse and asked his permission to accompany Drum, giving as an excuse the fact that in all the time they had been at Falconhurst, she had never gone even as far as Benson and felt that a little change would give her something new to see and talk about. Also there were a few purchases she wished to make. Drum was even more overjoyed when Narcisse gave his permission, so graciously that Drum could see he really wanted Claire to go with him. At times Narcisse surprised him. Often he would fly into rages so uncontrollable that it was impossible to talk with him; then he would be gracious and friendly, going out of his way to do small favours for Drum. Actually they saw very little of him except at meal times because he had developed a habit of staying in the overseer's cottage until late in the evening, oft-times remaining the whole night, excusing himself by saying that there was a great amount of clerical work to be done and that he had only the evenings to do it in. However, Drum had no complaints about him. Even Lewis Gassaway had complimented him on the cotton, saying it was the best in the county and that he was fortunate to have such a good overseer.

Although Claire did not seem entirely happy over Narcisse's frequent absences, she made no complaints, spending the hours after dinner with Drum and Mede outside on the portico and many times retiring earlier than they did. Drum had learned by experience that her door was always locked. He had tried it often, tiptoeing to her door and cautiously lifting the latch always to find that the door was securely bolted inside. He could not understand her. She claimed to love him, but she always ended by saying that she loved Narcisse too. How could she love them both?

This night, however, they all went to bed early, including Narcisse. But Drum did not sleep well. He was awakened in the night by the sound of violent quarrelling coming from the room across the hall. He was half tempted to interfere because he could hear Narcisse shouting and Claire crying, but he convinced himself that he had no right to interfere in family quarrels, regardless of how much he loved Claire.

They were on the road the next morning around six, with Mammy Morn's lunch basket on the front seat beside Ciceron. At that hour it was cool, so cool that Claire wrapped her Paisley shawl a little tighter around her shoulders, but Drum, taking advantage of the chilly air, drew her closer to him and put his arm around her shoulders, fearful at first that she would object but marvelling when she didn't. Encouraged by this, his other hand reached under the shawl, feeling the smooth contours of her breasts under the thin challis dress she was wearing. She allowed his hand to remain there, even when it started to unbutton a few buttons, until they began to pass an almost continual procession of Negroes on their way to work in the fields, followed by white overseers or owners on horseback. With their appearance she pushed his hand away, buttoned the little black buttons of her dress, slid out from under his encircling arm, and sat bolt upright on the seat.

Drum was caught off guard when many of the white men bowed to him and tipped their hats to Claire. It was evident, perhaps because of the high-stepping greys and the fine carriage with Ciceron in livery, that they were mistaken for whites. Drum returned their bows, tipping his own broad-brimmed Panama hat and wondering how these white strangers would react if they were to stop long enough to see that they had been so honouring a coloured man and woman. However, none of them did stop and the greys trotted along, with Ciceron flicking his whip, although he never touched the horses.

'Jes' a-keepin' the flies off my pretties,' he explained.

As the sun climbed higher it began to get hot and now the fields were peopled with workers. The passers-by were either white people in carriages – none of which looked as smart as Drum's own – Negroes on mules, or black children lugging water pails for the field hands. They passed no plantations as elaborate as Falconhurst and what they did see were mere shells of the big houses that had once marched so proudly across the Black Belt of Alabama.

Drum managed to secure Claire's hand, covering it with his own and keeping them both hidden under the folds of her shawl. Glancing at her sideways, he was once again over-whelmed by her beauty, although he felt that his eyes were playing tricks on him. He seemed to catch a resemblance to Narcisse, which he had never seen before. It reminded him of a silly superstition he had once been told – that when a man and woman are married, they begin to look like each other. That was, of course, ridiculous. She sensed his scrutiny and turned and smiled, giving his hand a warm clasp, which he returned. It caused the hot blood to rush to his groins and he was all too conscious of the throbbing urgency that demanded satisfaction. He realized that another second of physical con-tact with her would provoke a climax, which would be em-barrassing to both of them. He had to force himself to think of something else.

Fortunately they were just turning on to the long bridge that spanned the Tombigbee River. Claire was so excited over the length and height of the structure that Drum was able to forget himself in her enthusiasm over crossing it. The shoes of the horses and the tyres of the surrey made such a racket on the wooden planking that it sounded like distant thunder. The river was low now, sluggish and oily; but Drum had heard that in the springtime it was a torrent, washing away farms and livestock.

A short distance past the bridge they came to a place where the road dipped down to ford a small run, a tributary of the river they had just passed. Here the road sloped down to the stream and then rose again on the other side. Ciceron stopped the horses and undid the checkreins so that the horses could drink in midstream. It was an idyllic spot. On the farther shore a high pine tree cast a cool black shadow over the white sand. Lush ferns and a vine with flowers like orange trumpets climbed up the bank to meet the road. Willows trailed their leaves in the water; and to complete the pastoral scene they saw a small farmhouse across the fields, with smoke from the chimney making a white mare's tail across the blue sky.

Claire got out when Ciceron stopped to refasten the check-reins on the shore and said she wanted to stretch her legs. Drum accompanied her through a passageway between tangled shrubs into a small circle of pine trees, seeded from the big tree, which made a circular retreat, carpeted thickly with pine needles.

'If only it were time to eat' – Claire broke off a twig, freeing the resinous perfume – 'what a perfect place this would be.'

'Perhaps we can eat here on the way back.' Drum allowed his nose to be tickled by the aromatic needles. 'Ciceron says we cannot be far from Westminster now and if we allow an hour for my business and your shopping, we could be back here in time for a late lunch. Hope Mammy Morn put up plenty of food. We'll be hungry by then.'

'She did.' She took him by the shoulders and turned him around. 'Now you walk the other way back to the carriage and don't you dare turn around because I am going to walk in the opposite direction. Don't embarrass me by asking me why.'

'I won't.' He turned and kissed her and then resolutely marched back to the carriage. Here he found that Ciceron was availing himself of Claire's absence, standing by one of the wheels of the carriage and urinating. Drum recognized his own need and when Ciceron had finished, he stood in Ciceron's footsteps and proved to the grinning coachman that he was more of a man because his stream reached a foot farther.

'That ain' fair.' Ciceron's high-pitched laugh startled the horses. 'If'n I'd a known, could of pissed farther'n yo'.' He glanced down at Drum. 'Co'se I ain' hung so heavy's yo', but mine got plenty o' power behind it. So Esther a-sayin' anyway.

Hurry up! Git it in 'n' git buttoned up. Miz Claire she a-comin'. Got to git started. Reckon it 'bout 'n hour to Westminster.'

Ciceron was right. After about an hour's driving they came to the first straggling Negro cabins, which betokened they were nearing a town. At first these cabins were scattered, but soon they were standing cheek by jowl on either side of the road. Some listed drunkenly while others were sprucely painted, but each boasted its own chinaberry tree with leaves grey from the dust of the road. Naked children ran about; women were bending over washtubs; men were weeding in their small vegetable patches or sleeping in doorways. Strangely enough, Drum thought, they all seemed happy, without a worry in the world. Perhaps this was the way it had been back in Africa before they were transported to this strange new world. Would to God they had stayed there.

Westminster turned out to be a much larger town than Benson. Its business section extended along the four sides of the central square, which boasted a fretwork bandstand along with the inevitable granite statue of a Confederate soldier but, while the soldier in Benson was merely a pigmy, this one was life-sized, a moustachioed man leaning on his musket. A white church with a steeple reminded Drum of New England, and the shops around the square seemed prosperous and well kept. He dispatched Ciceron to the livery stable to inquire where Adolphus Barry lived and when they drove down the tree-shaded street of homes, he was able to pick out the Barry home himself. It alone was resplendent with a gleaming coat of white paint, a picket fence that was not missing a single picket, and a wide veranda supplied with rocking chairs and tables like a sitting-room.

Drum was not sure whether he should go up to the front door or have Ciceron drive him around to the back. He had already learned that only white people were allowed through the front door. Negroes and coloured must always use the back entrance. This time, however, he decided to use the front door. After all, he was not seeking work or delivering groceries. Why should he use the back door? With a word to Ciceron to take

Claire wherever she might want to go for her shopping and return for him in an hour, he lifted the latch of the white gate, walked up the gravel path bordered by pink and white begonias, up on to the shiny grey-painted boards of the porch, and rang the bell outside the screen door. He had only a moment to wait. An elderly Negress, in proper black with a white apron, appeared at the door, surveying him through the screen. When he inquired if Mr Barry might be in, she grudgingly allowed as to how he was. Then, peering at Drum again, instead of inviting him into the house she opened the door and pointed to a rocker on the porch, hidden behind a vine that climbed up over a trellis and that could effectively conceal whoever might be sitting there from anyone in the street. 'Mista Barry he a-comin' right out,' the woman said, still staring at him and trying, he supposed, to ascertain the mixture of white and coloured blood in him. Damn her! Nobody need try figure out whether she had any white blood. She was prune black and to hell with her anyway. At least she had not sent him around to the back door, but why should she? He was white and respectably dressed. Again damn her and damn all these niggers who took their prerogatives as white men's servants to insult others of their own race.

She had no sooner turned to enter the house than Mr Barry himself came out, waiting for her to open the door for him and close it behind her. Drum had not had time to seat himself and now, standing before this hearty white-thatched man, whose pale blue eyes did not seem entirely to condemn him, he wondered whether or not to offer his hand. He noted the momentary hesitation on the other man's part and was relieved when the hand was extended, grasping his own warmly.

'Well, what kin I do for you?' Again Barry hesitated and then added the word 'mister'.

Small though the addition of the word was, it meant a lot to Drum and when Barry motioned for him to be seated, he lowered himself into the cushioned seat of the rocker while Barry pulled up another chair to face him.

'I'm Drummond Maxwell of Falconhurst Plantation—' He started to introduce himself.

Barry slapped his knee and roared in laughter. He even went as far as to lean forward and nudge Drum in the ribs. 'Been wondering jest how long it's goin' to take you to find me. Had thought of goin' over to Falconhurst myself, but yo're here now. Don't need to tell me nothin'. Know all about you, I do. News travels fast in these parts. Now, let's see. You're a mulatto and a goddam fine-looking one at that. You're the son of that Drummage Maxwell that the Ku Kluxers kilt 'n' Miz Sophie Maxwell that married up with him, so you ain't no bastard. Heard that you been nawth all your life and they tell me you're richer than Croesus and then some.' He nodded his head with the assurance that he was correct, took a pipe from one pocket and a sack of tobacco from the other, then filled the pipe and lit it. After a few puffs he nudged Drum again. 'Right?'

'Right,' Drum agreed, 'although there may be a little exaggeration about my being as rich as Croesus. Guess there's nothing more I can tell you—'

''Ceptin' I say you're a goddam fine-lookin' young feller again and I mean it. Never seen a coloured boy with yella hair, but it becomes you. Would take you for a white man myself. You're a credit to your race. Most mulatto bucks are good-lookin', but they're sort of greasy-lookin' and they're a bad lot what with drinkin' 'n' whorin'. Far's I kin see, Mr Maxwell, you 'pears like a gentleman, even though you're coloured. Use' to know your grandfather, Mr Hammond Maxwell, onc't. Had the finest niggers in the world, he did. My pappy always wanted a Falconhurst buck but never did get one. Well, now that we're introduced, what kin I do for you? That's sort of a stupid question 'cause I'm pretty sure why you're here.'

'I understand you're an architect and a builder.'

'Whoa there, mister. I never claimed to be an architect, but I'm a goddam good carpenter, if I do say so. My daddy was a real fine architect 'n' he put up a lot of the houses 'round here. Didn't build Falconhurst, though. Mista Hammond Maxwell had a man from N'Orleans do that.' He puffed away on his pipe. 'You'd think I'd be the busiest man in the county with all the work that needs to be done 'round here, but the trouble is mos' folks 'round here ain't got a pot to piss in nor a window to throw it out of.'

Drum liked the man, liked his bluff heartiness and his frankness. He had an idea they were going to be friends because he sensed that the man already liked him.

'My idea is to restore Falconhurst.'

'Worth doin'. Worth doin'. Finest place 'round here except Fernwood, which I think a prettier house, though it ain't so big's Falconhurst.' He let out another puff of smoke and smiled at Drum, his smile making two dimples in his round cheeks. ' 'N' you want me to help you?'

'That's what I came here for, Mr Barry, although' – he sucked in his lower lip and looked straight into the blue eyes, which were looking at him – 'I didn't know if you would be able to help me – or rather if you would be willing to work for me.'

' 'Cause you're coloured? Hell, man, don' make me no nevermins. Dollar's a dollar so far's I'm concerned. And there are damn few dollars floating 'roun' this part of Alabama these days. Damn few! Now let's talk bizness.' He turned to the screen door and yelled, 'Mirey, bring us out a pitcher o' corn 'n' two glasses! I ain't one o' those goddam red-necks who are poisoned if they get in the shadow of a nigger. Not by a damn sight. Ignorant trash. My daddy sent me to school in New York. Sent my nigger playboy along with me and he was my daddy's git. Sent him to the same school 'n' damned if he didn't get higher marks'n I did. He's still with me. I'm not makin' it public, but he's my partner, though everyone thinks he jes' my foreman.'

And talk business they did to the accompaniment of glasses of corn whisky. Adolphus Barry, along with the coloured man he had just mentioned, whom he referred to as Daniel, together with three carpenters and two painters, would arrive at Falconhurst within a couple of days. Barry's wife's sister lived in Benson, so she could accommodate him and Daniel. The three carpenters and two painters could bed down in some empty cabin or – Barry snapped his fingers at a sudden inspiration – they might tackle a small barn first, rebuild it, and put in bunks for the boys, but it would be Drum's responsibility to feed them. They would probably be there a couple of months, considering the barns and all.

It was understood that Drum would buy all the lumber, nails, hardware, and paint. Barry would furnish tools, ladders, and all equipment. The job could be done on a daily basis of $15 (which would pay for all of Barry's work and that of his help) plus the keep of his five hands or, if Drum desired, after Barry had made an inspection of what needed to be done, he'd make him a flat price. They agreed to leave it until Barry arrived.

It was settled and Barry again yelled out in a voice loud enough to be heard at the livery stable several blocks down the street, 'Mirey, fetch out another pitcher o' corn. We gotta seal a bargain.'

The corn was raw and straight, without even water to go with it, and between the two of them for the second time they finished the pitcher. It made a ball of fire in Drum's stomach and his throat felt as though he had swallowed a cupful of lye. Not having eaten since morning, he was immediately drunk and weaved on his feet when he stood up to leave. They shook hands on the porch, again halfway down the walk, and again when Barry helped Ciceron get him into the carriage.

'Miz Claire she a-buyin' thin's. We a-goin' to pick her up soon's yo' finished 'n' reckon yo' finished now.' Ciceron sniffed. 'Reckon yo' had a li'l corn, Mista Drum.'

Drum straightened himself up in the seat. 'Not a little, boy, a hell of a lot. I'm drunk.'

'Uh-huh, man. Yo' shore drunker'n hell. Better start soberin' up afore yo' meets Miz Claire.' He started the horses, cramping the wheels of the carriage and heading back towards the square.

Drum was beginning to get control of himself. He was now able to focus his eyes on particular objects without their swinging around in circles.

'How you like that Esther gal, Ciceron boy?'

'She good ridin', Mista Drum. She shore a-likin' it.'

'Getting plenty?'

'Uh-huh.'

296

'Then, you do me a favour. When we stop for lunch, you eat yours in the carriage. Miss Claire and I are going to go somewhere else.'

Ciceron understood. He slowly closed one eye and agreed.

Claire was standing on the narrow sidewalk before a small store that bore the sign PAINTERS, PAPERHANGERS & UPHOLSTERERS. She waved gaily to them and Drum, assuming the dignity that all drunks do when they want to appear sober, descended from the carriage, doffed his hat to her with an exaggerated flourish, handed the large package that was sitting on the sidewalk beside her to Ciceron, and with extreme gallantry helped her up to the back seat of the carriage.

'All through with your shopping, my dear?' He sat as far away from her as possible so she would not smell his breath.

'All through,' she sighed, 'and oh, Drum, I made the most wonderful discovery. There's a young man and his sister in that shop back there, an absolutely darling pair of young coloured people, and he has just opened up this shop. Their father owned one of the big plantations here and remembered them in his will, so they took this money and went into business. They've been in business for three months and have scarcely had a customer yet.'

'Because they're coloured, I suppose.'

'Well partly, I imagine, but the main reason is that nobody around has enough money to buy wallpaper or have upholstering done. They do it themselves. But it's a wonderful opportunity for us. We need this fellow and his sister. Every room at Falconhurst needs repainting and repapering and every piece of furniture needs reupholstering. Most of the paper he had there was cheap stuff – not worth putting on the walls – but he did have a sample book from New Orleans with gorgeous French papers in it' – she pointed to the bundle on the front seat – 'and I'm taking it with me. Oh, Drum dear, I don't know whether you want to go to the expense or not, but I was just carried away with myself. Falconhurst seems like home to me now.'

'It's your home, Claire, as long as you and Narcisse stay with me. Go ahead! Pick out the papers you want. Have every

297

room repapered. Have the goddam furniture upholstered or throw it out and get new. Get that man and his sister to come to Falconhurst.'

'And I'll send to Madame Helene and get samples for upholstery and draperies.'

'Sure. Go ahead. Mr Barry's coming out to fix up everything for us.'

His head was getting clearer now and he looked at Claire beside him. To hell with wallpapers and upholstery! All he wanted now was her. He wanted her for his wife, but if he couldn't have her that way, he wanted her. Any way. Any way at all. He'd held himself in check as long as he could. A man had limits; he'd reached his. He couldn't go on much longer looking at a locked door at night and trying to make himself believe that the Negro girl who shared his bed was Claire. He lunged forward to kiss her, but she pushed him back.

'Behave yourself, Drum! I do believe you're drunk.'

'Boiled, we used to say back at college.'

'We'll stop and eat lunch at that charming little spot by the brook on our way home.' Claire patted his hand. 'Hungry?'

He looked at the tempting outline of her breasts under the grey challis. Just this morning he had touched them and his fingers had felt her nipples grow hard.

'Yes,' he answered. 'Hungry! Hungrier than I have ever been in my life. Starving, in fact.' His eyes lingered on the contours of her breasts.

CHAPTER TWENTY-SEVEN

WHEN CICERON WHOAED the horses to a stop under the big pine tree at the ford, Drum was snoring in a drunken stupor, his head against Claire's shoulder and her hand supporting it so that it would not roll from side to side with the motion of the carriage. His hat was on the floor, his hair down in his eyes, and the cravat around his neck had been loosened by his groping fingers. A thin cobweb of spittle spun from one corner of his mouth and his breath stank from the rancid smell of raw corn whisky.

Ciceron turned around. With lifted eyebrows he looked first at Drum and then at Claire.

'Pore Mista Drum, he mos' awful drunk, Miz Claire. He ain' been drinkin' none 't'all lately 'n' he must of put down an awful lot at that there Mista Barry's. Didn't look too drunk when he comed out, but it hit him all of a sudden. Wham! Never seen him like'n this afore. Even if'n he a-drinkin' in N'Orleans, he never passed out.' Ciceron felt he had to make apologies to Claire for Drum. It was one man's duty to defend another before a woman.

'I'm going to wake him up.' Claire lifted his head and shook him gently. 'We'll wash his face in cold water and if Mammy's coffee is still warm, it will do him good. He didn't intend to get this way and he's going to be awfully ashamed of himself when he comes to. Help me get him out of the carriage, Ciceron.'

Drum opened his eyes, his mind hazy. He did not know where he was or what he was doing there. Ciceron was lifting his feet down from the carriage and Claire was helping to steady his shoulders. Together they got him on his feet and between the two of them, one on each side, they led him down through the bushes to the little pine-carpeted circle. Putting one foot slowly before the other, he managed it and when they halted, he slid down from their arms on to the ground, closing his eyes for another drunken sleep, but Claire shook him awake and sent Ciceron back to the carriage to get the basket of lunch.

When Ciceron returned, Claire took a napkin from the lunch basket and wet it in the stream, wringing it out as she walked back to where Drum was lying like a disjointed doll on the pine needles. He opened his eyes again, conscious that some man was straightening his legs and trying to lift him up. Not recognizing Ciceron, he started to kick at him, but Ciceron nimbly ducked. Drum was now in a fighting mood and he managed to pull himself up to his feet, his fists clenched and an ugly look on his face.

'You goddam nigger son of a bitch. You looking for trouble? Well, I'll give it to you. Who the hell do you think you are?'

'Drum.' Claire walked up to him and slapped his face, albeit gently. 'Come to yourself. Stop it!'

He stared at her with lacklustre eyes, finally identifying both her and Ciceron. His fighting mood changed to one of maudlin affection and he stumbled towards her, grabbing her around the waist for support and squeezing her to him. 'Honey baby. It's you, honey baby. 'N' that's my good old friend Ciceron.' He took his arm from Claire and reached forward to shake hands with Ciceron but slipped and fell again. This time he did not close his eyes and he permitted Claire to wipe the spittle from his mouth and sponge his face. She took a comb from her reticule and combed his hair back over his forehead, straightened his cravat, and, with Ciceron's help, moved him to a more comfortable position. Although he had not achieved complete control of his thoughts, he knew that there was something he desired. While Claire's back was turned and she was busy with the lunch basket and pouring out a cup of coffee from the stoneware jug he motioned to Ciceron to leave. Ciceron helped himself to a chicken leg and a ham sandwich. He rolled his eyes, looking from Drum to Claire and then back again, denoting that he understood.

'Them horses been a-sweatin' 'n' ain' got me no brush nor curry comb with me. Thinkin' I a-goin' to walk over to that farm' he pointed to the house across the field ' 'n' see if'n I kin borry one.'

Drum watched him depart while he sipped at the lukewarm coffee in the cup that Claire held for him. He was far from sober, but he could feel some vague rationality establishing itself in his mind. It was all concerned with his desire for Claire and his reluctance to have her leave him as she started towards the lunch basket to get him some food.

'Don' want nothin' to eat, Claire dear. Just thinkin' 'bout food makes me sick. Come over and sit beside me.' He raised himself up on his elbow and fumbled with one hand to smooth a place for her on the pine needles beside him.

She poured herself a cup of coffee, unwrapped the napkin that held a ham sandwich, and walked back to where Drum was lying.

'Sit down.' It was a command with an edge of cruelty that she had never heard in his voice before. Something about the way he had spoken to her frightened her. Instead of sitting where he indicated, she sat about a foot away from him. She was hungry and bit into the sandwich, taking a swallow of coffee.

Suddenly he lunged at her, knocking the coffee cup from her hand and grabbing the sandwich, which he hurled into the bushes.

'Goddammit! This ain' no time for eating. Kin eat anytime. We're alone now. More important things to do, like lovin'.' The force of his body against her threw her backward on to the ground and he leaned over her, lowering his face to hers until their lips touched. Somewhere in his befuddled brain he knew that his breath stank of the whisky and he feared that he was stenchy from his own sweat, but this half-formed thought did not deter him. His mouth was avid for hers and his tongue entered her mouth, seeking a response from her that did not come. She continued to lie rigid beside him and the colder she became, the more frantic his efforts to kindle within her the same flame that was consuming himself. Despite his desperate attempts, she merely lay still but tense, looking up at him and staring at him with revulsion.

'Goddammit!' He pulled away from her a moment, his face flushed with anger and desire. 'What the hell's the matter with you? Froze up on me all of a sudden? I'll get you hot.' Freeing his own hand from holding her, he reached out and grabbed her hand, pushing it down between his groin, but it remained there motionless. Ripping at his buttons, he placed her hand inside. This time she made a violent effort to withdraw her hand, but he hung on to her wrist, clenching it like an iron spancel, forcing it where he wanted it. Her hand remained tightly clasped and he cursed her when she would not open her fingers and move them as he wanted.

'You were anxious enough this morning,' he gibed, 'out on the road with people passing by. You liked it then, but now that we're alone, you're skittish. What's come over you? Trying to pretend you never felt of a man before? A man like me?'

Still she did not answer him but continued to stare back at him whenever their eyes met. Her eyes despised him. She made no resistance when he took his arm out from under her head and released her cold, clamped fist, which he had tried to warm by the contact with the pulsating heat of himself. Awkwardly he pulled himself up to his knees, hanging on to a low-lying branch. Kneeling over her now, his knees straddling her waist, he manoeuvred her on to her back, spread-eagling her arms and pinning her hands down on the pine needles while he shifted the position of his knee to force her legs apart.

He realized, however, that by continuing to hold both her arms outstretched with his own hands, he too was powerless. Slowly, and trying to gauge her reaction, he took one of his hands away. He expected that she would use it to pound on his chest or to try to free herself, but much to his surprise she did not move.

With his free hand he pushed his trousers down, displaying himself with a pride of masculinity.

'Yo' a-wantin' it, honey baby?' He did not realize that he was reverting to the common verbiage of the Negro. 'Yo' a lucky gal 'cause yo' a-goin' to git all of it 'n' yo' shore goin' to love it.' She turned her face away and he abandoned his clutch on himself and wrenched her head around. 'Don' yo' like it? Ain' such a one as that fellow in New Orleans, that Harlequin had, but bet it better than your goddam Narcisse.' His hand fumbled with the little buttons of her dress and, unable to unfasten them, he ripped down the front of her dress, exposing her breasts.

Slowly then, in order to keep his balance, he inched backwards on his knees until he could pull her skirts up, swearing at the petticoats and undergarments she was wearing. Now he became rough and brutal, spreading her legs. Her words, after her long silence, startled him.

'Do you intend to rape me, Drum Maxwell?'

'Aw, honey baby, ain' a-rapin' yo' jes' a-goin' to pleasure yo' like'n yo' never been pleasured before. Drum kin do it for yo', baby.'

'It doesn't pleasure me!' She lifted her head and the force of her eyes caught his, so that he could not turn away from them. 'But if you are going to rape me, go ahead! If you are going to treat me like any nigger wench you caught in the weeds, I'll not struggle against you. My strength is no match for yours. I'm helpless against you. But let me tell you one thing, Drum Maxwell, and drunk as you are, you'd better understand it. If you do what you intend to do, there is nothing, no, nothing in God's world can ever make me care for you again. So if you want to spoil the love between us, go ahead and get it over with. Kill everything between us and I will leave you and Falconhurst. If that's what you want, go ahead!'

Her words managed to penetrate through the fog of his drunken stupor. Slowly, as though awakening from an evil dream, he pulled himself up, hanging on to the branches. He lifted one foot over her body and, still holding on to a pine branch with one hand, he reached down with the other and pulled his trousers up. Gaining a precarious equilibrium, he fumbled with the buttons. As he looked down at her the swelling desire for her subsided. He knelt beside her, gently touching her cheeks with his fingertips, and then clumsily tried to gather her torn dress together. Without warning he became violently ill and he could not prevent the sour vomit from spilling out, drenching himself and her. Too weak and confused to maintain himself any longer, he fell to the ground in his own filth, weeping like a child, begging her forgiveness, pleading with her not to leave him, not to stop loving him, not to abandon him. Through his sobs he became conscious that she was moving away from him and he wondered if she were really leaving him for good, but in a few seconds, to his relief, she returned and tried to lift him. She could only drag him a few feet from his spewed vomit, then she sponged off his face with a damp napkin, dabbing at the stains on his clothing and on her own.

'Claire!' It was a tormented cry that tried to explain his repentance without words.

'Hush, Drum.' She recognized his anguish. 'Can you stand? Let's get out of this place.'

She helped him to his feet and while he leaned on her, she again dabbed at his suit, removing such stains as she could. Then, taking her arm away, she pinned her dress together as well as she could with her brooch. Supporting him again, she led him back to where the carriage was. Ciceron was nowhere in sight, so she guided Drum to the edge of the stream, where he rinsed his mouth and laved his face. Then, with her help, he moved to the big pine tree and they sat together on the ground. Drum was almost sober now, but he remembered what he had done, or rather what he had tried to do, and the very thought of his own bestiality caused him to sob, while her hand on his head reassured him. He peered up at her through his tears and found that she was regarding him with affection and indulgence rather than with the cold hate he had seen in her eyes only a short time before. Something told him that she still loved him, despite the abuse he had forced upon her. He did not dare to kiss her, but he did take her hand and guide it to his lips.

'You'll never forgive me. Oh, Claire darling, what a beast I've been.'

'I have forgiven you already, Drum.' The hand that was on his head crept down and fondled his ear lobe. 'But I assure you, I would never have forgiven you if you had forced me. I'm no nigger wench to be taken in the high weeds. Neither are you a randy buck to throw me on the ground and force me. We are not that sort of people. But it was the whisky, Drum. That is why I forgive you. It made another person of you. You were not yourself. You were not the Drum Maxwell I love.' She bent towards him and kissed him lightly on the cheek. It was a kiss without passion, merely a kiss of comfort.

He had no desire to speak. Just holding her hand was all the comfort he needed. There were so many things he wanted to say, so many elaborate apologies he wanted to make, but he could not articulate any of these thoughts. He only knew that he loved her and that she knew he loved her and loved him in return. Yet, despite his repentance for what he had done, he still wanted her. He was jealous of Narcisse, who did not seem to appreciate her. His sobs had ceased and her arms assuaged him. He drew nearer to her, pillowing his head on her breast. It was strange, though, the touch of her breasts under the thin material of her gown did not rouse him now. Instead they calmed him.

'You do forgive me, Claire?'

'Hush.' She was cradling him like a child. 'Of course I do and we shall never mention it again.'

'I promise never to get drunk again. More than that – I promise I shall never take a drink again.'

'Don't be a silly boy. There are times when men drink and you are a man, but' – she laughed for the first time – 'don't ever try it again on an empty stomach and don't drink so much. You must have had an awful lot today.'

'Mr Barry called for a pitcher of whisky and we drank that and then he had it refilled. I was so excited that I was – well, stupid. Mr Barry's going to fix Falconhurst all up for us and it won't take a year either.'

'And I'm going to fix the inside too. Do you know, Drum darling, what strange things I was thinking about when you were trying ... Oh, I forgot, we were never to mention it again, were we?'

'But tell me of the strange things.'

'I was thinking I would never be able to pick out the wall-papers for Falconhurst and they are such delightful French papers too. That seemed to worry me almost as much as your strange actions did.'

He put his fingers to her lips. 'You'll never have to worry about me again, I promise. But I wonder—'

'What?'

'If the liquor didn't bring out some part of the real me. Perhaps it released the person inside all this veneer of civilization. Perhaps I am nothing but a randy nigger, raping a wench in the high weeds.'

It was her turn to put her finger on his lips.

They heard Ciceron's yell and looked up to see him halfway across the field, accompanied by another coloured man considerably lighter in colour than Ciceron. He had not wanted to surprise them, so he had given warning of his approach. The two of them descended the bank, crashing down through vines and bushes, to stand before Drum and Claire, who were now both sitting upright.

'This yere fella he a-wantin' to talk to yo', seein' as how I said we comed from Falconhurst. He a-called Youngstone 'n' he all-fired in'rested in anythin' to do with Falconhurst.' He nodded to the stranger who accompanied him. 'Go 'head, Youngstone. Tell Mista Drum 'n' Miz Claire what yo' tol' me 'n' how come this tree been called the Falconhurst Pine 'roun' here. Go 'head!'

Youngstone made a circle in the sand with his big toe, not daring to lift his eyes to look at Drum and Claire, but under further prodding from Ciceron he spoke.

'Yes, suh 'n' mist'ess, this ol' pine tree it been called the Falconhurst Pine so long's I kin 'member. 'Members my pappy a-tellin' 'bout it 'n' how Mista Hammond Maxwell he bought'n my brother which I never seen right here under this yere pine tree.'

' 'N' that ain' all.' Ciceron was anxious to add his share to the recital. 'Tell 'em more, Youngstone. Tell 'em 'bout the pretty lady what was raped here 'n' the man that was hung.'

Claire was startled. She clung to Drum's arm, not daring to look at him.

Again Youngstone became tongue-tied, but with sufficient urgings from Ciceron he managed to get the whole story out while Drum and Claire listened, dumbfounded by the first Falconhurst tragedy that had taken place under this tree, each of them mentally comparing it with a second, which had been so narrowly averted.

Youngstone himself had not witnessed the event* – he had not even been born at the time – but it had been discussed over and over again by his white father, who had formerly owned

* For a full description of the event, see the earlier novel in this series *Master of Falconhurst*.

the little farmhouse across the fields that Youngstone had inherited. It had happened a year or so before Youngstone had been born. One of Hammond Maxwell's slaves had come running across the fields, asking for help. It seemed that a male slave from Falconhurst Plantation was aiding two of the Falconhurst slaves to escape. The two slaves he was assisting were a handsome octoroon woman and her son, a boy about fifteen. It was night and they were on their way to Westminster to catch the early morning train for Mobile, travelling in a carriage stolen from Falconhurst. The buck had stopped the carriage at the ford, forcibly raped and then murdered both the woman and her son, and had then been picked up by the patrollers and returned to Falconhurst. Later in the day Hammond Maxwell with several of his slaves had arrived at the spot with the rapist tied in a wagon. Here Hammond had had the luckless Negro hung from a branch of this very same pine tree and had left instructions with Youngstone's father, a white man, for all three bodies to be buried 'over there'. Youngstone pointed to the little circle of pines where Drum and Claire had just been. Strangely enough, nothing had ever grown on that spot and no Negro in the neighbourhood would willingly pass the Falconhurst Pine at night because so many had sworn that they had seen a man's body hanging from it and could hear the screams of the woman and the boy who had been raped.

Drum found himself trembling during the awkward recital of Youngstone but listened while the Negro continued.

And that wasn't all. While the body of the dead nigger had still been swinging back and forth on the rope, Mr Hammond Maxwell had purchased Youngstone's brother. With the money he had received from the sale the white owner of the farm had purchased a wench who became the mother of Youngstone. Therefore Youngstone had always felt that had it not been for the Falconhurst Pine and its tragic history, he would not be alive.

Drum reached into his pocket and took out a silver dollar, which he handed over to Youngstone, who looked at it and then grinned his thanks to Drum. Drum shivered. How close he himself had come to committing just such another atrocity in this same place. He glanced at Claire and he knew she was thinking the same thing. But it had not happened. Thank God for that! It hadn't happened, although it was not Drum's fault that it hadn't. Claire had averted it and he was grateful. But, he tried to excuse himself, he had been rip-roaring drunk. That was his fault. He'd never get drunk again.

Never! Somewhere hidden in him, glossed over by the polish of civilization, was a rampant savage that could be released by liquor. He'd never allow that part of him to come to life again. For a little while he had been nothing but a nigger buck, rutting with some nameless wench in the weeds. He had been cock-crazy like some African black, lying in wait along a midnight trail for some woman to pass, to catch and rape her. He had felt exultant in his power over her. He was proud of his virility and his only desire had been to satisfy the over-powering urge within himself. He must never let that part of his nature have the ascendancy again. He must not forget that he was Drummond Maxwell. He had been brought up as a white man and he must keep that wild savage hidden at all costs. Damn this African blood! Damn it for the demands it made upon him.

They waited while Ciceron fetched the lunch basket and put it in the front seat. Then Youngstone bade them goodbye and set off across the fields; and Ciceron clucked at the horses and started them through the ford.

The silence between them continued until after they had rattled over the long bridge. He tried to think of some commonplace remark to make about the scenery, his mission in Westminster, the weather even. His hunger was the solution. 'Must be some sandwiches and chicken in Mammy's basket.' He smiled at her like a little boy, still seeking her indulgence.

'And you must be starved.' She leaned over into the front seat, delved into the basket, and unwrapped a sandwich from the napkin, taking a second one for herself.

He ate slowly. When he had finished, he brushed the crumbs from his lap, noting the grimy sweat stains his hands had made on his trousers.

'Perhaps we had better get Big Pearl to go to the Falcon-hurst Pine and see if she can't exorcize the haunts away.'

'They are already gone.' Claire moved closer to him. 'You see, Drum darling, the love that was there today destroyed all the hate that was there years ago.'

'Love?' he asked. 'That wasn't love. I was a beast.'

'Oh yes,' she insisted, 'it was love. It was love that reached you through the whisky and love that made you stop. Love was there, Drum. Perhaps we should be grateful to the Falcon-hurst Pine. It protected us because, even while you were kneeling over me, threatening me, there was something inside me that wanted you, even that false you. But we both saved ourselves. There will come a time, Drum, when we shall both enjoy each other and it won't be out in the fields.'

'Is that a promise, Claire?'

'It is, Drum, but don't ask me when.'

CHAPTER TWENTY-EIGHT

THE INCIDENT BETWEEN Drum and Claire was never mentioned between them again. Drum did, however, question Brute about the happening under the big pine tree so many years ago and Brute corroborated it. Drum also learned that his father had been present at the scene and that the young boy who had been raped and murdered was his own uncle, sired by Drumson on the mulatto girl at about the same time Drummage had been sired on Big Pearl.

Evidently, Drum considered, he was related through his father to almost everyone on the plantation. He had so often heard the phrase 'that's Drummage's git' applied to various men and women at New Quarters. What a potent man with the wenches his father must have been. His grandfather too, the legendary Drumson, who was buried under the white phallic finger of marble, must also have been equally potent. Now Drum could understand what it was that caused him to be so hot-blooded. It was his African inheritance. But, no! From what little he had heard about his mother, she had had a consuming passion for Negro men. He came by it from both sides of his family. Was it a blessing or a curse? Mostly, he decided, it was a blessing. He was a man made to please women and women pleased him.

In his remorse over his treatment of Claire he had fully intended to dispense with Debbie and for two nights he had dispatched her to sleep in the servants' quarters. He had not even allowed her to sleep on the pallet in his room. He had not known, and neither had Mede told him, that instead of going to the servants' quarters, where she would lose face from having been turned out of Drum's bed, she had sneaked into Mede's room and bedded herself with Mede and Rosanne. Mede had enjoyed these two nights and kept Debbie's secret, hoping that Drum would continue to dispense with her services.

Drum, however, was not cut out for a monastic life. By the third night his body made such throbbing demands on him that he reinstated Debbie, to her great pleasure and to Mede's sorrow. Even the mechanics of sleeping with her somewhat assuaged the desires of his healthy body but neither she nor Rosanne, whom he often demanded from Mede, were anything more than a means of relief. It was Claire he wanted, yet he would have to wait, even though sometimes the waiting was almost more than he could bear. But wait he must! He had tried the other way and it had nearly separated them. He could not take that chance again.

Drum was with Claire far more than Narcisse ever was and except for sharing her bed at night, Drum and she seemed more like husband and wife than she and Narcisse did. Theirs was a strange relationship. Narcisse seemed to live an entirely different life. He was either in the fields or in the overseer's cottage. He rarely had any word of endearment or caress for Claire and she mentioned him but seldom, although she insisted that she loved him. Then, why, if she loved him, was she not with him in the overseer's cottage? Why did she seem to want to spend all her time with Drum and not mind if Narcisse were there or not? Anyway, it was to Drum's advantage. He looked forward to the long evenings they spent on the portico together.

He could not claim that Narcisse was not doing a good job. The cotton was flourishing in long rows in the fields, carefully tended by Narcisse's field hands. And, after all, that was what Narcisse was there for and certainly the cotton was good. Lewis Gassaway had spoken of it. Brute was loud in his praises of it and even Mr Barry, when he arrived, said it was 'damned fine cotton'.

Yes, Mr Barry had arrived, along with his half-brother, the mulatto Daniel, and his helpers. He had come about a week after Drum's call on him in Westminster, along with a wagon-load of ladders, tool chests, and jugs of corn, all of which, except the corn, were piled on the front portico. Together with Drum's Rex, Fred, and Amos, they started such a whirlwind of activity that Falconhurst was transformed from a quiet and sometimes sleepy place to a hammering, banging, shouting scene where everyone was constantly rushing to and fro. Drum decided to work along with them, glad of the chance to stretch his muscles. Much to his surprise he discovered that by working he was no longer considered the master of Falconhurst but rather an apprentice to fetch and carry at the orders of Barry's men. He didn't mind and soon he had learned how to hammer nails straight and true and cut a board with a saw. Claire insisted that he wear a big straw hat like Narcisse and keep his hands covered with gloves. He didn't want to get black, did he? People with coloured blood tanned quickly in the sun and their skin took on a Negroid tint. He followed her advice, but he could not work with gloves on and he could see that she was right, because his hands and arms were several shades darker than his face and body. Mede followed Drum. He was naturally lazy and refused to learn carpentry, but he discovered that he liked to paint. No hat was needed for Mede and he stripped bare to the waist, flexing his muscles whenever any of the girls from the house passed by. He wondered why they giggled when they saw him. He had expected only admiration, but he did not realize how ludicrous he looked with his black skin speckled all over with white dots. Mede was not an expert painter and managed to get as much on himself as he did on whatever he was painting, albeit he enjoyed the work.

It was Barry's decision that they should start at once on the big house. He proposed, and Drum agreed, that it was only common sense that their own habitation be in order before they attended to the horses and the cattle. There was, he showed Drum, far more work to do on the big house than even Drum or his New Quarters assistants had realized. Wood that looked solid would disintegrate into powder at the touch of a hammer; hinges on shutters were so rusted that when they were moved, they came apart, and much that seemed solid was not. Drum gave him *carte blanche* and Barry did not disabuse the trust put in him. He started work immediately. Even though the combined forces of Barry and his men with Drum's own could do more in a day than poor Fred and Amos were able to do in a week, it seemed to Drum that the work still went slowly. No matter how many times he went to Benson to get kegs of nails or lumber, they were always out of something at the very time he needed it. Fortunately both the lumber yard and Hicks had no longer any qualms about dealing with Drum. He bought in large quantities and often. Furthermore, he paid in cash, which was in his favour. Although they would never address him as 'Mr Maxwell', they did defer to him by making some slight concessions, such as asking him to sit down or even offering him a tin cup of corn, although he drank little whisky these days.

Drum insisted that everything used on the house be of the best. He explained to Barry his desire for screens on doors and windows and Barry informed him that there was now something much better than the cotton mosquito netting that Drum had observed on the bank. He could have screens made of a woven metal mesh that would last much longer and be far more effective than cloth. Drum ordered screens for the whole house, even for the windows in the servants' quarters in the attic. When Barry suggested that neither flies nor mosquitoes bothered Negroes, Drum pointed out that if they had their windows open, and most certainly they would have, because the attic rooms were hot at night, the insects would come in and be all over the house. Barry recognized his short-sightedness but said that it was the first time in his life he had ever screened windows for servants. He had almost said 'niggers', but he had no desire to offend Drum, to whom he had taken a great liking.

While the outside repairs were progressing, Claire picked out samples of the French wallpaper she would order from New Orleans through the brother and sister she had met in Westminster. She had already sent to Madame Helene in New Orleans and when the samples arrived, she consulted with Drum as to what he might prefer, but in every case he yielded to her better knowledge of what was appropriate, his only stipulation being that he wanted something red in the drawing-room. The bolts of brocade and the boxes of elaborate fringes, silk ropes, and tassels arrived and were piled in the parlour. Then Claire astounded the womenfolk in the house, as well as many from New Quarters who begged to see it, with a marvel of marvels – a sewing machine. It was an elaborate affair of wood and cast iron with pedals that were pushed with the feet to make it go, and bobbins to put the thread on. When Claire demonstrated how quickly it would sew a seam, better than the finest seamstress, they were even more amazed. That too found its place in the parlour, awaiting the arrival of the Westminster brother and sister.

They turned out to be a charming young couple, nearly as white as Drum himself. The brother, a small man, introduced himself as Neal Turner and his sister as Laura Turner. Claire installed Laura in the big bedroom behind her own and Neal slept on a couch in the downstairs office, which had been turned into their workroom. Laura, an unusually pretty girl with long, dark curls, a piquant oval face, and a waist that could be spanned by a man's hands, caught Mede's attention and he argued that since all the upholstering and sewing was to be done in the office she would be more comfortable on the couch (thinking, of course, of the flight of stairs that led from his room to the office below), but he found that Claire was adamant. The gleam in Mede's eyes was all too apparent. Laura would, Claire insisted, sleep in the room behind her own. After seeing the searching glance that Laura shyly bestowed on Mede from under her long eyelashes, she wondered if Laura really wanted protection. Despite his dark skin, Mede was a handsome fellow, yet Claire was certain that a girl as light-coloured as Laura would never accept a mate as dark as Mede. Lightness of colour was something to be cherished and not thrown away. The sleeping arrangements remained and the big office downstairs soon became as busy a place as the outside of the house, with the whirring of the sewing machine and the pounding of the upholsterer's hammer.

What with the hammering, the ladders, and the constant activity on the outside, the inside became scarcely habitable. A gang of women was brought over from New Quarters to strip all the old wallpaper off the walls and scrape the plaster clean. When this long job had been finished, the women were retained to scrub the floors clean and to sandpaper off all the old varnish and stains. While all this was going on, Laura was ripping off old upholstery from the chairs and sofas and Neal was papering the walls with Fred and Mede painting the woodwork and ceilings.

For weeks there was no rest for anyone at Falconhurst. It reached a point at one time where there was no place to sit down in the house except in the kitchen and eventually that too was disturbed because Drum ordered the new stove that Mammy Morn had been begging for and Barry's men came inside to add extra shelves and cupboards and paint the entire kitchen. Mammy Morn grumbled about the extra work of getting meals in such confusion, but she was always thinking up something more for the carpenters to do. Drum discovered sawdust on his fried egg one morning and informed Mammy that she had enough cupboards and shelves and cabinets. She agreed and from then on they had meals on time and a place to sit evenings.

While Barry and his men worked on the outside; while Neal and Laura papered and upholstered inside; while Drum and Mede slimmed their waists and broadened their shoulders with hard physical work, the gardeners pruned and raked and weeded until the house, the lawns, and the gardens were all in order. All during this time Narcisse rode between the rows of growing cotton, letting his lash flick the backs of sweating field hands and raising a bumper crop.

Then came the happy day when Barry announced to Drum that the house was finished. The outside was completed down to the last window sash and the inside was as new-looking as it had been when Hammond Maxwell first built it. The familiar furniture, which, Claire had maintained, was far better than the Victorian atrocities that were then being made, was all polished and newly upholstered. Opulent brocaded drapes shaded the tall windows, which could now be opened because of the screens. The dining-room table gleamed, reflecting the big epergne, filled with summer flowers. The shelves of the butler's pantry held two new sets of dishes – one an elegant Meissen bespattered with flowers and the other an everyday set of pink and white Staffordshire. There was still enough Sèvres from the original set for a small dinner and, although Drum had approved of the new purchases, he wondered if Falconhurst would ever give a formal dinner for twenty-four people.

Out in the kitchen Mammy Morn's new stove gleamed like a black diamond and woe to anyone else who even as much as touched it. Matilda and Esther were watched by Mammy's hawklike eyes if they so much as neared it. It was her personal triumph and the slightest spot on the black polish brought her screaming invective for the luckless person who had spilled this drop of water or grease.

Throughout the house kerosene lamps replaced the candles. They gave more light than candles, while their silver standards and cut glass shades were more elegant than the candlesticks. There was now no further use for the big mahogany fan over the dining table. It did little to cool the room and with screens on the house, it had outlived its main purpose – that of keeping the flies away. Claire dispensed with it and in its place she substituted a hanging lamp, its shade painted with cupids and roses and its light reflected in a row of cut glass prisms around the circumference of the shade. It lacked the formality of the tall silver candelabra but made up for it by giving them plenty of light to eat by.

The day after Mr Barry had announced that the house was finished, he, with Daniel, his coloured half-brother, drove around from the barn and stopped his wagon at the portico of the big house, where Drum, Claire, Mede, and the Turners were sitting. Mr Barry as usual was more than a little drunk, but his taste for liquor had never interfered with his work. It almost seemed that the more he drank, the more sober he became.

'All finished, Drum.' He sawed on the reins of his horses to halt them. 'Tomorrow we'll start working on the barns. Think I'll start on the horse barn first. Don't need so much done to it as the others. Anything special you'd like me to do to it?'

Yes, there was something Drum remembered he wanted done. Why, he did not know, but he thought perhaps it was a way of perpetuating his heritage. One day while in the barn with Brute, he had noticed two large wooden pulley blocks, one suspended on each side of the big beams that ran the length of the barn from the big double doors. From one of them hung a length of frayed hempen rope to which an iron handcuff had been fastened. He was curious about it and questioned Brute, who climbed up on the beam and untied the rope, letting the metal handcuff fall to the floor.

This was where slaves had been whipped in the old days, Brute explained, pointing to first one pulley and then the other. Not that Hammond Maxwell had ever done much whipping – weals on the back of a slave lessened his value – but occasionally, and only occasionally, a whipping had had to be administered. Even Drummage had been whipped once, although according to Brute it was not his fault.

The unfortunate slave who was to be whipped was laid face down on the barn floor and held there by two strong men. The metal spancels were fastened around his ankles and then he was pulled up by the ropes, where he dangled, legs spread apart until he nearly split in two, his fingers above the floor so that all the weight of his body hung from his ankles. It was then that he was given the required number of strokes. The Maxwells had never used whips. Instead they had used a perforated leather paddle on the buttocks, which left no weals on a man's back but was even more painful. Ten strokes was a minimum – a hundred would kill a man.

The apparatus intrigued Drum and he decided he would like to have it renewed; not that he would ever have a person whipped, but it would be an interesting thing to show visitors to the plantation – a reminder of the old days when Falconhurst counted its slaves by the hundreds. He explained to Barry how he wanted new ropes and spancels put in. Outside of that there was nothing more he could think of that he wanted done except that the barn be restored to its original condition. He did, however, insist that all the outbuildings be painted white to match the pillars and trim of the big house. Having received Drum's instructions, the old fellow pulled out a jug of corn from under the seat and offered it to Drum and the other men on the porch, but Drum politely refused for all of them.

Mr Barry took a swig from the jug. 'I can guarantee you one thing. Big house's even better today than when it was first built. All the bricks pointed up. All the rotten wood replaced. Everything mended, puttied, painted, and plumb-lined. Looks good on the inside too. Glad you kept the old furniture. Most of this black walnut stuff today looks like it had been cut out on a jig-saw. Don't see that fine old Belter like you got any more. Worth keeping. Them Turners did a good job. Glad to recommend them anytime. Well, goodnight, folks. You won't have any more hammering and pounding 'round the house. Be all down on the barns now. Turned you and Mede into pretty good carpenters and painters, didn't I, Drum? Next time we'll give Mede some black paint to work with – won't show up so much.' He pointed his whip at Mede and guffawed. With a final courtly bow to the ladies, he was off.

They all sat in silence for a while after he left. The Turners had finished their work and were leaving in the morning. From now on, the Falconhurst family would be smaller and they would all miss the Turners, especially Mede, to whom Laura Turner seemed the most desirable girl he had ever met.

Claire brought her rocking chair to a stop, stood up, and opened the screen door. They could hear her calling for Rosanne and then, after the sound of the girl's running footsteps, they heard a whispered conversation between Claire and the girl. When Claire came back out on the porch, she promised them a little surprise but said she would have to wait until either Drumstick or Rosanne told her it was ready. Lights began to shine from the windows one by one and in a few seconds Drumstick came out on the porch and announced to Claire that everything was ready.

'We're all going to take a walk,' she said, turning her head to include all, then coming over to Drum's chair.

'A walk?' Drum stretched out his tired legs. 'But, Claire, it's almost dark.'

'All the better.' She tugged at his arm, forcing him to rise. 'And it will not be a very long walk, so I know you will do it to humour me.'

He stood up grudgingly and she took his arm, beckoning to the others to follow. They went down the steps and on to the gravelled drive, now free of weeds. It was darker under the long avenue of trees but still light enough for them to see. With Drum beside her, she led the company down to the tall brick gateposts with their granite pineapple finials and freshly painted iron gates.

'Now, everyone close your eyes,' she commanded, 'and turn around. Don't open your eyes until I tell you.' She waited for a moment until they were all turned in the direction of Falconhurst. 'Open your eyes.'

They did and the beauty of the big plantation house with every window brilliantly lighted, even those in the third-floor servants' quarters, burst forth upon them. The four white pillars gleamed in the fading light and the bright windows blazed a welcome into the oncoming darkness.

'Pretend that it's the first time you ever saw it,' she said. 'What do you think of Falconhurst?'

They were loud in their praises. The distance lent a new perspective to everything that had been accomplished. How different it was from the proud wreck that had first greeted them. Now it seemed solid and substantial, even though a bit imperious and imposing. It proclaimed to the night that it was a thing of substance and beauty – an important house that must house important people.

'All I can say' – Drum had never envisaged his home like this before – 'is that the people who live up in that house are very lucky people.'

'Like me,' Mede said, grinning.

'Like us.' Claire laughed.

'Like we'd like to be,' Neal and Laura sighed.

While they walked up the drive they kept getting new views of the house through the trees and each new vista was a cause of more comment, but when they emerged from the avenue of trees and saw it close up again, its glory subdued them. Claire led them up on to the porch and across it and opened the screen door. Drumstick, in a plum-coloured livery, stood inside and Debbie and Rosanne were beside him, both in shiny black dresses with white frilled aprons and caps. Over near the stairs Mammy Morn billowed in white dress and apron, while Matilda and Esther, Ciceron's girl, were in the background, decently clad in grey calico.

'Where's Lucy?' Claire whispered to Drumstick. 'I told you to find him.'

'Ain' a-knowin', Miz Claire. Sen' down to the cottage for him, but he ain' there. They ain' a-knowin' where he be at.' He bowed to her and then to the rest, while Mammy Morn and the girls dipped curtsies, after which Claire dismissed them all.

The inside of the house glowed with the light reflected on the white paint and the new French wallpaper. Claire had made the drawing-room all white and gold and red damask, while the parlour on the opposite side of the hall remained in its original green and gold colour scheme. The old wooden panelling and the staircase in the office had been painted white and gave life and colour to what had been a dingy room. The dining-room was resplendent with a scenic wallpaper above its mahogany dado, while the immaculate kitchen with its shiny new stove showed all the servants seated around the scrubbed kitchen table. Upstairs all the rooms had been newly papered and painted, with the furniture oiled and polished and new bedspreads and draperies in every room. All the rooms sported elaborate washstands with gaily decorated bowls and pitchers. Even the third floor, where the servants slept, had been painted and spruced up. Everywhere the floors shone with their coating of polished beeswax and everywhere there was a new brightness from the kerosene lamps and wall lamps.

Although they were all familiar with every aspect of the house, each one had to stop and point out various items in every room. There was so much to admire and exclaim about. Pride showed in every face and each one took pains to show the others what had been his or her particular handiwork. Mede strutted more than a little when he called Laura's attention to whatever spots he had painted, anxious for her commendation, which she gave unstintingly.

The tour ended up in the kitchen, where Mammy had Drumstick usher them into the dining-room. She had prepared coffee and little hot biscuits to be served with scuppernong jelly and melon rind pickle. For a long time they lingered over the food, still talking about the renaissance of Falconhurst with many a 'remember this' and 'I'm so glad I thought about that'.

The Turners finally excused themselves to pack for their early start in the morning. Mede watched Laura leave, his eyes following her to the door. Drum caught his glance, knowing that Mede was already in love with her, but he was sure that it would pass and Mede would once again be contented with Rosanne or any other wench from New Quarters. Mede, he felt, made no distinction between love and desire; and Drum, in analysing Mede, wondered if he did himself. Was this feeling he had for Claire merely his desire for her or was it love? He believed it to be love; he hoped it was.

Mede was the next to leave. His mounting desire for Laura had led him to thinking about Rosanne and now he was anxious to be up in his own room with her. He dropped his napkin and nodded a hurried 'goodnight'. They could hear his footsteps running up the stairs.

That left only Drum and Claire at the table. He pushed back his chair to walk around to her. 'You know something, Claire?'

She held up a warning finger.

'No, not that.' He was able to smile at her misinterpretation of his words. 'Only this. You took us down to the gates so that we could all see the front of Falconhurst. But we have not seen the back. Let's step outside the back door for a moment, just so we can get the complete picture.'

She smiled her acquiescence and took his arm. They passed out through the kitchen, where Matilda and Drumstick were preparing to wash the dishes and Esther was tidying up. Mammy Morn relaxed in a kitchen chair, her cumbersome shoes off to cool her feet while she fanned herself with the hem of her apron.

'It's a-gittin' late,' she reminded them. ' 'Mos' time to start brekkus.'

'We'll only be a minute, Mammy,' Drum assured her, as he held the back screen door open for Claire.

They walked out into the cool night over the dew-damp lawn to the very end of the kitchen garden, then turned back to look at the house, which still blazed with lights. A peaceful serenity enclosed them as they found each other's arms. Drum did not have to beg for a kiss from Claire; her lips were ready and waiting for him. As they stood there in the darkness, body pressed against body, their hands moving slowly and then faster as their kisses mounted in fervour, all thoughts of Falconhurst and its mansion were obscured by the consuming love that enveloped them.

'No!' His resistance to the pressure of her hand was feeble.

'Yes, Drum, yes, yes, yes.' She insisted and now he was powerless to resist. He gasped and suddenly his knees felt like water under him while he leaned against her. The stillness of the night enveloped them, broken only by the night noises of insects in the grass.

Suddenly she pushed him away. 'Drum, listen! Do you hear anything?'

The pounding of blood in his ears subsided and he straightened up, listening, too. He did hear a faint sound, like low moaning that seemed to be human and he wondered whether there might be another couple out in the darkness. Perhaps Mede and Laura! But, no! This was a sound of pain and anguish rather than passion. They both listened more attentively, trying to place this moaning and sobbing. It seemed to come from the high uncut grass that bordered the back lawn and the kitchen garden. Guiding their footsteps by the sounds, they walked through the dew-drenched grass until they stumbled upon a dark shape stretched out on the ground. Whoever it was was still moaning and when Drum leaned over and struck a match, he discovered that it was Lucy, stark naked in the grass.

'Lucy!' Drum got down on his knees beside the boy.

'Mista Drum, oh, Mista Drum! Yo' heard me.'

'What's happened to you, Lucy?' Drum started to lift the slight body, feeling the slipperiness of blood on his hand as he pushed it under Lucy's back. He lifted Lucy up in his arms and with Claire's help he carried the boy back to the big house and took him into the kitchen.

'What's the matter wid Lucy?' Mammy Morn was just preparing to ascend the stairs to her room. 'What he a-doin' nekkid as a jaybird 'n' what he a-screechin' for?' She motioned to Drum to precede her up the stairs. 'Whilst yo' a-totin' him better take him up 'n' put him in his bed. I'll fetch up a pan o' hot water 'n' some clean rags.'

Drum managed to get up the narrow stairs with Lucy in his arms – no small feat in itself. Claire straightened the mussed bed and Drum laid down his burden on the coarse sheet.

'What happened?' he asked for the second time, turning Lucy over on to his stomach. Bloody welts were criss-crossed in a regular pattern on Lucy's back and, although Drum realized that they must be painful, Lucy seemed to be more frightened than hurt.

'Cain' tell yo', Mista Drum, jes' cain' tell yo'.'

322

'Of course you can tell me. I'm a friend of yours, Lucy.' Drum took the dishpan of hot water from Mammy Morn, who had arrived breathless from climbing the stairs.

'Cain', Mista Drum. Done took an oath, I did. If'n I tells, I be daid.' Lucy turned his head to look at Claire, but she concentrated on washing Lucy's back.

'Don't press him, Drum. Probably he has some reason for not telling you. He's really not badly hurt. The skin is only broken through in a few places.'

'Somebody whipped you, Lucy,' Drum persisted, 'and I want to know who did it.'

Lucy winced under the touch of the warm cloth. 'A man done it. Ain' a-knowin' who he was. Ain' seen him. It dark. Happen on the way back from Mista Narcisse's cottage while I a-comin' home.'

'Then, where are your clothes?' Drum seemed to be aware of Lucy's nudity for the first time.

'Guess they down in the bushes somewhere. Jes' 'n ol' shirt 'n' pants. Wa'n't a-wearin' my new clothes.' Lucy seemed to fear Drum's displeasure over the loss of his good clothes. 'Never wear my good clothes to Mista Narcisse's house 'n' oh, Mista Drum, please, ain' a-wantin' to help Mista Narcisse no more. Skeered to come home now, I am. Please, Mista Drum, tell him I cain' help him no more. Tell him yo' a-needin' me here in de big house.'

Claire stiffened and dropped the blood-smeared cloth into the pan of water.

'The boy's merely frightened, Drum. Why ask him more if he doesn't want to tell you? You know Lucy's reputation as well as I do, as well as everyone in Falconhurst does. Evidently some man was laying for him on his way home and Lucy resisted him. That's all.'

'I wonder.' Drum looked down at Lucy and up at Claire. He seemed to sense some strange fear in both of them. They were both covering up for somebody and naturally that somebody must be Narcisse. By the number of weals and their even spacing in a diaper pattern on Lucy's back, Drum recognized that it would have been impossible for one man, in the dark,

323

to have put them there. Lucy must have been tied up and in a lighted place; otherwise the whip could not have been so expertly administered.

'Believe me, Mista Drum. Tha's how it happen 'n' tha's all. Yo' believe me, don' yo', Miz Claire?'

'Of course, Lucy,' Claire answered quickly. 'I believe you.'

' 'N' 'twa'n't no Falconhurst buck what did it. He a strangeh.'

'Of course,' Claire said, anxious to corroborate Lucy's protestations.

Drum looked up to see Mammy Morn returning. She had a jar of ointment in her hand and smoothed it tenderly over Lucy's welted back. She had never cared much for Lucy, but Drum noticed that the old arthritic fingers were trembling. Did she too know something Drum didn't know? 'That feel bettah, son?'

'Take all the sting out, Mammy Morn. Wa'n't no buck from New Quarters neither. It a strangeah.'

'We all believe you, Lucy.' Claire spread a smooth piece of cloth over his back and ripped off narrow strands to tie it with. 'Besides, he didn't hurt you too much. You'll feel fine by morning. Mayhap it's better for you to stay at the big house instead of helping Mr Narcisse. I'll speak to him about it.'

'I will,' Drum said emphatically.

Claire placed her hand on his arm. 'Better let me do it, Drum. Narcisse might get angry. I'll handle it all right.'

It was in Drum's mind to ask her whether Falconhurst belonged to him or Narcisse, but he thought better of it. Somehow Lucy's words did not ring true, even though Claire was so anxious for him to believe him. However, Drum knew how much he depended on Narcisse. He could never find a replacement for him. Moreover, if Narcisse should get angry and leave, he would take Claire with him. Let Claire speak to her husband. After all, what difference did it make?

'I'm sure you'll handle it all right, Claire.' It was better to humble his pride a little. He patted Lucy on the shoulder. 'You'd better stay here, boy. If anyone asks you, tell them I said that if you are going to be head servant in the big house, you'll need to be here evenings. Why, tonight we wanted you and we had only Drumstick.'

'Yes, suh, Mista Drum suh.' Lucy sighed with relief.

'Boys like'n him kin cause a heap o' trouble,' Mammy Morn said, starting for her own room. 'They's a lot o' 'em in New Orleans 'n' they a-gittin' theys throats cut alla time. Some bucks gits as jealous over 'em as they do a wench. Cain' understand it myself but knows about it.'

'You all right now, Lucy?' Drum pulled the sheet up over his bandaged back.

'Of course he's all right.' Claire urged Drum towards the door. 'He'll have forgotten all about it by morning. Come! We're awfully late and the Turners are leaving in the morning. You needn't get up to serve breakfast, Lucy. Drumstick will do it. Now, go to sleep and forget all about it.'

But Drum could not forget about it. After going to his room, he was still thinking about it and it bothered him so much that he opened the door of Mede's room. Mede and Rosanne were both sleeping, but Drum shook Mede awake and told him about what had happened to Lucy. Mede agreed with him. There was something strange about it. Lucy's story didn't ring true to him either, but there was no other explanation he could think of.

'Reckon that Lucy jes' a-goin' to keep on gittin' into trouble. First he gits himself knifed 'n' now he gits himself whopped. It the way he waggles that l'il ass o' his'n.' Mede sat up in bed, black against the white sheets. 'Even a-knowin' I got Rosanne here a-waitin' for me, they's times I want to reach out 'n' grab him when he goes sashayin' aroun' the house. Probably he been a-teasin' some other buck 'n' the buck jes' couldn't stan' it no longer.'

Drum nodded his head. That was probably how it was.

CHAPTER TWENTY-NINE

IT WAS HOT in the overseer's cottage. Not a breath of air came through the shuttered windows and the room stank of musky sweat and the smoky fumes of the oil lamp that sat on a deal table in the middle of the room. Its glare lighted the white walls while the moving figures splotched shadows – grotesque black silhouettes on the white plaster. The only decoration, if decoration it could be called, was a big piece of brown wrapping paper tacked to the wall, which bore a list of names – ten of them with an eleventh scribbled on the bottom. Each of the ten names was crudely printed in black paint and each had a cross beside it, finger-smeared in blood that had now turned a rusty brown. The list read: *Big Sol, Big Jock, Big Alecks, Big Tom, Big Ham, Big Dick, Big Harry, Big Bull, Big Porter, Big Danny.*

The name that was scribbled underneath these names was simply *Lucy* and the cross beside it was uneven and shaky, as though it had been traced with a trembling finger.

Narcisse sat on one of the few chairs in the room, facing the table, which was piled high at one end with heavy account books, while the opposite end was occupied by two stoneware jugs of corn whisky and a number of tin cups. A row of mattresses encircled the walls, salvaged from the big house when the new ones had been recently bought; and on these sat or reclined the ten men Narcisse had recruited as his drivers and whose names were inscribed on the wall. These men had two things in common – each was a giant in stature and each was pure Negro. Whether it was their size that had first brought them together or merely companionship, they had been a group long before Narcisse had arrived, but he had taken pains to weld them together even more closely. The ten men were now a unit, thinking and acting as one, because of the organization Narcisse had founded with its oath of absolute and undying loyalty to himself. The list of names on the wall denoted their initiation into the society of The Big Ten. Their recent initiation of Lucy had been more a matter of devilish fun than anything else, although they had bound him with the same oath that they had taken themselves. Narcisse lost no opportunity to pamper them. They were relieved of most work, paid far higher than the other hands, and given the freedom of the overseer's cottage, where Narcisse pandered to their desires of drink and women and had introduced them to the pleasures of the boys Lucy and Abel, the latter of whom Lucy had trained to a likeness of himself. Narcisse needed these men and their support. He had already gained it by their admiration for him and by all that he gave them. He never allowed them to know that their constant companionship was odious to him because they were Negroes and he hated Negroes. Far from it! He accepted them on his own level, making them his friends. They all thought that they were and they all looked to him for leadership.

Because of the heat in the room this night, all had stripped, but even the lack of clothing did not stop the sweat from channelling down their bodies. Three naked women from New Quarters were serving the men drinks, while two others were stretched out on the mattresses with men they had chosen or who had chosen them.

Some of the men were napping, others were merely sitting with their backs to the wall, while some little interest was engendered by Big Harry and his woman. Two of the fellows had laid bets on his completion of the act and one of them was holding Narcisse's silver watch in his hand, counting off the minutes as they ticked by.

'He gone pas' ten minutes now,' the man with the watch announced jubilantly. 'Yo' done lost, Bull. Yo' a-bettin' he goin' to come 'fore ten minutes.' He reached out his hand, slapping Harry's buttocks. 'Good boy, Harry, I gits to win fo' bits from Bull here. He a-sayin' yo' al'ays quick on the trigger 'n' yo' be all finished up'n ten minutes, but I a-sayin' yo' goin' to take mo' time.'

Without ceasing his motion, Harry turned his face towards them. 'Kin be quick if'n I wants but ain' a-hurryin' none tonight. Jes' slow 'n' easy. May take me half 'n hour.'

Narcisse had been watching too. He had shed his coat and pants but retained his shirt and while he watched the two on the floor through nearly closed eyelids he was fondling Abel, the only one in the room except himself who had any vestige of clothing. What he wore was more for ornament than from any sense of modesty. Someone, presumably Narcisse, had stolen a remnant of the green and gold damask that had been used to decorate the parlour at the big house. Abel had draped this around himself, tying it in the middle with a gaudy piece of turkey-red cotton. From the same material he had fashioned a headcloth from which sprouted a raddled ostrich plume that Claire had discarded. Big, shiny brass curtain rings, also purloined from the new ones purchased for the big house, were suspended from strings around his ears, and he had padded his adolescent chest to make it appear that he had breasts.

'Ain' I well tittied out, Masta Narcisse?' Abel snuggled up a little closer.

Narcisse was unaware that the boy had spoken to him. With his eyes still on Harry and the woman, he moved his hand down under the damask of the boy's dress and the folds of cloth were swaying with a slow rhythmic movement. Without answering Abel, he started to hasten the moment until Abel pulled away from him.

'Please don' no more, Masta Narcisse. It too early in the evenin', suh.'

'Too early li'l missy?' Big Ham, who was sitting up against the wall, spread his legs out before him, jeering at Abel in high falsetto tones. 'What yo' mean, li'l missy? What too early? Listen, ain' never too early, ain' never too late. If'n yo' wants to be one o' the Big Ten, yo' got to come early 'n' late bofe.' As if to prove his point he started manipulating himself, then stopped, beckoning to one of the girls to come and kneel before him. 'Hell, boy, yo' got to grow up.' He waggled an accusing finger at Abel. 'Now that Lucy boy, he ain' much older'n yo', yit he kin take it. Lookit how he took it the night he 'nishiated. 'Bout time we a-gettin' 'roun' to 'nishiatin' yo', ain' it?'

'Kin do what Lucy do if'n I want but don' wan' me no

whoppin' like'n Lucy got. Don' wan' no Big Ten criss-crossin' on my back.'

'Make a man o' yo.' Ham soon lost interest in Abel and devoted his attention to the girl before him.

'Reckon we shouldn't of whopped that Lucy,' Harry said, pushing his wench away and standing up. 'He a-goin' to the big house 'n' blab all he know. Now Masta Narcisse say he ain' a-comin' back. We a-goin' to miss that Lucy boy 'roun' here. He better'n Abel any day. Abel he al'ays a-whinin' 'n' sayin' that we a-hurtin' him. Lucy he never whine. He al'ays ready. Too bad Lucy not comin' back no more.'

'Reckon we too hard on Lucy,' Tom said, shrugging his shoulders. 'Jes' 'nishiatin' him tha's all. Jes' a-puttin' the mark o' the Big Ten on his back. We all got it 'n' we wa'n't a-screamin' 'n' a-screechin' like'n him.' Tom wheeled on one foot to display the criss-cross pattern welted across his own back in finger-thick weals. 'But, then, we all men and we kin stan' it. Lucy he not a real man, so's he whimper.'

'Yeah, man, but yo' didn' go through what pore Lucy did afore he got his stipin'. That pore boy nearly dead afore he gittin' whopped.'

'Pot a-callin' the kittle black.' Big Sol signalled for one of the girls to pour him a drink and waited impatiently for her to fetch it. 'Yo'-all pestered Lucy afore he a-gittin' whopped. Reckon as how yo'-all enjoyed it but thinkin' pore Lucy a bit used up afore he got his whoppin'. Whoppin' bad 'nough when a man ain' had ten big bucks like'n us plaguin' him, 'n' Mista Narcisse too. He the wust o' all.'

'That's why I waited until last,' Narcisse said, smiling. 'But Lucy he's used to it now. Don't see why he's complaining. Used to come around begging for it all the time.'

'Lucy marked jes' 'bout perfect, though. He marked better'n yo', Big Sol.' Dick, who was stretched out next to Sol, rubbed his fingers over Sol's back. He stuck out his thick lower lip and shook his head. 'Yores ain' even, Sol. Some o' them diamonds small 'n' some big. Now, look at mine.' He flopped on to his belly. 'Mine's perfect.'

Sol shrugged his shoulders. 'Tha's 'cause I gave it to you.

Big Jock did mine 'n' ain' so shore o' his aim. Me, I kin lay a blacksnake whip anyplace I wan'. Sort o' 'members, though, that yo' did plenty o' screamin'. Actin' like'n a baby a-gittin' his ass spanked. Didn' take it like'n a man o' the Big Ten.'

'Tha's 'cause yo' mad at me that night 'n' yo' shore poured it on. 'Member? I took a bright-skin gal over on Camelia Plantation 'n' yo' a-wantin' her 'n' I not a-givin' her up. Yo' jes' a-takin' it out on me.'

'Had that bright-skin gal later 'n' she a-sayin' she wisht she had me the fust time. Sayin' as how yo' ain' got no sap in yo'.'

'Got plenty o' sap in me 'n' kin prove it. Wan' to see? Kin prove it in jes' a minute 'cause I quick on the trigger, I am. Hey, come over here, yo' Abel. Wan' yo' should show Big Sol somethin'.'

'Hus that big mouf o' yourn. Knows yo' got sap, so's yo'd better save it. Too hot to arguify. Too goddam hot.'

For several minutes they were all quiet, feeling the stifling heat too much to make an effort to speak until finally Big Sol looked up at Narcisse, waiting for him to finish his drink and put his cup down on the table.

'That Lucy boy he ain' opened his trap, has he?' Sol asked.

Narcisse poured a remaining half-cupful out and handed it to Abel. 'Lucy doesn't dare to talk. He remembers his oath and he knows damn well if he opens his mouth, we'll cut his balls off.'

'Will do jes' that,' Big Alecks agreed. He pulled himself up to his knees and then stood up on the mattress, stretched himself, arms high overhead, his fingertips touching the ceiling. His big feet made no noise as he walked across the bare floor and poured himself a drink from the jug, downing the whole cupful in a few swallows, then filling it up again and drinking a second. The jug was empty so he took the corncob that stoppered another jug between his teeth and wrenched it out. This time instead of pouring the liquor into a cup, he tilted the jug over his shoulder and poured a draught into his mouth. Walking over to Abel, who was standing a few feet away from Narcisse, he asked, 'Wan' to play 'roun' a li'l bit, boy? See how it a-jumpin' for yo'.'

'Ain' hankering to jes' now, Big Alecks, jes' got ma bref.'

'Do's I tell yo', boy.' Alecks made a grab for Abel and pulled him to him, smartly boxing his ears. 'Yo' do like'n I tells yo'. Kin git yore goddam bref some other time when I through with yo'.'

Narcisse watched them with far more interest than he had watched Harry and his wench. He seemed to rouse from his lethargy and began to shout words of encouragement to both Alecks and Abel, inciting them on.

With only a desultory glance at the performers, Big Sol yawned and drew himself up to a sitting position, his back against the wall, picking his toes.

'Hotter'n hell in here.' He drew a hand down over his body, flipping off the sweat by snapping it from his fingertips. 'Jes' been a-thinkin' I'd like to haul ass outa here. Ain' got me no neverminds tonight for wenches, nor Abel, nor nothin' else. Le's get on our trogs 'n' take a ride. Got me a hankerin' for some good hog meat. Ol' McAllister got himself some nice shoats over on his place. Could git us one o' two 'n' bring 'em back here. Could roast 'em over the fire in the kitchen. Nice hog meat shore taste good tonight.'

'Ain' hankerin' for no black wenches tonight neither.' Big Jock pushed the girl beside him away and shoved her off the mattress with his foot. 'Ain' a-hankerin' for no hog meat, neither. Hankerin' to git me some white meat. Yassuh! White meat. Got to have me a change. Sick o' black wenches 'n' that Abel boy too. Wisht that Lucy back. He right good, though never tho't I'd ever be likin' it that way. Don' think o' nothin' I wan' tonight but white meat. Shore would jubilate me to git me a white wench tonight. M-m-m! That's somethin' different. White skin! Lawdee!'

'Hell, man, yo' wantin' to git yo'self hung?'

'I hung plenty, man.'

'Hung by the neck, I mean. Hung till yo' dead. White meat right risky for a nigger, man.'

'Haven't you ever had any white meat, Big Jock?' Narcisse asked, his eyes still on Alecks and Abel.

'Hell, no! Ain' no nigger 'roun' here never had no white

meat. Wisht I'd been bigger when the war was over. Sayin's how a nice-lookin' buck could git plenty o' white meat in them days. Look what Mista Drum's papa got for hisself. Nice pretty blonde woman what owned Falconhurst, 'though they a-sayin' that Drummage he likin' black meat better'n white. His git's all over the place. Ain' like'n that now. Nigger never gits hisself no white meat no mo'.'

'Whoa up there, boy!' Big Danny squatted on his knees, chuckling with a high-pitched ululating laugh that showed he was more favoured than all the others. 'Had me some white meat onc't. She right ol' 'n' fatter'n a sow, but she purentee white with red hair. Yes, suh! She that po' white trash what livin' over in Buck Hollow. Widdered, she was, with a passel o' young 'uns. I a-walkin' by there one day 'n' she a-settin' on the do'step. Kids all over the yard. Right hot day, it was, 'n' she a-fannin' herself with her skirt. Every time she a-liftin' it, I see that red bush, lookin' like it on fire. Nearer I gits, the higher she a-liftin' it 'n' I could see she a-crotch-watchin' me's I come along. Could feel that woman's eyes jes' a burning through my pants 'n' it make my pants stan' out 'bout a foot.'

'What yo' talkin' 'bout?' Big Dick said. 'Yo' jes' a braggin' fool. Ain' no one here but Big Sol 'n' Masta Narcisse kin say that.'

'Kin too if'n I wants.' Danny defended himself. 'Anyway I a-givin' her somethin' to look at.' He slumped down on to his knees and arched his body out proudly. ' 'N' she shore a-watchin'. Jes' a-passin' by her do' when she look up at me smiley-like 'n' say, "Mighty hot day, ain' it?" 'N' I 'lows as to how it was, but she not a-lookin' me in my eyes either 'n' she a-floppin' that ol' dress higher'n ever. Then she a-sayin', 'thout even takin' her eyes off'n my crotch, that she got some nice cold spring water in a crock ina house 'n' would I like a drink. 'Lowed as to how I would 'n' she shoos the kids away from the yard, a-tellin' 'em to go down by the brook 'n' play where it cooler. Then she a-lookin' up 'n' down the road for to see if anyone a-comin'.'

'Bet yo' a-comin' right 'bout then.' Big Sol had become interested in the conversation.

'Jes' 'bout,' Danny giggled, 'jes' 'bout. But ain' nobody 'roun', so she quick-like beckons me in. Slammed the do' shut, she did, 'n' pulled in the latchstring. 'Fore I a-knowin' it, she had my britches down 'n' she shore admirin', sayin' she never saw nothin' so purty afore. In two shakes o' a lamb's tail she drug me down ona bed. She wan' too good, though. Her belly so fat couldn' do much.'

Big Sol roared with laughter and pointed a derisive finger at Danny. 'Yo' shore a big boy, Danny, but yo' ain' like me 'n' Masta Narcisse. Now, if'n it be us, we'd have no neverminds 'bout a fat belly. I likes 'em fat. Jes' like rollin' on a feather tick. But now yo' a-talkin' 'bout it, reckon I could use some white meat too. A-gittin' tired o' black meat. It right good when yo' needs it, but it gits tiresome, mighty tiresome.'

'If'n yo' a-wantin' it that bad,' Alecks said, 'I a-knowin' whereat yo' kin git it easy. Purtiest white meat in the country too. 'N' knows whereat we kin git money too – 'bout three thousan' dollars. Yes, suh, man. Yo' not only gits yore white meat, but yo' gits paid for it too.'

Narcisse, who had been only half listening to the conversation, suddenly pushed his chair back from the table and swung it around on one leg to face Alecks. 'You said three thousand dollars, Alecks?' He clapped his hands together, 'You wenches, get your dresses on and get to hell outa here, 'n' you, Abel, now that you've finished with Alecks, get out in the kitchen and close the door. Go to bed. If I catch you listening, you'll be out working as a field hand.'

It was quiet for a few moments while the women dressed and left and Abel went into another room and closed the door.

'Tha's what I said.' Alecks continued where he had left off, grinned to show a row of even white teeth, and nodded his head.

'How do you know that?' Narcisse was tense with excitement now.

'Heard it, I did. Got me a wench over to Loralie Plantation. She the same wench what Stonewall Jackson Lee, that skinny

333

ol' nigger what works in the bank, so hell-fire crazy about. She got herself a husband what's a no-'count nigger that's al'ays road-chasin' from here to Mobile. Ol' Stonewall he so anxious to git it in her, he even went to Big Pearl to git hisself a conjure. Conjure ain' doin' him no good, not if'n she can have a real man like'n me 'stead o' that skinny jackrabbit. He al'ays comin' out to spark her, though, bringin' a bag o' lemon drops from the sto'. All she do is make a li'l sweet-talkin' with him while she a-waitin' for me.'

'Yes, yes,' Narcisse interrupted impatiently. He knew that once one of these fellows got started on a story, he would include all the details of his sexual ravishment of the wench and how she enjoyed it. He saw and heard enough of that in the cottage every night. 'Go on, tell me about the money.'

'Was jes' a-gittin' to that.' Alecks was the centre of attention now and he wanted to keep his audience. 'Well, this what ol' Stonewall he a-tellin' my wench 'n' she a-tellin' me. Yo'-all know that Miz Norrison what lives at Montvale Plantation 'n' her husban' what got gored by a bull 'bout a month 'go?'

'Ay-yuh!' They all nodded their heads while Sol spoke.

'She rather high-steppin' 'n' young for a widder 'n' she the one what got them two pretty gals. Prettiest fillies I ever did see. They 'bout seventeen, eighteen, 'roun' 'bout there. Man, tha's white meat for yo'. M-m-m!'

'What about the money?' Narcisse tried hard to keep Alecks from being sidetracked.

'Well, it seems that Miz Norrison a-wantin' to sell the place. It ain' been worked for a long time. Ol' man Norrison he shif'less 'n' let it run down, but it a big place onc't. That ol' man he so stingy he ain' wantin' to pay no fiel' hands no decent wages, so ain' able to git no niggers to work for him. Anyway Miz Norrison done sol' the place to some man from Tennessee. Place pretty well plastered with mortgages, but ol' Stonewall he a-sayin' she git three thousand dollars cash 'n' she tooken it home with her so's she could go to Mobile where her sisters live 'n' git them gals married up. That jes' two, three days 'go, so's the money must be in the house.'

'Hell with the money.' Big Sol shook his head violently and

pulled down his lower lip. 'What we a-needin' money for? Ain' wantin' no money, but I shore hankerin' to bust me one o' those purty li'l white gals.'

'You still wanting white meat, Jock?' Narcisse poured out a drink and offered it to him.

'Shore do, Masta Narcisse, shore do.'

'And what about the money? You want that too?' Narcisse anxiously awaited his answer while Jock gulped the corn.

'Hell no! Like Big Sol a-sayin', what good's money 'roun' here. Cain' spend it o' the sheriff a-thinkin' it stoled. Ain't got me no hankerin' to go to Mobile o' N'Orleans. Got all I want right here. I one o' the Big Ten boys 'n' we he'ps ourselves to anything we a-wantin' in the county. Ain' needin' no money for corn, no money for wenches, 'n' ain' needin' no money for new trogs.'

'But I need it.' Narcisse brought his hand down on the table. 'How about me going with you boys tonight? You take the girls and I'll take the money.'

'Don' wan' me the widder, wan' me one o' them gals,' Big Sol interrupted, his tongue circling his lips, wetting their dark purple. 'If'n one o' them gals a-gittin' married up in Mobile, she ain' goin' to need no bustin' 'cause she goin' to git busted by the best – that's me. Bustin's the likingest thing I do.'

Narcisse waited for him to stop bragging. 'Then, if you boys aren't interested in the money but only the girls, I'll go along with you. I'm not interested in the girls, so you won't have to share them with me and if you're not interested in the money, I won't share it with you.' He too wet his lips, thinking of how three thousand dollars, added to what he anticipated from the cotton crop and another scheme he had in his head, would enable him and Claire to go to Paris. Ah, Paris! No colour line! He and Claire with their good looks would find many means of living 'high on the hog', as the niggers called it. 'I'm going with you.' He stood up and surveyed the group.

'Yo' cain' go, Masta Narcisse. Yo're white o' almos'.'

'Who can tell I'm a white man under those hoods you wear. Got an extra one?'

'We made up one for Lucy, but he never worn it. Jes' fit yo', Masta Narcisse.'

They all agreed that they were not interested in the money. It was not that they did not know the value of money, those shiny silver dollars with which Narcisse paid them, but they had no conception of any large amount of money. Half the time they didn't even spend the money they earned but gave it away. A thousand dollars meant no more to them than the ten dollars Narcisse paid them every week. When they did spend it, they spent it carelessly, buying lemon drops or peppermint balls for themselves or some wench they wanted to impress. Occasionally they bought colourful bandanas to tie around their necks, a new straw hat when the old one was worn out, or a pair of boots. Their main interests were eating and drinking and wenching. For excitement they made midnight raids on other plantations. They all had their choice of wenches at New Quarters, but it was more fun to creep stealthily through the quarters of another plantation. The excitement added a new fillip of eroticism to their jaded tastes, which Narcisse had pandered to by every means he knew. When they had tired of wenches, they drove off livestock for which they had no use, stole pigs, which they roasted and ate or, just to be devilish, ran their horses around a big house, whooping and hollering for a few minutes before they rode off again.

They had started out with harmless pranks, but now they were getting dangerous. Narcisse's whisky and his continuous pandering to more and more perverse desires had changed them. Lately they had become more vicious. Their escapades were causing fear throughout the countryside. Their identity was unknown. They arrived in the night in black hoods and nobody had ever seen them, although it was rumoured that they came from another county. Certainly nobody would have suspected that the ten foremen on Falconhurst Plantation could be these night marauders. Only Narcisse knew and now, of course, Lucy. Even the wenches who served them were ignorant of their reputation and Abel, although he heard them talking, paid little attention to their words.

336

Narcisse had had a reason for making them his particular pets and he made a practice of pampering them, drawing them closer and closer to him, knowing that he was some day going to need them. They had reacted to his attentions and to the liquor and women he supplied, even to the boys, who were a new experience for them. Knowing that Narcisse was behind them, they had become more and more arrogant, lavishing their affection and devotion on him who had kept them from boredom and exaggerated their egos. They were willing to let him have the money. The novelty of having white women was enough for them. Although they did not anticipate the ready acceptance from any white woman that they were accustomed to receive in the Negro quarters, they were certain that they were such perfect specimens of manhood that no woman, be she white or black, could long resist them. Although they had heard tales of handsome black coachmen and butlers receiving favours from their white mistresses, they were aware that in touching a white woman, they were breaking the greatest law of the South. It was the most dangerous thing a Negro could attempt. Even had a white woman encouraged them, once they were discovered, she would have claimed it rape. The penalty was hanging, but that was only a legal penalty. When white citizens took the law into their own hands, a Negro caught with a white woman would be tied to a tree and burned.

Ee-jay! So what did it matter. They'd never been caught yet. They never would. Let the sheriff come around the day after and they'd be working in the fields at Falconhurst as innocent as though they had slept all night.

There were no servants, Big Sol assured them, at Montvale Plantation except an old Negress who cooked and she probably slept out in the kitchen, which was detached from the house. She could be easily gagged and bound, so they'd better take along some fishlines. The white women might thrash and holler but it wouldn't be necessary to tie them. Montvale was on an isolated road, far from any other farmhouses. So let 'em holler. Sol would attend to the cook himself or, he reconsidered, let Porter do it, he was like a cat, stealthy and noiseless, and he swore he could see in the dark.

337

'How yo' a-goin' to stop the ol' wench from yellin'?' Ham asked.

'Kin shore stop the young uns' – Big Porter grinned – 'but I ain' doin' this ol' wench no good turn. Stick a dishrag in her mouth. That good 'nough for her. Ain' wastin' nothing on no old wench when them purties a-waitin' for me.'

Narcisse had been pacing the floor nervously. It was the first time he had ever been out with the boys and he was frightened, but the thought of three thousand dollars offset his fears.

'All right, boys, get your trogs on and get started.' Narcisse walked up and down impatiently while the men dressed – a simple process, as they wore only shirts and pants and the black hoods. He peeked out into the kitchen and saw that Abel was fast asleep on a pallet on the floor, then blew out the lamp, and opened the door.

'Go and get your horses and saddle one for me,' Narcisse said. The cool air on his face was welcome after the heat and stench of the cottage. 'It's ten o'clock now. I'm going up to the big house and pretend to go to bed. I'll meet you all down on the main road in about half an hour.'

'Shore a-goin' to git us white meat tonight.' Big Jock slapped Sol on the shoulders. 'Yo' 'n' me fust, Sol boy. We'll bust the pretties, huh?'

'Shore, yo' 'n' I bust 'em, others kin have them later.'

Narcisse waited until he saw them disappear, black shapes swallowed up in the night's blackness, and then walked towards the big house. He was glad to see that there were lights on the first floor, which meant that Drum and Claire had not retired. They had, he knew, been sitting out in front, waiting for the upstairs rooms to cool off. Claire's dress made a splotch of white on the wide veranda and a sliver of light from the front hall made a highlight of brightness on Drum's polished boots. Mede was there too and for once he was glad of Mede's presence. The more witnesses the better, in case he should need to establish an alibi.

He started slowly up the steps. 'Hard day today.' He yawned. 'Now that Lucy's not coming, it takes me longer. Can't wait to get to bed. You about ready, Claire?'

'We were just talking about going up,' Drum answered for her. He stood up from his chair, stretched, and peered out into the darkness. 'How's everything, Narcisse?'

'Fine except that I'm dog-tired. Lucy ever coming back to help me?'

'That depends on Lucy. He's afraid of his own shadow these days.'

Claire took Narcisse's arm and walked inside with him. She went in the drawing-room to turn out the lamps and then turned down the wick of the lamp in the front hall, which always burned all night.

Narcisse pointed to the clock. 'Quarter past ten,' he remarked. 'Guess my watch is slow.' He made a pretence of taking it out of his pocket and setting it. 'Well, it's time we were all in bed.' Drum and Mede had waited for them and allowed Claire and Narcisse to precede them up the stairs. There were brief goodnights in the upper hall and then all three doors closed.

CHAPTER THIRTY

ONCE INSIDE THEIR room, Narcisse put his fingers to his lips, beckoned Claire to him, and whispered in her ear. She tried to dissuade him from leaving, pleading with him to stay with her, but he was adamant and his only excuse to her was that this one night's expedition would get them to Paris even more quickly than they had hoped.

'You do want to go, don't you, Claire?'

'Yes, for you, Narcisse, I want to go. I know how much it means to you.' She recognized the urgency in his voice and with it came the awful truth that she could never leave him. For years he had been planning on getting to Paris. His dream must come true. Yet even in his urgency she tried to dissuade him. 'Oh, Narcisse, my darling, why must you think always of Paris? We're so comfortable here and so ... so secure. Falconhurst has already begun to seem like home to me. I love it here.'

'And you love Drum too.' He pointed an accusing finger at her and smiled a crooked smile that raised one corner of his lips while it lowered the other. 'Don't deny it, Claire. You're head-over-heels in love with him and he is with you. Sometimes I think you love him even more than you do me. Maybe I don't blame you too much. I'm not much good.'

She shook her head in denial, pressing her lips closely together. Slipping from his arms, she sat down on the edge of the bed, her head lowered, not daring to look up at him. 'I'll never love anyone as much as I do you, Narcisse.'

'But you do love him,' he insisted.

'Yes.'

'And he's crazy about you?'

'He is.'

He rubbed his hands together and now his smile was turning into a grin.

'So! If you love him and he loves you, our little plan is going to be a hell of a lot easier when the time comes. You won't have to woo him with fluttering eyelashes and prim little kisses and he won't have to court you with gallant phrases. Just be sure he's all primed when the time comes. See if you can't get rid of that goddam slut he sleeps with about a week beforehand.'

'I already hate her' – Claire was vehement – 'hate her, hate her, hate her!'

'That's my girl! That's the spirit I like to see. You've been moping around too much lately, Claire. Hell, this backwater is no place for us. If tonight's venture is successful – and I shall not tell you what it is because it is better that you do not know - we may not have to wait for ginning time to get the money. We may be able to go very soon.'

'But I do like it here, Narcisse. For the first time in a long time I feel safe.'

'And who do you have to talk to but a lot of niggers. Oh,

Claire, if you could only know how sick I am of niggers. Black skins and gullah talk. I'm sick of their looks, their smell, their limited minds. Do you think I enjoy those evenings I spend at the cottage with them? No! I'd far rather be with educated white men. I want to be somewhere where nobody will ever say the word *nigger* to me again, where I can hold up my head, where I can be somebody. And the only place is Paris. We've got to get there while we're young, Claire, so we can enjoy it. We can't go like paupers as we went to New Orleans. We need money and the more of it the better. If my plans work out here at Falconhurst, we can go in the style we should and live in the style we should in Paris.'

She glanced up at him suddenly. There was a kindling of opposition in her eyes and a stubborn tilt to her chin. 'Have you ever considered, Narcisse, that I might refuse to go through with *your* plans? That I might have plans of my own?'

He raised his hand, the fingers opening on the upswing, to bring it down on her cheek. She flinched, letting out a small cry of pain and waiting for him to strike her again. The second time she did not flinch, although the sharpness of the blow had brought tears to her eyes. Without speaking to her, he rummaged through the wardrobe to find the oldest and most disreputable clothes he owned. He threw out a pair of black trousers, patched on the seat, and an old shirt, which he scuffled under his boots until it was soiled and torn. Stripping off his clothes, he came over to stand before her naked.

'Look at me, Claire. Look at me.' His hand was raised again.

She stared at him for a long moment.

'Have you any plans of your own?'

There was nothing but compliance in her eyes now. 'I have no plans of my own, my dear. You know the power you have over me. I cannot say "no" to anything you propose.'

'You never have, my dear. Don't start getting independent now. Just remember this. We came upstairs a little after ten and we went to bed. I was here all night. *Mais oui?*'

She arose from the bed and came over to him, putting her

arms around his neck and kissing him on the cheek. 'I'll remember, Narcisse, as I have remembered so many, many times before for you, but I shall not sleep until you are back safe. Oh, it's terrible to worry about you so when you are out nights. I never know whether you will come home alive or carried in on a shutter.'

'Silly Claire.' He kissed the red mark on the cheek where he had struck her. 'Don't forget, I'm not alone. I've got ten of the strongest, blackest bucks in the world to protect me. Any one of them would lay down his life for me, or at least I think the bastard would. God knows I've pampered them enough.' He kissed her cheek again. 'I'm sorry, dear. I'm always so hot-tempered, but I didn't mean to hit you so hard. Let's make up and be friends again. You know I worship you. You're all I ever had. I couldn't live without you. Say the *petit nom* you have always had for me and it will keep me safe. It brings me good luck.'

'*Mon petit Harlequin*,' she murmured, her fingers on his cheek. 'Oh, how long ago that seems, Harlequin.'

'*Au 'voir, Columbine*. Now, remember, I've never left this room.' He walked to the door, opened it gently, and then came back to pick up the pair of brogans he had taken from the armoire. Holding up one crooked finger to her, which she clasped with her own finger, he stepped out into the hall, traversing its length in his stocking feet. In his descent of the stairs he tested his weight on each step to ascertain if it would creak. The dim light in the hall showed him the outside door and he was glad that it was open and the screen door was unlocked. Thank God there was no moon. The darkness swallowed him up as he ran diagonally across the front lawn, down on to the main road. Once on the road, he started towards New Quarters, keeping close to the shadows so that no lone horseman coming back from the tavern in Benson might see him. When he passed a copse of trees, he heard the soft notes of a whippoorwill and stopped, listening for the faint noise of saddle leather creaking and the jingle of metal bits. The whippoorwill call was repeated and he stepped off the road into the thicket. Holding his hands before him, he touched the

342

warmth of a man's leg and felt the smoothness of a horse's flank. He lowered his hand to touch the bare foot that was in the stirrup.

'Which one are you?' he whispered.

'Big Bull. Danny's over there with a horse saddled for you.'

'Masta Narcisse.' He heard the voice raised above a whisper. 'I'se got yore hoss right here. Give him a hand, Bull.' Narcisse felt the wet warmth of a handclasp, which led him around the back of a horse, then another hand and still another until he reached a horse whose stirrup hung empty. He mounted and waited for some word of instruction.

'Yo' on, Masta Narcisse?'

He recognized the voice as that of Big Sol, who, as always, was the ringleader of the group.

'I'm ready,' Narcisse answered.

'We a-goin' by the roads,' Big Sol said confidently, certain now that nobody would hear him. 'Cain' track us on the roads, but we ain' a-ridin' together. Masta Narcisse 'n' I go 'long fust. Then yo' follows us two by two, but let us git outa sight afore the next two starts. No fas' ridin' neither. Keep yore hosses at a walk when yo' passes houses. Trot 'em when yo' gits a chanc't. 'Fore we gits to Benson, turn off to the right where that ol' dead tree at the crossroads. That'll bring yo' out on the Camden road 'n' Montvale right on that road. They's a grove o' pines jes' 'cross from the house. We all meet there. Don' wear no hoods till we gits there.'

Big Sol and Narcisse started out at a canter, slowing their horses down as they passed darkened houses. Once they heard a horseman approaching and turned off the road, waiting behind a clump of brush until he passed. When they reached the crossroads, they turned and climbed a hill, then went down into a valley. They forded a small branch and one rather wide stream with a sluggish current that reflected the stars like pinpoints of light in its slowly swirling water. It was a seldom-used road and they passed nobody else until they arrived at the stand of pines. Here Big Sol halted and they waited for the others to arrive. It took the other nine about an hour to assemble, and as each pair came in, Sol halted them and told them to dismount and tie their horses. They grouped around him, arms over arms until they made a complete circle; then, with heads bowed and almost touching, they listened as Sol spoke to them.

'We gotta have a plan,' Sol said. 'Ain' a-goin' to git this done less'n we do. Ain' nothin' to be fearful of, but this is somethin' new for us. Fust time we ever ina big house. Fust time we ever a-rapin' white women. This different 'n rapin' nigger wenches in the quarters where mos' likely they jes' a-waitin' for us 'n' likin' it too.'

'White women a-goin' to like it too onc't they gits it,' Jock said, snickering, but Big Sol ignored him.

'Now, yo', Porter, yo' more like'n a cat'n a man, so yo' goes fust. I worked here onc't for a few days a-choppin' wood. We et in the kitchen 'n' this kitchen ain' no part o' the house but separate. Doah to the house go into the dinin'-room. Porter, yo' go into the kitchen 'n' tie that ol' wench up 'n' stuff somethin' in her mouth so's she won't holler 'n' yell.'

'What yo' a-goin' to stuff in her mouth?' a voice asked, and a laugh followed it.

'Ain' a-goin' to pleasure that ol' wench,' Porter said. 'Dish-rag good 'nough for her. Got to save mine for them white wenches.'

'Shet yore mouth,' Sol said, in no mood for humour. He quite realized the seriousness of their escapade now. 'Look, Porter! Onc't yo' gits that ol' wench tied up 'n' quiet, yo' goes to the dinin'-room doah. Probably ain' locked. Mos' o' these ol' houses done los' the key years 'go. If'n it latched, yo' slips yore knife in the crack 'n' lif' it easy 'n' gentle so's not to make a noise. Onc't yo' gets the doah open, yo' makes that whippo'-will soun'. We goin' to be right near. We all comes inter the house. Now, le's git this straight. Big Jock 'n' me we a-goin' to bust the gals. That only right 'cause we the leaders. Who wants the widder fust?'

'I a-takin' her fust. Yo' knows me.' It was the voice of Alecks. 'If'n I stan' 'roun' waitin', I jes' a-goin' to lose it.'

'I a-gittin' seconds on one o' the wenches.'

''N' I a-gittin' seconds on t'other.'

344

'Widder good 'nough for me. She be nice 'n' easy after Alecks he gits through with her.'

'Lookin' like I got to take third.'

'Tha's all right, Bull, she all nice 'n' busted for yo' then.'

'Dick, yo' take thirds on t'other wench 'n' Porter he mounts the widder.'

'What 'bout me?'

'Look, Ham,' Sol answered him, 'by that time if'n yo' ain' come off in yore britches, yo' kin have any one yo' wants.'

'Mayhap we'll all git 'nother roun', a-changin' off like.'

'Not tonight,' Big Sol said emphatically. 'Bad 'nough, a-rapin' white women 'thout'n takin' seconds. We wants to git it over with 'n' git 'way fast's we kin. Ain' a-ridin' the roads home. Got to go 'cross the fiel's 'cause we'll be wearin' the hoods.'

'Ain' a-goin' to take me long. I jes' ready for it now.'

'Hush up 'n' stop braggin', Dick. We's all ready for it,' Big Sol continued. 'Now for yo', Masta Narcisse, 'fore Alecks he takes the widder, we find out jes' where the money is if'n that's what yo' want. 'N' keep yore mouf closed, Masta Narcisse. Yo' talks like'n a white man, so don' say nothin' 'tall. If'n the ol' bitch she won' tell where the money is afore Alecks tackles her, she will afterward. Mayhap if we tell her we ain' a-goin' to pester her purties, she'll tell anyway. Mos' white women would. Nothin' so disgraceful's havin' a purty young white gal birf a black baby. 'N' take off yore shoes, Masta Narcisse. They's a-goin' to make too much noise.'

They all slipped on their hoods and, with Big Sol leading the way, they stepped out of the pines and on to the road. The house was near the road. It lacked the long avenue of trees that graced the more important plantations. It was more of a farmhouse than a big plantation house; it was only one storey high, but at one time, as Narcisse could see, it had attempted some pretensions to grandeur, because there was a ghostly row of white pillars across the front. The moon had risen and gave a faint light between the scudding clouds, so they kept in the shadow of the overgrown crepe myrtle bushes that surrounded the house and made their stealthy way to the back of the house.

Big Sol was right. The kitchen, unlike the kitchen at Falconhurst, was separated from the house itself but connected to it by a roofed passageway, which led from the kitchen door to a door in the main house. Falconhurst was one of the few houses that had its kitchen as an integral part of the house; usually the kitchen was separate so that the heat and smells of cooking would not enter the main house.

They could discern Big Sol's hand raised and they all stopped and once again clustered around him. One of the group, whom Narcisse supposed to be Porter, crept around them like the cat to which Sol had likened him, keeping close to the house until he came to the passageway to the kitchen. They could barely see him as he passed between the white posts and disappeared into a doorway, closing the door noiselessly behind him. There was a muffled cry, which was immediately cut off. In another few moments Porter came out and once again they followed his dark shadow between the white posts until he came to the door of the big house. Evidently it was not locked, because they heard the mournful cry of a whippoorwill almost immediately. Big Sol beckoned to them to come on and they followed Porter into the house. Their eyes, now accustomed to darkness, told them that they were in a dining-room. A long sideboard made a blacker splotch against the wall and they encountered a square dining-room table, which they had to circumnavigate. They gained the next room, which was a parlour. Big Sol went first, his hands out before him, placing one foot cautiously down after another, exploring the uncarpeted floor. But even with all his precautions, he stumbled over a footstool, kicking it across the floor. Immediately they all froze, not moving a muscle, scarcely daring to breathe.

A voice came from across the hall. It was a woman's voice blurred with sleep. 'What yo' a-doin' up, Bonnie?'

There was no answer and they waited silently until the voice cried out again, 'Bonnie! Julie! Is that yo' a-walkin' 'roun' in the parlour?'

346

'Ain' me, Ma, 'n' ain' Julie. She right here aside me.'

'Tho't I heard something 'n' with this money in the house I nervous-like.'

'It was jes' the kitty, Ma. She al'ays a-prowlin' 'roun' at night.'

The answer must have been satisfactory because there was no further conversation. Sol waited for a few seconds, then, turning to Narcisse, he whispered, 'Widder a-sleepin' in the front room, gals in back.'

Once again he advanced slowly, Narcisse, Big Jock, and Alecks immediately behind him. Step by cautious step they crossed a narrow hall and entered the bedroom, where the bed, a lighter grey blur in the darkness, showed them where the woman slept. Quiet as they were, she had sensed their coming, because they could hear the rustle of the corn shock mattress as she started to get up. Sol was across the room in a leap and pushed her back on the bed.

She screamed, but the scream was muffled the second that Sol put his hand over her mouth. Narcisse was standing beside him and, although he could see only the dim outlines of the woman's body against the grey of the sheets, he could see Alecks' black hand pushing up her nightdress. The footsteps of the other men passed him going into the other room and there were short screams from the two girls, who were suddenly silenced.

'We a-hearin' that yo' got yo'self some money here, Missy.' Sol spoke softly to her, almost impersonally, as though he were talking to the bedpost. 'Tha's what we a-lookin' for. Give it to us 'n' yo' kin save yo'self 'n' those purty li'l gals a lot o' trouble. If'n yo' don' tell us, we shore as hell a-goin' to plant some black suckers in' em 'n' we shore a-goin' to plant 'em deep.'

'Take yore dirty han's off'n me, yo' black nigger.' She caught her breath, which had been stopped by Sol's hand, and struggled to free herself. 'Ain' got me no money here. It all ina bank. Now git o' I'll—'

'What yo' a-goin' to do, Missy?' The voice had changed from that of Big Sol's to Alecks'. 'My, my, what yo' a-goin' to do?'

Narcisse heard the metallic rattle of Alecks' belt buckle and heard him climb on to the bed.

'What yo' a-goin' to do?' Her words came between frantic gaspings. 'Oh, God help me. Not that! Don' yo' touch them gals o' mine. Don' yo' put yore black hands on 'em. My brother he a-sleepin' in the back bedroom 'n' he be out for yo'-all in a minute, a-bringin' his shotgun. He goin' to shoot yo'-all.'

'Yore brother he takin' a long time a-shootin' off his gun.' Alecks laughed. 'Got me one here what kin shoot quicker'n his ol' shotgun. Don' believe yo' got no man 'roun' here at all. Bet yo' been a-wantin' one, though.'

'Ain' got me no money here. Oh! Yo' a-hurtin' me.'

'Yo' a-likin' it, Missy? All the wenches a-likin' it 'n' that jes' a sample. Now yo' a-goin' to tell us 'bout the money?'

There was another scream from the back bedroom.

Narcisse was unaware that Sol had left them and was in the other room until he realized that the only voice he was hearing was that of Alecks.

'Yo' ain' a-goin' to rape my gals 'n' me too?' Her body thrashed on the bed, trying to get out from under Alecks.

' 'Pears like we a-goin' to, Missy. Jes' 'pears that way less'n yo' tell us 'bout the money.'

'If'n I tells yo', yo' go 'way 'n leave us 'lone?'

'Uh-huh.'

'Yo' promise?'

'Shore do.'

'Money's in the top drawer o' that chest o' drawers over there. It wrapped up in a silk scarf. Oh, please don' take it. It all we got. All we got ina world.'

'Yo' got yore hand on somethin' better'n money,' Alecks said, giggling.

Narcisse felt along the bed and across the room until his hand encountered the chest of drawers. He pulled open the top drawer, but it stuck and he gave it a vicious yank. It came open and the contents of the drawer spilled on the floor. His hands pawed through a mess of things – several fans, a small jewel box, which he put in his pocket, some bundles of letters, until finally he felt the smoothness of silk with the wallet inside. Striking a match, he held it down near the floor, opening the wallet and making sure that it was stuffed with greenbacks. He glanced towards the bed, but all he could see was Big Alecks sitting up astride the woman.

'Yo' got it?' the woman was sobbing. 'Now, yo' a-goin' to go 'n' leave us 'lone. Bonnie!' she called out. 'Julie! Yo' gals all right?'

'They shore fine,' Alecks answered her. 'They a-goin' to be the happiest gals in the world tonight. Ain' yo' happy, Missy? Now ain' that nice?'

'Oh, stop! Please! Even if you're a nigger, yo' must have some heart. Oh-h-h-h!' Her voice trailed off into a scream of pain and despair.

'Yo' ain' never a-goin' to wan' no piddlin' white man 'gain, Missy.'

Narcisse could hear the constant screech of the bed ropes and the rustle of the corn shocks under Alecks' driving. Narcisse heard him gasp, drawing the air into his lungs like bellows. The woman was still weeping, but she controlled herself long enough to plead for him to move, saying that his weight was killing her. He heard Alecks roll over and then saw that he was standing up while another black figure was taking his place. This time the woman did not seem to complain as much, although she was still sobbing, but her sobs turned into little gaspings for breath and then, the small throaty noises and the soft-spoken curses betokened that, even against her will, she had been caught up in her partner's all-consuming passion.

'Bet yo' ain' had nothin' like that afore, Missy. Ain' no man in the worl' kin pleasure yo' like'n I kin. Yo' shore a lucky woman.'

Narcisse thought the voice was Big Dick's, but he was not sure. He wished he might have held a candle over them, he so wanted to see what was happening, but now another black figure materialized and this time the woman did not struggle. Narcisse walked through the doorway into the other room, colliding with a figure.

'Jes' a-waitin' my turn,' the man said. 'Don' seem like'n that Big Sol ever git himself finished.'

The back room was somewhat lighter than the one Narcisse had been in and by the moonlight that filtered in through the bushes around the windows Narcisse could make out two black forms on the bed. Again he listened to the creaking of bed ropes and a hysterical sobbing, which seemed to come from only one of the girls. The other, instead of sobbing, was encouraging the man above her. Dark shadows around the walls betokened the rest of the Big Ten.

'Ain' yo' mos' through it?' one of them asked.

'Ain' never a-goin' to finish with this one.' Narcisse recognized Big Sol's voice. 'She a-likin' it too much, ain' yo', li'l gal?'

'Don' stop, oh, don' stop.' It was a girl's voice, but her cries were so different from the whimperings of the other.

'Goddam! Oh, holy goddam! Tha's the best I ever had. Only wishin' I could see that purty white skin. That better'n any nigger wench I ever had.'

'Bes' I ever had too, yo' stinkin' nigger buck.' It was the girl's voice. 'How 'bout one of them other'n what standin' 'roun'.'

The black form on the bed moved and stood up and another came running across the room to take Big Sol's place.

'Yo're nice, black boy, yo' shore are nice' – the same girl was speaking – 'but yo' not so good's t'other one. He the bes', but go on, go on. This's what I been a-wantin' since Cousin Bertie lef' 'bout a month 'go. Don' care if'n yo' white or black, yo're better'n Bertie.'

'I'm nex', li'l missy, 'n' yo're a-goin' to like me better'n him.'

'Oh, Bonnie!' The girl who was sobbing spoke. 'Oh, Bonnie, this black brute he a-killin' me.'

'Tha's 'cause yo' wouldn't let Bertie bust yo'.'

'She busted now.' The man who was with her laughed. 'She shore busted 'n' nex' time she goin' to like it's much as that Bonnie girl. She likin' it now, ain' yo', Missy.'

'Ain' never a-goin' to like it. Oh, Mama, Mama, Mama.'

'Hush, Julie, Mama can't do nothin'. She a-gittin' raped too. Yo' gotta jes' grin 'n' bear it. Sometime yo' a-goin' to love it's much as I do.' She waited for the man with her to quit her and then asked, 'Where that fust one? He the bes' o' all.'

'Yo' a-wantin' me 'gain, li'l missy? If yo' a-wantin' me, I shore goin' to 'commodate you, but this one gotta be quick.'

'Mama, oh, Mama!' Julie cried out again, but there was no answer from the other room.

Narcisse did not know how much longer he stood in that room, but he was enjoying everything, although he could not see it. The movements of the men, their words, the squealing delight of Bonnie, and the sobbing of Julie, along with the anguished pleading of the mother in the other room, all excited him. He felt the pressure of the wallet in his pocket and that too excited him. He wandered around the room, letting his hands caress the men and wishing again that he could have seen rather than heard what was happening.

'Everyone got 'nough?' Sol spoke, rising from the bed. 'If'n yo' have, every man gits his britches on. Time we a-leavin'.' He walked to the window and peered out. 'Only 'bout two hours to daybreak 'n' we got a lot o' ground to cover afore we gits back to the next county. Got us a lot of miles to ride.'

'What 'bout the women? We a-goin' to leave 'em untied?' It was Jock speaking.

'Might's well. Nearest place 'bout a mile 'n' ain' none o' 'em a-goin' to do any runnin'. They all spraddle-legged by now.'

They departed with far more noise and less caution than they had entered, laughing, whooping, and yelling. Once on his horse and headed back home, Narcisse felt easier. He knew that the black-hooded figure who was leading them across the fields was Big Sol and he rode up beside him.

'I know how we can cover up and nobody will ever suspect that we came from Falconhurst.'

'Ain' a-goin' to suspect nohow,' Big Sol answered. 'Kin track us through the fields if'n they want, but we a-comin' out ona road 'bout two miles 'bove Falconhurst.'

'Even that's too near. Listen, Sol. This is serious. Raping a white woman means hanging for all of us if they ever find out.

351

Now, listen to me.' Narcisse spoke rapidly and Sol saw the wisdom of Narcisse's plans.

They rode on through the darkness, skirting the fields and keeping in the shadow of the trees until the first rays of dawn brightened the sky, illuminating the white pillars of Falconhurst. Narcisse quitted his horse by the overseer's cottage and ran up to the big house, letting himself in the back door and creeping up the stairs. When he entered the room, Claire sat up in bed.

'Oh, thank God you're safe. I've been so worried about you.'

'Hush!' He shucked off his clothes and donned the nightgown that hung over the foot of the bed. As an afterthought he took the wallet from the pocket of his pants and, opening the door of the armoire, dropped it into one of his boots.

He pulled down the sheet, straightened the pillow, and was about to lie down when he straightened up. 'Claire, do you hear something?'

She listened. 'There is somebody walking across the portico.' She had no sooner finished speaking than there was a crash of glass from one of the downstairs windows.

Narcisse reached in the drawer of the small bedside table and drew out a pistol. He ran to the window and pulled the trigger, shooting the bullet through the screen. Claire ran to stand beside him. There was a sound of running feet, then the pounding of horses' hooves. Another shot exploded from Drum's window and Narcisse prayed that Drum's aim had not been good enough to hit any of the ten black-hooded figures that were racing down the drive. Not one of them fell from his horse and Narcisse saw them turn at the gates and head in the direction of Benson. They were safe. If one of them had been wounded, he would have had to go out and shoot him.

Frantic poundings on the door nearly loosed the bolt. Narcisse opened it to see Drum standing there.

'What's happening?' Drum still had his pistol in his hand.

'Damned if I know.' Narcisse shook his head as if to wake himself. 'Claire heard a noise down on the porch. Then we heard the glass break and I got up. Saw a hooded man on horseback and fired at him. Then I heard you fire and I saw them riding down the drive. Must be that same gang that's been riding around the country. Sheriff's been looking for them, I understand.'

Drum backed away from the door. He remembered Big Pearl's words, yet it was inconceivable that Falconhurst men would try to rob the big house. These were his people. They might go out stealing chickens or indulge in petty devilry, but they would not rob the house. Then it dawned on him that these men might be white men who held a grudge against him for his rebuilding of Falconhurst. That was it.

'Bet those black hoods covered white faces,' he said, biting his upper lip.

'Well, we didn't lose anything.' Narcisse looked sufficiently awake to grin now.

'Maybe we'd better report it to the sheriff anyway.' Drum took a step towards his own room.

'We certainly should. You ride in today to Benson and do it, Drum.'

Drum nodded his head and returned to his own room.

CHAPTER THIRTY-ONE

EVERYBODY AT FALCONHURST had either heard the shots, seen the horsemen pounding down the driveway, or at least heard about it second-hand from someone who had seen it. Big Pearl was over before breakfast to remind Drum of what she had told him about Narcisse's foremen, but he cautioned her to say nothing about it to anyone, adding that he was sure these were white men and not Negroes. Why would his own men want to break into Falconhurst? She agreed with him, albeit only partially, he was afraid, but at any rate she left to go back to her own cabin. Mammy Morn carried an iron poker in her left hand while she prepared breakfast with her right. 'Jes' let any man walk in that back door' – she brandished the poker – ''n' he a-goin' to git clobbered over his head. Matilda she got the meat cleaver 'n' she a-goin' to whack him too.'

Drumstick and Lucy, the latter ashen-coloured, served breakfast with trembling hands. Lucy suspected the truth, but the rest of the household, including Narcisse, confirmed Drum's suspicions that it was probably white men who, instead of wearing the ghostly sheets of the Ku Klux Klan, were now adopting a new uniform of black hoods. Therefore, Drum's intention of going in to Benson to report the matter to the sheriff met with approval from everyone. Narcisse was vehement that he go. Drum certainly should have the satisfaction of knowing that whatever stood for law and order in Benson was cognizant of the affair. Not that it would do much good, Narcisse added. There was only one law in the South and that was the white man's law. Probably they wouldn't believe him if he thought white men were behind the outrage.

Drum dispatched Lucy to the barn to tell Ciceron that he would be going into Benson as soon as breakfast was over and Lucy ran out the back door, heading straight for the barn. As he passed the smokehouse, where one of Barry's men was already at work putting on a new roof, he spied Big Sol, passing up a bundle of shakes to the man on the roof. He knew Big Sol was waiting for him, while he was merely accommodating the carpenter with a good-natured gesture of assistance. As soon as Big Sol saw Lucy, he left the smokehouse and fell in step beside the boy, placing his huge arm around Lucy's shoulders.

'Been a-missin' yo', Lucy boy, down at the cottage. Ain' yo' a-comin' down no more? Like yo' better'n that Abel boy. He ain' so good's yo'.'

'Yo' ain' been very good to me, Big Sol. Al'ays liked yo', I did, till that night yo' whopped me.'

'Hell, boy, we jes' a-funnin' with yo'. Jes' 'nishiatin' yo'. We-all tooken that whoppin' jes' like'n yo' did.'

354

'But yo' didn' take the other thin's.' Lucy's lower lip stuck out in a pout. 'Cain' come down no more nohow. Mista Drum a-sayin' as how he needs me at the big house every night.' Lucy started to run, but he could not shake off Big Sol's arm. 'Gotta hurry, Big Sol. Mista Drum he a-sendin' me out to Ciceron 'n' tellin' me to go quick-like.'

'Shore, shore.' Big Sol patted Lucy's shoulder. 'Probably Mista Drum he a-goin' in to see the sheriff.'

'How yo' know?'

'Jes' figured it out, tha's all. Hopin' he goes. Cain' have no doin' like'n that 'roun' Falconhurst.' The fingers of Big Sol's hand on Lucy's shoulder bit deep into the flesh. 'That wa'n' the Big Ten this mornin', even if'n yo' a-thinkin' it was. But yo' ain' openin' yore trap 'bout the Big Ten.'

'No, Sol, ain' a-sayin' nothin'.'

'Yo' recollects that oath yo' took?'

'Never fergit it after what yo'-all did to me.' Lucy shivered.

'Yo' opens yore big mouf 'bout the Big Ten, 'n' yo' know what we a-goin' to do to yo'. Don' think Mista Drum kin perteck yo' neither. We kin git yo' jes' like'n I got yo' this mornin'. But if'n yo' keeps still, ain' nothin' a-goin' to happen to yo'.' The hand relaxed and now it stroked Lucy's shoulder affectionately. 'Shore been a-missin' yo', boy. When yo' comin' back?'

'Sometime,' Lucy said, glad to slip out of Big Sol's grasp. 'Gotta hurry now.'

''Member, boy, that wa'n' no Falconhurst niggers what rode 'roun' the big house this mornin'. That 'nother gang. 'Member that.'

But Lucy was away, running as fast as he could for the barn. Sol was gone when he came out; he ran back to the house, arriving there breathless. He paused for a minute in the kitchen before going into the dining-room to announce that Ciceron would be at the front door as soon as breakfast was finished.

Drum did not want to take the trip into Benson alone. He felt somewhat in awe of the sheriff, whom he had never seen, and he was not sure what kind of reception he would receive.

Claire said it was impossible for her to go. There was a sick child over at New Quarters that she had been looking after and she felt she must go over there. Narcisse insisted that he had too much work awaiting him. Mede made several invalid excuses and then admitted he just didn't want to go. He was afraid of the sheriff and told Drum that lawmen scared him, begging Drum not to take him.

As a result Drum set off for Benson alone, wishing that somebody were beside him on the back seat. Claire, of course, was the one he really wanted, but he would have been tempted to make love to her on the back seat and, after the disastrous trip to Westminster, he did not trust himself. It was difficult, but he was trying to reconcile himself to the fact that life would have to go on the way it was going. He would love Claire at a distance, be grateful for an occasional moment alone with her, and satisfy himself nightly on Debbie. That was his only prospect, as far as he could see. It was a somewhat discouraging one.

Halfway to Benson he met Mr Barry and his half-brother coming out from town for their day's work at Falconhurst. Mr Barry stopped his horse and Ciceron halted the greys, so that the surrey and the buckboard stood in the road wheel to wheel.

'We're 'most done on the barns, Drum.' Mr Barry wound the reins around the whipsocket and reached under the seat for his demijohn of corn, offering it to Drum, who declined. He took a swig. ''Most done,' he repeated, with a regretful note in his words.

Drum shifted to the other side of the back seat so he would be nearer to Barry. 'You're not finished yet. That is, if I've got any money left after paying you.'

'Ain't going to cost you much,' he answered. 'These old houses and barns were pretty well built. Replace the rotten wood, put in some new sills, add a few beams, pound a few nails here and there, and slap on some paint. That's all. They come out as good as new.'

Drum nodded in agreement. There was more he wanted to talk about with Mr Barry, but that could wait. But why should it, he asked himself? Mr Barry could go along with him to

356

Benson and they could discuss the further improvements that Drum had been contemplating. He realized, however, that this was not the real reason he wanted Mr Barry to accompany him. Might as well admit it: he had become a coward before white men now, with the possible exception of Lewis Gassaway and Mr Barry. He would welcome the respectability that Mr Barry would give him merely by accompanying him. Mr Barry had always treated him as an equal.

'Mr Barry' – Drum moved over in the seat as a gesture of invitation – 'stop your work this morning and drive into Benson with me. I've got a lot of things to discuss with you and I never seem to find the time to sit down and go over them with you. We're always so busy at Falconhurst. I've got plans for New Quarters if I can afford them.'

'How long you goin' to be in Benson?'

'Just a short trip to the sheriff's office and then I'll be all through except for some things Mammy Morn wants me to get at Hicks'.'

Barry climbed down from his buckboard and signalled to the mulatto to drive on to Falconhurst. He climbed up into the surrey, surprisingly agile for a man his age.

'Heard you had trouble at Falconhurst last night. Gang of niggers broke into a plantation not far away, raped three white women, and stole three thousand dollars. Then they tried to get into Falconhurst. Ol' Aunt Sukey who's our cook told us about it at breakfast. Beats me how news travels among the niggers. Go into your room, close the door and sneeze, and in five minutes everyone will know about it.'

'You say a gang of Negroes, Mr Barry. How can you be sure they are Negroes and not white men?'

Barry looked at Drum, conveying in his look that Drum might be more than a bit stupid.

'White men go to steal money and they steal money. White men are not rapers as a rule, but of course they'd do it if it was around. But niggers ain' interested much in money. It's women they want and this is the first case of niggers raping white women around here since reconstruction days when a nigger could get away with anything if he promised to vote Republican.'

'When they came to my house, I felt sure they must be white men with a grudge against me. Can't imagine any Negroes wanting to get into Falconhurst. No white women there to rape.'

'What about Miss Claire?' Barry asked.

'You and I know that she's not white.'

'She's goddam white to a black nigger.'

Drum shook his head, unwilling to believe Mr Barry's reasoning. 'No, I still cannot believe that they were Negroes. Can these other people prove that they are?'

Barry shrugged his shoulders. 'Have to wait to see what the sheriff says. What was it you were wanting to talk about to me?'

Drum laughed and spread his palms in a gesture of futility. 'All depends on how much money it's going to cost me.'

'Don't worry about that. I'll take ten per cent off for cash.'

Drum thanked him. Mr Barry was a good man to deal with. He not only liked him but respected his knowledge. Drum had always had plans for New Quarters as well as Falconhurst. The two seemed inseparable. For a long time he had considered bringing the people back and establishing a settlement where the old slave quarters had been over at the old place and where Big Pearl now lived alone. Mr Barry advised him against it.

'These people have achieved freedom and they consider it freedom to have removed themselves from the vicinity of the big house, where they once were slaves. Bring them back and you'll bring them into bondage again. Better to leave them where they are. They've got their own plots of land and they feel that they own them, along with the cabins too.'

Drum placed two fingers to his nose and squeezed them together. 'It's pretty bad over there. Cabins falling down and the whole place reeks of poverty.'

'Those cabins have probably never been moved. A nigger cabin should be moved about every five years. Stuff accumulates under them and gits to stinking. Howsomever, those cabins ain' worth moving. Yo'd better to rip them down and build new ones. Won't cost you much and I can save you money too. Make cabins for two families. Two rooms on one side and two on the other with a dog-trot between. Cheaper that way. Saves you making two separate cabins and niggers somehow like to be together.

'We'll build 'em some good privies out'n back and teach 'em to put wood ashes in 'em to keep down the stench. Teach them not to throw their dishwater out the back door too. You know, Drum, niggers never were dumb animals. You can teach them. Trouble is, nobody ever took much pains with 'em. It ain' that a nigger really likes to be dirty. They jes' ain' been trained to keep clean. They'd rather be clean than dirty. I'll bet if you were to go into those cabins, regardless of what shape they are outside, you'd find 'em clean inside – swept floors, nice clean quilts on the beds, everything picked up. You know, they always have a shelf with something nice on it, even if it's only a cracked teacup, salvaged from what was thrown away at the big house. Or it may be a little jug of flowers. It's something to cherish because it's pretty. Call them their "purties", they do.'

'Rather pathetic, isn't it?' Drum began to realize what a wide gulf there was between him and his people. 'Not many years ago they were considered as nothing more than animals. Now we acknowledge them to be human beings, but nobody does anything for them. By God, Mr Barry, I'm going to try.'

Barry nodded his head slowly, considering the matter. 'Carpetbaggers said they tried. Scalawags said they tried too, but none of 'em ever really did anything. You can't make a silk purse outa sow's ear overnight. The damn Yankees were all for making these people jump from slavery to citizenship overnight. Can't be done, Drum, except in a few cases like your father and my half-brother. They gotta have an education. They gotta be shown how to work and how to live and how to enjoy themselves. Now, like'n I say, 'bout this half-brother of mine—'

Drum interrupted him, excusing himself for his rudeness, but Barry's words touched off an idea in his head. 'You've hit on the key, Mr Barry. Teach them to work, teach them to live, teach them to enjoy themselves. That's what I'm going to do.' He hesitated a long moment, envisioning a Utopia that he realized could exist only in his imagination but for which he could, at least, lay foundations. 'If I've got money enough, I'm going to make a real village out of New Quarters. Real windows in the cabins, brick fireplaces, everything new and clean and spotless and painted white. Then I want you to build a large building right in the centre of town. I want it to be part store, part school, and part social hall. Let's make it something that looks pretentious, that they can be proud of. The store and the school on the first floor and a big hall on the second that can be used for church on Sundays and for dances and other social events. Let's give these people something else to live for except eating, sleeping, and fornicating. Will you draw up the plans for me and let me know how much the whole thing is going to cost?'

' 'Pears like I'll be here another two or three months, Drum, but I'll do it. We'll have a model community here at Falconhurst that will make the red-necks realize just what sort of pore white trash they are.'

'Will there be any bad feelings? Will we be getting anything on our hands to engender hatred and envy? Is it possible to have a clean, wholesome, Negro community, owned by a nigger like myself?'

'Stop calling yourself a nigger, Drum Maxwell.' Mr Barry turned sideways and offered his hand. 'For my money you're the whitest man I ever met and I mean it, goddammit. I'm right behind you and to hell with the pore white trash. They'll hate you anyway, but decent people will respect you all the more.'

Drum shook the proffered hand, noticing as he did that they had entered the town of Benson and that Ciceron was heading for the hitching rail in front of Hicks' store. Hicks, seeing the carriage approach, came out on to the cluttered veranda, which was crowded with men.

'Hi, thar, Maxwell.' He waved a hand in greeting. 'Anythin' I kin do for yo', Mista Maxwell?' Drum's ear was quick to catch the title. He had never been addressed as 'mister' before in Benson. Perhaps it was the fact that he was giving Hicks so much business – so much cash business.

'Yes,' Drum called from the surrey. 'You can tell me where the sheriff's office is.'

'Ain' no need,' Hicks answered. 'He's right here in the store. Come in.'

Drum turned to Barry. 'Will you come with me? I'd feel better with a white man alongside of me.'

Mr Barry answered by getting out of the carriage and Drum followed him up the steps of the store porch and into the store. It was as crowded inside as it had been outside. Men were sitting on all the chairs, on the counters, and on barrels, while more were moving back and forth in the limited space left. All of them were at a fever pitch of excitement, shouting and waving clenched fists.

'If'n we only know where to lay hands on them goddam niggers.'

'There'd be a hanging party.'

'Or a burnin' party.'

'Burnin' not good 'nough for them bastards.'

'No white women safe any more.'

'That pore Miz Norrison. Lost all her money 'n' had her daughters raped.'

' 'N' she got raped herself.'

'Them gals both a-goin' to birth black babies, shore's shootin'.'

'Ain' no white man a-goin' to marry 'em after they been raped by niggers.'

A florid-faced man who had been sitting in a chair got up and came over to Drum and Mr Barry almost as soon as they entered the door.

'Yo' Maxwell?' he asked.

'I am and this is Mr Barry from Westminster.'

'I'm the sheriff o' this county and was jes' 'bout to ride out to see yo'.' The man reached out a hand to Barry. 'Name's Tucker.'

'Then, I have saved you the bother of the trip.' Drum bowed slightly.

'Le's git outa this place.' Sheriff Tucker gestured towards the door. 'Too much hollerin' 'n' screamin' here. Cain' even think in all this ruckus.'

He led the way towards the door and Drum and Barry

361

followed. The sheriff's office was in the back of the courthouse, its door adjoining the barred windows of the cells. Tucker unlocked the door, standing back for Barry to enter, then going in himself and letting Drum follow. Once inside, however, he offered chairs to both Drum and Mr Barry, then seated himself at a long table, facing them.

'What yo' a-wantin' to see me 'bout, Maxwell?'

Drum glanced at Mr Barry, meeting his eyes and receiving encouragement from them. The sheriff's voice was not unkind but rather encouraging.

'I came in to report that about five o'clock this morning a gang of mounted men with black hoods tried to force an entrance into our house. We were awakened by the breaking of a window. Both myself and my overseer, Mr Brantome, fired at the men and they rode down the drive and away.'

'Heard all 'bout it. How many men did you see?'

'I was too excited to count them. I would say there were more than five or six and probably less than twenty.'

'We already trailed them from Miz Norrison's place across the fields to where they came out on the road about two miles from your place. Couldn't figure out how many there were but figured it at quite a number. Miz Norrison she pretty hystericky jes' now 'n' she a-sayin' they 'bout twenty men.'

'Were those men Negroes?' Mr Barry asked.

The sheriff waited for a moment to reply, peering up at them with his head bowed. Drum thought he had never seen such bushy eyebrows on any man before.

'How come yo' askin' that, Mr Barry? Miz Norrison 'n' her daughters a-sayin' that they was.'

'Just seems rather strange to me, that's all. If it was purely a matter of rape, I'd blame it on the niggers – the horny bastards. But I understand there was a theft too.'

'Matter o' 'bout three thousand dollars.' The sheriff raised his head and stared at them both. 'Yo' a-thinkin' 'cause they's stealing, it could of been white men and not niggers?' He continued to stare at them both. 'Mayhap you're right. Mayhap. I know one thing, though – at least one o' 'em was a white man.'

362

'How do you know that?' Drum had wanted to ask the question, but Barry had spoken first.

'The man what picked up the money struck a match. Miz Norrison she on the bed 'n' she saw this man's hand holding the match. She a-swearin' it a white man's hand, but she a-sayin' that the man a-rapin' her a black. But it mighty pitch black in there 'n' she could be mistooken, though from what she 'n' them gals o' hers say, sounds mighty like them black bastards.'

'You mean? . . .' Barry did not complete the sentence, but Tucker seemed to understand.

'Kinda delicate question to ask a lady, suh, but it seems these niggers pretty well hung boys if'n they were niggers. They al'ays a-sayin' that's one way yo' kin tell a nigger even on the darkest night. Niggers is hung different 'n white men.'

'Heard tell,' Barry said, nodding his head wisely, 'but they's white men hung's well as niggers 'n' niggers what ain' hung so well. Now, I got a mulatto half-brother 'n' he hung more like'n a peanut. So that ain' no proof these rapers're niggers.'

Although the sheriff had not been talking to him personally, Drum felt a hot rush of blood to his cheeks. Now, it seemed, that which he had always been proud of was a curse.

He tried to control his voice as he spoke to the sheriff. 'Mr Tucker, if one of the men was a white man, and the unfortunate Mrs Norrison seems to think he was, wouldn't it be possible for all the rest to be white, regardless of this distinctive means of identification? Furthermore, if the girls were virgins, as I suppose white girls of that age would be, how could they tell the difference?'

The sheriff let out a howl of laughter and slapped his knee. 'Damn good idea, boy. Goddam good. If'n they be virgins! Ha, ha! Virgin wouldn't know a big one from a small one. Mayhap they weren't, though. They had a likely lookin' young fellow a-visitin' them – some cousin. Could be that he might have busted them gals while he there. Tha's the only way of knowin'.' He grinned at Drum and that grin made Drum feel almost an equal.

'I believe they were white men.' Drum's voice had a positive ring to it. 'I'm sure of it. I think the raping of the women was incidental. They went to the Norrison's to steal the money. They came to Falconhurst to steal too. After all, they must know there's money there, with all the repairing and building I've been doing.'

The sheriff seemed more or less convinced. He nodded his head slowly in agreement.

'We been having us some trouble with a band o' hooded horsemen. Been trying to track 'em down. Mostly they been a-rapin' wenches and a-stealin' cattle. Al'ays tho't they be niggers, but now I jes' wonderin' if'n they ain' some o' that pore white trash what lives just over the line in the next county. Live worse'n niggers, they do. Poorer'n Job's turkey. Won' do any harm to investigate. Yo' might be right, boy. Yo' jes' might be right.'

'Tell me' – Drum had lost some of his awe of the sheriff – 'something about this woman who was robbed.'

'Kinda pitiful case.' The sheriff eased the pistol in his holster and leaned back in his chair. He looked searchingly at Drum and for a second he seemed to be wondering if he might be facing the man who had lit the match and exposed the whiteness of his hands. Bringing the front legs of his chair down on to the floor with a thump, he leaned over the table, looking at Drum's hands. They were brown as berries from the exposure to the sun and the fact that he, unlike Narcisse, did not wear gloves. They were, to be sure, not black, but on the other hand they were certainly not white. 'Yes,' the sheriff continued, 'it be kinda pitiful case, that Miz Norrison. This pore woman jes' sold her farm 'n' that three thousand dollars all she got in the world, 'ceptin' she a-hopin' she could marry off them two daughters o' hern – both pretty gals. Miz Bonnie she the prettiest. Now pore Miz Norrison she ain' got nothin'. If'n it niggers what raped 'em 'n' they knocked up 'n' birth black babies, who ever goin' to marry up with them? Gal gits knocked up by a nigger 'n' even if'n it not her fault, ain' no decent white man a-goin' to marry her.'

Drum looked first to Mr Barry, but Barry's face showed only concern for the unfortunate Mrs Norrison. Then he looked at the sheriff and saw the same sympathy for this woman in his expression. He realized for the first time the utter tragedy that had overtaken her, over and above any physical suffering she might have endured last night. He rose from his chair and came to stand beside the table.

'Sheriff Tucker.'

The sheriff looked up at him. 'What kin I do for yo'?'

'I'd like to start a fund for this Mrs Norrison. I'll contribute five hundred dollars. I'd rather not have you mention where the money comes from, but I'd appreciate if you'd solicit the fund among the people of Benson.'

'Ain' none of us what kin give that money. Any collectin' I'd do'll be mostly dollars or small change.'

'I'll contribute fifty dollars,' Barry said.

'Then, I'll see what I kin do 'mongst the folks 'roun' here. Anything she gits is goin' to help her 'n' dollars 'n' small change do mount up. This yere's a wonderful thing yo're doin', Mista Maxwell. Man kin feel sorry, but when he reaches down in his britches pocket 'n' gives hard cash, that shows he's willin' to help out a pore widder. Thank yo', Mista Maxwell.' The sheriff reached across the table and shook Drum's hand. 'We're right glad to have you back at Falconhurst. Ever have any trouble, jes' let me know. I'll do anything I kin to help yo'.'

The handclasp was firm and genuine.

'Thank you, Sheriff Tucker.' Drum felt in some strange way that regardless of his father, he had been accepted into the community of Benson.

' 'N' ain' a-goin' to keep it quiet what yo' did, neither. Goin' to shout it from the church steeple. Ain' a-goin' to hurt yo' none 'roun' here. None 'tall.'

Drum thanked him again and when he turned to walk out the door of the sheriff's office, he felt he had suddenly grown in stature. A white man had addressed him as 'mister' and had shaken his hand – the sheriff, no less.

CHAPTER THIRTY-TWO

When Drum and Mr Barry arrived back at Falconhurst, they spied Mede standing beside one of the brick gateposts. It was evident that he had been watching for them because when he spotted them coming down the road, he started waving frantically. When they drew nearer, Drum could see a piece of paper in his hand and wondered what it might be that was so important as to station him in the hot sun as a lookout. Ciceron stopped the carriage at the gates and Mede jumped out on to the driveway and up on to the front seat, still clutching the paper in his hands. He turned sideways to face Drum, ignoring Ciceron and Mr Barry, his words tumbling forth in a gush of emotion.

'Got me a letter, Drum. First letter I ever got in my life. See!'

The letter was damp and crumpled and the address in violet ink was almost obliterated from the sweat of Mede's hands, but it was still legible. It read, 'Mr Mede Maxwell, Falconhurst Plantation, Benson, Alabama.'

'Well, why didn't you open it and read it?' Drum asked.

'Cain', jes' cain'. I not a-knowin' what it a-goin' to say o' who it from. Jes' too put out to open it 'n' see. Lucy he rid into town to get the mail. Miz Claire she a-sayin' as how yo'd forgit it 'n' she 'spectin' the magazine she a-readin' a story in. Lucy he got back afore yo' 'n' Miz Claire she give me this letter. She a-sayin' she'd read it for me, but I tol' her I could read but jes' ain' got the nerve to open it up.'

'Of all the damn-fool notions.' Mr Barry laughed and slapped his thigh. 'Here's a coloured boy got a love letter from his sweetheart and don't dare to read it.'

'Ain' got me no sweetheart, Mista Barry. None, that is, what would write to me. Got me Rosanne for a bed wench, but she ain' no sweetheart 'n' that reminds me, Drum, got something to tell yo' 'bout Rosanne too, but this letter more 'portant now. Reckon it the mos' 'portant thing that ever happen to me.'

By this time, they had arrived at the front steps and Ciceron pulled on the reins to halt the greys, obligingly cramping the wheels so that they could all get out.

'Yo' got yo'self really truly letter, Mede?' Ciceron jeered, his head shaking in doubt about such a rare occurrence. 'Who a-goin' to write to such a big black gyrascutus like'n yo'?'

'Ain' yo' forgettin' something, Ciceron?' Despite his excitement, Mede's voice took on a tone of authority.

'Yes, suh, shore is, *Mista* Mede' – Ciceron stressed the title – 'but I never did hear o' no nigger a-gittin' hisself a letter afore.'

'Yo' be goddam careful who yo' callin' a nigger, boy.' Mede reached up strong hands to pull Ciceron down from his seat, but Drum slipped in and stopped the quarrel. He grabbed Mede's hands, loosening them from Ciceron's jacket, and pulled Mede away, at the same time gesturing with his head for Ciceron to drive on. Mede was getting very uppity of late, insisting on his equal rank with Drum and, while Drum had encouraged him to do it, many of those who had arrived with them – Lucy, Mammy Morn, and Ciceron – often forgot the new title of respect that meant so much to Mede. Although his skin was almost as dark as Ciceron's, he resented being called 'nigger'. That was a word for field hands and servants and he was neither of those. Drum managed to quiet him down, realizing that his excitement over the letter had made him even more touchy than usual. Mr Barry left them when he saw, to his disappointment, that there was going to be no fight and Drum and Mede mounted the steps of the portico, each one choosing one of the rocking chairs.

Deliberately, in order to keep Mede in suspense a little longer, Drum drew a small, pearl-handled knife from his pocket and slowly opened the large blade, then painstakingly slit the envelope. Mede watched his every motion, his tension increasing, as Drum drew out the damp and crumpled piece of paper. The violet ink had not run as much on the letter as on the envelope and Drum was able to read the words more easily.

'Well, what do it say?' Mede was gasping with impatience.

'You want me to read it to you or do you want to read it yourself?'

'Kin read it myself. Yo' knows that. Kin read it good too. That is, if'n I want to read it by myself but thinkin' now yo'd better read it to me, Drum. All excited like. All nervy, if'n yo knows what I mean. First, though afore yo' reads it, tell me who it from.'

'From Laura.'

'Laura?' Mede seemed scarcely able to comprehend such a stupendous fact. 'She's my real sweetheart. She so pretty 'n' so bright-skinned 'n' it was so nice havin' her here when she a-fixin' up the furniture. Never did git a letter from her, though. Oh me, oh my! Ain' she wonderful to write me a letter? Read it quick, Drum.'

Drum had skimmed through it quickly to gather its contents and its news was now no particular shock to him. He read it slowly, watching Mede take in every word. He had in mind giving Mede a lecture later.

Mr Ganymede Maxwell
Falconhurst Plantation
near Benson, Alabama

MY ESTEEMED MR MAXWELL:

'What do "*esteemed*" mean, Drum?'

'That means "highly respected", but shut up if you want me to finish it.'

Mede settled himself back in his chair, a wide grin on his face, his white teeth shining, his fingers beating a tattoo on the arms of the chair.

Drum continued to read:

I take my pen in hand to write to you and regret that this letter comes from the depths of a sorrowing heart. It is indeed indelicate for a young lady to put such words on paper but I must let you know of my condition as I do not dare to tell my brother.

It was as much my fault as it was yours, dear Mede, because I was and am truly in love with you. You are the handsomest man I have ever met and indeed the truest and kindest and that night when you suggested that we stroll across to visit your mother, I was happy to go with you. Even when we walked home, I was happy to have your strong arms around me; happy to give you my kisses; and glad that you wanted them. I was also happy when those kisses led to other things and in my love for you I did not think anything bad would come from it.

But it has, dear Mede. It has. I do not know how to put the words to you as a proper young lady should but, then, I am not a proper young lady after what I did with you, am I?

Drum paused for a moment to turn the sheet and looked sternly at Mede.

I can only put it bluntly, dear Mede, although it makes me blush to read these words. I am going to have a baby and you are its father because you are the only man I have ever been with.

What are we going to do, Mede darling? The Negroes call a child like this a woods colt and I do not want to have a child that has no lawful father. I beg of you, dear Mede, to marry me so that our child will have a father and not be condemned for life as a woods colt.

Please let me hear from you. If I don't, I'll drown myself in the river because I cannot bear the disgrace.

Your ever loving

LAURA

Drum pointed an accusing finger at Mede. 'So you went and did it after all the precautions Claire took to keep you apart?'

Mede was meekly humble. He explained that he had nothing in mind – certainly nothing like that when he had invited Laura to walk over to Big Pearl's cottage with him. It was evening and there was a full moon and it had seemed like something to do other than sit on the front veranda and talk. Laura had slipped away, pleading a headache, and a few minutes later Mede had left the group, meeting her out by the barn. They had walked over to Big Pearl's and she had brought out chairs for them because it was cooler under the chinaberry tree. When Big Pearl went inside to bring out something cool to drink, Mede had excused himself to Laura and went in with her.

Alone with Big Pearl, Mede pleaded with her for a charm – something to make Laura love him. She reached for the un-glazed jar that had been hanging in the window to keep the contents cool, and poured a drink made of vinegar and molasses into one of her prized possessions – a goblet from the big house. Taking his hand, she reached for the shears on the table and snipped a tiny sliver from one of his fingernails, repeating a mumbo-jumbo of words that Mede did not understand. Then she dropped the tiny sliver of fingernail into the goblet. She then poured drinks into two small gourds, telling Mede to offer the glass goblet to Laura, which he did.

All the time that Laura was drinking, Big Pearl had kept her lips moving, chanting some litany, and when Laura had finished her drink, she had, so Mede swore, looked at him with adoring eyes.

'Don' see how no finger-parin' could of done it' – Mede shook his head with doubt – 'but reckon it did.'

'Mighty powerful conjure our mammy has,' Drum said, half convinced himself.

At any rate, Mede went on to say, Laura continued to gaze at him and even moved her chair closer to him so she could touch his fingers with her own. A few moments later she suggested to Mede that it was getting late and they had better get back to the big house. With an imperceptible nod of her head Big Pearl had bid them go and her parting words were: 'Everythin's a-goin' to be jes' like'n yo' wants it, son.'

They had started out from Big Pearl's walking hand in hand. Soon Mede's arm slipped around her waist and she did not object. When they turned at the old cemetery and made their way down the ravine, Mede stopped her and kissed her and she gave him her lips with no denial of his advances. His tongue entered between her teeth, exploring the smooth warmth of her mouth while she nearly swooned in his arms.

Reaching the ruined bridge, Mede picked her up in his arms and carried her across the stream. Then, when he let her down, they stood close together, her body arching to meet his while he continued his kissing, letting his lips nibble at her ear, then down her throat. With one huge hand, unaccustomed to the tiny buttons of her basque, he managed to undo them slowly, his lips seeking the hard nipples of her breasts. She continued to make little wordless moans while he guided her hand to his already rigid maleness. She pulled her hand away at first, but he held it there until it grasped of its own accord.

Unbuttoning his trousers, he let them slip to the ground and reached to lift her skirts, finding difficulty with the over-abundance of her petticoats. Now her hand moved more rapidly and she seemed unaware of anything else in the world but the contact of lips and hands with each other. With his arm under her, he lowered her to the grass. Once again she protested, but his kisses smothered her words and then – gently for Mede – he commenced. She screamed in pain as he entered her and he withdrew momentarily, but now it was she who urged him on and did not deny his re-entrance. Slowly, so as to cause her as little pain as possible, he proceeded. Several times he had to withdraw because he did not want to attain a premature climax, but each time she sought him again until in one burst of flaming rockets of scarlet and gold he spent himself, moved his weight from her body, and lay panting on the grass.

For long moments neither of them spoke and when she finally did, she merely whispered, 'I love you, Mede.'

He assured her over and over again of his love and pleaded with her to marry him. Her hands slid gently down over his cheeks and along the glabrous flesh of his chest until they rested on his nipples. He pushed them down farther, but this time she did not allow his strength to force her.

'No, Mede, not again, although in truth I want to. But I must speak to you of marriage. I am happy that you asked me to marry you, but I cannot. Never! It is impossible. My brother would never permit it. You see, I am almost white. My mother

371

was an octoroon and my father was white. So you see, there is only a tiny drop of coloured blood in me and my brother would never let me marry a coloured man. He insists that I marry a white man or at least an octoroon. He says we have come too far already from black to white and that we must not go back and start all over again. So, my darling Mede, marriage is impossible.'

That was what had happened, Mede explained to Drum. It was not his fault and it was not hers. It was entirely the fault of the fingernail-paring and Big Pearl's conjure, but how that could accomplish it, Mede could not explain. However, now everything had changed. She wanted to marry him and that was just what he wanted. Her brother could not deny his suit now that he had planted his black seed in her. Mede was exultant.

'Yo' gotta admit I real potent, Drum. Jes' one time with Laura 'n' she knocked up.'

Drum shook his head in reproof. 'With wenches you can say that, but with white ladies – and Laura's almost white – you have to use another word. You can say "pregnant", although that is not as delicate as the French word *enceinte*. I believe the favoured phrase is "in the family way".' Drum looked at his watch. It was only mid-morning. 'And speaking of Laura's being in a family way, mayhap we'd better drive over to Westminster and see her before she carries out her threat of throwing herself in the river. It will set her mind at rest anyway just to know that you are willing to marry her. Perhaps we'd better take Claire along with us. It will be late before we return, though. She may not want to go.'

But when Drum explained the circumstances to Claire, she volunteered to go. 'Laura needs a woman to console her. In times like this a girl wants a mother or a sister to lean on and she has neither.'

While Mammy Morn was packing a lunch for them Mede and Drum changed their clothes and Mede took particular pains with his appearance. He was certainly a handsome buck, Drum realized, and he was not surprised that Laura had yielded to him despite his colour. Well, she could do worse than Mede. He'd seen too many of those namby-pamby bright-skinned bucks in New Orleans to compare their worth with Mede. As a wedding present he'd make over a part of Falconhurst to them. He'd even build them a house if they preferred a home of their own. Why was he being so sentimental over Mede? Why? Mede was the only person in the world that he had been with all his life and now he really felt, as he remembered the ceremony at Big Pearl's, that Mede was his brother. Why shouldn't he do something for him?

They left, with Mammy Morn waving her apron from the back door and Lucy standing on the front portico waving a dustcloth. Drum wondered if another trip to Westminster would bring back unhappy memories to Claire, but when they forded the little stream and passed the Falconhurst Pine, she seemed completely unperturbed and even placed her hand on his while he squeezed it warmly, knowing that he had been completely forgiven. This simple gesture proved it.

The interview with Laura's brother in the back room of the little store in Westminster started out to be stormy with vituperative name-calling on his part towards Mede. But after the first outburst he accepted the affair more or less calmly, particularly when he was advised by Drum that Mede would have a share of Falconhurst. This seemed to please the brother to the extent that he granted Mede the privilege of marrying Laura and suggested that under the circumstances it be done at once.

Ciceron drove Mede and Laura to the tiny parsonage of the Negro church in Westminster, then returned to the shop for the others. When they all reached the house of the pastor, he had donned a worn but decent black suit and a Roman collar, which seemed a bit incongruous with his avowed Baptist faith. They were ushered into a tiny parlour whose closed shutters and musty air proclaimed that it was but seldom used. A horsehair sofa, bursting at the seams, a rag rug, and a stand with a gaily coloured lamp were the only furnishings. The lamp was lighted and Drum wondered if the sacred rites of marriage were supposed to be more effective if pronounced by lamplight.

The ceremony took only a few moments. The minister had

evidently memorized the marriage lines and rattled them off in a rapid monotone. Drum wondered how these carelessly chanted words could make a man and woman one. It was so different from the weddings he had attended in Boston, with their elaborate rituals.

After the ceremony – if such it could be called – was over, they all signed the marriage register, including Ciceron, who had some difficulty in writing his name. He painstakingly spelled out Ciceron Daubigny and it was the first time Drum had ever realized that the fellow had a last name. Mede presented the pastor with a neat little pile of ten silver dollars, which so overjoyed him that he filled out and gave him in return a fanciful marriage certificate on which a happy bride and groom (both white) were surrounded by doves, garlands, and cupids, all intertwined.

It was dark when they arrived back at Falconhurst. Mammy Morn had left a lunch for them and there was a steaming pot of coffee on the back of the stove. While they ate, Drum managed to get Mede away from Laura and mentioned that there was a matter of immediate urgency. Rosanne was probably even now sitting beside Mede's bed waiting for him to return. Mede was unable to think of anything to do with her, but, since she was a house servant, he persuaded Drum to take her above to one of the servant's rooms on the third floor. She departed not very happily because she too was in love with Mede.

That night there was a new occupant in Mede's bedroom – his wife. With Mede now happily – ecstatically – married, and with both Claire and Narcisse across the hall, sharing the same bed, Drum looked at poor Debbie with distaste. She was all he had and she was damn little consolation – merely a piece of warm flesh to relieve him. Her function, as he could see it, was merely to rid his body of a certain superfluity of secretion, thus enabling him to sleep more easily.

He was surprised when he heard a knock on the connecting door between his own room and that of Mede's. At his 'Come in' Mede entered, still fully clothed. Drum had imagined that the bridal couple had long ago been bedded, but Mede merely grinned and closed one eye.

374

'She kinda modest, my li'l Laura. A-sayin' as to how she a-goin' to git herse'f undressed and into bed afore I do. But I a-tellin' her I don' mind this first night. No, suh! She kin get into bed afore I do, but I ain' a-goin' to turn down no light whilst I take off my trogs. She shore a-goin' to see what she a-gittin' 'cause I ain' ashamed o' it 'n' she ain' a-goin' to be neither.' His grin turned into a high-pitched chuckle and he motioned to Debbie. 'Yo' h'ist yore ass outa here a minute. Got somethin' I wants to tell Drum privately.'

After she had departed, Mede drew Drum closer to him.

' 'Members what I a-sayin' that I had some news for you 'bout that Rosanne wench?'

Drum nodded, wondering why Rosanne should occupy Mede's thoughts on his wedding night.

'Well, she knocked up higher'n a kite.'

'Don't wonder. I've been hearing those bed ropes squeak all night and every night.'

'Ah, but that ain' it. Mammy a-sayin' it yourn. She a-lookin' into the fire 'n' she a-seein' a bright-skin sucker. Sayin' as how it yourn 'cause only yo' 'n' me been a-sharin' Rosanne. Shore's hell I cain' git no bright-skin sucker off'n her. I too black.'

Drum laughed, poking Mede in the ribs. 'You mean to tell me that I'm more potent than you? Listen, boy! I had her only a few times. You've been riding that filly every night. How can you think it's mine?'

'Mammy say so 'n' she ain' wrong. Never! She a-sayin' it yourn. She a-knowin'.'

'Well, I'm damned if I'm going to marry Rosanne.'

'Don' have to marry no bed wench. She don' 'spect it, though she a-wantin' to marry up with me. She cain' now. After all, hern ain' the first sucker born what have no pappy.'

Drum was silent. It was no matter to joke about. If it should turn out to be true and Rosanne's baby was born light-skinned, he would certainly be the father. It would be his own child, his own flesh and blood. He could not abandon it. It was ridiculous to think of such a thing . . . yet, he remembered the children he had sired up North. It appeared that he had only to sleep with a woman once to get her pregnant. That was mighty potent sap

375

he had in his loins. Rosanne should be married to someone, but whom? He looked at Mede, who seemed to understand his unspoken question.

'That Drumstick boy he mighty tired o' sleepin' with Lucy. He a-wantin' himself a wench. Whyn't yo' marry him up with Rosanne? They both house servants 'n' he a good boy, that Drumstick. He yore half-brother too, if'n it true that he Drummage's git.'

Drum nodded. He was smiling now. His tongue circled his lips. Yes, why not keep it all in the family?

'Shall we wake them up and do it tonight? Get a minister from Benson?'

'Hell, no.' Mede started for the door to his room. 'All they got to do is jump the stick 'n' they all married up. Mos' niggers jes' jump the stick 'n' that all. They kin do that tomorrow. Gotta go now, Drum.' Mede reached down and clutched his crotch. 'This ain' a-goin' to last much longer. It so hot now it goin' to sizzle like a hot iron if'n anyone put a finger on it.'

'Better not let it sizzle all night. I want some sleep. Goodnight.'

'This not only a good night but the bestest night I ever had.' Mede closed the door and Drum went out into the hall to summon Debbie. Black she might be, but tonight he needed her. Just thinking about Mede and Laura in one room and Narcisse and Claire in the other was enough to make him sizzle too.

CHAPTER THIRTY-THREE

WHETHER IT WAS Brute's planting, Narcisse's expert cultivation, or the beneficent weather they had been favoured with all summer, the cotton crop at Falconhurst was the best, so Brute averred, in many years. When Drum had arrived in the spring, the fields had been green with the young plants. Later they were a garden of blossoms and now they were white with the bursting bolls. During these months they had been carefully tended by the field hands who had kept the long rows free from weeds and hoed up the dirt around the plants to conserve the moisture.

Now picking time was upon them and it was the big time of the year. This was the time of fruitage, the final result of all their labours. Everyone prayed for good weather so that the bolls would not get wet; and this year fortune continued to smile on Falconhurst. The sun climbed high into the blue skies every day and only once or twice were there threats of rain, when towering castles of white cumulus clouds appeared in the sky, threatening thunderstorms. Everyone watched the clouds anxiously, praying that they would not send torrents of rain, but the feared storms never materialized and all the cotton that was picked that year was dry as tinder.

This was the one time when everyone on the plantation turned out to help – men, women, and even children bent their backs and dragged the long jute sacks after them. Even the house servants were not exempted and Matilda, Debbie, and Rosanne worked along with the field hands. Drumstick, now the husband of Rosanne and very much in love with her despite the fact she was carrying another man's child, picked alongside her, still entranced with his sudden marriage to the girl he had secretly adored. Only Lucy and Ciceron were excused from picking, the one to take care of the house and the other to be on hand for driving. Mammy Morn, although not asked to pick, refused anyway. She affirmed that she was a city nigger, had never been near a cotton boll, and wouldn't know one if she saw one. Besides, as she reminded them, somebody had to stay in the house and get the meals. Three good meals a day were more important than the small amount of cotton she could pick. Drum explained to her that he had never expected her to go out picking anyway, whereupon she said that she'd go if she wanted to, but he knew she was only putting on her usual show of bravado. Mammy Morn refused to accept the challenge of old age and anything that might point to her declining physical powers was something she vigorously negated by doing just that thing. Nobody, she was determined, would ever think of Mammy Morn as getting old.

Drum and Mede, along with Narcisse, were riding the fields every day and Drum came, albeit grudgingly, to admire the ten big men whom Narcisse had appointed foremen. They too rode horses up and down the rows but, whereas Drum was always greeted with smiles on uplifted faces, it was plain to see that all the people detested the foremen. They would hurry their work when one of them appeared, slacking off as soon as his back was turned. Yes, Drum agreed, they certainly got the work out of the field hands, but Drum disagreed with their methods. Brute, however, assured Drum that everyone was nervous and high-pitched at picking time and that the big fellows were not unduly harsh. Drum kept silent, although he did not like the long black whips the men carried. This was free, not slave, labour and nobody, he felt, had the right to flick a whip over the bowed back of a free man. True, it was only a flick, he was told, but he imagined even flicks could be painful, especially when wielded by experts, as he could see that the ten big fellows were. No matter how much he counselled against the whips, he knew they would be used. They and the horses were the signs of authority that the foremen depended upon and they would not relinquish them. They were proud of their prowess and one day one of them – it was Big Sol – demonstrated his ability to handle the whip. He handed Drum a sheet of folded newspaper and while Drum stood, holding it at arm's length, Big Sol sliced it into ribbons. Then he asked Drum if he would mind making another test and when Drum consented, Big Sol let his whip sing out, touching Drum on the shoulders, but the touch was so light Drum could scarcely feel it. After that he consented to the use of the whips, but he always wondered if Big Sol and the others used the same technique on the field hands' black backs as Big Sol had used on him.

While the picking was going on in the fields Mr Barry and his men, along with the Falconhurst men who helped him, were putting the finishing touches to the new village of New Quarters. They were so nearly finished, it would now be a matter of only a few days. Drum was amazed at the transformation of the poverty-ridden settlement. It was now something to be proud of and he could see the transformation of the village in the faces of the people who lived there. Despite the hard work and long hours involved in cotton picking, which started as soon as the sun had burned the dew from the bolls and lasted until it was impossible to see a white boll in the fading light, the people of New Quarters marched home singing. The new village was a never-ending marvel to them; and Drum, riding through the village one evening, saw one of the women holding a lamp while her man spaded in the garden and this even after a long day's work in the fields.

Sturdy, white-painted cottages with brick chimneys and glazed windows replaced the old slab-sided cabins that had leaned at such crazy angles along the village street. Each cabin boasted a chinaberry sapling in its front yard, and already gardens were being laid out, and flowering shrubs planted to take root through the winter and blossom in the spring. The dusty road, which became an impassable mudhole after a rain, was now gravelled and at the end of the street stood that wonder of all wonders – the combination store, school, church, and dance hall. Barry had attempted the style called Steamboat Gothic, borrowed from the palatial boats that sailed on the Mississippi. The building was two storeys high and its roof eaves sported a decorative edging of crocheted wooden lace. There were upstairs and downstairs galleries with slender pillars and fretted railings. Downstairs was divided between the store in front and the schoolroom at the back, whereas the upper storey was one enormous room. One end of the room was a platform on which two fiddlers played on Saturday nights and on which a pulpit was placed on Sunday morning for the visiting minister, who came from the coloured church in Benson. His evangelistic sermons had already resulted in one mass baptism in the river and the minister looked forward to several more.

It was in this room that Drum held a big celebration when picking time was over. All from the big house attended, sitting uncomfortably on the hard chairs on the platform. They knew that the real fun would start after they left. However, they were also aware that the people wanted them there – for a short time at least. Drum announced that there would be two weeks of light work, during which time all of them were free to work around their own cabins, doing only what plantation work was necessary and then on half-day shifts only. He bowed to the clapping of hands and the broad grins that greeted his announcement. They all worshipped him, loved Miz Claire, liked Mede and his new bright-skinned bride, and looked up to the house servants in their calico and sateen dresses as superior beings. They too were glad that the cotton had all been picked, drawn in big wagons to Benson, where it had been ginned and baled and then brought back to Falconhurst, where the bales were piled high, protected by tarpaulins, in one of the fields. They were proud of the bumper crop that they themselves had had a hand in raising.

Cotton brokers had swarmed the plantation even during picking time and all had agreed that Falconhurst had produced a superior grade of cotton. Drum could easily have sold his bales in Benson, but the highest bid had come from a broker in Mobile, representing an English firm, who was willing to pay transportation from the railhead at Westminster to Mobile and give them a higher price than any of the local brokers were willing to offer. Narcisse advised accepting the Mobile offer. It came to around $30,000, which was $2,000 more than any other offer. It also seemed good sense to Drum to accept it. After Narcisse's share and other expenses were taken out, he'd have more than $20,000 and, frankly, he would be glad of the cash because two of the iron kettles under Big Pearl's bed had been emptied of their gold. The cotton money would go into the bank, but he intended to keep the remainder of the gold right where it was. It would be safe with Big Pearl. Nobody would ever dare enter her cabin because of Big Pearl's conjure powers.

Narcisse volunteered to accompany the cotton to Mobile and make the financial arrangements with the broker there. It was his suggestion that Drum allow him to deposit the money in a Mobile bank and, when he returned, Drum could draw a draft on that bank for Narcisse's share. This too seemed like a good idea to Drum. One train trip between Westminster and Mobile was all he could ever stand. He could never quite forget the horror of it. Now he was somewhat accustomed to the colour distinction between himself and whites, but at that time he hadn't been. Nevertheless, he did not relish a ride to Mobile on a freight train, which would be even worse than his ride in a baggage car.

Besides, Claire was remaining at Falconhurst. A freight train was certainly no place for a woman, but, Narcisse suggested, he would like to take his ten foremen along with him. He'd pay all their expenses and it would be a well-earned treat for them, as none had ever been more than a few miles away from Falconhurst. It would be a good way to keep them contented at Falconhurst. It was well to pamper them. Witness the good crop they had produced this year. Few plantations had such a fine group of head men and he wanted to keep them. To this also Drum assented. Narcisse suddenly seemed to be full of suggestions and all of them made sense. Let the men go with him. There was little work for them to do now and if Narcisse paid their expenses, Drum would not be out of pocket.

The morning of their departure was quite a gala occasion. The big wagons (some rented from neighbouring plantations whose owners were willing to accept Drum's cash despite the colour of his skin) were piled high with bales and the oxen decorated with flower wreaths and coloured streamers of torn calico. Narcisse led the procession on horseback with his ten mounted foremen following. Owing to the slow progress of the plodding oxen, it had been decided to stop overnight along the way, making camp for the evening meal. The men could sleep either on the cotton bales or under the wagons, then start off early in the morning for Westminster in time to get the cotton loaded on the special freight train that was to take it to Mobile.

Drum had rather wanted to accompany them at least a part of the way to Westminster, but Narcisse was quick to point out that the highstepping greys would have difficulty in slowing their pace to the oxen and Drum would require the utmost in patience to cover even five miles. Besides, he decided, it would serve no purpose and he might as well bid them *au revoir* from the portico of Falconhurst as along the dusty roadside. Once again Drum assented to Narcisse, but it was his own cotton and now he was rather sorry that he had not decided to go along with it to Mobile. Yet that was an overseer's job.

The whole household assembled on the front portico to see them depart and Mammy Morn stood waving her apron long after the procession had turned between the brick gateposts and headed down the road in the direction of Westminster. Then, after the enthusiasm of their departure, the house became suddenly quiet. Laura and Claire, along with Lucy, Drumstick, Rosanne, and Debbie, all went out to the kitchen with Mammy Morn to arrange the daily schedule of cooking and housekeeping. Mede decided to visit his mother and asked Drum, but he declined. He somehow had no desire this morning for the dark mysteries of Big Pearl's cabin. Instead he had Ciccron saddle his horse and started out to ride, heading for no place in particular. The whole plantation seemed strangely empty. There were only a few workers in the fields, working under Brute's direction, and when Drum stopped to talk with him, he said that he had sent a group of men up into the woods to chop down trees that would eventually provide firewood for the winter months ahead. With nothing else to do, Drum followed the sound of chopping and came to the woods, where he found a group of about twenty men working leisurely. They had no overseer or head man over them, yet their work did not increase in tempo as Drum arrived. They did, however, cease work as he dismounted from his horse. He picked an axe up from the ground and worked along with them for a while. It gave him a physical relief to find some vent for his energies. There was a sharp bite in the air, but he worked so hard, he had to remove first his coat and then his shirt. It was nearly noon when he decided to quit, and rode back to the plantation in time to change his clothes for the midday meal.

After dinner, time still hung heavy on his hands. Claire had finished her morning chores and suggested that they all take a drive in the surrey. It could seat five, but that was uncomfortable and both Laura and Mede, who had far rather be alone, suggested that Ciceron take only Claire and Drum. They took the road towards Benson, paid a short call at Lewis Gassaway's, and then Ciceron took them along narrow country roads.

Before leaving for the drive, Drum had made up his mind that he would not indulge in any lovemaking with Claire. As much as he wanted to, he now realized that it would lead to nothing; yet somewhere in the back of his head he was conscious that this was the first night in all the nights they had spent at Falconhurst that Narcisse would be away. He was sure it would make no difference to Claire. Although she vowed that she loved him, she had always been faithful to Narcisse, admitting that she loved him too.

Claire's hand touched his under the light laprobe and the mere brushing of skin against skin kindled a fire in him. It was like a match touching pitch. Immediately his whole body became a holocaust of raging flames and he knew he would never be content with merely holding hands. Yet he was loath to continue further, knowing his nature to be such that once the fire was kindled, he would have no control over himself.

He pulled his hand away and hers sought it, clutched it, and then released it to slowly edge its way over the smooth cloth of his trousers. Now she became the aggressor. His resistance was futile, although in truth he was able to resist very little. He felt the warmth of her hands through the cloth of his trousers and then against the tumescence of his flesh. All at once he had to push her hands away and he groaned in desperation at the unfulfilment. It was too much. No man, especially himself, could be so tempted.

'Oh, Drum, I love you so much.' Her small hands appeared above the laprobe.

'But you love Narcisse more.' He was not content with her declaration of love. He needed further assurance.

'No, no, no! Oh, my dear Drum, you cannot understand. I do love Narcisse, but the love I have for him is something entirely different from the love I have for you. I can't explain,

383

not even to myself. But believe me, Drum, it is you that I do love with all my heart. I do, I do, I do!'

'And yet our love must go lamely on depending on these chance meetings, these little stolen moments that do not satisfy either of us? Things cannot continue like this for ever.'

She bowed her head, the rim of her bonnet hiding her eyes from his. When she finally lifted her head and turned so that Drum could see her face, he noticed tears in her eyes. She threw herself into his arms, sobbing.

He tried to comfort her, but she was inconsolable. His big handkerchief wiped away her tears. His soothing words brought some sense of calmness to her and when she was able to speak, he questioned her, seeking to find out the source of her grief.

'It's only because I love you so much, Drum. Only that. I have not been fair to you. I have allowed you to love me, yet I have given you very little in return. Believe me, on that trip back from Westminster I would have let you take me, only that you were drunk and I did not want you that way. Oh, believe me, I have wanted you as much as you have wanted me. I can stand it no longer.'

'That is up to you, Claire.' Drum tried to be consoling, but his words were jubilant.

She hesitated a long time before answering and her whispered words were scarcely audible. 'Then, tonight, Drum, while Narcisse is away.'

'Tonight?' He could hardly believe that she had yielded at last. He clasped her tightly, drawing her so close he could hear her heart beat.

'Yes, tonight,' she answered, and he thought that she was going to faint in his arms. 'Tonight, Drum, but remember this, oh, my very dear, remember this, it will kill your love for me for ever. For ever.'

CHAPTER THIRTY-FOUR

THAT EVENING, as they had so many evenings in the past, Drum and Claire sat with Mede and Laura outside on the veranda. They watched the purple shadows of the gathering dusk change into the blackness of night and listened to the nocturnal song of myriads of insects. Mede and Laura sat on one side of the doorway, their chairs close together, hand in hand. Drum and Claire sat on the other side, but their chairs were separated and, although Drum longed to reach out in the darkness and take her hand with that same freedom with which Mede clasped Laura's, he hesitated to move his chair closer to hers. A thin sliver of light from the lamp in the hall painted a path of brightness between them, which separated them even more. Mede and Laura were content with their physical nearness. Neither of them spoke and occasionally Mede detached his hand from Laura's to stroke her neck or brush back wandering locks of hair. Their silence was echoed by that of Drum and Claire but, whereas there was rapport between Mede and Laura, the separation between Drum and Claire seemed to grow with every moment.

Drum envied the others' intimate oneness and wished that he too had the right to make these little gestures towards Claire – gestures that only a husband or a lover could make. To be sure, he was her lover. She had assured him of that this afternoon. But she did have a husband and, although he knew that neither Mede nor Laura would report any of his actions to Narcisse, Drum did not feel privileged. There was something that had caused Claire to withdraw into herself. What could it be? She had offered herself to him freely, even without his importuning her and now, he felt, she regretted her promise.

He could not understand her attitude. He had not urged her. He had not begged and pleaded with her until she had consented reluctantly. The promise had come from her and yet, since she had returned home from the drive, she had seemed depressed and unhappy. Despite Mammy Morn's best efforts, she had eaten little and as dinner progressed she seemed to erect a barrier between herself and the rest of the world, particularly Drum. Now, as he sat beside her, he noticed that there was an occasional movement of her hand – a white blur of her handkerchief as she wiped her eyes. What could be causing her all this anguish? Was her conscience hurting her? Had it not meant so much to him, he would have released her from her promise, but that he would not do. He was too selfish. He wanted her too much. But why, he asked himself again, had she offered herself to him in the first place if she could not even anticipate it with pleasure? Surely she must realize that he did not want a weeping, sorrowful woman whom he would have to coax from frigidity to warmth. He wanted her desire to equal his; and God knows – or perhaps it was the devil in this case – his desire for her was growing as the moments passed. He could feel it even now, burgeoning within him, and he was grateful for the darkness, which hid it from Mede and Laura. Damn it! Women were strange creatures. One moment they were fire and laughter; the next moment they were teary and cold. He reached his hand across the path of light to touch hers and, although she looked towards him and smiled wanly, there was no answering touch from her hand. Damn it again!

He glanced across at Mede and Laura and noticed that Mede was yawning, his mouth open wide like a red wound in his black face. Laura yawned more discreetly, her hand covering her mouth and patting it delicately as she exhaled.

'Reckon it 'bout time we all went up to bed,' Mede said, pushing himself up with the arms of his chair. He yawned again and stretched out a hand to help Laura. ' 'Thout Narcisse 'round, reckon we got to git ourselves up early 'n' git things started 'round here come mornin'.'

'Not much to do.' Drum tried to sound casual, but he could feel his voice tremble in his throat. For the moment he actually dreaded being alone with Claire. Which of them would be the first to speak and what would they say to each other? 'Brute can take over,' he added, 'there's just a few odd jobs for the hands to do.'

'I'se tired anyway.' Mede yawned for the third time. ''N' Laura she tired out too. Reckon we two'll h'ist ourselves upstairs.' He winked surreptitiously at Drum while he opened the screen door with one hand to allow Laura to precede him. Drum stood up and followed him into the hall, waiting for Laura to start up the stairs before he detained Mede.

'Tell Debbie I'll not be wanting her tonight. No need of her sitting up there, waiting for me.'

Mede eyed him curiously but said nothing. Together he and Laura ascended the stairs and Drum returned to the veranda to sit once again beside Claire, searching for something to say to break the awful stillness.

'Let's sit awhile longer.' He realized as he spoke the words that it was the last thing in the world he really wanted to do. What he wanted was for Claire to be beside him, following Mede and Laura up the stairs, but it seemed expedient at the moment not to rush things. Perhaps if he let matters take their course, they would resolve themselves.

The tone of her voice surprised him when she spoke. Neither melancholy nor depression seemed to tinge it. Perhaps she had been waiting for Mede and Laura to leave.

'Yes, Drum, do let's sit awhile longer, but draw your chair closer to mine. We've seemed far apart this evening and I know it's been my fault. I've been sad, Drum. I've been thinking that this may be the last evening we shall ever sit here together. Oh, how I've longed to reach out my hand and touch you, Drum, but something stops me. You've seemed far away this evening. You've scarcely spoken to me.'

'I've been waiting for you to speak, I guess. Or perhaps I've been thinking too much about the promise you made me this afternoon.'

She was silent for a long time and her silence was broken only by the rocking of her chair. Again he noticed her dabbing at her eyes with her handkerchief.

'Will you believe me if I tell you one thing, Drum?'

He squeezed her hand in assent.

'I love you, Drum. I do not say it idly or without meaning. I do. I love you so much it hurts. That's why I made you that promise this afternoon. I feel that whatever happens, I owe myself this one night. I need to be loved, Drum. *Mon Dieu*, how I need to be loved. I've exhausted myself with loving someone else and now it's my turn to be loved. That love I am sure I will find in your arms.'

'You shall.' Drum slid from his chair and sat on the floor beside her, leaning his head in her lap. 'No other arms in the world have longed to hold you like mine. Oh, Claire darling, what is this mystery that envelops our love? No, don't answer – I know it's Narcisse.'

Her hand played with the tight curls of his hair, her fingers twining among them. He reached up with his other hand, discovering that her handkerchief was wet with tears.

'You weep, my dear. Is it because of Narcisse?'

She shook her head in denial. 'No, Drum, it's because of you. I am going to hurt you, Drum, and that I do not want to do, but I cannot help it. Yes, I weep, but I do not weep for Narcisse, I weep because of him. I love him, but I cannot explain my love for him. He's been an evil influence over me and yet I cannot stop loving him. I am like a bird being hypnotized by a snake, knowing that in the end the snake will devour me, yet I make no effort to run away. You too will see what an evil influence Narcisse is. As much as I love you, Drum, and that is more than I can put into words, I would sacrifice my love for you for Narcisse.'

'You are merely speaking words, Claire. They don't make sense.'

'Of course not. I wish I could tell you all about him, but I cannot. You'll find out soon enough and then you'll hate me and I cannot blame you.'

'Hate you?' Drum buried his head deeper in her lap, feeling the warmth of her body through the thin cotton dress. His fingers started upward, unbuttoning the tiny buttons of her basque until they were able to make their way under it to the soft flesh beneath. 'I could never hate you, Claire, no matter what happens.'

Instead of denying him, she helped him unbutton the buttons, feeling the hugeness of his hands as they cupped her breasts.

'Don't speak too soon, Drum, or too rashly. Love can be turned into hate in an instant. Yet remember what I told you. Whatever happens, I love you.' Now she pushed his hands away and stood up. 'Come, Drum, let us go upstairs. Tonight we shall go together and there will be no barrier between us, neither closed doors nor these cumbersome rags of clothing. Tonight I offer myself to you. Now I want you more than ever. I know that you want me. I've never been wanted before. Can you believe that, Drum?'

He shook his head in denial. Her words did not make sense. If she loved Narcisse, then certainly he must have wanted her.

'I've always wanted you,' he whispered.

'Then, why deny ourselves any longer? Come! I know I shall regret this as long as I live, but I cannot deny either you or myself any longer.' She stood up, reaching down an outstretched hand to help him up.

He opened the screen door to let her pass into the hall and noticed that she looked up at the tall clock as if, for some reason, the time might be important to her, before she turned down the lamp, leaving only a tiny flame. Arm in arm they crossed the hall, took the stairs slowly, one by one. Each step provoked a lingering dalliance, a loosening or removing of some constrictive garment until, by the time they had reached the top of the stairs, each one was carrying the other's garments and they were entirely naked. Here they stopped for a long moment, letting their hands wander restlessly over each other. Drum lifted the latch of the door into Claire's room and they entered, dropping the shed garments on the floor. There was no light in the room and Claire extricated herself from Drum's tight embrace long enough to strike a match, take the chimney off the lamp beside the bed, and light it.

'The better to see you in all your glory,' she said without embarrassment. 'I must see you as you are, Drum. For too long I have wondered what the shoulders of your coat were hiding and although I did know, shameless hussy that I am, what the bulge in your trousers accounted for, I must see it now, free and unemcumbered.'

He arched his body towards her with male pride and backed

away from her a few steps the better to see her. He had expected perfection and now he saw it. Her corsets had made little red marks on the clear ivory of her skin, but they were imperfections that he knew would vanish. His eyes glazed and he shook his head in unbelief that such beauty existed. He revelled in the round breasts with the dark rose of the upstanding nipples. He followed the curves of her hips, the curves of her legs and then allowed his eyes to centre on the dark spot that promised the hidden delights he was so anxious now to attain. She in turn gloried in the thick column of his neck with its pulsating vein, down to the wideness of his chest with the paps like round copper pennies peeping out through the mat of curly blond hair. His belly was flat and her eyes travelled down to his strong, bulging thighs and calves, then back again to rest on his manhood in all its glory.

He made a move to turn down the lamp, but she reached out a restraining hand.

'Let the light remain, Drum. With light we shall both enjoy everything more. We are not about to do anything that should be hidden in darkness. Rather it is something in which we can indulge all our senses. Each one must be involved, else we shall not gain the fullness of our desires. We must see each other, feel each other, taste each other, hear each other, yes, even smell each other if we want to truly enjoy ourselves. So, Drum dear, leave the light burning that I may glory in you as you do in me.'

He picked her up in his arms to carry her to the bed. With one arm she clutched him around his neck while with her free hand, she reached down, fiercely clutching at him. He fell on the bed with her, pushed her hand away, and for a moment they remained immovable, he asprawl across her, scarcely daring to breathe, so nearly had she come to destroying him. She realized what she had done and remained still until she heard him breathing normally, then pushed the quilted coverlet down, leaving only the smoothness of the linen sheet. He straightened himself on the bed, pulling her close to him, so that their flesh made contact from lips to toes. Speech was forgotten in the ecstasy of the moment and only lips and fingers were left for all those delicate explorations that tempted each of them to discover the hidden parts of those bodies that had never before been explored. His lips moved from the warm wetness of her mouth, down her neck, stopping for a moment to explore the little hollow of her throat, then to her breasts, where the tip of his tongue touched and teased the hard, upstanding nipples. He explored farther, listening to her little moans and exulting in the writhing of her body until his lips returned to hers.

But only momentarily! She was not to be denied and her lips engulfed his bronze paps, her teeth biting the tightly curled hair of his chest. They discovered the shell-like convolutions of his navel and now it was his turn to moan and for the second time he had to check her, pulling her head back up to meet his own and holding his breath. Each tempted the other with love play that demanded more and more until he felt he had reached the limit of his endurance. Fingers and lips had almost proved his undoing. Now, before it was too late, he must seek his ultimate goal.

Gently he turned her over, his mouth still fastened to hers while he eased himself over on to her. She gasped a little under the weight of his body, shifting her own to accommodate it. His knee, entering between, gently forced her legs apart and she allowed him his will.

'Now?' he begged her. The one word came hoarsely and in a whisper.

'Yes, now, Drum,' she murmured. 'Now.'

'Oh, Claire, we have waited so long.' He forsook her lips, raising himself on his arms so that the muscles in his shoulders supported his whole weight. Slowly he shifted his weight to one arm while the fingers of his other hand sought and guided. Only then did he open his eyes, looking down at her, seeking the same look of expectancy that he realized was in his own, but instead he saw only fear. It was more than fear, it was terror. She gazed back at him with all the apprehension and dread of a virgin about to be ravished.

'Slowly, Drum, slowly,' she pleaded. 'Slowly and carefully.'

He promised her, trying to reassure and comfort her to remove the fear from her eyes, but his words accomplished nothing. He tried to lower himself slowly, but now he was not accountable for his actions and he plunged, quite unprepared for her scream of pain. He did not withdraw but sought her eyes, only to see that they were not looking at him but staring with horror at the door.

It was then that he heard it – the mere click of a latch being lifted. For a fleeting second he damned Mede, for there was nobody else in the house that would intrude. But it was not Mede. The door crashed open, banging against the wall. Narcisse stood, feet wide apart, in the doorway, brandishing a pistol and a revolver in either hand. There was a sardonic grin on his face.

'Well-timed, my dear Claire.' He stepped into the room. 'By your scream and your lover's position I take it you are no longer a virgin.'

Others were behind him, black faces that were indistinguishable in the dim light of the hall but edging through them was the cringing figure of a white man.

'So!' Narcisse did not raise his voice, which was more tinged with amusement than anger. 'When the cat's away, the mice will play. Ah, what charming mice. Drum Maxwell and my wife both bare-assed naked in bed. One wonders how long this has been going on. No, don't bother to answer. It doesn't make a goddam bit of difference. I've finally found out and I've got a witness to prove it. Meet Mr Jeremiah Wellington of Westminster. He may be the town drunk, but he's a white man and his word will be accepted in court, whereas mine might not be. Jerry, allow me to introduce my wife and Mr Drum Maxwell of Falconhurst. Do you see what I do, Jerry?'

'Shore do, mista, shore do. If'n that my wife, I'd shore shoot that bastard what's got it in her. Ain' no jury in the world a-goin' to convict yo'. Ain' jes' fornicatin' – adultery it is.'

'Mr Wellington used to be a lawyer before he took up drinking.' Narcisse's elbow shoved Wellington back. 'Get the hell out, Jerry, but stick around. Remember, there's ten dollars in it for you and that will buy a lot of corn, enough to keep you drunk for a month.'

Wellington sidled out, passing Big Sol, who stepped into the room. Drum slumped on the bed, then managed to sit up, his bare legs dangling over the edge of the bed. Claire, her face buried in her hands, was weeping. Drum reached for a corner of the coverlet to cover his nakedness, noticing that he was encarmined with blood. Then, what Narcisse had said about Claire's being a virgin was true after all.

'No need to cover it up.' Narcisse laughed. 'You can well be proud of it, Drum, although after me, Claire must have been a trifle disappointed.' Suddenly his voice changed from one of sardonic humour to dead seriousness. 'Don't move, you bastard. I can kill you and there's not a jury in the land that would convict me. But I have no desire to kill you, at least not yet. You're worth nothing to me dead, but alive you're worth plenty. You're going to solve all my problems, Drum. You're going to give Claire and me everything we want, everything we've ever wanted.' He walked across the floor to where Drum was sitting on the edge of the bed, stuck the revolver – Drum's own six-shooter – under his chin, and lifted Drum's head until their eyes met. 'Do you know what that is, Drum?'

Drum shook his head.

'Money, Drum Maxwell! Money! And a lot of it. Enough to take Claire and me to Paris and keep us there the rest of our lives in luxury. That's what you're going to give me and if you do, I may let you live.' He turned, handing the pistol to Big Sol. 'Lock that black bastard Mede in his room and tell him if he steps out, he'll get shot. Then go up and rouse Mammy Morn. Tell her to cook up the best dinner she ever cooked. We're all going to be damn hungry after we get through with this business. Come on, boys, take him down to the barn.'

Before the black hands of Narcisse's Big Ten grabbed him, Drum felt a light caress on one arm. He turned to look at Claire.

'I told you you were going to hate me, Drum.'

Even now, in the shock of realizing her complicity, he could

393

not genuinely hate her. But he could find no words to say to her. The black hands grabbed at him, yanking him to his feet and marching him from the room. The last thing he heard was Claire's weeping.

CHAPTER THIRTY-FIVE

DRUM THOUGHT HIS arms would be pulled from the sockets as he was dragged down the stairs. Big Sol on one side of him and Big Porter on the other showed him no mercy. As they progressed through the drawing-room they kicked over chairs and tables that were in their way. Big Alecks ran ahead of them, tipping over the dining-room table to make room for their progress, and Drum heard the crash of the crystal epergne. For a brief moment he saw it as it had been at dinner that night, with the flowers Claire had arranged in it. Damn her! Damn her and her protestations of love!

In the kitchen black hands grabbed at him, propelling him out the back door, while Big Sol's hands gripped his arm like a steel vice. On his way out the back door he slipped and fell, but they did not give him a chance to regain his feet. Instead they dragged him along the gravel path and he could feel the lacerations of his knees and legs as the sharp gravel tore at his skin. He struggled to get away from them, but they held him tight and he finally relaxed limply in their grip. Only once did he raise his head to see Narcisse walking ahead of them with a lantern towards the blaze of light that was coming through the wide-open barn doors.

It was there that they were dragging him and when his knees caught on the doorsill and he was thrown on to the barn floor, he felt a momentary sense of relief, although Big Sol's hands still gripped one of his arms. Despite his pain, his mind was back in the bedroom. Claire! She had not lied when she said she loved Narcisse. She had done all this for him. No wonder she had said that Drum would hate her. And how he hated her for luring him into her bed when she knew all along what was going to happen! She had been a party to this all along. But there was one thing he could not account for – she was a virgin. And how could she be, married all this time to Narcisse? Then all thoughts of her fled as Big Sol brought him painfully to his feet and released him to face Narcisse.

'It was well planned, wasn't it, Drum? We arrived at just the right moment.' Narcisse held up the lantern to Drum's face, staring at him, the sardonic smile still on his lips. 'My wife and I have been planning this little event since that first day you walked into Madame Helene's in New Orleans. There was only one complication, however; the little fool fell in love with you and you, you idiot, fell in love with her. But it made no difference. As infatuated as she was with you, she did as I told her in the end, although if it will give you any satisfaction to know it, she did it unwillingly. It was a question of her hurting you or me and, of course, she chose to hurt you.'

'But why?' Drum still could not understand.

'Because I have a life I want to live and you are going to help me – and Claire too – live it. All my life I have wanted to live in Paris, where there is no distinction between a man who is white and a man who is white but not quite. I'm sick of being a *nigger*. I'm sick of living here in the South and having every white man's face turned against me. I'm as good as they are.' His voice was raised in a frenzy. 'Goddamit, I am and I'm going to be. I'm going to be white. By God, I'm going to be white and you are going to give me that chance. You, Drum Maxwell, are going to do it.'

'How?'

'With money, *mon ami*. Money! You have it and I do not. I need it – plenty of it. It's not that I have anything against you. I've always liked you, but you've got money and I haven't.'

'I'll not pay you a red cent. It's blackmail.'

Narcisse lowered the lantern and laughed softly. 'Blackmail? That's not a very pretty word to come from a man I just found in my wife's bed and in my wife too.' Narcisse laughed louder and the Negroes around him giggled and guffawed at the joke.

'Shore did have it in her.'

'Shore did.'

'That man he a-goin' strong.'

'Bet she not a-likin' it as well's Masta Narcisse.'

'Ain' nobody in de worl' like Masta Narcisse, not even yo', Big Sol. Yo' met yore comeuppance when Masta Narcisse comed 'long. Cain' go braggin' 'roun' now.'

'Shut up!' Narcisse silenced them.

The brief moments of standing unmolested had renewed Drum's strength and although he knew full well it was useless to struggle against Narcisse and his henchmen, whom he recognized now as the Big Ten, he resolved that he would not go down without at least a token struggle. Big Sol was still beside him and still grinning over Narcisse's feeble joke, his face turned away from Drum. He crouched to gain a better leverage and suddenly pounded his fist into Big Sol's face. Big Sol was stunned for a short moment; then Drum felt the impact of the giant's fist against his chest. It nearly knocked him over, but he regained his balance and, with his two feet planted firmly, he dodged Big Sol's next blow, coming up under the ham-like fist to thrust one finger, rigid as iron, into Big Sol's eye. With all his strength he twisted his finger, gouging out the eyeball and hearing Big Sol's scream of anger and pain. Drum looked up to see Big Sol's left eye dangling from the red socket, held only by a thread of shiny muscle. Brushing it away as if it were no part of him, Big Sol lunged at Drum, his fists hammering at him with an insane frenzy until a word from Narcisse halted him.

'That's enough, Big Sol. I don't want to kill him. Dead he will be of no advantage to me. Alive he is. To the floor with him, men, and fasten the spancels around his ankles.'

As he heard the ropes being pulled through the big wooden pulleys on each side of the barn Drum remembered how he had had Barry repair the old whipping machinery; but he did not have long to think about it because black hands grabbed him and flung him face-down on the floor.

'I'm a-goin' to whop him, though,' Big Sol was howling above his pain. 'Ain' no one kin keep me from whoppin' him onc't he gits strung up. Not even yo', Masta Narcisse. Yo' cain' keep me from that.'

'You'll whop him if I say so and you won't if I don't. I give the orders around here.' Big Sol cowered before the cold voice of Narcisse, his hand covering his eye. 'Big Alecks, you got those spancels fastened?'

'They right tight 'roun' his ankles, Masta Narcisse.'

'Then, up with him boys.'

The pulleys creaked and the ropes whined as Drum felt himself dragged across the floor. Splinters from the rough planking tore at his skin. He tried vainly to support his weight as much as he could, but the ropes were pulling too fast and he was drawn up so high that not even the tips of his fingers could touch the floor. Now the torture was in his crotch; his legs were so spreadeagled that he felt he would split through the middle. He heard himself shrieking with the pain, although he was unaware of making any sound. Opening his eyes in an effort to orient himself and control his screams, he could see, albeit upside down, Narcisse's boots and he could hear the curses Big Sol was yelling in a futile effort to lessen his own pain. Then came a blessed oblivion as Drum felt himself slipping into a maze of soft black cobwebs, but it was only momentary. A bucket of cold water splashed over him and brought him back to the awful reality of his situation.

'Can you see to whip him, Big Sol?' It was Narcisse talking. 'I think a few lashes might do him good – might put him in the right mood. It will convince him that we are in earnest and not just playing a game.'

Drum opened his eyes to see Big Sol's bare feet move away and, by twisting his head, he could see them circle behind him and then pass out of his vision. It was only a second before he heard the swish of the whip through the air and felt the stinging pain as it bit into the soft flesh of his buttocks.

He screamed. It felt like a red-hot iron searing into his flesh.

'I'se a-goin' to put the mark o' the Big Ten on this bastard's back so he'll always remember us.' Big Sol reached out to stop Drum's swaying body. 'Cain' do it well's I could when I had both eyes, but don't make no neverminds how it looks.' Again the whip sang and again the searing lash of fire struck Drum's back, then again and again and again until life had become nothing but a fiery hell into which he descended deeper and deeper. He wailed, he begged, he pleaded, and screamed. In a vain attempt to dodge the blows he used all his strength to double up his body to keep the lashes from his back, but he was losing his strength.

'That's enough, Big Sol.' Narcisse seemed almost reluctant to give the order.

Despite Narcisse's words, Drum tensed for another blow, but it did not come. Instead he felt Narcisse's hands slide down over the calf of his leg, then slowly, and almost like a caress, down the inside of his thigh. Narcisse's other hand started on a similar journey down Drum's other leg until the two hands met in the middle to fondle him. 'That's just a taste, Drum, *mon ami*, but we might give you more if you insist on being stubborn. But you won't. You won't.' The hands continued their caressing motion until Narcisse took them away momentarily.

Drum opened his eyes with difficulty; able to see but dimly now, all he could make out was Narcisse's boots.

'Let's get down to business, Drum. Can you hear me?'

Drum nodded his head weakly.

'I want money, Drum. Money and plenty of it. Claire and I are going to need it if we go to Paris. We want our own home, our own carriage, and money to live on in style. See this piece of paper? Can you read it?'

'No.' Drum uttered the single word with difficulty.

'It's a letter to your brokers in Mobile. It's all written out correctly and legally by that stupid fool, Wellington. All it needs is your signature, Drum. That will give me about thirty thousand dollars. But that's not enough. You've got money. You have some in the Benson bank, but you've got more. Where it comes from, I don't know, but you've got it. I've searched the house thoroughly, but I cannot locate it. It's the source of all those gold pieces you've been handing around here. Where is it, Drum, and how much have you got?'

Drum raised his head as far as possible to look up at Narcisse. Suddenly he remembered something. Ciceron slept out in the barn. He had probably been awakened by the noise below but had not dared to come down. Instead of answering Narcisse, he gathered all his strength and cried out Ciceron's name.

'Goddamit,' Narcisse said, turning towards Big Sol. 'We forgot that nigger bastard that sleeps out here.'

'He ain' a-goin' to show his face 'gainst all of us.' Big Sol had wadded up his bandana and was holding it against his eye. 'He's scairt shitless by now.'

'He won't help you, Drum,' Narcisse continued, but an edge of exasperation, even nervousness, was apparent. He was blaming himself for having forgotten one item in his carefully laid plan. 'Come on, now. Sign the paper and tell us where the money is.'

'You'll not get it. Not a goddam penny of it.' Drum's anger gave him strength. 'Go ahead, kill me if you want, but I'll not be the means of your getting away with this. You won't be living in Paris on my money.'

'Oh, yes I will. But really, Drum, I've no intention of killing you. There are, you know, worse things than death.' Narcisse's hands returned to him, stroking, caressing, and manipulating. 'You've had a lot of fun out of this during your lifetime, haven't you, Drum? No, don't bother to answer, I know you have. Anything like that would make any man happy and any woman too. Women have loved you for it, Drum, and you've enjoyed their loving it. Even Claire has been in love with you. I'll not deny it, she loves you far more than she does me, but she's faithful to me, Drum. She has to be. There's more between us than her love for you. But to return to this' – Narcisse lifted Drum's inert member. 'Just suppose you didn't have this. Suppose I were to make you less than a man. It would be easy, you know. Just a single slice with a knife.' Narcisse pulled a blade from a sheath in his belt and knelt down to hold it before Drum's face. 'Just a single stroke, that's all.'

'My God, Narcisse, you wouldn't do that!'

'Willingly unless you sign this document and agree to furnish me with all the money you have at Falconhurst. Isn't this bit of flesh worth that amount of money to you?'

'Yo' a-goin' to let me do it?' Big Sol came close to Narcisse. 'Him jes' a-gougin' my eye out 'n' everythin'.'

'I'll attend to that myself.' Narcisse elbowed Big Sol away. 'He'll not die from it. We'll cauterize him well. Is that iron hot?'

'Red hot.' Big Dick lifted a glowing soldering iron from a bed of coals in a bucket. He was the nearest to the barn door, so he was the first to hear the sound of running feet.

'Someone's a-comin', Masta Narcisse.'

By now they had all heard it, but they were scarcely prepared for Big Pearl, clad in long white robes. Behind her were Mede and Lucy.

'What a-goin' on here?' She pointed to Drum. 'What yo'-all a-doin' to my boy, a-hangin' him up there stark-naked 'n' whoppin' him!'

'Get out of here, old woman.' Narcisse made a quick motion towards Big Alecks, who was carrying the pistol. 'Keep her covered, and that Mede boy too. If they move, shoot them. Lucy, remember you're still a member of the Big Ten. You took the vows. Stand there and warn me if anyone else comes.'

'Yes suh, Mista Narcisse.'

'Yo' ain' a-shootin' me,' said Big Pearl coolly, walking forward. 'I'se put a conjure on yo'-all. I'se started a fire in yore necks, a tightenin' in yore throats. I'se callin' down a curse on yo'.'

'Conjure?' Big Sol and one or two others roared with laughter. 'Conjure ain' a-doin' yo' no good tonight, ol' woman. Yo' ain' a-goin' to live to start no fire in my neck.' He snatched the gun from Big Alecks and fired point-blank at her. For an instant she stood, her hand raised in some unholy condemnation. A small spot of blood on the breast of her white robe spread rapidly across and down. She swayed and then

400

crumpled in a heap on the floor. Mede bent over her with a cry, putting his hand on her and drawing it back smeared with blood.

'Yo' done kilt my mammy!' He burst into sobs.

Big Sol reloaded the pistol and handed it back to Narcisse. 'Whyn't yo' kill the bastard now? Git him outa the way so he won't blabber afterwards.'

Narcisse regarded the pistol, then handed it to Big Alecks. 'Keep him covered,' he said, gesturing at Mede, who was cradling Big Pearl's head and moaning. 'His time comes when we're through.' He flourished the knife, stooping so that Drum would see it. 'Well, which is it? The money or the thing you value most in the world? Come, make up your mind! We've got to get back to Westminster to get the cotton loaded.' He rose and laid the keen edge gently against Drum's groin.

'I'll sign,' Drum said in a thin voice. His black grandmother lay dead or dying on the barn floor and he was icy with the dread of the horrible maiming. 'Let me down and I'll sign whatever you want. I'll give you the gold too. Just don't do . . . what you're threatening.'

'I knew you'd sign. We'll let him down,' said Narcisse, jubilant. 'He can't write his name in that position.' He stood spraddle-legged as the pulleys creaked and the ropes slowly lowered Drum to the floor. Black hands brought him to his feet, although the spancels were still on his ankles.

Should he hurl himself at them, even now? No, that was suicide. He'd give Narcisse what he wanted . . . and pursue him to the end of the world and murder him slowly, slowly. Black hands shoved a piece of board, a paper, an inkwell, and a pen upon him. Laboriously Drum signed, his fingers so stiff he could scarcely hold the pen. Narcisse took the paper and waved it to dry the ink. 'Now the gold.'

'It's in Big Pearl's cabin.'

Narcisse walked to a lantern and examined the document, making sure that Drum's name was legible. He folded it and stuffed it into his shirt pocket, then came back to Drum, pulling the six-shooter from his belt. 'I'm afraid I'll have to kill you, after all, Drum, you and Mede. You'd have the

401

sheriff on us before we reached Westminster. I must protect myself, you understand. Get over here, boys. Alecks, bring that nigger over, we'll send him to hell along with his brother.'

Mede looked up over Big Pearl's body at Drum. 'They a-goin' to shoot us, true?' His teeth chattered so much that he could hardly speak.

'Looks like it, Mede.' He stared over Narcisse's shoulder, grim and helpless. Then he saw Mede launch himself upward in a vicious leap for Alecks and would have done the same at Narcisse but for the menace of the steady revolver. Alecks clubbed Mede on the side of the head and shoved the pistol muzzle into his face. Mede, terrified, collapsed; Big Alecks dragged him over and threw him down beside Drum, where he knelt shaking with fear. 'Goodbye, Mede. You've been a real brother to me,' Drum said.

' 'Bye, Drum,' said Mede, catching hold of his hand.

The Big Ten stood, five on each side of Narcisse, forming a semicircle with their leader in the centre. Drum squeezed Mede's hand hard, determined that he would show no sign of weakness. Death was, after all, better than the horror with which he had been threatened. He did not look at Narcisse now, but stared beyond him to the semi-darkness where only Lucy stood.

Yet was it only Lucy? No, for there was Claire, materialized out of the blackness behind the boy, staring at the lantern-lighted tableau before her – Claire, dressed in a hastily donned gown, her face drained of blood, and holding in her right hand a small blue derringer. Had she come to attend to his killing herself? Drum's wits spun. Only moments ago he had embraced her, had felt her respond—

Then he saw it coming, a shining streak of steel in the glow of the lanterns. It struck Narcisse in the back, embedding itself to the hilt. The man staggered forward, his face amazed, then dropped like an ox, sprawling out at Drum's feet, the hilt of the knife standing upright and the white shirt fast reddening around it.

A voice from up in the darkness of the hay mow shouted, 'Got yo'-all covered with a rifle.' It was Ciceron. Then Brute spoke from the other side of the barn, ' 'N' so've I, 'n' we got six men from New Quarters outside, so don' move, none o' yo'.'

Lucy walked into the light. 'I stuck him, Mista Drum. He a bad man, Mista Narcisse. All the rest o' 'em bad too. Sheriff's a-lookin' for all o' them. They's the ones what stoled from that white woman 'n' raped her 'n' her girls. Mista Narcisse he with 'em. Yo' look in his hip pocket 'n' yo'll fin' the money he stoled from her.' Lucy knelt, tugged his knife free and, after wiping it on Narcisse's shirt, thrust it into his belt. He shoved the man over on to his back. 'I kilt him a'right.'

Drum released his ankles from the spancels, walked with halting footsteps to where his enemy lay, and pulled open his shirt to feel for a heartbeat. There was none. It was then that he noticed the birds, one tattooed over each nipple. He had seen them before, but where? He could not remember, his mind was too full of other things. He tottered, barely able to move his legs, to Big Pearl, a small mountain of white on the floor. Feebly he sat down beside her and took her limp hand in his own. 'Grandmammy,' he said brokenly. 'My grandmammy.' He had felt no real kinship to the old conjure woman while she was alive, only gratitude and perhaps a little awe. But now in his physical weakness and relief, he was drawn to her as he was no longer to any living thing. 'Grandmammy, don't die,' he said, sitting naked and bloody and helpless on the barn floor. But she would never hear him again.

He saw Claire walking slowly past him, and turned his head to watch her. She fell to her knees beside Narcisse and lowered her cheek to touch his. The folded piece of paper was still in his pocket and in a moment she took it out, scanned what was written on it, then tore it slowly, tore it again and again and released the handful of tiny white bits to drift like snowflakes over his body.

'*Mon Harlequin*,' she sobbed, '*mon Harlequin!*'

Just before he fainted, Drum remembered. Harlequin! The famous Harlequin of New Orleans. He had had two flying birds tattooed on his chest. Harlequin was Narcisse.

And Harlequin was dead.

CHAPTER THIRTY-SIX

SOMEWHERE WITHIN THE deep, soft darkness there came a faint stirring of consciousness. Drum fought against it. He preferred the blackness and its absolute forgetfulness to awakening because even this faint stirring warned him that he would awaken to a reality he dreaded to face. He tried to sink back into the welcome nothingness, but the harder he tried, the more he was forced to accept awakening. Finally, when he could fight it no longer, he opened his eyes, trying to orient himself in this new world of reality. He discovered one thing at a time slowly. He was lying on his belly. One hand was under his cheek, the other stretched towards the side of a bed. He blinked and opened his eyes wider, seeing his own dim reflection in the polished mahogany headboard of the bed. He recognized it as his own bed because now he could see the peculiar graining of the wood at which he had stared so often when he had been there with Debbie.

With the return of consciousness, he began to feel a pain that centred in his back. Testing it, he moved ever so slightly and the pain became worse, so he lay still and allowed it to subside for a moment. Turning his head slightly, he saw a veined and toil-worn hand, black, with a pink palm, reach out and rest on his forehead.

'He ain' got no mo' fever. Yo' a-goin' to give him mo' o' that laud'num?'

Soft footsteps came across the room and then a white hand, smooth and cool, replaced the black one on his forehead.

'I think we'd better let him come to himself, Mammy Morn. It's been three days now and it's time he woke up. His back's better and his fever has gone.'

'Yas'm, Miz Claire, I'm a-thinkin' so too. He jes' got to come to sometime 'n' this as good a time's any. Needin' food, he do. Ain' et nothin' for three days. Goin' to h'ist myself down to the kitchen 'n' hotten up that chicken broth I been a-makin' for him.'

Slowly lifting himself on his elbows, Drum turned his head to see Mammy Morn leaving the room and Claire standing beside the bed. His first reaction was great relief; she was still there, and that comforted him until he realized that she was the cause of his present condition. She, Claire, whom he had loved – still loved – had done this to him! Searching further into his memory, he recalled the scene of horror in the barn, the lashing of his naked body, the cruel caresses of Narcisse as his hands slid down the insides of his thighs, Big Pearl sinking slowly to the floor, the hurtling blade of Lucy's knife embedding itself in Narcisse's back, Claire taking the paper to which he had signed his name and tearing it to bits. He looked up again; Claire was still watching him.

'You are . . . still here?' He found the words difficult to say, though he managed to put particular emphasis on the word *you*. He knew that he loved her even yet; and at the same time he abhorred her for what she had done. How close she had brought him to gelding, nay, even complete emasculation! Once she had said to him that there was little distinction between love and hate, and certainly she had proved it, was proving it now. He loved and hated her almost equally. He would beg her to stay . . . he never wanted to see her again. He was about to touch her hand but recoiled from it.

'Yes, Drum, I could not leave until I knew you were all right. I'll go now. My bags are packed. Ciceron can take me to Westminster to catch the train. Goodbye, Drum. You will not believe me . . . but I really love you. I can't blame you for not believing that. But it is true,' she cried suddenly, her face twisting, 'oh, my God, it is true! Goodbye, Drum, and try to believe that I love you, that I always have.'

She touched his forehead and let her hand linger in a fleeting caress; then, without looking back, she walked to the door. He watched each slow footstep, watched her hand raise to lift the latch, and then he called out weakly, 'Not yet, not yet!' He sat up, turning his body, oblivious to the pain. 'There are things to say.'

'There is nothing to say,' she answered, her fingers on the

latch. 'You remember what has happened, don't you? You will never trust me again and without trust there is no love.'

'You claim that you still love me. When you would have let Narcisse despoil me and then kill me when I had done as you and he wanted.'

'As he wanted, not I.' Reaching into her dress pocket, she drew out a small derringer. He remembered it now. 'I have kept this with me, wondering if it might be the best way for me. It has been cold in my pocket since that dreadful night.'

'When you were going to shoot me with it.'

'Narcisse! I would have *killed* Narcisse before he could harm you. I knew that when I saw you dragged away from my bed, when they locked me in. I tried to break down the door, and failed. Then I tied sheets together and got down from the window and ran to the barn. When I arrived and saw what was happening, I was actually lifting this to shoot him . . . but Lucy, thank God, did what I meant to do.' She stared at him. 'Goodbye, Drum.' She opened the door and stepped out into the hall.

Gathering all the strength left in him, Drum managed to crawl out of bed. That he was naked made no difference; in his haste he did not even bother to snatch a sheet from the bed to cover himself. He found it difficult to walk, and stumbled across the room, opening the door she had closed. Haltingly he managed somehow to cross the hall to her room. He saw the strapped valises inside.

'No!' he shouted. 'Don't go!' He dropped his voice, pleading, clinging to the doorjamb. 'Wait, wait! Until I am strong enough to talk. Promise me you'll wait.' His head reeled, his knees buckled, once more he was afraid he would faint; but a strong black arm supported him.

'Yo' better git back to bed, Drum,' said Mede, with Lucy and Mammy Morn behind him. They half carried him back to his bed. Claire came in hesitantly, taking the bowl of broth from Mammy Morn and beginning to spoon it into Drum. The hot stuff made him feel better almost at once.

'You won't go until we've had a chance to talk?'

'No – but I can't imagine why you wish it.'

'You stayed,' he said.

'Yes, to be sure you were out of danger I stayed to reassure myself, and if you wish it, I can stay a little longer, for you.'

'There is so much to speak of.'

'Later. I give you my word, if that means anything to you now, that I will be just across the hall, waiting. I'll let Mede and Lucy talk to you now,' she said, straightening up, 'for they can set your mind at rest about certain things.' She went swiftly across the room and shut the door behind her.

Mammy Morn, scolding him for not eating more of her broth, departed also, grumbling that she would *make* him eat, ram it into him. Drum was left alone with Mede and Lucy. His brother-uncle sat on the edge of a chair, while Lucy perched on the edge of the bed.

'Has she said anything to you two? Anything to explain her actions?' he asked them.

'She ain' been downstairs since that night, Drum. Hear she ain' even had her clothes off. She been right here aside o' you all the time.'

'Ever' mornin' she a-sayin' to Ciceron, hitch up the horses. Then soon's he gits 'em hitched up, she sendin' word she ain' a-goin'. 'Pears she not knowin' what to do 'cept sit here aside you.'

Drum was glad that she had not spoken to the others, for these were matters between him and her. But it was an enigma. That she had been ready to kill her husband to save him, yet had been a party to the whole plot simply for money – it made no sense to him at all. That she had been married to Narcisse and remained a virgin, that she had loved both of them . . . oh, there were so many questions, but they must wait. Even those concerning his own attitude towards her must wait. He loved her, he felt strangely happy that she was near by, yet he hated her; he realized that he had always been ruled by his heart and not his head, and now the conflict between head and heart was torturing him sorely. Dammit! He loved her as much as he had before that night, even as he hated her in the same breath. Meanwhile there were other matters. There were Mede and Lucy.

407

'Thank you, Lucy.' Drum reached out and took Lucy's smooth hand and held it tight. 'You saved my life and Mede's too.'

'That Masta Narcisse he a bad man. If'n ever a man deserved killin', he did, 'n' so did the others. That Big Ten a bad bunch. Nearly killed me, they did, one night. Raped me 'n' whopped me. But they all gone now.'

'All gone? What do you mean all gone?' Lucy's words conveyed more than a mere physical absence.

'They swung. Sheriff was out here, took 'em all into Benson. Had 'em a trial that lasted 'bout half an hour 'n' foun' 'em guilty o' rapin' them there white women 'n' stealin' from 'em too. Got himself a posse together 'n' took 'em all out 'n' hung 'em. Some of the folkses were all for burnin' 'em, but no, sheriff said this's a civilized country even if'n they be varmints in it like'n them ten big niggers, so he had 'em hung. They already bad when Mista Narcisse, he come here, but he made 'em worse. He bad all the way through, that Mista Narcisse.'

Drum looked to Mede for confirmation. Yes, he agreed, it was true. Ciceron had ridden into Benson and fetched the sheriff, while Brute, Mede, and Drumstick kept the Big Ten covered with their guns. The sheriff had brought men out with him and they spancelled the big fellows and took them back into Benson, keeping them in the jail the remainder of that night. The missing money was discovered in Narcisse's wallet, just as Lucy had said it would be. The sheriff had larrupped first one and then another until Big Dick – at least that's who Mede thought it was – broke down and confessed. Trial was held the next morning and by noon they were all hanged. The sheriff marched them out to a grove of oak trees the other side of Benson and hung them all, two or three from each tree. Just mounted them on horses, tied nooses around their necks, then whipped up the horses, and that was that. Next day they cut them down and buried them. At first the sheriff was not so sure but what Lucy might have been mixed up in it, he knowing that Narcisse had the money and all but, although Lucy confessed that he had been initiated into the Big Ten, displaying the welts on his back to prove it, he insisted that he had not gone with them and Mede was able to convince the sheriff that Lucy hadn't been out of the house at night in months. Then there was the indisputable evidence that Lucy had killed Narcisse to save Drum and Mede. That stood in his favour, especially when Mede explained to him all that had taken place that night. He told them in detail how Narcisse and the Big Ten had strung up Drum and how they were going to geld him if he didn't give them all the cotton money.

'The cotton!' It was the first time that Drum had thought about it. Thirty thousand dollars' worth of baled cotton abandoned somewhere on the road to Westminster.

'That ain' nothing for yo' to worry 'bout,' Mede assured him. 'Laura she had Ciceron drive her to Westminster 'n' she went to see Mista Barry. He comed right out here with her, while that light-skinned brother o' his'n guarded the cotton. Took 'bout twenty fiel' hands back with him to git it loaded on the train 'n' he say he a-goin' to Mobile with it for Drum. A-sayin' he a-goin' to charge only five per cent commission for sellin' it.'

So everything had been taken care of while Drum lay in bed. Justice had been done. Narcisse was dead; the Big Ten had been tried, found guilty, and hanged. The cotton was on its way to Mobile and he trusted Mr Barry to take care of all the details. Only one thing remained to trouble him. Claire!

He wanted to think about her and he wanted to be alone while he thought about her. Pretending sleepiness, although his mind was racing in circles, he asked Mede and Lucy to leave. But there was something else he must do – reward Lucy for saving his life.

Calling Lucy back to him, he once again took the smooth hand in his and held it. 'You saved my life and Mede's, Lucy. What can I do to repay you for that?' Mede was looking on with interest.

'Ain' nothin' yo' kin do, Mista Drum.' Lucy stood up proudly beside Drum's bed. 'Ain' nothin' yo' kin do but keep me here. All I askin' is that yo' don' kick me out. Ain' got no other place to go. Ain' got no other folkses I love. This my home, Mista Drum. Wants to keep it always. Ain' foolin' 'roun' no more, at least tryin' not to. Sometimes cain' help it no matter how much I try, but *tryin'* not to. I ain' bad, Mista Drum. Don' know why I this way but jes' am. If'n yo' kin forgive me for what I am 'n' keep me here with yo' always, that's all I'm a-askin'. 'Specially if'n yo' don' be too hard on me if'n I slips sometimes.'

'I promise, Lucy.' Drum could not understand the boy and his strange predilection, but he knew that nobody could be more loyal than Lucy, despite his shortcomings, which Drum sensed were not actually his fault. 'Just try to keep yourself out of trouble. You see where it got you with Narcisse and the Big Ten.'

'Ain' never goin' to git mixed up with no more black devils like'n they were.'

'You'll always have a home here, Lucy, and I'm going to put a thousand dollars in your name in the bank at Benson. That will protect you in case anything should happen to me. You'll be the richest boy at Falconhurst.'

Lucy lifted Drum's hand to his lips and kissed it. 'I always a-goin' to be yore boy, Mista Drum.'

Drum pulled his hand away but then overcame his distaste for the boy's affectionate gesture and patted him on the head. 'You will be, Lucy. I'll always look out for you.'

'Thank yo', Mista Drum. 'Pears like'n we three come a long way together since that first day out o' Boston. Ain' nothin' a-goin' to separate us, nothin'.' He left, his face glowing with happiness, pulling Mede along with him.

Drum sank back on to the pillow. And now Claire! He thought about her for a long time. He tried to imagine never seeing her again, and it was impossible. Her perfidy, though, had nearly killed him. Does a man keep a rattlesnake in his breast after it has bitten him once? Even a man who is ruled by his heart?

Yet he knew that he was on the point of forgiving her. He was a fool, a fool . . .

Drum Maxwell fell asleep.

CHAPTER THIRTY-SEVEN

IT HAD TURNED unseasonably cool that evening – cool enough
for Lucy to light a fire of fragrant pine knots in the fireplace in
Drum's room. Drum was sitting up in bed and the heat from
the fireplace felt good on his bare arms. The chill in the air had
forced him to pull the sheet up to his chin so that only his face
and arms were exposed. Lucy had shaved him, ridding him of
three days' growth of beard, and then bathed him, rubbing his
body with Florida water. Mammy Morn had then rebandaged
his back, renewing the ointment, whose disagreeable odour
completely overwhelmed the scent of the Florida water.
Debbie, with a longing look at his body, had changed the sheets
and he luxuriated in the feel of the smooth linen against his
legs.

Drum had matured during his stay at Falconhurst. His face
had lost its adolescent look and he was now a man. The
responsibilities and experiences had strengthened his face,
robbing it of some of its youthful beauty and adding a firmness
that had never been there before. His hair had grown longer.
It was not as closely cropped as it had been and was now a
mass of crisp golden curls. The excitement, shock, and pain
he had been through the last few days had left their marks too.
He had sent word to Claire to have supper with him, but he
felt that it made little difference what she might say. She must
love him or she would not have remained. He was sure that
whatever it was she might tell him could not change his love
for her either, although what he could do about it, he did not
know. What could her story be? Perhaps ... he pondered a
minute ... perhaps Narcisse had sold her favours to other
men. He would not put it past him, remembering as he did
how indifferent Narcisse had been to Drum's own attentions
to Claire. In fact, now that he regarded it in retrospect, it
almost seemed that Narcisse had encouraged their being
together and it was possible that he had used the same method
of blackmail before. But no! The most important argument

possible remained to negate this. Claire had been a virgin that night he had been with her. Of that one fact he was certain. So she had never been with any man before, not even her husband, and this puzzled Drum badly. If she loved him as much as she claimed she did, how had she been able to sleep with him all these years without having relations with him?

Reaching across the bed, he pulled the other pillow towards him and placed it behind his head to bolster him up in the bed, gritting his teeth at the pain it caused him. The fire was beginning to warm the room, and he threw down the sheet, until it covered only his belly. It was growing dark outside and he stared down at his body, noticing how the flames from the fireplace glinted on the hair on his chest, turning the close tendrils into little curls of burnished gold. Remembering Harlequin, he realized that he could never be such a man as Narcisse. But who would want to be? What woman, other than a seasoned prostitute, could either accommodate or enjoy such a man as Narcisse? No, he was not the gross male animal that Narcisse was, yet he was more of a man for not being.

The old clock in the lower hall struck seven, while he counted the booming strokes. They died away and then he heard steps on the stairs and the voices of Mammy Morn and Lucy. They entered without knocking, Mammy Morn nudging the door open with the toe of her worn carpet slipper. She was toting a big japanned waiter and Lucy followed with a folding table and linen over one arm. He set up the table beside Drum's bed, smoothing the cloth over it to the accompaniment of Mammy Morn's constant grumbling that he hurry because she could not hold the tray another moment. When he had finished, she set the tray down on it.

'Everything yo' likes for yore supper, Mista Drum.' She left the steaming food for a moment to place her hand on his forehead. ' 'N' yo' ain' got no fever now. A-hopin' yo' feels hungry.'

Drum realized that he was hungry, ravenously so. 'Hungry enough to eat a horse, Mammy Morn,' he said.

'Well, this yere ain' no horse what I been a-cookin' for yo'. It chicken 'n' I means chicken. Ain' no scrawny ol' hen neither.

It fried chicken 'n' candied yams 'n' some okra soup 'n' some beaten biscuits 'n' I went 'n' made a Lady Baltimore cake for yo'. Heap o' lot o' work, that is, if'n yo' don' know it. We ain' got no champagne what they always a-servin' in N'Orleans, but mixed yo' up a good hot toddy, which is better anyway. Yo' start a-sippin' on that 'n' Lucy he a-gone to call Miz Claire. I a-goin' to light the lamp.'

'Candles tonight, Mammy Morn.' The soft light of candles, supplementing the flickering of the fire on the hearth, seemed more appropriate for the meeting that was to take place than the glaring light of the kerosene lamps. Whatever confession Claire was about to make would not be a pleasant one and the softness of candlelight might help her.

Drum sipped the hot toddy, feeling it in his stomach like a warm ball and then feeling its warmth spread through his whole body. It relaxed him and he lay back on the pillows, hearing the door of Claire's room open and her footsteps coming across the hall. For a moment she hesitated on the threshold before entering his room. She no longer wore the drab calico she had had on earlier in the day but a peignoir of some soft white fabric, trimmed with billows of lace. He had never seen it before and he wondered if she had worn it this evening for any particular reason. The soft fabric outlined her body and the sash of blue taffeta seemed to make her waist small enough so he could encompass it with both hands. The deep neckline plunged below the cleft of her breasts and through the thin fabric he could see the soft yet firm outlines of her breasts. She had even done her hair differently. It was parted severely in the middle and gathered together in a large chignon behind, which was topped by a tortoiseshell comb. Her paleness had been somewhat obliterated by a skilful use of rouge, but it was not too successful, for the rose of her cheeks was nothing more than a painted spot that did little to hide the pallor but only accentuated it. Lucy followed her and pulled up a chair beside the table.

'I would have been able to eat downstairs tonight, could I have appeared without a shirt.' He noticed that she was trembling. 'Come, let's eat before all of Mammy Morn's

413

efforts become cold and tasteless. I find myself absolutely famished.'

She managed a wan smile. 'And so you should be, after nothing to eat for three days.'

'I doubt if you've had much more.'

'I can't remember whether I've eaten or not. I'm not even hungry now.'

'But eat,' Drum insisted, 'and when we've eaten, we'll talk, but don't dread it so.'

'I'm afraid that when one's life appears before one in all its horror, it is terribly difficult to acknowledge it, let alone confess it to another. But you are hungry! Eat and enjoy it. You need food to regain your strength.'

Acknowledging this need, he tackled the meal that Mammy Morn had prepared and did it full justice. When Claire pushed away the slice of Lady Baltimore cake that Mammy Morn had served her, Drum reached across for it, adding it to the generous slice he had already eaten. They drank their coffee silently, neither finding any words for small talk. When the last drop of coffee and the last crumb of cake was gone, there seemed nothing else for Drum to do but resign himself to whatever Claire had to say. He dreaded the ordeal, but in spite of this, he was curious. He pulled the bell cord beside the bed and, when Lucy appeared, indicated that he was to remove the remains of the meal; when Lucy departed, Drum moved over in the bed, hoping that Claire would sit beside him, but she refused, preferring to remain in the straight chair alongside his bed. When his hand reached out for hers, she ignored its mute appeal.

'It would be easier for you and a hell of a lot easier for me if you were here beside me.'

She shook her head in denial. 'It would be more difficult, Drum, at least for me. I might be tempted to leave out some of the things I have to say to you. I might be tempted to think them too awful even to speak about and try to spare both yourself and me. Being near you, touching you, feeling our love or what remains of it, would make things harder. Let me talk. Let me conceal nothing. My bags are still packed. When I have finished speaking, if you want me to go, I shall and I am quite sure you will not want me to stay.'

She got up and moved the candle from the bedside table, then carried it over and placed it on a chest of drawers on the opposite side of the room. Then she snuffed out the other candles so that the room was all but in darkness. Although the one candle shone on Drum's face, he could see only the dark silhouette of Claire, like an ill omen of things to come. She sat with her hands folded in her lap and for several minutes she did not speak. When she began, the words came slowly, her lips reluctant to pronounce them.

'In the first place, Narcisse and I were never married. We were never husband and wife.'

Drum was startled but made light of it. 'So you weren't married. That's not unforgivable. Why, even you and I—'

'That was different, Drum. We could not be married. You see, Narcisse's mind was warped. I must admit it now, though I have tried to imagine it was not true, have tried all my life. For I have known him, been with him, all my life, Drum.' She sighed. 'Narcisse was not like other men. He possessed a physical abnormality, which, I believe, produced the mental abnormality.'

Drum remembered that night in New Orleans when the painted Harlequin had appeared before him. The man's prodigious endowments were indeed abnormal. They were truly more bestial than human. Drum nodded slowly. 'Go on.'

'Narcisse was evil, yet I loved him. I adored, worshipped him, more than anyone else in the world. He was a part of me, he was my god, though I shudder to say it. It is sacrilegious, but it is true. I wonder now if he did not mesmerize me. Time and again I tried to break his hold on me, especially after I had met you, Drum, and realized that my love for you was far deeper, cleaner, more normal than the emotion I bore for Narcisse. But I could never do it. His grasp on my heart was too tight. We had been separated for very few days as long as I can remember; and, I regret to say, for no more than a few nights. I always did everything, *anything*, he wanted me to do. It was my way of life, obedience to Narcisse. He had only to

415

say the word, and I . . . even agreed to his plans for destroying you . . .'

'But when it came to the final moment, you could not destroy me,' said Drum. His heart was thawing towards her as she spoke, for she was so obviously telling him the truth, muddled and strange though it seemed so far.

She shook her head. 'I could not and that was the turning point for me, dear Drum. From my love for you I found the courage to break his hold on me. Yet I could not hate him, can never hate him, and if I had been forced to kill him, I would have died by my own hand, I swear.'

'Don't speak of such things. Lucy saved your life as well as mine, then.'

'Yes. I have thought that something of me died with Narcisse; but I begin to think that it was a wicked portion of my soul and I should not mourn it.' She took a deep breath, gathering her courage. 'Let me tell you of our life together. Perhaps you will understand how a lifelong devotion to his demands, insane as they were, corrupted me into what you see before you.'

'Go on,' he said.

'I am trying. I must pretend that I am alone, speaking my thoughts aloud, and that you are far away. Otherwise I could not tell you – you, Drum, whom I loved and lost.'

CHAPTER THIRTY-EIGHT

CLAIRE WAS GRATEFUL that she was sitting in the shadows. She almost wished that the room were in complete darkness, because the flickering flame of the candle illuminated Drum's face, pinpointing dancing highlights in his eyes. Seeing him, she had an irresistible desire to stretch out her hand and touch him. Her fingers longed to lose themselves in the crisp golden curls; to touch, ever so delicately, the throbbing artery in his neck; to wander down to the copper pennies on his chest and pinch them gently; then to let her hand slide under the sheet to the flatness of his belly and down farther to grasp that warm, pulsing maleness of him. But no! She must not think of that. That was something she was about to deny herself for ever. Yet she had nobody to blame but herself – unless it were Narcisse and the strange hypnotic power he had always held over her.

Where would she begin? Once again she lifted her eyes to look at Drum. His slight smile encouraged her.

'Narcisse's father,' she said carefully, 'was Aristides Brantome.' It seemed almost irrelevant, yet it was a start. 'It means nothing to you, Drum, but on that glittering façade of a world that existed before the war, the Brantome name was one of the brightest. It was one of the oldest and most distinguished names in that tight circle of Creole aristocracy that ruled New Orleans and southern Louisiana. Of all the Brantomes, Aristides was the richest and handsomest. Even in his forties, when I knew him, he was one of the finest-looking men I ever saw. Narcisse took after him, and Narcisse was handsome. Even you will have to admit that?'

Drum shrugged. 'I can't exactly consider a man handsome who's attempted to mutilate and murder me, Claire.'

'I suppose that is true. Well, Aristides Brantome was the owner of Mon Plaisir Plantation, which was situated on the river just north of New Orleans. It was a cotton plantation and had made him a wealthy man before the war changed everything. It was a grand place, enormous, with fifteen bedrooms and huge double parlours that opened up to make a ballroom. At one time there were nearly thirty house servants. I can't remember it in all its glory, that was before I was born; but when I was little, a ghost of its former beauty still clung to it.

'When Aristides Brantome's wife died, he contented himself for some years with a fine-looking mulatto wench named Sarah, a house servant. Then, at the last of the great octoroon balls in New Orleans, he bought Narcisse's mother, who was the daughter of André St Aubin and his octoroon slave Phoebe.

She was beautiful, and Aristides was madly in love with her. He installed her in the big house at Mon Plaisir. Despite his love, I think he always regarded her as a slave, but later, to legitimize Narcisse, he married her. She was his property, though, and I'm sure he always felt the same way about Narcisse. And about me too, for I belonged to him as well, a little orphan girl whom he gave to Narcisse as a companion because Narcisse wanted me. It was born in him to feel that way about slaves, or former slaves, and he could not change his way of thinking. Although he and his new wife were happy together.

'That happiness lasted a short time only. She died when Narcisse was six, and his father brought Sarah back to the big house to care for us both, Narcisse and his innocent playmate.

'Sarah was jealous of Narcisse and even of me. Her son Etienne was ten years older, the result of Aristides' carelessly planted seed. But he never acknowledged him, although he doted on Narcisse, spoiling him completely. Narcisse played cleverly on his affection. Whatever mischief he got into, he was never punished. He was brought up, almost deliberately it seemed, to be selfish and wilful. He always had his own way. And because I too adored him, I always did as he wished. It was a way of life for me.

'Soon after Sarah moved to the big house with Etienne, the boy ran away to become a sailor. Things continued at Mon Plaisir as usual until Narcisse, and I too, were about fourteen. Then something happened that had a profound effect on my playmate's character. There was a large marble fountain within the horseshoe curve of the driveway before the house. It had not worked for many years and its marble nymph had fallen from her pedestal, but after a heavy rain the marble basin would be filled with water and Narcisse and I used to take off our clothes and play in it.

'It was at one of those times when Aristides noticed us and, although he did not scold us for playing together naked, accepting that as natural in children who were not quite human, he did pay special attention to Narcisse. He stared at him, astonished at his unusual development, and called

Narcisse to him, admiring him and actually fingering him as he had done when he purchased slaves in the old days. I remember him exclaiming, "*Mon Dieu*, such a phenomenon cannot be possible on a fourteen-year-old boy! He's a veritable stallion already. What will he be when he grows up?" I can also recall him saying, "You're going to make a lot of women happy, boy. Never, in all the years that I've bought niggers, have I seen anything to match my own son."

'From then on, whenever male company came, Narcisse was exhibited as one of the few remaining glories of Mon Plaisir. His father would call him in after dinner, make him climb on to the dining-room table, take his clothes off, and make a spectacle of himself for the men assembled there. Narcisse enjoyed being admired, and yet I believe he also resented the fact that he was shown off as a prize slave would have been before the war, when he might have been commanded to "shuck down 'n' let these men finger yo', boy". Nevertheless, it built up a strange and unnatural pride in Narcisse, which increased as he grew older and made him feel superior to other men. After he had been exhibited, he would rush upstairs to me, telling me what they had said about him and how proud his father was of him. He would show himself to me, strutting like a peacock and boasting that there was no other boy like him in the world. Then, like as not, tears would come into his eyes and he would weep in my arms, sobbing that if he were all white, his father would not do such a thing to him.'

Claire dabbed at her eyes with a tiny handkerchief and Drum again motioned for her to sit beside him on the bed, for she seemed so alone with the horror of her story. She shook her head and continued.

'I could see nothing unusual in what he was so proud of. I had taken it for granted that he was like all other boys. As small children we had always slept together and it was not till we were about fourteen that we were separated – does that shock you? – because Sarah said it wasn't decent for such a big boy and girl to sleep together. We were put in adjoining rooms at Narcisse's insistence and always when we had gone to bed he would come through the connecting door and crawl in with me. I must admit to you, Drum, that I welcomed him. We were so accustomed to being together that I could not sleep nights without him beside me. We saw no harm in it. Indeed, at that time there was none. But it was not long before Narcisse, with the help of a Negro boy from an adjoining plantation, discovered that his own body could be a source of exquisite pleasure.

'This discovery led him to make me do things to him that seemed strange to me, but he would grab my hand and force me to fondle him, saying he would die if I didn't. Naturally I did what he wanted, although from his moaning and tense arching I believed I was causing him more pain than pleasure. But when I stopped, he would urge me wildly to go on, screaming at me in hoarse whispers to continue. He knew it was wrong, because he made me promise that I would never tell anyone about it.

'When we were both sixteen, his father died. He had never been able to adjust to the changes that came after the war. He had continued to spend what little money he had, then went deeply into debt as the plantation deteriorated. Finally he could no longer entertain his friends at Mon Plaisir. There were no servants except Sarah. Family after family had moved away from the cabins, which fell into ruins. When Aristides died, Narcisse tried to do what he could, but that was no more than to keep us in food. You must give him credit for one thing – Narcisse was a hard worker. He did well here at Falconhurst,' she said defensively.

Drum nodded silently, waiting for her to continue.

'Some months later Etienne returned. He was Narcisse's half-brother, but we barely remembered him. He was a grown man in his late twenties. He was very handsome, but what impressed us was the intricate tattooing all over his arms and chest. He had had it done in Japan. Being light of skin, he was proud of the designs and seldom wore a shirt. He had learned the art of tattooing from the man who had embellished his own skin, and soon he was practising on Narcisse, tattooing two birds on his chest. Narcisse was proud of them, but he would never let Etienne put further decorations on him.

'He developed a fanatical hero-worship of Etienne. I was inconsolable, because I had never shared his affections before. He even stopped sleeping with me to share a bed with Etienne. But the sailor would often disappear for a night or two, and on those occasions Narcisse would return to me, weeping and telling me that his friend had gone to sleep with women on other plantations and that it was a great sin for a man to do such things with a woman.

'On those nights when Etienne was away, Narcisse would force me to do things to him that seemed repulsive, but as always I was so under Narcisse's spell that he won out and I finally did whatever he asked me. Although I did it unwillingly at first, when I found that it was giving him so much pleasure, I came to do these things voluntarily. You must understand, Drum, how Narcisse always came first with me. Whatever he wished, no matter how repugnant it was to me, I would do. I was a slave to him and his passions and, I must admit, not always an unwilling slave.

'He convinced me that there was no harm in doing such things with him but that I must never allow another man to touch me. He explained what other men might want to do to me and he frightened me so by explaining what would happen to me and the pain it would cause me that I promised him I would never let anybody touch me. I realized what might happen if Narcisse did such a thing and I had no reason to know that all men were not like him.

'In another year or so Etienne first began to notice me. He would put his arm around me, stroke my hair, and call me endearing names. Whenever he did this before Narcisse, it would throw Narcisse into a rage and he would storm against Etienne and me both, saying that I was trying to take Etienne away from him.

'One night after we had all gone to bed, I became very ill with cramps. Ordinarily I would have gone to Sarah, whose room was on the third floor, but I felt unable to make the stairs, so I went out into the hall and was glad to see a sliver of light under the door of a room. I pushed it open without knocking. Several candles were lighted and Narcisse and

Etienne were on the bed. They were doing the same things to each other that Narcisse had forced me to do to him. Somehow it had not seemed so evil between Narcisse and me, but between Narcisse and Etienne it was revolting. I stood in the doorway for a moment and then fainted. I did not recover from the shock for weeks. Narcisse did his best to convince me that there was nothing wrong in it. He told me it was only right and natural. It was only when a man did the other thing to a woman that it was wrong. He frightened me so about it that in the end he convinced me he was right.

'One day when I had stretched out on my bed, naked because of the heat, I heard my door open. I looked up to see Etienne with his fingers on his lips, closing the door softly behind him. He was clutching an old pair of pantaloons about his waist and when he released them and they dropped to the floor, I could see that he was excited. But, even more, I was fascinated by the tattooed designs that continued down from his upper body all the way down his legs to his ankles. As he walked towards my bed I longed to touch them. Oh, Drum, can you understand what an ignorant, untutored ingenue I was? Can you realize how I did not know right from wrong? No, don't answer, Drum. I must not try to excuse myself. Let me go on.

'He lay down beside me on the bed and kissed me in a way I had never been kissed before and excited me, so that when he guided my hand to him, I did not resist. His hands on my body set me on fire. It was the first time in my life that somebody was doing something to give me pleasure. Hitherto, I had only done what Narcisse asked to give *him* pleasure. Now it was different. Very gently he turned me over. It was only then that I became frightened and would have cried out, but he put his hand over my mouth and talked low, quieting me and telling me that he would not do anything to hurt me. To prove it, he showed me how unlike Narcisse he was and how easy it would be for me to accommodate him. He continued to kiss me and run his hands over my body. Suddenly he was upon me and I realized by his fumbling that he was about to do to me what Narcisse had repeatedly warned me against doing. It was then that I started to fight him off and screamed for help. What Narcisse had told me changed my desire for Etienne into fear. Narcisse heard my screaming and rushed into the room. He had a long knife with him, the kind they use for cutting cane, and he plunged it into Etienne's back. Etienne slumped forward on to me and I could see blood staining the sheets.

'Etienne lived only a few moments and after he died, Sarah ran to the barn, mounted our only mule, and rode into the village, fetching back the constable, who arrested Narcisse. He was taken to jail. Sarah left and I was all alone during the months that Narcisse was awaiting trial. How I got along alone, I do not know and when Narcisse's trial came up, I knew nothing about it until he walked into the house, joyful over his acquittal. He had merely told the jury the truth – that he had killed Etienne to protect me from being raped.

'Now, once again, Narcisse tried to carry on alone, but it was impossible. There were many days when we went hungry. Narcisse was so happy to be back that he never blamed me for Etienne's death. Once again he returned to my bed and I was happy to have him and glad that Etienne was gone. So we lived, amid the decaying splendour of Mon Plaisir.

'Finally, when we were nineteen, we had to abandon Mon Plaisir. The kitchen roof fell in and the house was a shambles. Narcisse found twenty dollars that his father had hidden in a book and a gold eagle in the bottom of a bureau drawer. I had a string of pearls and a diamond brooch that had belonged to my mother. We bought a few clothes and left for New Orleans. We had heard of Madame Helene's, so we went there. It was then that Narcisse decided to pass us off as husband and wife. It would be far cheaper, as we would need only one room instead of two.

'The little money we had did not last long and although Narcisse tried hard to get work, his colour and his lack of education were against him. He knew only how to raise cotton. With nothing to do, he became a hanger-on at Hermione's and then started pimping for her and earning a little extra money by satisfying the tastes of those very few of her clients who preferred him instead of her girls.

'Hermione was aware of Narcisse's unusual attribute and it was she who thought up the idea of the Harlequin entertainment. Although any relationship with women was distasteful to him, he was willing to go through with it for the money, which was considerably more than he had been earning. Also, Hermione gave him drugs that stimulated him to carry on his performance. At first I used to go to Hermione's with him to paint the harlequin diamonds on his body. Of course, he never appeared without a mask, so he was still able to take his place in the little social group that gathered at Madame Helene's. Everyone believed the fable that we had inherited enough money to live on.

'While we were living with Madame, we heard a lot of talk about Paris and how people of colour were accepted there. Poor Narcisse, he always felt unhappy over his mixed blood and longed to be accepted as white. His one ambition was to get enough money to take the both of us to Paris and live there.

'Then you arrived at Madame Helene's and Narcisse said you must be very rich because you were travelling with two servants and you owned Falconhurst. It was then that he devised the plan of having me make you fall in love with me and then compromising you and blackmailing you. When you asked him to come to Falconhurst, he realized that it was going to be easier, although, I must admit, he was pretty disappointed when we arrived here. I didn't want to go through with his scheme, even at first, but the power he had over me compelled me to. But, there was one thing he had not counted on.'

'That I should really fall in love with you?' Drum asked.

'No' – she shook her head sadly – 'that I should fall in love with you, fall so deeply and madly in love with you that at the last moment I could not go through with it. No, I could not, despite my love for Narcisse and the influence he had always had over me. When I realized he was going to kill you, the spell, the fascination that he had always exercised over me, was broken. You know the rest.'

She rose from the chair. Slowly she began to unfasten the

soft white peignoir, unclasping the blue sash and then separating the lacy fabric slowly down the centre, past her breasts, past her body. 'Now you know my story. Now you know why I went so far along the road to hell down which Narcisse led me. I had no one to tell me the difference between right and wrong, not ever. But my own conscience should have told me, so I have no excuse whatever.'

As he watched, his eyes wide and the desire stirring in his groin despite his weakness, she removed the robe and laid it slowly, almost sensuously, over the chair. The candlelight turned her to a living and infinitely desirable statue of warm white marble. 'Now,' she said, looking at him, 'I am going to ask one last favour of you, Drum Maxwell, you who have done so much for me. I want you to take me now, to finish what you began before Narcisse broke in upon us. You know I was a virgin then and I feel I will remain one till I die except for this single time. I want you to take me, oh, not with love! I know I cannot have that from you now. But with the simple passion, even if you hate me, the plain *lust* with which you would take any nigger bed wench! It is much to ask, perhaps. You're weak. But, oh, Drum,' she cried, stretching her hands out towards him, 'I love you, and I must, must, must have one night to remember! I'll do all the work. I—'

'You will not,' said Drum, hurling the covers back from his eager body. 'Not as long as I'm Drum Maxwell and more than half alive!'

She stepped to him and he clasped her around the naked waist, but even at that point she suddenly put her hands on his shoulders and held him back a little.

'No, wait. I lied to you. I have told you nine-tenths of my story and—'

'And the rest doesn't matter. Do you think I couldn't tell you just as sordid a tale of my own life? But far worse, because everything I have done was done deliberately and not through ignorance. We are together and the past is past.' He rested his cheek against the smoothness of her belly. 'Before you began to speak, Claire, I had not made up my mind, although I knew I would love you till I died. But as I realized that you were

425

only a victim of a heartless and selfish brute, I fell more in love with you than ever, if that is possible.'

'But the rest does matter, dear Drum. Oh, God, I love you too with such a clean feeling in my breast! But if after all I've told you, you still love me, then you must know everything. It is the only fair thing I can do, my Drummond. Listen!' She wrenched herself back from his grip. 'I was *not* a little orphan girl given to Narcisse as a playmate. And of course I was never married to Narcisse, but not simply because he preferred men to women. We could not have married. Narcisse was my brother. More than that, even – my twin brother. We were born together and lived together, his flesh mine and mine his, and though we did not think alike, our blood and brains were one. There. That is all.'

'And it is no more than you had told me already, except that it makes even more plain why his hold on you was that of a mesmerist,' said Drum, smiling. This final revelation was almost a relief, explaining so much of what had gone before. 'Come here again, Claire, my dearest. See how much love is waiting for you.'

'But that is not love,' she protested, gesturing at it, 'for if it is, you have loved Debbie and—'

'And forty other wenches? You are partly right. This is a portion of love, though, and when it and what I feel in my heart for you are fused together, then it is all that a man can want for a lifetime.'

'You love me. Yet you know what Narcisse was and I am his twin.'

'Yes. He was cold, selfish, and evil, and you are warm, unselfish, and good. The elements of your natures, instead of being mixed in both of you, were divided between you. Poor Narcisse. I can feel sorry for him now, Claire, for he was born with a curse. And so were you, but it is gone now, buried with your brother.' He swung his legs over the side of the bed, but instead of catching hold of her again, he simply looked into her eyes. 'So you want a night to remember?' he said, smiling. 'Then, put your robe on again. You shall have your night.'

'I don't understand.'

'You will.' He rose and, feeling his strength renewed beyond all expectation, he lifted her in his arms and kissed her long and gently. Then he set her on her feet and tugged at the bell cord beside his bed. Far below in the kitchen they heard the jangle of the summons. Drum slid back into bed. 'You'd better get that robe on,' he said, 'you haven't much time.'

She hastened into it. She was just knotting the blue sash when Mede's heavy footsteps sounded in the hall and Drum hastily pulled the sheet over himself. Claire's eyes shot a question at him. He would answer her shortly.

'Heard the bell a-ringin'' – Mede was rubbing the sleep from his eyes – ''n' thinkin' yo' might be took bad. Yo' a-wantin' som'thin? Lucy he a-gone to bed 'n' ain' nobody up, but I kin git anythin' you' a-wantin'.'

'Yes, Mede, there is something I want.' Although he was speaking to Mede, his eyes were on Claire. 'I want you to ride into Benson.'

'At this time o' night? Yo' a-wantin' a doctor, Drum?'

'Not a doctor, Mede, just a minister.'

'A minister, Drum? Yo' a-*dyin*'?'

'Dying, Mede?' Drum laughed and circled Claire with his arms. 'No, Mede boy, I'm just starting to live. Go into town and fetch that coloured minister. Rouse him out of bed. Tell him he'll get a gold eagle if he rides back with you tonight. Tell him there's a marriage ceremony for him to perform out here at Falconhurst. Claire and I are going to be married tonight. Now, get going.'

'Mus' be in an awful hurry if'n yo' cain' wait till mornin'.' Mede grinned, gathering up the long nightgown around his knees. He ran out of the room, only to stick his face back in the doorway. 'If'n yo'-all a-goin' to git married up, I better rouse Mammy Morn 'n' Lucy 'n' all the rest. Mammy Morn shore a -goin' to be mad if'n she don' git yo' a weddin' supper or mayhap a weddin' breckus.'

'And I'm going to be mighty mad if you don't get started.'

They both listened to Mede's bare feet running down the hall. Drum pulled Claire down beside him. 'In a few moments you'd better go in and unpack your valises. Even if I can't get

427

dressed for my wedding, there is no reason why my bride cannot.' His lips sought hers again, but she pushed him away gently.

'But you know, as well as I, that if I stay here, the valises will never get unpacked and I shall never get dressed.'

'Then, don't bother. What you are wearing is good enough for a midnight wedding.'

She shook her head, placing her fingers on his lips. 'You can wait and so can I. I'm going to get dressed and when I come in that door again, you are going to see one of the happiest brides in the world. All of the sadness and evil in my life have suddenly disappeared and I am happy. Yes, Drum, really happy for the first time in my life. You still want me and that is all that matters to me. We've come a long way together, Drum.'

'And we've got a long way to go, my dear, a long, long way that's going to be filled with happiness for us both. From this moment on, we shall never speak of the past.'

She kissed him lightly on the forehead and ran from the room.

'Leave the doors open, Claire.' Drum lay back on the pillows. 'Even if I can't see you, I want to hear you.'

Her voice came from the other room. 'We'll never be separated again, Drum.'

'Never,' he answered.

Ashley Carter
Master of Blackoaks 95p

The latest bestseller from the publishers of *Mandingo* . . . Behind the respectable facade of the Baynard plantation at Blackoaks ran a hot stream of scandal and perversion. Ferrell Baynard lived only for his black slave mistress, Jeanne d'Arc ; his son burned with lust for the town whore. When the cotton prices plummeted, only Styles Kenric, Baynard's power-hungry son-in-law, saw the way to survival.

William Goldman
Magic 80p

Corky Withers was the all-time loser. He could do card tricks, but the people didn't like card tricks all that much. So Corky added a new twist to his act. The twist was going to make him a star, but instead, it pitched him into horror . . .

'Exceptionally skilful . . . totally readable' GUARDIAN

Douglas Fairbairn
Shoot 70p

Why should six ordinary guys on a weekend hunting trip take with them 'the Armalite and the Uzi and the Stoner and the Sten and the Beretta and a Schmeisser and the AR180 and plenty of ammo'?

When you've seen action in Korea or in Vietnam, you can get a thing about guns . . . and for some the war is never over.

'Exceptionally gripping . . . men and their obsessions, courage, sex, toughness and weapon-worthiness . . . a riveting read'
SUNDAY TIMES

Sir Arthur Conan Doyle
Tales of Terror and Mystery 75p

From the creator of SHERLOCK HOLMES . . .' What a tread it was!
My skin grew cold as I listened to that ponderous footfall . . .'
Thirteen tales of murder and vengeance, crime and detection,
hideous and unspeakable horror from one of the very greatest of
storytellers.

Tales of Adventure and Medical Life 75p

'The features were human, but the eyes were not. They seemed to
burn through the darkness . . . ' Fifteen tales of the strange and
bizarre, of adventure in the far-flung East and on the windswept
English fells.

Bernard Packer
Doctor Caro 80p

Who is DOCTOR CARO ? He is a man with a past. A man who
refused to die. His face and body were remade by wartime surgeons.
He has changed his name and nationality again and again. As
Henry Carr he comes ashore in the steamy South American port of
Puerto Acero. Among the seamen and exiles, the whores and
whoremasters, he stalks the man who condemned his family to the
holocaust twenty years ago and half a world away . . .

'Superbly wrought' NEW YORK TIMES

Colin Forbes
Avalanche Express 80p

'When the luxury Atlantic Express pulls out of Milan Central
Station it has aboard the highest-ranking defector ever to leave the
Soviet Union.

In the care of British and American agents, he is pursued across the
Continent by the massed network of the Soviet's European agents.
A blizzard is roaring across Europe and airlines are grounded.
Tension mounts unbearably as *Avalanche Express* develops to its
spine-chilling conclusion' LONDON EVENING NEWS

Patrick Alexander
Death of a Thin-Skinned Animal 75p

Winner of the John Creasey Memorial Award for the best first crime
novel of 1976.

A Grade One Foreign Office nightmare when President Njala — now
an officially approved African statesman — arrives in London for
top-level talks. Two years ago he was a dangerous psychopath and
dictator . . . two years ago Whitehall sent out a man to assassinate
him . . . that man spent two years in Njala's hell-hole jails, and now
he's back in London with a gun to finish the job . . .

'A first class thriller' EVENING STANDARD